LJ BURKHART

An Ember in the Dark

Realm of Queridian:Book 1

First published by L.J. Burkhart 2023

First edition

ISBN: 979-8-9859102-3-0

This book was professionally typeset on Reedsy.
Find out more at reedsy.com

To my mom and sister for believing in this story when others didn't.
P.S. Fuck you Aurora

Contents

Map

QUERIDIAN
N
NIGHTSHADE ECLIPSE
Familiar Forest
TWIN FANGS CITY
White Heights
Moonlit Mountains
Vision Lake
Elisora Forest
BLACK MOON CITY
THE IMMORTAL CITY
WICKSHIRE
NYLALUNA
Thunder Peak
THE HEALING SPRINGS
MYSTIC MOUNTAIN
MERMACOVIA
Lodge
THE MORTAL SANCTUM
Stone Fields
SR & AB
SAPIEN CITY
MUTABLE MEADOWS
Ironwood Forest
Sand Dunes
THE EVERCHANGING GLADES
ALLURE ISLE
Savage Sands

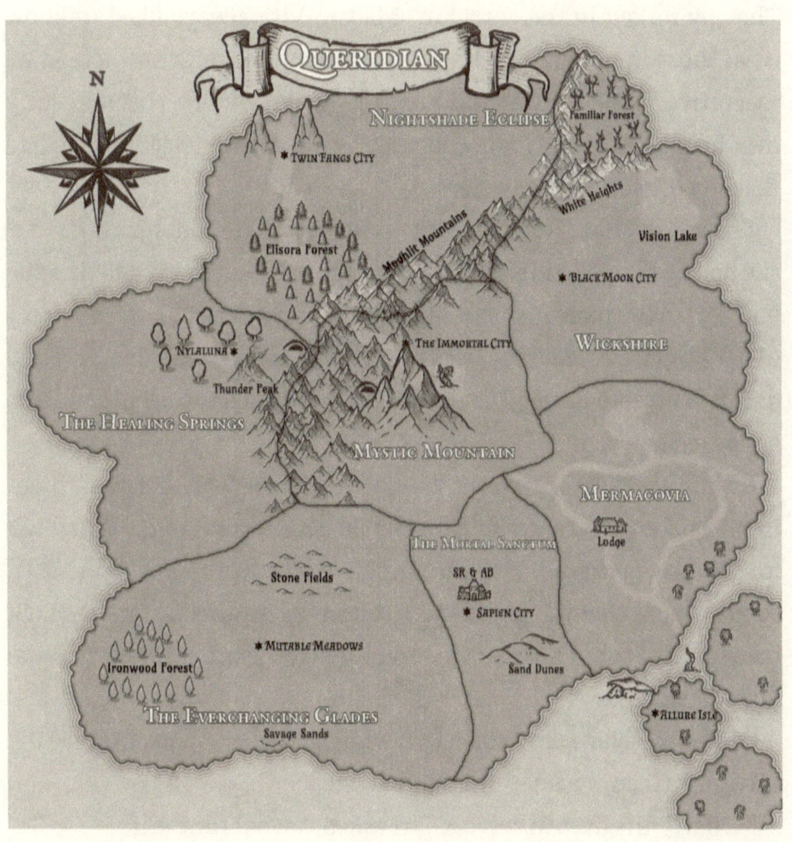

Prologue

The spy lurked in the corridor. Madam Vita always liked to know what those in her employ were up to, and this interaction screamed "secretive." The spy had followed the witch, who had been looking over her shoulder and hiding something under her cloak until she had reached the servants' quarters.

The spy did not know the witch well, or much about her, only that she had been sold to the madam years ago by her parents, and that she had gotten the madam out of many tight situations with the accuracy of her prophecies. The spy tried not to get too close with those around her. It was more difficult to do her job if she liked the people she was supposed to watch.

No one knew, no one except the spy and the madam, that every room in the building had a spyhole that could be accessed from the hallway for this exact purpose. Well, the ones in the "client rooms" were used to make sure that the guests adhered to the brothel's standards. Of course, the Sacred Rite was much more closely monitored than the Abandoned Bliss.

"Catalina! Wake up!" the witch whisper-yelled upon entering the servant's room. "Something came to me."

"What?" the human servant girl asked. "What time is it?"

"That doesn't matter, Catalina! Get up! I *saw* something."

"What is it, Penelope?" the servant girl asked as the witch started taking out the items she had hidden in her cloak. Among them was a small bowl, which she then filled with water, and a tiny pouch that rattled, the contents clacking.

"I had a dream about your daughter." The servant was pregnant? This was news. And definitely something the madam would want to know.

"I'm having a girl?" the human asked, placing a hand on her slightly swollen belly, a tear slipping free from her eye.

"Yes. She will be strong. And important. That's all I saw, but a prophecy came to me:

"The child you bear
  Won't be yours to care
  For though her blood will be the call
  You won't be there to see her fall
  She will be an Ember in the dark
  She will bring the spark
  Through her pain
  She will end the fae reign..."

"Wait. I won't get to see her grow up? Am I going to die?"

"I can't *see*. That's why I brought my things. We need to do some scrying." The witch grabbed the pouch, pouring out small bones with symbols on them. "I need to decide which are the right questions to ask."

"Am I going to die?" the human asked again.

"Well, I can't ask that. You will eventually die, so the answer would be yes."

"Will I survive childbirth?" the girl asked.

The witch nodded that it was the correct question. She shook the bones in her hand before tossing them onto the table. All the symbols were facedown.

"No," the witch said quietly, taking her hand.

Before the witch could do any more divinations, the spy heard someone coming down the hallway. As much as she needed to hear the rest, she could not get caught. She snuck away from the spyhole and returned to the madam to reveal all she had discovered.

Chapter 1

I'm sitting on my couch with "You Should See Me in a Crown" by Billie Eilish playing, looking for archaeology jobs on my laptop, when there's a knock on my door. As I never get visitors, I am thoroughly confused. I'm about to ignore it, figuring it's a salesman, when I get the strange sensation that my life is about to take a drastic turn, almost like déjà vu. There's a swooping sensation in my stomach, and chills erupt on my skin as I shut the music off. Another knock comes, this one more insistent. My heart rate increases slightly, but I take a deep breath to calm myself.

I look through the peephole to see a middle-aged man in a button-up shirt on the other side. Figuring I'm being paranoid, I open the door, fully intending on telling the man that I'm not interested in attending church, since he looks like the preaching type. I can't explain why I feel this way, but I just get that sense from him.

"Hello, miss. I'm Chaplain Jenkins."

At his introduction, my face pales and my heart sinks. There's only one reason a chaplain visits a home.

"Are you Ember Amor?"

"Yes," I say quietly, nausea starting to build in my stomach.

"Miss, I am so sorry to tell you this, but your mother, Evelynn Amor, died in a car accident today."

The chaplain continues to talk, but I don't hear one word out of his mouth. My mother was the only person I had in my life. I've always been a bit of an outcast, and never fit in anywhere or made friends, but my mom and I were close.

"Miss?" Chaplain Jenkins asks, and I realize that he asked me a question.

"I'm sorry, can you repeat that?"

"Of course," he says sympathetically. "I was letting you know that you will need to come to the morgue to identify her body as soon as possible. I can give you a ride?"

I think I'm in shock. I can understand the words he's saying to me, but my emotions have shut down. I usually pick up on others' emotions fairly easily, but it's like as soon as mine closed off, the ability to feel his went right along with them.

"Yes, I can come now. I would appreciate a ride. Thank you."

On the short drive to the morgue, we don't speak. It would be awkward if I wasn't in the state I'm in. As it is, I take note of everything around me. He has a cross hanging from his rearview mirror. The station is tuned to something religious. His car keys dangle and swing as he drives and turns corners. There's a long black thread hanging from his right sleeve. His dark hair is receding into the shape of a horseshoe. His glasses are dirty.

Noticing these little things helps me to not think of the only important thing: my mother is dead.

We pull up to the morgue, and I stare at the building. I can't believe that only twenty minutes ago my life was normal. It's strange how quickly things can change.

"Do you need me to come in with you, miss?" Chaplain Jenkins asks.

"No, I'll be fine on my own. Thank you."

"All right, well, I will be waiting right here in the parkin' lot, and when you're done I can give you a ride back to your house."

"I appreciate that. I'll be back soon," I reply, genuinely thankful for his help. I know that I'm in no state to drive myself.

I walk into the building and tell the receptionist I'm here to identify the body of Eve Amor. I'm escorted to a bare cold green room. There's a body on the table covered by a sheet. I know logically that it's my mother's body, but I'm so detached that in my head, it's not.

It isn't until the sheet is pulled back to reveal her face that any of this feels real. All of a sudden, my legs give out, and I can't get any air in my lungs. Luckily, there was a chair immediately under me, otherwise I would've fallen on my ass.

"Miss, can you put your head between your knees for me?" the coroner asks me kindly.

I do as she says, and am finally able to get a full breath down. When I've taken a few deep inhales, I raise my head.

"That's her," I state.

She jots down something, and I'm asked to sign off in confirmation, which I do, and then she leaves me alone with my mother.

I uncover her hand and wrap it in my own. I almost drop it because I'm so startled by how cool and stiff it is. All I can do is stare at her features, committing them to memory.

She looks so different from me. I've known for my whole life that Eve is not my birth mother, so it's no wonder. She had very fair skin, freckles covering most of her face, golden hair, and bright blue eyes. She was also model thin, which I've always envied.

I, on the other hand, am not considered plus size, but I definitely have some curves on me that refuse to go anywhere, no matter how many diets I've gone on. I have olive skin, and most people think that I am Mexican or Native American, which I very well could be, but have never known for sure, since I was adopted. I have dark brown, almost black hair, with a strip of white in the front on my left side. I also have amethyst eyes.

It is often assumed that my eyes and my strip of white hair are artificial, but they are one hundred percent real. They also didn't show up until I started getting older. I used to have plain dark hair and brown eyes until I hit puberty, then they started slowly and subtly changing. Around that time, my ears also started developing a point on the tops. The last identifying feature is a beauty mark under my right eye. I always hated it when I was young, but it grew on me.

I stay there, simply looking at my mother for an undetermined amount of time, knowing that I might never get to see her in person again after this.

I still don't know what exactly happened to her. Someone might have told me at some point, but I've been too out of it to comprehend anything said to me. I can see blood staining her blond hair on the left side of her head. I'm sure there are plenty of other injuries that I can't see, but I don't want to look. I don't want to remember her body broken. I want to remember her vibrant and alive.

"Oh, Mom." My voice breaks, and the emotions finally burst open inside of me. I start sobbing as I rest my head on my mother's stomach. I long to feel her arms around me, comforting and holding me, but I cry harder knowing that will never happen again. Her body is wrong underneath my cheek, and I can't catch my breath.

After what seems like equally forever and no time at all, I pull myself back together. I stand on shaky legs and bend over to kiss her forehead.

"I love you, Mama. I'll miss you so much."

I cover her back up with the sheet and make my way out to the front desk. The coroner asks what I would like done with her remains, but I've never had to think about it before. When I tell her I'm unsure, she replies that it's fine. They can call me in a few days, and that everything is taken care of for now. I nod and head out to the parking lot. Chaplain Jenkins is right where I left him, and he gently waves at me as I approach.

I open the car door and climb in. Now that I've left my mother behind,

I'm back to a similar state, noticing that the car smells like stale coffee.

"All set, dear?"

"Yes. Thank you for waiting for me. I know I was in there for a while."

"Of course, of course."

The drive back is just as silent as the drive in, and I'm grateful when we pull up to my house. I open the passenger-side door and am about to step out when Chaplain Jenkins stops me and hands me a brochure.

"I just wanted to give this to you. If you need any sort of support during this difficult time, we are here for you." I look down to see it's his church's pamphlet. "We also have group counseling for individuals who've lost family members." At my silent nod, he reaches over to squeeze my hand. "I'm so sorry for your loss, Miss Ember. My number is on the back if there's anything at all you need, okay?"

I nod again, not having the strength or energy to thank him, and head to my front door. He waits until I'm safely inside the house before taking off.

I look around my place to find everything the same as when I left it, but everything is different now.

I sit on my couch and stare at the blank TV. I don't know for how long, but when I finally force myself up to use the restroom, I realize it's dark outside and my stomach is rumbling. I have no appetite, but I do get myself some water and head to bed. There's a picture of me and my mom sitting on my nightstand, staring me right in the face, and my heart stops when I spot it.

The picture is one of my favorites of the two of us. We had gone to Santa Fe on vacation and were at the pool having drinks. We had the pool attendant take our picture. We were laughing our asses off after spilling our drinks attempting to cheers each other. She looked so young, she could've easily passed for my sister.

I've always been curious about that. It's like she never aged at all in my whole life. I don't know if everybody feels that way about their parent, but the more I'm thinking about it now, the more it bothers me.

I get up and start digging through the back of my closet where all my mementos are. I finally locate the box I'm looking for and pull it out before sitting back on my bed. I take out every picture I can find of my mother, all ranging from when I was a baby up until now.

It hurts, and I have tears in my eyes, staring at her beautiful face and knowing that I'll never get to speak to her again. I'll never have her hold me, or give me advice, or lecture me. Before I can start down that path, I drag my gaze over every picture I have. I'm somewhat shocked to discover that she barely aged. She was fifty-three, but she never looked a day over thirty-five. Now with the pictures in front of me I can see that in my twenty-seven years on this Earth, there are hardly any signs of her aging.

I don't know if she had fantastic genetics, or if something else is going on here. I know it sounds ludicrous, but I have this strange sense that there is a lot I don't know about her. That there is something deeper going on than looking young. Maybe I want to focus on anything other than her death, but there's something whispering to me that's not the case.

"Mom, were you keeping secrets from me?" I whisper as I drag my finger over her loving face staring back at me. This one is us after my high school graduation.

As I'm gathering all the photos together to put them back into the box, I notice one of her holding me when I was a baby. My gaze catches on a strange-looking necklace she's wearing. I've never seen it before, but it's very unique. It's a stone or a crystal with a peculiar symbol on it, and it appears to be glowing. I shake my head and put the picture with the others. It's probably just a trick of the light or the flash going off.

I return the box to my closet and get ready for bed. When I finally lie down, the day catches up with me, and I cry myself to sleep.

Chapter 2

A few days later, I'm contacted about what I would like to do with my mother's body. I'm going to have her cremated. I already bought a necklace that holds ashes so you can always carry your loved one with you. They asked me if I wanted them to do an autopsy, but I decided against it. The cops notified me that there was a malfunction with her car, something with the steering wheel, and that's what caused the accident, which in turn caused her to hit her head on the window. The doctors are pretty sure she died from blunt force trauma to the head. I don't want them opening her up to learn what they are almost positive they know anyway.

The police told me I could sue the car company if I wanted to. I still haven't made a decision, but I do know that I have to start going through her things and figure out what I want to do with her house. I already have a nice home for myself, so I don't want to keep it. I know it's going to be a lot of work, and I'm not looking forward to it.

I start with her bedroom, because it's where I feel closest to her. It still smells like her in here, and this was always her space. As I'm going through her closet, I put on articles of her clothing that I've always liked. Obviously since we weren't the same size I'm not able to take any of her pants, but she used to like dressing in baggier clothes, so most of her shirts fit. It's a bit like a warm hug from my mom. I sort out my keep and my give-away piles, slowly making my way through the room.

I finish with her closet, and I'm about to move on when I notice something on the wall. I'm unsure what it is, only that it catches my attention as chills erupt across my skin. I crawl into the space and touch it. It seems like a normal wall, and I almost chalk it up to something with the paint, but then I knock on it. It sounds hollow and not at all like the wall surrounding it. As I'm inspecting, I notice a little piece of cloth sticking out of the wall. I carefully pull it, and an entire panel pulls away, making me gasp and my heart pound harder.

Inside is a small box. The sight of it brings tears to my eyes because I now know that my mother had secrets. I mean, who has a secret compartment in their closet if they aren't hiding something?

I take a deep breath as I grab the box and take it out of the closet. When I open the lid, I'm surprised to find that it's mostly empty. My eyes instantly spot the necklace from the photo, and I inhale sharply seeing it in person. It's stunning. It's almost clear, with maybe a hint of pink, making me think that it's rose quartz. It's ovalish in shape and has a bit of copper wiring wrapped to hold it in place. There's a symbol carved onto the front that I don't recognize, which is saying something since I'm an archaeologist. There's a barely there glow, nothing like in the picture of my mother wearing it. There's also a warmth to it, which shouldn't be possible considering it was sitting in a box for God knows how long.

Without giving it another thought, I reach up and clasp it around my neck. As soon as the stone settles between my breasts, the glow gets brighter, flaring for a moment before dissipating. I am completely stunned. I have no idea what could cause it to do this. Heart pounding, I turn my attention back to the box. There's a piece of paper inside that's yellowed and weathered, like it's been read a million times. I carefully open it to find only two lines.

Thank you, Eve.
  Take care of her.

There are water stains on the sheet, like someone was crying when they either wrote it, or read it, possibly both. My thoughts start spinning before I can control them. This means that Eve knew my birth mother. She knew her. She lied to me, and I don't know why. A droplet falls from my face onto the page, and I realize that I'm sobbing. With shaking fingers, I carefully put the note away before I damage it.

There's another note in the box. This one doesn't look nearly as worn, and it's attached to a strange object. It's got a long piece of string, and at one end is a small metal piece, almost like a medallion, and at the other is a delicate purple feather. Upon touching the feather, I know it's real, and above it on the string are ten wooden beads. They are all slightly different, and the bottom one, closest to the feather, looks the oldest. I open the note to find the same handwriting, and I trace my thumb over the letters. This is a piece of my birth mother right in front of my eyes. More tears well, but I push past them so I can read, even though it gives me a headache.

Give this to her when she turns twenty-eight. It was passed on from the women in my family, and each added a bead before they gave it to their first daughter. She needs to braid it into her hair to signify that she is officially a woman.

Twenty-eight. My birthday is in a month. Where was she from where twenty-eight was officially a woman? Here you were considered an adult at eighteen, or maybe even twenty-one.

I counted the beads again, running my fingers over each one, trying to feel a connection with the women of my heritage. They had left little pieces of themselves with me. Before I know it, I'm sobbing again. My whole life I've wanted to know where I came from and more about my ancestry and family. Now I have these connections, and I feel a small, sad piece of me mend a little bit.

Frustration and resentment also build in my chest. How could my mother never tell me about all this, or show me these things? And now she was dead. The only person on Earth who knew the answers to my questions was now gone forever.

I slowly pull myself back together and look at the final item in the box. It's a small ancient-looking iron key. The bow is a unique shape; there are four hearts touching each other in a circle, the points all in the middle. I have no idea what it's for or to, but it must be important.

I put everything back in the box and place it next to my purse by the door so I can take it home.

After that, I'm able to finish going through her room, not finding anything else secretive or life-changing. It takes me most of the day, and by the time I'm done, I'm equally drained, relieved, and devastated. I go into her kitchen and find a half-drunk bottle of wine in the fridge. I pour myself a glass before plopping down on the couch. At the first sip, my eyes tear up again. This was our favorite wine, and we always used to drink it together. The taste of it reminds me of late nights spent drinking and laughing.

Even after all of this, it still doesn't feel like she's dead. More like she's on vacation. But I know as soon as I finish clearing out her house, that will no longer be the case.

As I'm sitting there basking in my misery, I have an idea. One that has been in the back of my mind for a while, but suddenly comes roaring in with a ferocity that takes my breath away.

What if I did one of those DNA tests? I know that it won't tell me who my parents are, or any other family members, but it would at least give me more information on my heritage. Mind made up, I finish my wine and head out the door with all of the belongings I want to take with me.

Ten minutes later, I'm pulling up to my local drug store. Twenty minutes later, I'm sitting at my kitchen table reading the instructions and spitting into a vial a million times until my mouth is as dry as the desert.

I get everything sealed up and ready to send out the next day. For the first time since my mom died, hope and excitement make their presence known. In a few weeks, I might actually know a little bit more about where I come from.

Chapter 3

It's been four weeks since I sent out the DNA test. It's also my twenty-eighth birthday. Apparently I'm officially a woman now. As I'm lying in bed, I look over at my nightstand to see the feather hairpiece sitting there staring at me.

I get up and take it into the bathroom, holding it up to see which side it would look better on. With the white stripe on my left side, I figure it should go on the right. I find the middle of the string and bring it to the top of my head, wrapping it around the strands there a few times before braiding it in with a small section of my hair. When I'm finished, the feather and the medallion lie next to each other, and as I look in the mirror at myself, the glow from the necklace flares, making me gasp. It hasn't done that since I put it on the first time. I meet my own eyes in the mirror, and I see a warrior princess staring back at me. It's also probably due to the fact that my eyes have gotten colder and harsher since Mom died.

Deciding to go with the warrior princess look, I do my makeup dramatically, with heavy eyeliner and dark lips. I put on a black V-neck T-shirt with a bohemian-style float skirt, tucking the shirt and adding a brown belt.

In years past, my mom and I would always have brunch and get pedis on my birthday, so that's what I'm going to do. I've also been thinking about getting a tattoo to honor her. I've always wanted one and feel like this is a good reason, and a good time for it.

I find a shop close by that opens at ten called Tit for Tat. I make my way there, and am glad to see when I pull up that they're not busy. I head in and am greeted by a friendly, but eccentric blonde.

"Hey! How can I help you today?"

"I know it's last second, but I was hoping to get a tattoo today? It's my birthday and my mom passed away recently, so I wanted to get something in her memory."

Her face softens in sympathy. "Well, first off, happy birthday," she says, smiling kindly at me. "Secondly, I'm sorry to hear about your mom. I lost mine too, if it's any consolation. Third, you got lucky because Savannah had a cancellation this morning, so she's free. Savannah!" she sings loudly.

A woman covered in tattoos, with fiery red to blond ombre hair, comes up front, rolling her eyes as she does so.

"Are you scaring our customers away again, Anna?"

"Of course not. We're best friends already. Aren't we?" she asks, looking at me expectantly.

"Old friends, actually," I chime in, earning a smile from Anna.

"Yes! This is..."

"Ember," I supply.

"Yes. This is Ember, and it's her birthday, and she wants a tattoo for her mom who passed away recently. You had a cancellation, so I thought I would give her over to your lovely hands."

Savannah gives me a warm smile. "Nice to meet you, Ember. I would love to give you the perfect way to remember your mom. Do you have something in mind?"

"Well, her name was Eve so she got a tattoo a while ago to represent the original Eve." I bring out my phone so I can show her the exact tattoo that my mom had. A black, gray, and white snake wrapped around her wrist, its mouth open and about to bite a red apple on the back of her hand. I hold it out for them to see. "I want the same thing."

"I can definitely do this," Savannah tells me. "Do you have any tattoos?"

"No. This is my first one. I've always wanted one, but I've never been committed to an idea enough to have it on me permanently."

She nods in understanding. "Okay, well, I'm going to sketch this out on my tablet, and then once you're happy with it, I'll print out the stencil, put it on your skin, and that's when the fun starts. Which arm do you want in on?"

I'm about to say my left, because that's where my mother had hers, but something stops me, a strange sensation I can't identify. I look down at my left wrist and I see a flash of a star. Weird. Maybe that will end up being my next tattoo.

"My right."

Since I have the exact picture of what I want, it doesn't take her long to sketch it, and soon I have the stencil on my arm and am on the table watching her get the tattoo gun ready.

"Here we go. Take a deep breath."

I do, and in the next second I hear the tattoo gun. The needle stings as it connects with my skin. The first few minutes aren't very fun, but then the endorphins kick in, and it's not too bad.

We talk as she works, and she tells me about her husband and about how they started dating after he came in to see her for a tattoo. I'm tempted to ask what else happened, because I feel like there's more to the story, but I don't want to be rude.

The door dings a moment later to signal that someone came in, and Anna exclaims loudly at the front. I almost jump before I remember that I have a needle to my skin. Savannah, on the other hand, doesn't look fazed in the slightest.

"She's a loud one, isn't she?" I ask.

She laughs. "Yes. That's one way to describe her. Plus, her girlfriend walked in, so she's even more excited than usual."

I look up front to see an adorable redhead walk around the counter and kiss Anna on the mouth. The two men who also work in the shop are staring and groaning at the sight.

"I thought after months of us dating and you guys seeing this on a regular basis you would be used to it by now," Anna shouts at them.

"We will never get used to it," one of them replies. "It will always be the most glorious sight to ever grace us in this place, and you're both being selfish by leaving and taking our favorite part of the day away from us."

Savannah rolls her eyes affectionately and scoffs.

"Are they moving?" I ask, even though it's none of my business.

"Yes. They're moving to Colorado Springs in a week."

I watch the two of them interact with each other and a deep yearning settles in my chest to have what they do. Even though I don't know them, I can tell they have something special.

Savannah finishes up the tattoo not long after, and I admire it on my wrist before she wraps it up. I tear up slightly seeing it on my skin as opposed to my mom's. I'm glad I can always carry her with me.

I pay and thank Savannah, and Anna comes up and gives me a warm hug before I leave.

"Happy birthday. And I'm sorry you don't have your mom with you to celebrate."

"Thank you, Anna." I give her a grateful squeeze before I untangle myself from her arms.

I head to our favorite brunch spot and order the peach mimosa with the huevos rancheros and a side of French toast with blueberries. I know it's overkill, but it's what we always get, and it's my birthday, so fuck it.

After three mimosas, I'm thoroughly stuffed and well on my way to drunk. I stumble slightly as I cross the parking lot to get to the nail salon, figuring I should be sober enough to drive by the time they're finished.

As I'm sitting there getting pampered, my phone dings. I pick it up to discover that my DNA report has been sent to me. I'm eager to see what it says, and I open the email, even though I should probably wait to read it when I'm home.

My excitement turns to confusion and dread though the more I read.

Miss Amor,

We must admit that we are baffled by your results. You had a small percentage of Native American and Mexican heritage (both of those lines are ancient; we couldn't find anything recent), but the remainder of your DNA is inconclusive. It is nothing like we have ever seen before. Would you be willing to come do more testing? We are always looking for new developments in the healthcare industry as well as any changes in our knowledge of the human body. We would love to speak with you more. Our contact information is below if you would be interested.

I sit there and stare at the screen for minutes. I reread the short email again and again, and regret that I've had so much to drink.

"Miss? Is this the color you want?" the nail technician asks, startling me out of my spiral. I can feel her annoyance with me, and I think it's probably not the first time she asked. I nod absentmindedly before clicking my phone off. I need to look at this more when I'm sober and not around a ton of strangers.

My panic is still at the forefront of my mind, and without my phone I basically end up staring at the nail tech. If I wasn't I might've missed the way her breathing accelerated and her hands started shaking. She closes her eyes and takes a deep breath. It's then that I realize that I'm still connected to her emotions, and I have a crazy thought that I might have affected her feelings somehow. Did I push my anxiety onto her?

I'm suddenly completely sober, and she finishes with my pedicure quickly.

In a daze, I drive home, trying not to hyperventilate. Once I walk through my door and drink a ton of water, I sit down and reopen the email. The words stare back at me, just as unfathomable as before. How is this possible? They get DNA samples from literally all over the world, and yet mine is basically inconclusive? It's disconcerting that they did get *some* results. If it was entirely inconclusive, I could chalk it up to me not doing the test right, or something going wrong. What does any of this mean?

"I know you know what all this means, Mom," I say, picking up the necklace with her ashes I wear around my neck. "Why didn't you tell me any of this? I would say it's all pretty *fucking* important." I'm yelling now, angry about all the lies and everything I don't know about myself and her. "What's happening to me? Why did you leave me? Why am I all alone?" I scream, furious tears rolling down my cheeks.

The tight leash I've had on my emotions since she died snaps. I'm sobbing, I'm shrieking, I'm out of my body, I'm exploding. There's a strong gust of wind pounding furiously at my face and sweeping my hair up in a tornado. Then I feel a spark of heat, and I think that my fury must be burning me alive. I open my eyes, and through my tears I see a wall of flame in front of me. I gasp and jump back, but by the time I blink, it's gone. I look around, stunned. Nothing seems to be damaged, but I can't tell if things have moved. But how would that even happen? The window in front of me is open, which explains the wind I felt. The fire must be my vision going as wonky as my emotions.

"What's wrong with me?" I whisper quietly as more tears stream down my cheeks.

I collapse on my floor, not caring that I'm probably messing up my pedicure, or that I need to sweep. I sit there and cry, until my attention randomly is pulled to my coffee table, where all my junk typically ends up, and the brochure that Chaplain Jenkins left me catches my eye.

I get up on unsteady legs and walk over to pick it up. I need to talk to someone about all this. And I have no one. I turn it over to see his number scrawled in messy handwriting. Before I can think too much about it, I'm dialing.

It rings three times before he answers. "Hello?"

"Is this Chaplain Jenkins?" I ask, regretting my decision to call him as soon as I speak. He probably won't even remember me.

"Yes, can I ask who's calling?" His kind voice puts me at ease, and I realize it doesn't matter if he remembers me or not.

"This is Ember Amor. I don't know if you remember me. My mother died about a month ago, and you drove me to the morgue."

"Yes, of course, Miss Ember. How are you?"

I take a deep, shaky breath, laughing somewhat hysterically. "Honestly, not great. I need someone to talk to. Is there any chance you would be able to meet me for coffee today?"

"I would be able to actually. Does an hour from now work?" he asks, surprising me. I didn't think he'd be willing to, or at least not able to meet up so soon.

"Yes, that would be great. I'll meet you at the Caffeinated Moose." We hang up and I'm relieved knowing that I'll be able to talk to someone soon.

I drink some more water before heading into the bathroom. I cringe when I catch sight of myself in the mirror. My makeup is completely ruined. I have tear tracks cutting through my foundation, my eyeliner and mascara are smudged and running down my face, and my lipstick is smeared and starting to flake off. I take a quick shower, needing the hot water to calm me, and wash my face so I don't look like such a hot mess.

I dress in the same clothes but forgo the makeup in case of another meltdown. I have some more water, adding some lavender oil to calm myself the fuck down, and walk out the door. It doesn't take me long to get to the coffee shop, and I'm here early, but I couldn't sit around my house anymore waiting to meet him. I grab a tea with honey before taking a seat in a secluded, quiet corner.

He also arrives early, so I'm sitting there for only about ten minutes before he walks in. I wave to him, and he waves back before going to stand in line. Once he has his coffee, he joins me.

"Nice to see you again, Ember. I'm a little surprised you called me."

"I wasn't planning on it, but I don't have anyone to talk to. I've recently made some discoveries about my mother, and I don't know what to do about them."

He nods patiently. "I don't know if I can help, but I can definitely be a sympathetic ear and lend you whatever advice I can."

"Thank you, Chaplain Jenkins. I really do appreciate all you've done for me."

"You can call me Frank, dear," he says, smiling warmly.

I smile back genuinely. The sensation is foreign, and I don't remember the last time I smiled for real. The thought is slightly upsetting, so I move on to why I called him in the first place.

"Well, Frank, I think I'm having an existential crisis. A lot of strange things have happened since my mother died, and I don't know what to do or what is true anymore."

"That's pretty normal, Ember. A lot of people feel lost after the death of a loved one."

I don't want to be rude, but he's not understanding what I'm saying. "This isn't quite like that."

"Isn't it?" he asks. Not in a condescending way, just in a way that gets me to examine myself.

His concern and amusement trickle toward me, but I shut that shit down so I can focus on how all this is making *me feel.* I don't want his emotions clouding my thoughts right now, so I sever that connection.

"Okay, well, that might be part of it, but it's definitely not all of it."

"I'm assuming you want to talk to me about it. That's why you called me, isn't it?"

I nod. I take a deep breath and tell him everything that's happened since her death, with the exception of my crazy meltdown this afternoon. By the time I'm finished, his eyebrows are halfway up his forehead, and he looks as shocked as I was.

"Inconclusive?" he asks quietly, referring to the DNA test.

"Yes. Frank, do you think it's possible that..." I'm about to ask him what's been swimming in my brain, but it sounds way too crazy to actually say out loud.

"Possible that you come from somewhere that's...not here?" he volunteers.

I nod, waiting for the judgment to enter his eyes. I suddenly get the urge to take it all back. Why did I think telling him would be a good idea? He's a pastor, I don't think they usually think anything else exists besides heaven and hell.

"I think that's a very likely possibility," he says, stunning me. My mouth must be hanging open because he chuckles quietly. "Just because I'm religious doesn't mean I'm close-minded, Ember. There's clearly more at work here than we can comprehend. And I know there's a bigger purpose for you."

"A bigger purpose?" Instead of the comfort I'm sure he meant to instill in me by those words, anxiety blooms in my chest instead. I don't want to be a part of any *greater good* kind of thing.

"I have this sense that *he* has more intended for you."

I almost roll my eyes at the mention of God. I'm not a religious person at all, but I have to remind myself that I asked him to come talk to me, and that he's been very open-minded and respectful. Instead of addressing that, I simply nod.

"Thank you, Frank. I appreciate you coming to meet with me and for not calling me crazy."

"Of course, Miss Ember. You call me again if you need anything else, okay?"

I nod again before giving him a hug. When his arms wrap around me, I almost break down into tears again. It's been so long since I received affection. He pats my back in a fatherly way, and I break away before I start crying.

I smile at him before heading home. I cook myself a quick dinner, making sure to drink more water to make up for all the booze I drank this morning. I can't believe that was only eight hours ago. It seems like a lifetime has passed since then. Wow. Some birthday.

Feeling a little sorry for myself, I make some more tea and lie in bed watching a show until I get sleepy.

As I'm dozing off, I hear a voice in my head. It sounds like my mother. It's barely a whisper, and I almost don't catch it.

The Forbidden Ground.

Chapter 4

When I wake in the morning, the words are burned into my brain. I know they mean something. Something important. And I have to figure out what. I somehow know that if I find the Forbidden Ground, I will find the answers I'm looking for.

I open up my laptop after I make some tea, and type the words into Google. At first all that comes up are novels and movies. I add the word *places* to my search, and after some more digging, I find something called the Oregon Vortex. Intrigued, I click on the link.

It's a tourist attraction. Some kind of natural phenomenon. There was a small structure built on the land, now called the House of Mystery. It appears to be falling into the ground, tilted on one side. The website also has pictures of people standing in different places and it appears to change their height based on the magnetic field surrounding the area. However, before the structure was built, the area dates back to the Native Americans. Their horses would not go near the area, thus they refused to as well. They called the area the "Forbidden Ground."

I read through the scientific information section as well, my curiosity piqued. I don't understand what this has to do with me or my heritage, but there's clearly something strange going on there. I debate on what to do. I could do more research from my computer, but I doubt I'll find much.

My other option is that I could actually go there, talk to people, check it out. That's the one I'm leaning toward, but it's quite the commitment when I don't know if it will lead to anything.

As I think about it, I consider that this is probably the best time to do it. I have no people in my life, no job, and once I sell Mom's house, I'll have a shit ton of money. Mind made up, I book a ticket and hotel for a month away. That will give me time to finalize the sale on her house and be financially set.

A month later, I'm at the airport, getting ready to fly halfway across the country based on a whisper. I can't tell if I'm crazy or not. Probably. I'm flying into Medford, Oregon. That's also where I booked my hotel. My rough plan is to fly in, check in, and then relax for the rest of the day. The Forbidden Ground is only about twenty minutes from there, so I can go tomorrow and have plenty of time to explore, go on the tour, and then maybe talk to the owners and locals if I still haven't found anything.

My plane takes off, and I clutch the armrests as the ascension turns my stomach. I hate flying, but it's much quicker and easier than driving. When the flight attendant comes around, I order a Bloody Mary, needing a little liquid courage for the rest of the flight, not to mention the trip. A few hours later, we're landing, and nerves flutter in my belly. I don't know if I'll find anything out, but it would sure be cool if I did.

I take an Uber to my hotel, nothing fancy, just a Holiday Inn. Like I planned, I take the day to settle in. I take a nap, and then I figure out a place to eat down the street. I have a drink and a relaxing dinner before heading back to the hotel, where I take a bath in the big tub, and then watch mindless TV all night. It's almost like I'm on a normal vacation just for the hell of it. Not like I'm searching for clues regarding my heritage based on a whisper I heard right before I fell asleep. Did I seriously do this? Am I crazy? My thoughts spiral for the millionth time since I booked this trip.

It doesn't matter, I tell myself. I'm already here, the money is already spent, I might as well see what I can find. With my mind made up, I finally drift off into a somewhat restless sleep.

The next morning, I eat the continental breakfast, even though my stomach is churning with nerves. I also have multiple coffees, which I know is a bad idea. If anything it will make my anxiety worse, but since I didn't sleep well, it's necessary.

My tour isn't until noon, so I go back to my room, take a shower, and get ready. By the time I'm done, it's eleven. I'm about to lock up and head downstairs to order my Uber, since I'm sick of waiting, when I have a feeling that I'm forgetting something. I look through my purse to find everything I would need in it—wallet, phone, key to my room. I look through my suitcase to be on the safe side. As I'm about to give up, I spot the key I found in my mother's closet. I threw it in here on a whim, and when I touch it, my necklace flares the tiniest bit and I get the sensation that I should bring it with me.

Not questioning myself, I throw it in my purse. I already have both of my necklaces around my neck, the notes from my mother in my purse (I've read them more times than I care to admit), and my feather hairpiece in, so I have everything with me that was left in the box.

I grab a sweater and my purse and head downstairs. Before I know it, my ride's here, and I'm nervously fidgeting in the back seat. Like I calculated, twenty minutes later, we pull up. It's basically in the middle of a forest with nothing else around, and of course has a huge touristy sign on the front. I have to admit, this moment is a bit anticlimactic. I was anticipating...something? This place looks like a run-down shack. How am I going to discover anything here?

I shake my head, attempting to clear my thoughts. I thank my driver and get out of the car. My tour doesn't start for another twenty minutes, so I visit the gift shop. It's exactly what you'd expect. It has some apparel, some shot glasses, and then some natural stuff, like different kinds of rocks and then a copper pipe with some magnets. I know from my research that they do some sort of trick with it during the tour, so I'm sure I'll find out the significance behind it.

At noon, the tour starts, and we're given the history of the space, starting with the Native Americans and their horses, then how it was used for mining, and finally, how John Litster invested interest in it in the 1920s and opened it to the public in the '30s, doing thousands of experiments during his time here.

I find all the information fascinating, but as the tour continues, I begin to feel motion sick. I push through and focus on the guide, who's now on to doing demonstrations outside the gift shop and getting closer to the House of Mystery. I also researched this online before coming; they have two people stand on opposite sides of a level surface and then switch and you can see that their height appears to change. I have to admit, I was skeptical, but seeing it in person is pretty incredible.

I look down and realize that my necklace is glowing. Not subtle flares like I've noticed in the past, but a steady glow, visible even outside at noon. We're now directly outside the House of Mystery and doing more demonstrations. I back myself up closest to the house so I can get a look inside while everyone else is busy. My necklace suddenly flares even brighter, lighting up the entire house, making me cry out in amazement. I look behind me to discover that no one is paying me any mind. Good.

I carefully inch my way into the space, my necklace continuing to go crazy. I get a sudden wave of strong sickness, and I have to close my eyes and take a deep breath in order to get it to pass. When I open them, I use my necklace to guide me, avoiding where it gets dimmer and continuing when it gets brighter, almost like it's playing the hot and cold game with me. It directs me to the window on the left side of the house. A flash emits from it so bright that I close my eyes and begin to stumble. I start falling, and when I open my eyes I can't see anything at all.

Chapter 5

I land on my ass, hard, with an *oomph.* My vision is blurry, and my ears are ringing. What happened? Do I have a concussion? My vision finally clears, and I inhale sharply. This is definitely not where I was a moment ago.

The House of Mystery that I was standing in is nowhere in sight, and the landscape is completely different. The view in front of me is picturesque. I'm on a huge mountain, and there's a similar one right across from it. Below me is a sprawling city located between the two peaks, with a river running through it that leads out to an ocean I can barely see in the distance. Everything is green and open as far as I can see. I look down at myself and notice that my purse is still slung across my torso, and I thank my lucky stars that I didn't lose it in whatever the fuck happened.

It takes me another moment to realize that someone is talking to me.

"Who are you?" a rough voice asks me angrily in a slight accent I can't place.

I look up and to my right only to be stunned into silence by the most gorgeous, albeit stern-looking man I've ever seen in my life. He looks like a Viking. His wavy, dark blond hair comes down a little past his collarbones, and the top portion is braided back out of his face, which allows me to see his heavily pointed ears. He has a strange but alluring mixture of features, some hard and striking, while others are soft and almost feminine. His cheekbones and nose are so sharp they look like they could cut glass, and he has a long scar running from the center of his hairline down in between his eyebrows and then trailing off to the left side of his nose, ending right above his lip, where a full but trimmed beard frames soft, pouty lips. His warm dove-gray eyes hold judgment in them, like he can see straight through to my soul, and they get more harsh the longer I look into them.

"Did you hear me? I asked you a question. Do you have a permit to travel through the portal?"

"A permit?" I parrot back, probably sounding like an idiot, which is evident by the way he's looking at me, but I have no clue what the fuck happened.

He rolls his eyes and huffs down at me. "Yes. A permit. You came through the northwest portal. You can't travel here without permission."

"And here is...where exactly?"

"The realm is Queridian. The territory is Nightshade Eclipse. The city is Twin Fangs."

I swallow. That's a lot of information he's given me, but I have zero idea what it means. "I'm in a different...*realm*?"

I can feel his frustration bleeding toward me, and now that I focus on it, I realize that this ability I have is much more heightened. I can't tell if it's because I'm no longer in my *realm* or if I can pick up on *his* emotions easier. I usually find it too draining to focus on others' emotions instead of my own, but I keep that connection open between us because it's helping me stay at least a little bit calmer.

"How? I was on a tour, and now I'm here in the middle of fucking *nowhere*."

"I guess I'm going to need to take this slow. You came out of our portal, which means that you must have traveled here from...Earth,

I'm assuming?"

At my nod, he rolls his eyes, but continues and offers me his hand so I can stand.

"And you didn't know you were traveling through a portal?"

I shake my head, too stunned to do anything more than that.

"And you've never heard of Queridian?"

"No! I didn't even know that there were other realms. I have never been here or heard of this place or anything affiliated with it. I don't even know what the hell *happened*."

"Okay, then. It seems like I'm going to have to explain some things before we figure out how exactly you got here. Earth is a non magical realm. Queridian is Earth's magical counterpart. Our world is a lot like Earth, although we are ten degrees cooler since we're technically underneath it." He pauses, as if to give me a moment to digest everything he's told me. I nod for him to continue. "Right now, you are in Nightshade Eclipse, which is vampire territory."

At the word *vampire*, my eyes nearly bug out of my head and I almost fall back down on my ass. He notices my reaction and gives me a wicked smile, complete with a set of fangs. I gasp and take a step back.

"It's all right, little doe, I won't bite. At least not right now."

My eyes narrow in irritation and challenge at being referred to as "little doe."

"What I don't understand is how you say you've never been here before, but you certainly have other species in your blood. You *smell* human, even though you have mermaid eyes and elf ears, which isn't exactly *unheard* of in humans, but it is very rare that you will get physical traits of your mixed blood."

My heart stops beating. In just a few glances and sentences he already knows more about my heritage than I do. Normally I'm not so quick to trust or listen to a perfect stranger, but his words are resonating deep within me, and there's a sense of rightness that accompanies them.

"You can tell what heritage I have?" I take a step closer in my eagerness to hear more.

"Let's walk and talk," he says, pointing to a building close by.

Suddenly, I start to panic. I don't know this man. I don't know where I am. He could do anything to me once he gets me in that building. "No. I think I'd like to talk right here."

"I'm not going to answer your questions unless you cooperate with me. I won't hurt you, but this way we can sit down and I'll get you some food and water."

I glance at the building again as I weigh my options. Supposedly, I'm in a different realm, which means I'm on my own no matter what. I have no clue where I am, or how to get back to Earth even if I wanted to. Within two minutes, this man has given me more answers about myself than I've ever had before, and now that he's told me a little bit, I want to know so much more. I won't get that if I don't go with him. I hesitantly nod and start walking alongside him.

"Most humans don't have any traits of any other bloodline except human, but there are a few rare exceptions that will have another physical attribute. That usually happens when the magical blood is especially powerful. It's too bad you are human. I bet you'd have quite a bit of magic in you if you weren't." He licks his lips as his eyes latch on to my throat.

"Excuse me, can you stop eye-fucking my neck, please?" I say, snapping my fingers in front of his face.

He blinks and shakes his head slightly as if to clear his thoughts. "Sorry, vampire trait," he says, slightly sheepish.

"So, because I'm human, I won't have any powers that a mermaid or an elf would, even though I apparently also have their blood?"

"Humans have their own abilities. Nothing as strong as what the other species have, but they're able to pick up on what others feel. Especially here, the magic in the realm amplifies your powers, where on Earth you might not have noticed anything like that because Earth doesn't produce or support magic. Although those who do possess magic are able to wield it on Earth, it's simply not as effective as if they were to use it here. But enough about that," he says as we arrive at the building, holding the door open for me. "For now, I need you to sit down so I can ask you some questions about *you*."

I look up to see a symbol above the door. From here it looks like fangs with blood dripping from them. Nice. Real nice.

"Are those fangs?" I ask him, gesturing.

"Yes. It's the symbol that represents us. Every species here has a different crest, and they are used to show others what we are. Sometimes it can be hard to differentiate between the races, so you'll see it on different buildings or on clothing to identify them."

Wow. That sounds a little like 1940s Germany to me. "Why do you need to tell the difference between them at all?"

He looks at me strangely for a minute, not answering me before gesturing for me to go in.

The building is small. It looks like housing quarters for some government project. The man leads me to a table and brings me a glass of water. I almost collapse into the chair, my mind a jumbled mess, and my body a wreck from whatever it went through when I traveled through the *portal*. Jesus. I still can't believe that happened. I detect a feeling similar to what happened when my mom died coming on, and I wonder if I'm going into shock.

Before I can spiral too far, the man sits down across from me, a bottle in one hand and two small glasses in the other. He sets a glass down for each of us and pours some amber liquid into both, pushing one toward me before taking the other. "I thought you could use something a little stronger, considering what you've been through."

I blink at the thoughtfulness, not expecting it from this harsh and to-the-point man.

"Thank you..." I stall, not knowing his name.

"Alexei. Alexei Dreymonde."

"Thank you, Alexei."

"And what is your name?"

"Ember Amor."

"Nice to meet you, Ember."

"You too, Alexei."

"So, how did you get here?"

"It's kind of a long story," I say, taking a sip of the amber liquid.

It burns going down, but it helps to clear my head a little bit, so I take another. Alexei waits with his eyebrows raised for me to continue. I sigh, not wanting to talk about it, but I tell him everything that's happened from the moment my mom died to going on the tour and the necklace freaking out.

"Then the next thing I know, I'm falling, and your grumpy-ass face was staring down at me asking why I don't have a permit to travel through the portal."

"What necklace?" he asks, as if that's the most important part of my story.

I pull it from underneath my shirt collar and extend it out in front of me to show him. He immediately gets into my personal space, grabbing the necklace and coming closer to have a better look.

With him so near, I struggle to breathe. I can't explain it, but it's almost like there's a heat to him, and I have a feeling that if he were to touch me that there would be a zing. With Alexei so close, his delicious scent is filling up my nostrils, making my brain almost fuzzy. He smells like leather, whiskey, a hint of blood, and something sweet that I can't quite place. Maybe honey?

"Where did you get this?" he asks, snapping me out of my stupor.

"It was in the box of things from my birth mother."

"This is a Queridian necklace. You see that symbol on it? It's a rune.

It means love. In order to travel through the portal you need to have a stone with a rune on it. Our language is recognized by the magic and that allows us to move between the realms and the stone simply channels it. It's uncommon for any of us to go between them even *with* permission. But in your case, the only time I've ever heard of this happening is when the humans first came here hundreds of years ago. According to their legends, a whole group of them traveled here at the same time. Apparently, their gods told them what they needed to do, and where they needed to go to get here, and here they came."

"So, my mother lived here?" I ask.

"I think she would have had to. With your heritage I don't see how you could be from the Mortal Realm. I'm guessing your birth mother was in some sort of danger and didn't want you involved so she had your adoptive mother take you where she knew you'd be safe."

I think this over for a moment. It's definitely possible.

"Either way, you need to be taken to the king," he says nonchalantly, like it's not a big deal.

"Excuse me?"

"You heard me." He gives my attitude right back to me, and I struggle not to slap him across the face.

"I'm not going anywhere with you, especially not to see some stuck-up asshole king who will choose to do God only knows what with me."

"I'm sorry to be the one to tell you, *Ember*, but you don't have a choice."

"Oh, so you're going to kidnap me then? 'Cause I can tell you right now that I'm not going," I say like a petulant child.

I don't know where my snippiness is coming from, but I'm in a different place, and what seems like a whole different time period, I'm getting information overload, now this man who seems to be getting on my last nerve (and thoroughly enjoying it) is talking about taking me to go see the *king*.

"I'm not going to kidnap you. You are my prisoner," he states simply.

"*Prisoner?!*" I practically scream at him, popping up out of my chair and leaning in close to his face. I'm attempting to be intimidating, but by the smirk on his face and the amusement trickling toward me, I'm not accomplishing it. "How did you come to that conclusion?"

"It's simple. You traveled through the portal without a permit. That is breaking our laws. I am here for this exact reason. I am the *guard* of the northwest portal. There are specific protocols for this very situation. Anyone who travels through the portal without a permit, even if by accident, is to be taken to the king immediately."

I sit there staring at him with my mouth hanging open, not knowing what to say.

"We will leave for Mystic Mountain and the Immortal City tomorrow. I'll cook us up some dinner, and then I suggest you get a good night's rest. It's going to be a long journey." Without giving me a chance to reply, he gets up and leaves me alone at the table.

I sit back down and take another drink of my whiskey. The fucking *nerve* of that man. He's lucky he left when he did, otherwise I would not have been responsible for the damage I would've done to him. Although, by the look of the weapons he's carrying, and the muscles he's got on him, I don't know how much I would've been able to inflict.

My next thought is about what a *vampire* is going to cook me for dinner. A hysterical bubble of laughter bursts free from my lips, and suddenly I am in full-blown stress-induced howling, tears streaming down my face, not able to catch my breath.

Alexei appears moments later, brows furrowed, a plate of cheese and grapes in his hands.

"Should I be concerned about you?" he asks skeptically, making me laugh even harder.

I lean over, putting a hand to the stitch in my side. I hear him set the plate down on the table, and I start to pull myself together. It has been so long since I laughed like that. My heart instantly lightens. My mom used to call that "frozen face," where you're laughing so hard you're crying and your face is literally frozen in a smile. The last time that happened to me was with her. Thinking of that memory fully snaps me out of it and brings a sad smile to my face. I miss her.

I take another drink of whiskey, and wipe the tears from my eyes. When I've calmed down enough, I reach over and grab a grape from the plate, popping it into my mouth. I moan as the flavor explodes on my tongue. I don't know if it's because of where I am, or the fact that I've had some crazy shit happen today, but it is the most refreshing fruit I have ever eaten in my life. I try the cheese next, and it's so smooth it melts in my mouth. Before I know it, I've eaten more than half the plate.

"I guess it's a good thing this isn't all we have to eat," Alexei remarks like a smartass.

I fight the urge to give him a filthy gesture and keep eating as he goes back into the kitchen. I finish off the snacks as he walks in with two steaming bowls. He sets mine in front of me before taking the seat across from me. My mouth is watering at the smell of the delicious-looking stew and crusty bread. What is it about traumatic experiences that makes you so hungry?

I start scarfing my food in a very unladylike manner, which is another reason that I'm not fit to meet royalty. I finish my meal before Alexei and push my bowl away, chugging my water. When I set my glass down, I feel fully satisfied. I don't think I've ever had a meal that good. And I was worried about what a vampire would feed me. I mentally roll my eyes at myself.

My eyes suddenly have weights on them, and I struggle to stay awake. At first, I panic, thinking that maybe my food was drugged, but that snaps me out of my exhaustion enough that I realize it's only the events of the day and the fact that I just had a wonderful, fulfilling meal.

"You can sleep in my bed tonight. I'll take the couch. We leave at first light." Alexei gets up upon finishing his meal and points to a closed door, which I assume is his room.

I nod and head that way. Little does he know, I have no intention of leaving with him in the morning.

Chapter 6

I close the door behind me and sit on his bed. I need to wait probably at least an hour to make sure he's asleep before attempting to escape. Luckily there's a window in the room that I can sneak out of. Now all I need to do is make sure I don't fall back asleep before that happens.

As much as I want to know everything about myself and where I come from, I don't want to go on a long trek to see the king with a man I don't know or trust who claims that I'm now his prisoner. Plus, I already discovered quite a bit, like where my mother was from and the other species I have in my blood. I definitely have more answers than I had yesterday. It's time for me to go home.

To keep myself occupied, I take note of everything in his room. It doesn't entertain me for long though. There are no personal items anywhere, and it is very clean and orderly. The bed is neatly made with the most boring bedding ever, there's a lit candle on the bare nightstand, a trunk full of weapons in one corner, and a trunk full of clothes in the other. That's it. I grab a knife from one of them to be on the safe side.

After snooping, mostly unsuccessfully I might add, I rummage through my purse, deciding to take my phone out. I open it to find that he did indeed tell me the truth. I have zero service here and no internet. Not that I thought it would be different, but I was holding out hope that maybe he was crazy. I turn my phone off to save the battery.

I look at my belongings with new eyes. This is all I was able to take with me from the Mortal Realm, as Alexei likes to call it, and in case I'm not able to get back, it will be nice to know what I have in here that could be useful. I dump all my stuff out on his bed and sift through it. I have my phone (the battery is at 80%), a wireless portable charger that is fully charged, a small Bluetooth speaker that is also fully charged, a new stick of deodorant, ChapStick, some makeup, my wallet, which will be no use to me here, headphones, painkillers, Dramamine, my favorite scrunchy, a compact mirror, a lighter, gum, Kleenex, and then the small key and the notes I found from my birth mother. I put everything back in my purse and sling it over my torso.

I press my ear against the door and hear Alexei snoring softly on the other side of it. I smile to myself as I ease the window open. We're on the first story, so I don't need to drop down a level from an open window. The last thing I need is a broken ankle in the middle of the night in a magical realm where I don't know anyone.

I crawl out, the knife firmly in my grip, and start walking. A few minutes in, I regret not rummaging through his clothes to grab something warmer. I forgot that it is ten degrees colder here than on Earth. Another few minutes later, I realize that I'm going the wrong way. I huff in frustration, turning around to head back to the house so I can find the correct direction, when someone appears in front of me. Literally right in front of me.

I cry out in alarm, stumbling back and almost ending up on my ass. The male in question is extremely ragged, almost homeless looking. His clothes are ratty and dirty, hanging off of him, either like he lost a lot of weight since getting them, or those were the only clothing options he could find and they just didn't fit. He has streaks of dirt on his face, dark circles under his eyes, and a very unruly beard, nothing like the trimmed, clean facial hair that Alexei has.

It also dawns on me that before he suddenly appeared, he was nowhere in sight. If I were on Earth I would chalk it up to me not paying attention, but here, my intuition tells me he has a power that I'm not aware of.

"Well, don't you look tasty" are his first words to me, making me shudder. I have no clue what he means, but it could be several different things, none of which bode well for me.

"Excuse me," I say, attempting to ignore him and walk away, knowing that it probably won't work in the slightest. I grip my knife tighter in my hand.

"Oh, I don't think so."

He rushes at me, and I slash at him. It knicks him in the stomach, a little bit of blood seeping through his filthy shirt. He looks down and snarls, actually snarls, at what he sees.

"That wasn't very nice."

Before I can attack him again, he disappears right in front of my eyes. I'm about to turn to look for him when I feel one of his arms come around my neck, his other gripping my hand that's holding the knife, and twisting until I have to release it, or risk a broken wrist.

"Now, I'm going to let go, and you're going to come with me. If you don't—" Before he can finish his sentence, I whip my head back, slamming it into his nose and giving me an instant headache, but the result is worth it.

Warm wetness gushes down the back of my neck, and I smile in satisfaction, pretty sure that I broke his nose. His hold on me loosens, and I take advantage of it, elbowing him in the stomach for good measure. He releases me fully then, and I take off toward Alexei's. I don't get far, and as I'm about to scream, he appears in front of me again. I stop in my tracks, and he punches me right in the face. I feel my lip spilling blood, and then I lose consciousness.

I wake up freezing, goosebumps peppering my skin, my body shaking so hard my teeth are clacking together. I try to rub my hands over my arms, but find they're bound behind my back. It's then that the memories flood back and my panic starts to set in.

I open my eyes slowly (in case it makes the pain in my head worse) so I can figure out how bad my situation is. At first I can't see anything at all, but then as my sight adjusts, I realize that I'm in a cave. The moon is shedding just enough light that I can barely take in my surroundings.

I'm at the mouth of the cave, not too far in, but enough that I can smell the mustiness and humidity that clings to me like a second skin, making me even colder. Farther in, there's a large pile of something—it's not bright enough for me to see what it is, but it causes my heart rate to speed up as though I've run a mile.

My purse is still with me on the floor. He must have figured that there was nothing of value in there, and probably didn't recognize anything inside. I can feel dried blood on my chin, and the hard rock wall I'm propped against is jutting into my back. My mouth is dry as cotton and there's a faint taste of iron, likely from my lip splitting open, and I have the worst headache I think I've ever had in my entire life. My eyes finally make their way to the man strolling into the area with a bunch of wood gathered in his arms.

"Oh good, you're awake. I was afraid I hit you too hard and that you'd never wake up."

I swallow loudly, not knowing what to say to the man who captured me and actually did kidnap me. He starts building a small fire in front of us, and soon the heat penetrates the chill that won't leave my bones. I'm torn between wanting to move closer to warm up and scooting far away from him. Eventually, my discomfort wins, and I get as close as I can manage to the fire without burning myself.

It's then that my eyes make their way back to that pile I couldn't quite see earlier. It takes a few moments for my brain to comprehend what it is, but when it finally clicks, I almost throw up. The full reality of my situation sinks in, my breathing accelerates along with my heart rate, and I almost pass out again.

My captor notices my reaction and smirks in my direction, his fangs peeking out at me. If I wasn't sure if he was a vampire before, I am now.

"Don't worry, lovely, you'll join them soon," he says, reaching out to stroke my cheek, making me flinch and gag.

He's referring to the pile of bones on the other side of the cave. There's no way to know how many people that pile contains, but it's got to be in the double digits. High double digits. His words finally sink in, and I realize he intends to kill me. What I don't know is *why*.

"What do you want with me?" I ask, my voice hoarse.

"Your blood, of course," he states simply as he continues stoking the fire.

Even though his words are nonchalant, his intense hunger hits me harder with every breath. I don't want to be connected to his emotions right now, but as I'm about to sever the connection between us, I realize that would be stupid of me. If I can sense them, then maybe I can anticipate his moves.

"Well, in that case, wouldn't it make sense to take a little bit of blood so you can keep me alive longer and get more out of me?"

I absolutely loathe the idea of being kept hostage and used as a blood bag for an undetermined amount of time. I do, however, want to give myself the best chance I can to survive, which means talking him into using me for as long as he can.

"That way you can get more blood over a longer period of time and won't have to go looking for someone else until after I die."

"While your logic is sound, it doesn't apply here." He is extremely well spoken, which takes me by surprise.

I figured that since he looks so disheveled and is living out of a cave that he would speak unintelligently. And while he looks raggedy, the face beneath is deceptively handsome. Maybe it's a vampire quality?

"There's a group of us who can't afford to go to the alchemist, or to pay a private donor for blood, so each night we go hunting and see who we can find. We meet back in this cave and then everyone shares. So, while if it was only me, I would keep you alive for as long as I could, that's not the way this works. The others will be here around sunrise."

My heart sinks. I don't know how far off that is since I was unconscious, but at most it's a few hours. My only chance is talking my way out of it, or giving Alexei enough time to find me.

Although, when he finds me missing he'll probably think that I was able to get back through the portal and not even give me another thought. No. I have to figure this out on my own. No one is going to rescue me. Since my hands are already behind me I have an advantage. My body blocks any movements that he might see, but I need to keep him talking so he's distracted. I scoot back toward the wall where I started, making a show of wanting to lean against something.

"What's the alchemist?" I latch on to the first question I can think of.

He seems like a talker, so hopefully he won't realize what I'm trying to accomplish. I start moving my hands along the wall behind me, looking for any sharp bit of rock that I can try to sever the rope with.

"The alchemist is a shop. They have volunteers come in and donate blood, for a price, of course, and then if you are a vampire, you can go in and mix and match whichever kind of blood you want. The more blood options you choose, the more expensive your visit will be, and let me tell you, even just *one* type of blood is expensive at the alchemist."

I finally find something that might be useful, and I get to work on the rope.

"What's the benefit of drinking different blood types?" I may be stalling, but I am genuinely interested in the answers to these questions.

"How do you not know any of this?" he asks, brows furrowed.

I halt my movements when he stops working on the fire to look at me questioningly.

"I'm not from here. I traveled through the northwest portal from Earth."

His eyes widen in surprise. "Well, that would explain it. You've had quite the introduction into our world, haven't you?" He winks at me as though my being kidnapped and about to be made a blood bag is something that every human being from Earth should want. "If we drink the blood from another type of species, we can temporarily use whatever powers they possess. So when you go to the alchemist, if you are incredibly wealthy, you have the opportunity to have access to all the powers in Queridian."

I swallow; that sounds both amazing and terrifying.

"It's rare, however, for someone to mix more than two blood types when they go. Especially because the more blood types you mix, the faster they lose their effectiveness."

I'm starting to make progress on freeing myself, but blood coats my wrists. I must be messing my arms up since I can't see what I'm doing and using a fucking *rock* to cut through my bindings. I'm surprised I don't feel any pain from it, but then I realize that my adrenaline must be working overtime.

"Does every species have their own power? What even *are* all the races here?" I figure this question will take him a while to answer.

He sighs dramatically, and I can sense his frustration and mounting hunger, but he obliges me, probably figuring the least he can do is answer my questions since he's about to kill me.

"There are seven different species in our realm. Vampires, obviously, with the ability to teletravel. Mermaids, power of persuasion and allure. Elves, healing. Witches, premonition. Mimics, shapeshifting. Fae, elemental magic. Last, and definitely least, humans, with the power of empathy." Disdain drips from his mouth as he talks about humans, and I wish I could kick him in the balls to show him who's *least*.

"Is that how you captured me then? You teletraveled?" I think he's talking about teleporting, but I can't be sure.

"You mean like this?" One second he's standing across the cave from me, in the next he's standing immediately in front of me.

I suck in a sharp breath and press myself against the wall so he can't see what I'm doing as he towers over me. He takes a sharp sniff and his eyes dilate. He crouches down in front of me.

"I smell blood," he says quietly, his voice rough and full of what I can only assume is bloodlust.

"Well, I have dried blood on my lip from when you punched me earlier." I inject as much venom as I can into my voice so that he doesn't start questioning it. Apparently, I'm not successful, because in the next second, he's pushing my body forward.

"You sneaky little *bitch*," he snarls, backhanding me across the face.

My lip splits open again, and I gasp against the amplifying pain in my skull. He hoists me up in his arms and unceremoniously drops me in the middle of the cave where there is nothing I can use to free myself. He crouches behind me and tightens my bindings even more. The next thing I know, he's teletraveled (as he likes to call it) to the other side of the cave, breathing in the fresh air deeply. His shoulders are almost all the way up to his ears, and he looks tight as a bow string.

I feel through our connection that his self-control is on the verge of snapping, and I know he's struggling to wait for the others. I suddenly recall something that I think may have happened before, and it gives me an idea. I have no idea if it will work, or if it can even be *done*. But I have to try. I can't sit around here waiting for death.

I focus on the connection between us until my blood is humming with it, and I visualize the emotions I'm sensing as if they were another person. Once I've accomplished that, I try to push an emotion toward him.

I picture what it feels like to be extremely full, like I was earlier in the night, and completely satisfied. I manifest it and gently nudge it toward him, like an old friend coming to tap him on the shoulder. Almost immediately, he visibly relaxes, and I sense his hunger slip away from him. He takes another deep breath, probably equating it to the fresh air and not to me. That's what I need. I think it worked? It's so hard to tell, but there's no harm in trying.

The next thing I visualize is guilt and shame. I swirl them both together until they are an ugly mess of angry colors, black and gray and brown, fighting for dominance. I don't know if I'm actually seeing the emotions I'm attempting to make him feel, or if it's just my imagination making this easier. Before I push it toward him, I need to say something that he would equate to triggering these emotions.

"This realm is so beautiful. I wish I could've been able to explore it. I haven't been able to even see much of *my* world. It would've been nice to travel"—I sigh regretfully—"before I died."

I inject as much pitiful whininess into my voice as I can, even going so far as to sniffle before I gently push that swirling mass toward him. I don't let it hit him all at once, instead it trickles slowly. I can see when it hits him. His head hangs low, and he runs his hands through his hair like he can pull the emotions out of his head. I instead do the opposite, feeding him more and more of the mass until it's all disappeared inside of him. His breathing accelerates, and I think I hear his breath hitch. A sweat breaks out on my brow. I think because I'm pushing a more complicated emotion onto him than before, it takes more of an effort, but from his body language it seems to have worked.

"How old are you?" he asks, his voice tormented.

"Twenty-eight." I make an effort to put more misery in my voice.

"*Fuck.*" He stands there looking out at the world. I can see the faintest trickle of light along the horizon, and I know I'm almost out of time. He turns around and appears in front of me, quickly untying my binds. "Go" is all he says. I blink in surprise. I can't believe that worked. Before he can change his mind, I take off.

Just as I get through the mouth of the cave and turn the corner, I run into someone. They grip my arms to make sure I don't fall. I look up only to discover a group of equally grungy-looking individuals to the man inside. I immediately know who they are, and attempt to pull away and run from the man holding me.

"Well, hello. I can already tell you are going to be a fun one, your blood smells *delicious.*"

Chapter 7

I scream, kick, thrash, bite. I do everything I can think of to try to escape, all to no avail. The man holds firm, and I almost break down in tears at how unfair it all is. I rescue myself, only to not do it quickly enough. I can't do what I did to...seven people all at once. I could barely do it the first time, and now that it's over, I don't even know quite *how* I did it.

"Keep fighting me, adrenaline-soaked blood is my *favorite*." The man leans down and smells my neck before dragging his fangs gently down the same path. I freeze. One simple move and he could impale my throat.

"Mosher, let's take her in the cave," a delicate female voice sounds behind him.

He takes another long sniff and licks up my neck before pulling away and dragging me back into my prison.

"Let our meal escape, did you, Shindar?" he says to the man who captured me.

Shindar is closer to the entrance than when I left, and he looks fairly confused, but he says nothing and stands away from the group. The next thing I know, I'm surrounded by seven hungry vampires, all looking at me like I'm the best breakfast they've ever seen. As I meet every one of their gazes, and see nothing but ravenous monsters staring back at me, I decide to go out guns blazing, doing as much damage as possible.

"Come at me, motherfuckers." And they do.

Mosher first, and quick as lightning, I thrust my open palm out and up toward his face. I hear a crunch, his nose breaking under the pressure. Someone else approaches me from behind, and I throw an elbow into their abdomen. I'm throwing out every trick that I know (granted, most of them are from *Miss Congeniality*, and I've had no real training), and am actually surprised to see how much damage I'm inflicting, but before long too many close in on me all at once and I'm subdued.

I scream again, but it's abruptly cut off by a sharp inhale when someone's fangs pierce my throat—Mosher, I think. I whimper at the pain. I've always read about vampires and found them sexy and intriguing, thinking that a bite from one sounded like something I might even enjoy. I'm dead wrong. This is horrible.

Lightning shoots through my veins, burning me from the inside out. Another sharp bite lands on my inner right wrist, and I open my eyes to see that it's Shindar—guess he got over the guilt and confusion quickly enough—and then another bite at the skin between my neck and shoulder. And then, I'm being bitten everywhere, and my body is on fire. I can't tell where I begin and the pain ends. It's unclear how long it's been, seconds or an eternity, but the next thing I know, the pain stops. No one is biting me, and as I start to come back to myself, I realize that at some point, either my feet came out from under me, or they laid me down.

I blink my eyes open to see Alexei creating carnage throughout the entire cave. He's so fast and skilled that it takes me a moment to recognize him, but there he is, stunning, like an avenging angel. There is pure fury on his face and nothing but wrath written in every line of his body.

He bellows his rage as he teletravels around the cave, slashing with two mighty swords, and before I know it, everyone except the two of us are dead, bleeding out on the cave floor around us. Only then does he look at me. When our gazes meet, there's so much relief in them that it brings tears to my eyes. Let me rephrase, fresh tears to my eyes, because there's wetness on my cheeks from when I was being drained.

"Ember," Alexei says, his voice rough.

He drops his swords and slowly walks to me. He's doing it purposefully so as not to startle or scare me, which I appreciate. If he were to teletravel, I don't think I could handle it. The tears start coming faster now. Everything hurts. I look down and see bite marks on my arms; my pant legs have been hastily rolled up, and I have some there as well. I bring my fingers to my neck to feel two sets of marks there too.

My eyes are so blurred with tears that I can't see him clearly, but he's crouched next to me, gently moving my fingers away from my neck. "Don't touch them. We don't want you to get an infection. Can you sit up?"

I take a deep breath and try to pull myself up. Alexei brings his hand underneath my back to help me, and when I'm finally upright, I look around at the carnage in the cave. There's blood everywhere, some heads disconnected from bodies, bellies slashed open, blood, blood, *blood.*

Alexei notices the direction of my gaze and picks me up before gently setting me down on the ground outside the cave. Then he takes off his jacket, draping it around my shoulders. I snuggle into its warmth, his unique masculine scent calming me. I take a few deep breaths of fresh air, closing my eyes and trying to come back to myself. After I'm somewhat composed, I open my eyes again, only to see the most breathtaking sunrise on the horizon. I enjoy it for about two point five seconds before I remember something and start to freak out.

"Alexei, you can't be out in the sun!" I exclaim, attempting to shove him back toward the cave.

"Says who?" he asks with a perplexed look on his face.

"Every vampire story I've ever read. Don't you die or wither away or something when you're exposed to sunlight?"

"Aww, little doe, are you *worried* about me?" he asks, a teasing glint in his voice.

I shake my head as I give him a little half smile. "Well, you did save my life. It seems like the least I can do is to make sure you don't burst into flames. Or erupt into sparkles. That would be embarrassing."

He gives me a small smile before looking at me with concern. "Are you all right?"

I look down so I don't have to meet his gaze, taking a deep breath before asking a question to change the subject. Because no. No, I am not all right.

"How did you find me?"

"I woke up before first light, and got a bad feeling. I knocked on your door, and when you didn't answer I went in to find your window open. I figured you were trying to go back home, but I could see footprints leading in the opposite direction. I followed them and found the knife and two different blood scents. I knew one was yours, and I was able to track the scents here. Then I heard you screaming," he finishes quietly.

"What else isn't true about vampires?" I ask, wanting to change the subject.

He indulges me. "Probably nothing in the Mortal Realm is true about our different races. Or at least not much."

"Clearly you can die other ways than a stake through the heart?" I gesture toward the cave. None of them were stabbed through the chest, at least not that I saw.

"We can die from anything a human can, but it usually takes a little more effort. We have a higher chance of healing from things than a human does. We can die of old age, but we live to be about three to four hundred years old. The same is true for all races except human. You guys only live to be about one hundred and sixty. We also don't get diseases or anything like that, and that pretty much applies to every magical creature in this realm. Except again, humans, of course. You guys are exceedingly fragile." He winks at me, trying to distract me and put me in a better mood. I appreciate the effort, but I am so tired. "Can I pick you up? I can carry you back to the house."

"I can walk. Can you help me up?"

He reaches a hand down for me to grab, hoisting me up. When I'm on both feet, however, I am immediately light-headed, and I sway.

"I don't think you are going to be able to walk, little doe," Alexei says as he sweeps me into his arms.

I almost protest, but I clearly can't even stand, let alone walk. Plus, as much as I hate to admit, it feels nice being in his arms. Soon the gentle movement of his walking and the heat from his body lulls me to sleep.

I wake sometime later, the sun fully up now, and his house in view. I wipe the sleep from my eyes, yawning right in Alexei's face.

"Good morning, sleepy head."

"You can set me down now," I say, embarrassed.

He does as I ask. I'm grateful that this time around, I seem to be steady. We continue walking toward the house at a slower pace than when he was carrying me.

"How long was I out?"

"Only about forty-five minutes."

"That long? How on Earth did you carry me for that long?" I am not thin. I'm not overweight either, but I have no clue how he managed to keep that up for the length of time that he did.

"Well, that's just it, isn't it, little doe? We aren't on Earth," he says cryptically, winking at me for good measure. "Vampires, and most magical creatures here in general, are much stronger than humans.

Especially humans on Earth. The magic of the realm amplifies our bodies. You should notice a difference here too. You will be stronger, faster, and your senses should be amplified as well."

Now that he's mentioned it, I do notice subtle differences. Everything looks crisper, sharper. I'm sure some of that is the realm itself, but I also remember eating last night. The food tasted better too. I bet some of that was the food itself, and some of it, my newly heightened senses.

"Why didn't you teletravel us here?"

"We can't carry anyone or anything over a few pounds with us when we teletravel."

We arrive at the house, and I am about to walk straight to bed to go back to sleep, nowhere near rested enough, when Alexei grabs my arm, halting me, and shakes his head.

"We need to clean those bites before they get infected."

"Is there always a risk of infection with vampire bites?"

"No. Rarely does that ever happen actually, but those fuckers were filthy, and Gods only know what had been in their mouths before that. Also, if we bite someone, we usually have the common courtesy to close the wound for them."

My eyebrows jump up in surprise. "You can heal people?"

"No, not in that sense. That ability belongs to the elves. But there is a quality in our saliva that, when we are done feeding, can close the bite. It's done out of respect for the donor. Once we wash your wounds, I can do that for you. We need to make sure there's no risk of infection before we do that so that I don't seal the bacteria into your body and make the problem worse."

I nod, intrigued to see how it's done. He guides me to the bathroom and gestures for me to step into the large tub.

"You want me to bathe in front of you?" I ask.

He looks me up and down, heat flaring in his eyes. He turns the water on for me, and I'm surprised to find that this realm has running water. They seem stuck in the old ages. Not to mention that I hadn't seen any form of technology since I got here.

"Why don't you bathe on your own first, and when you're done, wrap up in a towel and I will help you clean all of them individually before we close them up. I'm sure you'd like to bathe, and if we were to clean them beforehand, they would just get more dirt in them from the bathwater." With that, he turns and leaves me on my own.

I eye the bath longingly as I strip off all of my nasty ass clothes. I wince as I pull my pants down, the material scraping against the raw and, honestly, brutal-looking bites. I guess that they didn't care about biting me nicely, since they were planning on killing me anyway.

I sink down into the warm, soothing water, making an almost sexual noise as it envelops my body. Alexei was right, the dirt is already coming off my skin, tainting the water. I dunk my head under before it gets too bad. I find soap next to me and quickly lather it between my palms before running it all over my body, paying special attention to the bites. When I'm about to use it in my hair, I spot a little bottle of what looks like shampoo, or at least something similar. I sniff it cautiously, and am pleasantly surprised by the smell of rosemary and mint. I squirt some in my hand and massage it into my scalp, sighing at the scents and the feel of getting clean.

When I'm done washing myself, I look down to find the water so murky and disgusting that I can't even see my own body underneath it. Grossed out, I drain the tub and fill it again with fresh water. I soap down my body once more before wrapping in a towel and calling for Alexei. He enters, and his eyes flare again at seeing me clean and basically naked. The towel is barely large enough to cover the important bits.

"I'll clean the bites, and then I'm going to put a liquid on them that draws out any potential infection, and then I'll seal them for you," he says, his voice husky.

I nod, stepping back into the now-empty tub. He turns the water on, lathers the soap between his hands before gently and methodically cleaning every bite. I wince at the first touch, but I know it needs to be done and that he's being as gentle as possible. Once the wounds are thoroughly cleaned, he retrieves a bottle of clear liquid from underneath his sink.

"This is going to sting a bit. I'm sorry." I nod for him to continue, preparing myself for the inevitable.

He starts with my neck, and sure enough, the first splash of whatever the fuck that liquid is burns like a sonofabitch. I inhale sharply through my nose, closing my watering eyes. It lessens quickly, and before I'm ready for it, he moves on to the next one. I'm glad he's getting it over with, but it's not a pleasant experience. When he's finally finished, I exhale in relief.

"Now what?"

"Well, you may want to put on some clothes, because I have to lick you."

"You have to do *what*?!"

"I mean, I'd be more than willing to do it as you are now," he teases, his eyes glinting. I narrow mine back at him.

"I don't have any clean clothes here."

He grabs my hand, guiding me out of the tub. "You can wear some of mine until we clean yours and get you some new ones."

I nod as he directs me back into his room. He rummages through his trunk, fishing out some shorts and a soft shirt. They're going to be absolutely massive on me, but at least they're clean. He steps out so I can change, and as I had guessed, I'm swimming in them. The shirt comes down to my knees, and when I put the shorts on they immediately fall off, however, they have a drawstring so I'm able to keep them up that way. Of course I don't have any panties, and while I considered putting my dirty ones back on, I really do not want anything on me from the night before.

Alexei comes back a moment later, huffing what sounds like a laugh upon seeing me drowning in his clothes. I narrow my eyes at him again—I seem to be doing that a lot since we met—and he makes his way over to me.

"So, you really have to *lick* me?"

"Yes. Our brain can send a signal to our mouth that creates enzymes that will close the bite when we're done feeding."

"You mean you have to bite me again?" I ask, terrified at the thought.

"Not right now, little doe. I only need to tell my mouth to close the wound, and it will." I visibly relax at his words. I do not want to be bitten ever again. "Most vampire bites aren't painful. Actually, most people find them quite pleasurable," he says, his voice dipping low, making a slow heat spread through my body and settle in between my legs.

"Well, I've been bitten. Seven times, in fact, and none of it was pleasurable. It felt like my blood was on fire."

"Those *fuckers*. They could have at least made it pleasurable for you. My guess is that they either were too lost to bloodlust to remember, or they enjoyed having you in pain."

His eyes are full of rage, and his body is taut with anger, his fists clenching as if he wants to kill every single one of them again. I swallow at the intensity. I'm surprised he's reacting this strongly *for me*, or maybe that's wishful thinking and he would have felt this upset about anyone they would have attacked.

"So, closing my bites?" I ask suddenly, trying to distract us both.

He nods, moving in closer to me. He looks every bit of the predator I know he is in that moment, and I feel exactly like the "little doe" he claims I am. He wraps his arms around me and draws me against his chest. I press my palms against the smooth planes, and he leans down.

His nose skims my throat, and it's already such a different experience than Mosher.

My heart beats an excited pattern, and I know he can hear it. A moment later, his tongue makes a wet glide against the bite on my neck. Instead of hurting like I anticipate, pleasure zings through my body. A moan breaks free from my throat, and Alexei's heart jumps against my palms in response. He slowly draws back and repeats the process on the bite on my shoulder. I thought I would be prepared for it the second time, but it's even more intense. I squeeze my thighs together to try to get some relief, but it doesn't seem to help.

The next ones aren't quite as overwhelming, either because he's no longer in my personal space, or because the areas themselves are less sensitive. Although, I do almost combust on the spot when I glance down to see him on his knees before me, licking my legs.

"See, little doe? It doesn't have to hurt."

"Yeah, but you weren't biting me."

"But I was still able to make it more pleasurable than it would've been otherwise."

"You mean, you made it feel sexual when it didn't have to be?" My palm is twitching with the desire to slap him.

"I was demonstrating what *my* bite would be like," he states smugly, winking at me before walking out, closing the door behind him.

Dick. Now I'm a mess of need, and it's all his fault. I walk over to the bed, discovering that he's left me a glass and a pitcher of water on the nightstand. I scowl at the thoughtfulness, chugging half the glass before collapsing into bed. I thought that I would struggle to sleep after the events of the night, but I'm out as soon as my head hits the pillow.

Chapter 8

When I wake, I have no clue how long I slept. It's light outside the window, so it's either still the same day, or I slept a full twenty-four hours. I stretch satisfactorily in bed before wincing at how badly I need to use the restroom. Once I've taken care of those needs and freshened up my mouth with something I can only assume is toothpaste I find next to the sink, I go in search of Alexei.

I find him in the kitchen. It's small, but plenty bright since there's a large window above the sink with multiple different herbs and plants on the sill. It's also very warm here, due to the roaring fire, which is where Alexei is. He has a teapot on a grate over the fire and in the next breath is pouring steaming water into two mugs.

"Good morning," he says, extending the cup toward me.

I blink in surprise. I didn't even realize he knew I was up, let alone in the room with him.

"You too," I reply, taking it from his hands.

I inhale deeply, the steam soothing my sore throat and lungs from screaming earlier. I take a tentative sip, the licorice root, echinacea, and lemon, doing wonders for my tender vocal cords. I drain half, drinking it as quickly as I can without scalding my throat. Before I can finish, Alexei sets down breakfast in front of me—eggs over easy, potatoes, and some sort of meat that reminds me of bacon.

I mix my eggs and potatoes together, something I learned from my mother, and dip my strip of meat in the egg yolk. I scarf it, like the first meal he made me, and he once again looks at me in amusement. When I finally come up for air, I look at him. He's slowly and carefully eating his meal, a perfect gentleman with exceptional table manners.

"How long was I asleep this time?"

"About a day."

I was right, and honestly, I'm not surprised, with the way my stomach is growling. Not to mention that a lot has happened since I arrived here. I needed that rest.

"How are you feeling?"

"My throat hurts a bit, and I'm still tired, but overall pretty good." I bring my tea to my lips, only to stop.

My eyes snag on the healed-over bite mark on my arm. It looks fine, like normal skin, except it's scarred.

"Ah, yes. Normally, bite marks don't scar because we usually close it immediately after, but these were rougher, and we weren't able to heal them right away, so unfortunately, you will have them the rest of your life. Unless you wanted to see the elves for it. They have specific healers for scars."

I nod as I continue looking at it. I'm not sure what I want to do about them. The whole experience was godawful, and something that I never want to go through again, but I came out on the other side of it. And I was strong enough to escape Shindar on my own. If the others hadn't come when they did, I would've been in the clear. I need to remember my strength, and these are good reminders.

"They had bodies in that cave. Well, actually not bodies exactly. They had *bones.* So many that they had to have done this to at least fifty people, but I'm guessing more."

"I know. I saw them."

"Why weren't they bodies? There were none actually intact. It couldn't have been *that* long since they'd fed, right?"

"When a vampire drains all the blood from its victim, the body deteriorates and all that's left are the bones. It's called 'skelling,' it's barbaric, and illegal for that matter, but unfortunately, it's common among groups like this. They can only feed when they hunt because they can't afford a donor, and as a result are all lost to bloodlust, draining their victim entirely."

I shudder at his description, knowing all too well the feeling of what he's talking about. Not the extent of being drained completely, obviously, but enough to never want to experience it again.

"Are there other groups like them?"

"A few. The enforcers are usually pretty good about finding them and taking care of the issue." I know that's his way of saying they execute them. "While you were sleeping I teletraveled to the enforcer's base and let them know that I found a nest. They are going to identify their victims from their remains and notify the families."

"So, what happens now?"

"I'm going to give you a few days to rest, and then we're going to see the king."

"Still? Alexei, I thought things had changed between us."

"My orders are still the same, Ember." It's one of the only times he's used my real name, and I know he's not going to budge on this. "Why did you run?"

His question catches me off guard, and for a moment I don't know how to respond. I want to be mad at him for still insisting on taking me, but he did rescue me. And he's done a lot for me since I got here in general. He's fed me multiple times, let me sleep in his bed, cleaned my wounds, and looked after me. The least I can do is answer his question.

"I'm scared to go see the king," I say truthfully. "I was trying to go back home, but I ended up going the wrong way in the dark, and then Shindar found me and kidnapped me."

"First of all, going to see the king will not be bad. I promise. You won't be in trouble. The worst thing that would happen is that you would be sent back to Earth. Second, I know that you were able to do some damage to those that were trying to hurt you, and I'm glad that you did. I wish I could've let you take your revenge on them yourself, but I was more concerned about making sure you were safe."

I think that over for a moment. Why am I scared to see the king? One of the things I was worried about was traveling across the country with a man I don't know or trust, but after what happened, I find that I actually trust him with my life.

The second thing is that I don't want to be in any sort of trouble for traveling here accidentally, but from the sound of it, that won't be an issue either. I also realize that there's a chance that I could meet someone during my travels who knew one of my mothers and might be able to tell me more about them or where I come from, or what happened to make one give me up and the other take me to Earth. It would be stupid of me to go back home now.

"Alexei, there's a few things I want to ask you."

"You're acting like this is the first question you've had," he teases, a glint entering his eyes as I roll mine.

"Something happened in the cave, and I don't know if it's normal for the humans here or not." He nods at me to continue. "In the cave with Shindar, I was able to not only feel and see his emotions, but I was able to influence them. I actually escaped on my own when it was just the two of us. I got him to release me by pushing emotions onto him. Can all humans here do that?"

He doesn't say anything for several seconds, and it seems I've stunned him silent.

"Are you sure that's what happened?"

"Yes. First, I took away his hunger, and I could see when it hit him because he visibly relaxed, but then I did it again. I pictured a huge ball of guilt and shame mixing together in a cloud, and then I pushed it into him. I could see the mass disappearing inside of him, and then moments later he released me. He wasn't feeling any of those things before I intervened."

He thinks this over for a minute, and then shaking his head as if he can't come up with any other reason as to why all of that would happen, he responds. "It certainly sounds like that's what you did, but I have never heard of something like that happening before. Your blood must be very potent indeed."

His gaze lingers on my neck again like it did the day before, only this time, I'm not insulted. A steady heat builds between my legs again, the fire from the previous night reigniting, my heart pounding steadily.

He licks his lips as he visibly struggles to look away from my neck, and when he finally meets my eyes, his are slightly dilated.

"What was your second question?" he asks roughly.

"Oh. I was actually hoping you'd be willing to train me." Embarrassment creeps into my voice.

"Train you?"

"You know, like combat training. It would be nice if you could also help me with my gifts too, but I don't know if you can since yours are different."

His slow blink is the only sign that he's surprised by my question. "You want to learn how to fight?"

"I realized that I don't know how to defend myself, and I don't ever want to be in a position like that again. I don't want to have to wait for some man to come and save me. I want to save myself." *I am an independent woman, damn it!*

Alexei smiles as if he heard what I said in my head before nodding in understanding. "I can teach you on the road when we take breaks. I can attempt to teach you some magic stuff, but no promises there. The combat training I can definitely help you with."

I return his smile wholeheartedly, excited despite myself. I thought about taking self-defense classes back home, but never went through with it. I figure this will be even better. I'm sure that Alexei could kill those instructors on Earth without even putting in any effort at all.

"When do we start?" I ask, anxious to begin.

"First, you need to rest. Second, you need new clothes. I will teletravel down to Twin Fangs today to buy you something suitable, as well as supplies for the long journey. Third, we will be traveling to Mystic Mountain on horseback, so I should probably get you one of your own, since I only have one."

"I can't ride a horse!" I exclaim, panicking slightly.

The thought of riding my own horse for days, through an unfamiliar land, is terrifying. What if I did the wrong signal with the reins and got left behind as Alexei rode on, not noticing I was no longer with him? What if it got spooked and ran me right off a cliff? I know my fears aren't super realistic, but hey? Who said anxiety was realistic?

He huffs in frustration. "Of course you can't." He pauses. "I suppose we will have to share a horse."

Even though his words are annoyed, I can sense his delight and lust at the thought. The sensation brings a blush to my cheeks, and I bite my lip to hide my smile. I know that I'm falling fast for this guy, but who can blame me? He is absolutely *gorgeous*, and he saved my life from evil vampires.

"Can I come with you to town? I would like to pick out my own clothes."

"Are you going to wear that?" he asks, pointedly looking at my baggy attire that clearly doesn't fit me.

I narrow my eyes. "Fine. But only buy me one set of clothes, and then tomorrow we can go down together so I can pick out my own things. Please," I remember to add. He's already doing so much for me, but I know men. I'm sure he will come back with something that either doesn't match, is slutty, or doesn't fit.

"Oh, all right," he agrees, making me smile. His gaze locks on to my mouth for several seconds before he abruptly stands up. "Well, I guess I'll get going so that you have something to wear." I nod, standing up myself. "Feel free to do what you want, but please don't leave again. I know it's light outside, but there are worse things than vampires that prowl these areas," he states cryptically.

Before I can ask what kinds of things, he's disappears. I startle, not quite used to him doing that yet.

On my own, I meander back to the bedroom, still tired despite the fact that I slept for an entire day. The large meal combined with the tea makes it easy for me to fall back asleep in no time at all, and soon I'm dreaming.

I'm in the cave again. My hands are tied behind my back, and the entire group is looking at me like they can't wait to finish what they started. The pile of bones is now three times as large and takes up nearly the entire cave. I know I'm going to join them shortly. No way can I escape this again.

They crowd around me, circling me like hungry sharks. A scream builds in my throat, and before I can release it, they shoot at me, lips and teeth latching around any exposed skin they can find. The pain is as bad as the last time, maybe even more so. It feels like they are biting and draining before moving and biting again and again and again.

An unknown blast of power explodes. I have no idea if it's from me, or one of them, but suddenly, all of them are off of me, burning. Alexei comes through a moment later, slashing through their charred bodies, and before I know it, we're out of the cave and the moment from the bathroom slams back into me. I'm standing there, dripping wet in my barely there towel with him staring at me as if I'm his next meal, nothing like the vampires in the cave. Only this time, instead of having me change into his clothes, he undoes my towel.

"I need to make sure they didn't bite anywhere I can't see." His voice has taken on that sexy timbre. He slowly drags his gaze down my body, making

it a caress even though he isn't touching me. He crouches in front of me, looking up into my eyes as he drags his tongue over the bite, immediately igniting the fire in me from the last time he did it, only now it's heightened. He licks his way up both legs, stopping at the juncture of my thighs. He inhales deeply, growling low in his throat, but just as I think he's going to tongue me there, he stands. He licks up both my arms as well before pulling me close and closing the wounds on my neck. When all of them are taken care of he doesn't step back, and instead whispers against my neck.

"You smell so good. Your blood calls to me."

I moan as I tilt my head to the side, giving him access, even though I told myself I would never be bitten again. He drags his fangs up the side of my neck before gently sliding them into my vein. He groans at the same time I do, and my body is on fire in a whole different way than the last time I was bitten. This is pleasure. This is bliss. This is heaven. His impressive length grinds into my hip, and I match his movements. We move faster and faster as he pulls more and more from my neck. I am on the edge, and just as he's about to push me over...

My eyes snap open, and I grumble in frustration. It was only a dream. It felt so realistic. I reach down and drag a finger through my folds to find myself absolutely *drenched*. My body is extremely sensitive, and my pussy is on fire. I listen closely, but don't hear any movements. I don't think Alexei is back yet, and I should take care of this before he is. His scent envelops me from his sheets, and I pretend it's him pinching my puckered nipples. I pretend it's his hand flicking my clit and plunging his fingers deep inside me. It takes no time at all to build, and then I'm arching into my hands, crying out as my pleasure breaks. There's a knock at the door.

"Ember? Are you all right?" Alexei's voice is on the other side, full of concern.

My face turns the shade of a tomato. The absolute last thing I need is for him to come in here and find me with my hand down my shorts—well, technically *his* shorts—and my shirt pushed up around my chest to give myself access to my breasts.

"Yes, I'm fine," I say, my voice as high as I've ever heard it.

"Are you sure? You sound strange."

I clear my throat this time before speaking and sound a little bit more normal as I say, "Yes, I'm sure."

"Okay, well, I was able to get some clothes for you, so come on out whenever you're ready."

I hear his footsteps fading away from the door and I breathe a sigh of relief. I slowly get up, and when I'm as put together as I can be, I walk out to greet him. I can't meet his eyes, and my face is still burning with embarrassment, but I push past it. My plan is to snag the clothes he got for me, and then book it to the bathroom to take another bath and wash my arousal off of me.

"Here's what I found," Alexei says, not seeming to notice my discomfort, and gestures to the table where he's laid a pair of tight-fitting brown pants, a simple white shirt, and some black boots. "Hopefully they all fit. And, I also got you some...uh...underthings. They're underneath all the clothes." His face is now bright red, and I smile at his awkwardness.

"Thank you," I say as I move forward to snag everything off the table. It's then, when I'm in his personal space, that I hear him sniffing. I turn to look at him to find his eyebrows halfway up his forehead, and a look of satisfaction and heat in his gaze.

"Is that...? Are you...?" Before he can finish his question, I take off to the bathroom.

I shut the door behind me, leaning against it and breathing heavily. I set the clothes down before starting the water and quickly stripping out of Alexei's clothes. I sink into the water when the tub is full. I need to get my shit together. I'm clearly attracted to the man, but I don't need to be behaving like a bitch in heat around him. I mean, he hasn't made a move on me, so there's a chance that he's not interested. Of course, things could be different here than back home. With the feel of this place, I would guess they are more old-fashioned. Maybe they don't think it's appropriate to have sex before you're married, and I don't want to be stuck somewhere where that's true. I wouldn't consider myself a slut by any means, but I am a fairly sexual person. From what I can tell, he seems interested in me. There's definitely been times where his eyes flare with want. Or at least I think that's the case, but if it is, why hasn't he made a move yet? I guess I'll find out sooner or later, especially since it looks as though we're about to spend quite a lot of time together. In the meantime, I need to settle down so that I don't have the urge to do what I just did when we're on the road together with no privacy. I huff in frustration again. This is going to be a long trip.

Chapter 9

The next few days are fairly uneventful, and we spend it much the same. Eating, sleeping, resting before our big trip. Unfortunately, I've never been great at sitting around doing nothing. I like to be busy, and there's nothing to do here. He has a few books, but nothing that I would enjoy reading. They're all about war strategies, and I scoff at the macho-ness of it all.

On my second day of sitting around not doing anything, I think of something he said to me when I first got here.

"How can you tell that I have elf ears?"

"Because they're pointed," he says as if I'm being dense.

"Are you part elf then? Yours are pointed."

"No. I'm part fae. The fae also have pointed ears. The two races actually look very similar."

"So how do you know that I'm part elf and not part fae?"

"Fae don't breed with other species. Ever. I'm the only exception," he states matter-of-factly.

"You?"

"Yes. I have a fae father, who is also advisor to the king, and a vampire conduit mother."

"What is a conduit?"

"Conduits are human women who contain the blood of another species. Humans are the only race that can mix our lines. For instance, if an elf wanted their son to also have mermaid traits, he would have to breed with a human woman who had a mermaid father."

My head is spinning from all the information. I'm struggling to wrap my brain around it. "So, an elf and a mermaid wouldn't be able to get together and have a child that had both traits?"

"No. They would have to go through a human conduit to do it. And even then, it's only the males who acquire the traits. The women are all born human, no matter what species they breed with."

"*What?*" I practically yell. I know it's not their fault but that seems *so* unfair. "So, what happens to the females?"

"They would then become a conduit. So, for instance, the son of a vampire father and a witch conduit human mother would then have the traits of a vampire and a witch, but if that child were a female, she would then be a vampire conduit human. When she became of age and joined the Sacred Rite, then someone could go to her if they wanted to have a son with vampire traits."

I nod in understanding, even though it's complicated and a lot to digest. I skip over the obvious question of what the Sacred Rite is. I don't think I want to know right now, even though I'm pretty sure what the answer is. I steer the conversation back to my original topic. "Why don't the fae mix with the other races?"

"Because it has always been forbidden. The fae rule because they are considered the most powerful of all the species of this world. They don't want anyone else to taint the line." Again with the Nazi parallels.

"They sound like a bunch of stuck-up assholes," I mutter, to which he scoffs. "What makes you so special? Are you the only mixed fae?"

"Yes. That we know of at least. The king made an exception for my father, since he is the advisor. When they were young, they all went to the human territory, the Mortal Sanctum, to have a night of fun. They went to the Abandoned Bliss, and my father slept with one of the girls, not realizing that she was a conduit. She *should've* been in the Sacred

Rite, but she lied to him, and here I am."

Something else occurs to me after I take a minute to think about all he's said.

"How would a mermaid breed with a human?"

"What?"

"Like how would that work? Don't they live in the water and have fins?"

"They *can* live in the water, but they don't have to. When they come out of the water they take on a more 'human' form. They don't look much different than me or you."

We end the conversation there. It leaves me reeling, and I need time to fully comprehend everything he told me.

Finally, a day later, Alexei tells me it's time to go down to the city. "We're going to be leaving tomorrow. You've rested enough and are fully healed from the bites. It's time. We'll get supplies and more clothes for you today in the city and leave at first light tomorrow. For real this time."

I nod in excitement. I'm so ready to get out of this boring house. And I'm also looking forward to seeing the city. I've barely had any interactions or seen anything in this realm besides Alexei, this house, the crazy homeless vampires, and a gross run-down cave full of bones.

I quickly get ready, and soon we're heading down the mountain. Clouds gather in the distance, and I wonder if there's going to be a storm. I'm thankful we aren't leaving today, and hope that it doesn't keep up for our travels.

"So, what all are we getting in town?" I ask.

"Well, you need more clothes. We also need to get some food that will last awhile. And I need to stop by the alchemist before we leave."

"Are you running low on blood?"

"No, but I need to make sure I'm set for a few weeks on the road. I usually only need to feed about once every two weeks. It seems to be less than a full-blooded vampire. They feed about once a week."

"Is it always once every two weeks? Or are there any times that you have to feed more than that?"

"If I get injured I need to feed. If it's something small I won't need to right away, but still sooner than I normally would, but if it's a serious injury then I need to feed immediately."

"What happens if you don't?"

"If I don't feed when I need to? I start out feeling hungry but am not satisfied no matter how much I eat. If I still don't feed, I get stomach pains and body aches. If I were to be badly injured, my body wouldn't be able to heal as quickly, and it would take as long as a human to heal. If we aren't able to feed for an extended period of time, we suffer a fate worse than death."

"Are there only vampires in this territory? Also, what is the fate worse than death?"

I know he's frustrated at the number of questions I'm asking, but I don't care. "Mostly. You have to have permission to travel into any other territory. Usually if there are other species in another territory they have a visa to be there, or in cases like me where you have some connection to the crown, you're able to travel into any territory. And I'll tell you about that fate another time."

"Why is everyone so divided?"

"It's the way we've always been. The species don't get along very well because we're all so different. You would think that mixing the bloodlines would help with that issue, but usually they only do that if they want their son to carry a certain trait for something specific. For instance, a politician might want their son to have mermaid blood to help with drawing people in and gaining them more support. It hasn't helped to bring anyone together, and honestly, most of the mixed individuals aren't looked at as equals and are normally just used for their abilities."

"That's terrible," I tell him. My heart aches for the children born in that scenario. I bet they aren't loved like they should be. "Is that what happened to you?"

"My father's never been the loving type. Probably because of the fact that I was an accident and almost cost him his position at the palace."

I reach out to touch him when I feel his loneliness and dejection. As soon as my hand makes contact with his arm, his emotions hit me even more strongly, as though the connection heightens my ability.

"I'm sorry."

He puts his hand over mine, gently squeezing before removing it and giving me a grateful smile.

I had only seen the town from a distance, but now that we're nearing it, I can see that it's even more spectacular in person.

"Welcome, my lady, to Twin Fangs City," Alexei says dramatically, sweeping his arm in front of him for me to walk ahead. I smile before taking off, excited to see for myself.

I enter the first street and pass by the cutest-looking little houses. We make our way deeper into the city, closer to the river that runs through it. We arrive at what appears to be the main hub of the town. There are street vendors selling everything from food to fabric to weapons. The smell of the food overwhelms my senses, and though I ate not long ago, my stomach growls and my mouth waters. I stop in front of a stall that has food reminiscent of the carnival. They have what look like turkey legs, beer, and bread that smells sweet. I'm standing there salivating over it all when Alexei walks up next to me.

"Hungry?" he asks with a knowing smirk. I nod, licking my lips at how delicious everything looks. "What do you want?"

"All of it?" I ask.

Guilt sneaks in because I don't have any money. Well, that's stupid since I actually *do* have money. A lot of money. But none of it is good here. It's frustrating. He chuckles good-naturedly before nodding.

"We'll take two of everything, please." The vendor hands everything over, Alexei pays him, and we sit down at a table and chairs close by. I bite into the meat, and just like when I ate in Queridian for the first time, the flavor bursts on my tongue, and I rip into it. Within minutes I've devoured the leg and drank half of the berry-flavored, somewhat sweet ale. Alexei, as always, eats his food much slower and looks my way in amusement.

"Why is everything so fucking *good* here? It's not fair. I've never had food like this in my entire life."

"Probably because where you're from they pump everything full of chemicals and mass-produce it."

I almost choke I'm so surprised. "You've been to Earth?"

"Once. When I acquired my guard position I was taken there as part of my training in case someone ever came through. I was there for about a week to see how humans act in the Mortal Realm. You're right. The food there tastes horrendous. I almost couldn't eat my first few days."

I chuckle as I try the sweet bread. It's cinnamony, buttery, and covered in brown sugar and honey. It's the best thing I have ever eaten, and when I finish it, I lick my fingers clean of all the sticky goodness, wishing I had more. While Alexei finishes his meal, I look around in wonder at everything and am curious if every territory is this impressive, or only Nightshade Eclipse. I guess I'll be finding out soon enough, and instead of worrying about it, I decide to enjoy this in case the other territories are different. The sun beats down on me, although it doesn't seem like it's as close as it would be back home, and then I remember that we're underneath Earth, which is why the sun feels farther away, especially since it's colder here.

We're close to the river that runs through the city, and I make my way over to it, washing my hands of any leftover lunch while I'm at it. The water is so clear and blue that I can see the stones on the bottom, and when I lean down to dip my hands in, I gasp at the crispness of it. I cup my hands and let water pool in them before bringing it to my mouth and taking a long drink. It's so refreshing that I have multiple handfuls, and when I get up and turn back to see if Alexei is done eating, I find him staring at me with an amused smile on his lips. I furrow my brows in confusion, and I head back over to him as he gets up to clean up our lunch mess.

"What's so amusing?" I ask.

"You'll find out soon enough."

"What do you mean? Do I have something on me?" I start running my hands down my face to make sure there's no food on it.

"No, you look fine," he assures me, and I let the subject drop.

"So, where to now?"

"Want to get some more clothes?"

I nod gratefully. The set that he bought me a few days ago is starting to get dirty, and it will be nice to get into some clean clothes before our trip.

Instead of stopping at another stall, we walk into an actual shop. The bell chimes as we open the door, and I look around at the charming store. There's a warm ambient light coming from the back, but large windows at the front that give the shop plenty of natural light, which is always nice while shopping for clothes. I feel like the sunlight always enhances the colors, and makes it easier to see. They have everything here that you can think of, from practical traveling clothes like I will need, to extravagant ball gowns that I could never picture myself in. They also have shoes for all occasions, and multiple hats that I immediately have the urge to try on to see how silly they look on me.

"Can I help you?" a plump older-looking woman asks when she spots me. "Oh, Alexei. How wonderful to see you again, dear." She walks over and pats him on the cheek.

"Sisilla, this is Ember, the young woman I bought those clothes for a few days ago. We're about to make a trip to the Immortal City, and she needs some more outfits. Ember, Sisilla was a big help in picking out clothes for you."

Ahh. That explains why he did such a good job. He had a woman to help him.

I shake her hand as she turns her attention to me. "Nice to meet you, Sisilla."

Suddenly her name is so *funny* to me, and before I can stop it, a giggle works its way free. My eyes widen in alarm as I pray that I haven't offended her. Her nose scrunches up and she looks at me funny. Her facial expression makes me giggle again, and I am mortified that I'm making such an ass out of myself. She looks at Alexei like he might be able to explain my strange behavior.

"She drank from the river."

Realization dawns in her eyes before her lips pull up in an amused grin. "I see. Well, let's look at some outfit choices then, shall we?"

"Wait, what's wrong with the water I drank?" I ask, panicking slightly, which makes me start nervously laughing.

"Don't worry. The water is fine. It just makes people laugh until it makes its way out of your system. It's actually very good for you. Laughter is the best medicine after all," Sisilla says completely seriously.

Well, this should be fun. Alexei catches my eye and smirks. "Why didn't you stop me, asshole?"

"Because this is much more amusing."

I want to be pissed. I *am* pissed, but I'm laughing again, because even though I find everything funny right now, I know I will be amused by this even after the water is out of my system. He grins and starts laughing along with me as we follow Sisilla.

"You need traveling clothes then, dear?" I nod. "What colors do you usually prefer? We can get you a few different color options for basically the outfit you have now so that you can have some variety. Since you're traveling we'll leave the crest off of the clothing as well."

"I usually prefer neutrals, but sometimes I like some colorful options too. I also wouldn't mind having a nice flowy skirt. I know that it's not ideal for traveling, but I would like to wear it every now and then."

She nods, showing me a pretty plum skirt. I reach out and touch the material. It's flowy, like I asked, but it's also a little heavier so that it has some substance to it, which will be nice if it ends up being a little chilly. She also shows me some variations of the outfit that I'm wearing now. We get three pairs of pants, four shirts that are a mix of sleeve lengths, and the skirt. She also shoos Alexei off when she shows me the undergarments, and I get multiple sets of those, more than any other item, not wanting to have to wear my underwear for multiple days in a row and not knowing how the whole cleaning process is going to be on the road.

Alexei has also gotten some clothing items for himself, but I can't see what they are. He pays, and we thank Sisilla for all of her help. We step back outside, and I look around at everything. It really is the perfect day, and the scenery is wonderful. The sun shining down on me brings a smile to my face.

"So, where to now?"

"I think we should get food for the trip next."

We stop at a stall outside, and they have a selection of all kinds of foods, but for our trip we will need stuff that will last a while and that we don't need to cook. Alexei gets a fairly big selection of dried meats, a tin of spices so that we can season any meat that we hunt on the road, a huge bag of nuts, cheeses that are wrapped in wax so they don't need to be chilled, some dried fruits, and a few loaves of bread.

Once we're satisfied that we have everything we need, we make one more stop to the alchemist. We walk in front of the shop, which looks dark and dusty and mysterious, as I expected it would. The words

Bloody Shaker hang above the door, and I think of how appropriate that is for essentially a vampire bar. We walk in, and there are a few snobby rich-looking vampires here. They have fancy goblets in their hands and are swirling the blood around before holding it up to their noses and smelling it, like they would with wine. I almost scoff at the ridiculousness.

"Does the shop provide the goblets?" I ask Alexei under my breath.

He actually does scoff. "No. They must have brought their own from home."

My giggles kick in before I can stop them, and the two with the sticks up their asses glare at me.

"How can I help you, sir?"

"I need a full serving of vampire blood, please." The man nods before turning around and moving to a cooler across the room.

"Why did you order vampire blood? Can't you use other abilities if you drink a different type of blood?"

He looks surprised at my question. "How do you know that?"

"Shindar told me. The one who kidnapped me."

His eyes darken in anger at the mention of him. "Well, vampire blood is the cheapest since it doesn't give us any other abilities. And I don't need any other abilities right now. I have my elemental magic and my teletraveling. Plus, the abilities don't last long. Only a day or two."

"You have elemental magic?" I ask, surprised and impressed. I thought he could only teletravel.

"Yes. I'm part fae, remember?"

"So, what exactly *is* elemental magic?" A blush rises to my cheeks as I realize how naive and stupid I sound, but this is all so new to me.

"Elemental magic is control of one of the four elements. Air, water, earth, fire. All fae have control of at least one ability. It's very rare to have two, but it does happen on occasion."

"What is yours?"

"Earth."

"I've never seen you use that ability."

"I did in the caves, but I'm sure you were too distracted to notice at the time," he says quietly.

The man from earlier walks up, interrupting our conversation. He hands Alexei a cup, not a glass, thank God, because I don't know if I could stomach watching him drink blood. I mean, I *know* that's what I'm watching, but I can't actually *see* it happening. From here, it looks like he's drinking a cup of water.

I watch the smooth motion of his throat gulping down the liquid, and for a moment I'm mesmerized. An inappropriate giggle rises, of course, and I flush. He meets my eyes and raises his eyebrows in question, but I can't very well tell him that I was turned on by watching him swallow. I laugh again at my ridiculousness, shaking my head, and that only seems to make him more intrigued.

"What are you laughing about this time, little doe?"

"Nothing," I try to lie, but a snort comes out this time, and I blush again as my eyes move to his throat again, giving me away. He smirks at me knowingly before paying for the blood and walking out.

"I need to go to the bathroom," I tell him. I don't want to have to go in the middle of nowhere as we're walking up the mountain back to the house. Although I should get used to it since that's about to become my life as of tomorrow for the foreseeable future. He takes the bags from me and points me in the direction I need to go.

When I return, the urge to laugh has disappeared, and I'm relieved to find that the river water is out of my system. Alexei is right where I left him, but all the things we bought are nowhere to be found. He must see the question written on my face.

"I teletraveled to the house while you were going to the restroom so we wouldn't have to carry the bags up with us."

"Well, that was thoughtful."

"You sound surprised."

"I guess I keep forgetting that you have these abilities. I'm actually jealous, if I'm being honest," I tell him.

"You're forgetting your own power. That's pretty spectacular too."

"Not as cool as teleporting though," I grumble.

"Teletraveling."

"Oh, whatever."

"It looks like the effects of the river have worn off," he remarks, noticing my somewhat sour mood.

I don't reply as we start our hike back to the house. We walk in silence for a while, and I try to enjoy the scenery around me. There are these two mountains, lots of open space, and the ocean in the distance. The sun is starting to make its descent now, and a bird is telling everyone that it's almost time for bed with his song.

"Are you all right, Ember?"

"Yeah, I'm not looking forward to being on the road on a horse for weeks. And this has been a lot to take in. I miss my world, although I don't know why. I didn't have any friends. The only person in my life was my mom up until she died. I think I'm also pretty bitter toward her for not telling me about any of this, but I still miss her at the same time. I'm so in the dark, when she clearly knew about all of this. It would've been so cool to come here and experience it all for the first time with her by my side." Tears well in my eyes, and I turn my face away from him, embarrassed. I wish I wouldn't have unloaded all of that out on him, but I have no one else.

"I'm sorry that she didn't share any of this with you. But I have a theory that she was trying to protect you. That makes the most sense to me. Maybe if you start looking at it that way, it'll make you feel loved instead of lied to and betrayed."

"Yeah, but she still didn't trust me with it. I'm not fucking five years old. I could've handled it, and we would have been able to figure out what to do *together* instead of her leaving me completely fucking clueless and ending up here on my own anyway." I take a deep breath, trying to calm down the raging storm inside of me. I am so angry with her. And I miss her so much. It's a hard combination to come to terms with. The tears finally spill over and flow down my cheeks.

Alexei grabs my hand, forcing me to stop walking. I keep my face angled away from him, but he cups my cheek with his palm, turning my face toward him. I keep my eyes down, not wanting to see whatever is going to be in his eyes. His thumbs brush my tears from my cheeks, and I inhale sharply at the gesture. Heat spreads from that point of contact to the rest of my body, and while my grief still cuts me like a sharp knife, he's starting to slice through it with something completely different.

"Little doe," he says, his voice rough. His tone catches my attention enough that my gaze snaps up to his. He doesn't have pity in his eyes, or annoyance. Just understanding and acceptance. I didn't realize how much I needed him to look at me like that until that moment. "Your mother knew how strong you are. It's written on every line of your face, and every act of defiance against the world. You are more fierce than you realize, and before long, I will make sure you see how incredible you are. Believe me, she knew. She just loved you too much to risk you."

I'm pretty sure that I'm not breathing. No one has ever said anything like that to me before, and it lights up something inside of me that's been sorely neglected, like it had been hiding in a corner of myself that I never knew existed. But with those words, a sliver of light shines on it, making it grow the smallest amount.

Heat flares between us, and I'm sure he can hear my heart pounding out a furious rhythm, especially because of how close we are. Our eyes are still locked, and we seem to be gravitating even more toward the other. His eyes flick down to my mouth, and I lick my lips in anticipation. He lets out a low sound, almost a growl, that I feel in the very core of my being. When I'm sure he's going to kiss me, he blinks and the heat in his gaze is gone, replaced by steely determination. Before I know what's happening, he releases me and makes his way up the mountain.

"We should keep going if we want to make it back before dark," he says, walking ahead of me.

Embarrassment slides through me, but before it can take root, I focus my gift on Alexei's emotions to see if I can figure out what happened. I can sense his disappointment and longing. Resolve is the strongest out of his emotions, and I wonder why he's so resolute in his decision. Maybe he already has a partner? That would be my luck, wouldn't it? Before I travel down that road with myself, I take off after him.

We reach the house right as the sun sets over the ocean. Alexei has the best view. You can see everything from his house, and it makes me a little sad that we won't be able to enjoy it for who knows how long. I take a deep breath and head inside, and we immediately go to bed. After all, tomorrow is the first day of a long journey.

Chapter 10

I wake up the next morning to Alexei banging on the door.

"Ember. Get up and get dressed. We have to get going."

I groan, looking out the window to see it's still dark outside. I grumble loudly enough for him to hear me.

"Don't go back to sleep," he warns.

"You're not my mother!" I yell petulantly. I almost want to cry, that's how tired I am. Why on Earth would we ever leave this early?

"Little doe, don't make me come in there. You won't like it."

By the tone of his voice, he's hoping that I won't get up so he can come in. I throw my pillow at the door in response. I know I'm being extremely childish, but I've never been a morning person. And I am absolutely *never* up before the sun rises. Ever. The door opens a moment later, and Alexei strides in looking way too good for the time of day. I wince at the bright light that he's letting into the dark room and pull the other pillow over my head.

He climbs up on the bed with me, and for a second I entertain the idea that maybe he will wake me up in a sexy way. That would literally be the only way to get a happy Ember out of bed. His hands run up my legs, and I turn over, thinking that I might get my wish, but he suddenly jerks me halfway down the bed, making me squeal. In the next moment I'm thrown over his shoulder, my ass bared to the world in my short nightgown. Luckily there's no one else here.

"Hey! What the fuck do you think you're doing?" I yell as I reach around to cover my backside.

"I told you you wouldn't like the way I got you up," he states smugly.

He takes me into the bathroom and sets my feet down in a tub full of warm water. Even though he had perhaps the worst way of waking me up in the world (just kidding, tickling me would take the cake), it was thoughtful of him to draw me a bath. I even see a fresh cup of steaming tea sitting on the rim of the tub.

"You have a half an hour." He strides out of the room before I can reply.

I step back out of the tub, taking off my nightgown and emptying my bladder before sinking back into the warm water as I try to enjoy my last bath before our trip. I know that most of the time we won't have this luxury, so I soak it in while I can. I finish my tea before washing myself.

As I'm finishing, Alexei knocks on the door. "Are you almost done?"

"Yeah. Give me another few minutes." I drain the tub and step out, drying myself off as I go.

I look around only to discover that I don't have any clothes besides my nightgown. Oh well. It's his fault for throwing me in here first thing in the morning. I wrap the towel tightly around myself before waltzing out. Alexei looks over at me, seeming pleased that I stuck to his timeline. I meet his gaze, and then his eyes are sweeping over me. They heat, and lust pours my way from him. I have water dripping over my body from the bath, and I smell like his products. He clears his throat and turns away as disappointment sinks through me again. This guy is seriously giving me whiplash, I think as I head to the bedroom.

Ten minutes later, I'm dressed in warm, practical traveling clothes. I quickly pack the rest of my clothing in the bag that he left on my bed for me, adding my purse to it. I've braided my long hair back out of my face, so the wet strands aren't freezing my cheeks off. I look in the mirror, and I have a sense of déjà vu from my birthday when I thought I looked like a warrior princess. Now with my attire and my braid I really do look like that, more so than before. Almost like a medieval Lara Croft. The thought makes me feel incredibly badass, and I straighten my shoulders and lift my head a little bit higher.

I step out to find Alexei outside, the door swung open. I bring my bag to him, which also has my purse in it, and find that he's packing up a beautiful gray mare. I reach out and pet the side of her face and she nuzzles into my hand. I love her immediately.

"What's her name?" I ask.

Alexei looks at me quizzically. "Why would I name her?" I gape at him.

"Are you a total fucking animal? Why *wouldn't* you name her?"

"We don't typically name animals. Some do if they have more than one to differentiate them, but I only have her," he states simply, like it makes perfect sense for him to not name his pet. I roll my eyes so hard that I fear they'll get stuck in my head.

"Well, once I get to know her a little bit better I will give her a proper name," I tell him. "Won't I, sweetie?" I say in a baby voice that I use solely for animals. She neighs softly in appreciation, nudging my hand more firmly. I smile at her as I scratch behind her ears.

"Oh Gods. Please don't talk to her like that. She's an animal, not a baby. Not that I would find it any more acceptable for you to talk to a child like that."

"Are you a heathen? Like seriously, what is wrong with you?"

The mare glares at him like she can't believe he's never given her this kind of treatment before, and I mentally promise her that I will make up for it. He rolls his own eyes at me in response, and the action is so unlike him that it makes me laugh. He takes my bag from me, adding it to the mare. He goes back to the house, blows out any candles, and locks the door before coming back to me.

"All right. It's time," Alexei says.

He holds a hand out to help me up, and I take it as I try not to think about how right it feels having him support me. I put my foot in the stirrup and grab the saddle with my other hand. I push myself up with his help and swing my leg over the horse. I almost don't make it, and there's a moment where I'm terrified that I'm going to fall, but Alexei steadies me, and the next thing I know I'm seated. Alexei swings up after me, making it look all too easy, and I scowl at him. I'm sure I looked like a beached whale getting up here.

He settles in behind me, scooching closer until he's firmly pressed against me and supporting my weight. I can't deny how intimate this position is, and I know it's going to take me a while to get comfortable with it. Right now I am so aware of him, and it makes an unbearable heat build between my legs. His arms wrap around me to grab the reins, and I swallow at being boxed in. It's not unpleasant, but it does make me all the more aware of him. To break the tension that's risen in me, I make an ass out of myself.

"Let's roll, Horsey," I say seriously.

Alexei chuckles behind me, and I feel the vibrations through my torso. He digs his heels into the mare's sides, and we start moving.

"And we're off like a herd of turtles." I smile sadly.

My mom always used to say that when we would go on a road trip together. In this case it rings true. It's going to take longer than I've ever traveled to get there.

"So is the mare's new name 'Horsey'?"

I bust out laughing, not used to him joking with me. "For now. I'll think of something perfect for her. She's such a majestic animal, she deserves an equally majestic name."

He chuckles at me as we make our way down the east side of the mountain. I can see the first hint of sunlight in the distance.

At first, I'm pretty nervous about riding. I haven't ridden a horse in *years*, and it was only like an hour-long tour, but I do remember that even from that short ride I was extremely sore the next day. I try to prepare myself because I know the first few days will be the worst, but hopefully after that my body will become accustomed to it.

"I just thought of something. If you are taking me to the king, who is going to be guarding the portal?"

"There's another guard that's always on standby in case of an emergency or something like this. I teletraveled to him last night. He's going to arrive at the house today and take over. And since it's such a long journey, he will probably be there indefinitely, and they will probably send over another spare guard when we get to the Immortal City."

As the sun steadily rises in the sky I get more comfortable, the rhythm of the horse surprisingly comforting. However, now that I'm not worried about the horse, I become more aware of Alexei pressing up against me. My blood starts heating, and I can't help but focus solely on the contact between my backside and his groin, and the way that his hips cradle mine. I subtly try to put some distance between us, moving my hips forward as much as I can and straightening my back.

"Are you getting uncomfortable already?" Alexei asks me, his confusion as well as concern seeping toward me.

"No, I'm fine. Readjusting is all." I attempt to keep my voice as natural as possible, but I'm sure that instead I sound squeaky and awkward.

I mentally slap myself as I maintain the uncomfortable posture. I don't know how long I'll be able to keep this up, but after developing an attraction to him, I know I need a little distance for as long as I can because otherwise I am going to combust on the spot. Before long, my back starts aching from sitting stick-straight, and my core muscles are burning. I almost give in and lean back against him, but I'm too stubborn for my own good.

By the time we get to the bottom of the mountain (which was much quicker than when we walked down yesterday), I feel like I'm going to die. I am also shivering my ass off, despite the fact that the sun is now shining down brightly on us.

"Why are you torturing yourself?" Alexei whispers in my ear, making me jolt in surprise and something more delicious.

"I don't know what you're talking about," I lie.

He huffs in frustration, but he's also amused. He reaches up and tugs my shoulders back so that I have no choice but to collapse against him. I sigh in relief at the combination of his body heat and the fact that my muscles don't have to hold me up anymore.

"This is going to be a long journey, Ember. You won't last the day if you sit like that the whole time. Besides, I won't bite. Not unless you want me to," he teases, even though I know he's not kidding. He would bite me the second I asked him to, I'm sure.

"Never going to happen, Dracula."

"Who's Dracula?" he asks in confusion, and I bust out laughing.

"He's like the most famous vampire in the Mortal Realm. He's the reason I thought you couldn't be in the sunlight. He also can't eat garlic, and you can kill him with holy water or a stake to the heart."

"Why would holy water kill him?"

"Because vampires are supposed to be demonic. Soulless creatures from hell. Evil. So you're supposed to be able to kill them with help from the heavens."

He scoffs in response.

"How is it that humans on Earth know about all of the species here? It seems like most theories about them are wrong, but we know about mermaids, vampires, etcetera," I muse.

"My guess is that someone long ago thought it would be funny to go to the Mortal Realm and mess with the humans. That's happened quite a bit. It's not such a thing anymore, especially now that we have humans living here, but it used to be some people's brand of fun. A lot of the weird unexplainable things that happen on Earth are usually someone from Queridian playing a prank on the human race."

"Like what?"

"Well, there are several, but a big one that I know of is what I believe you all call Stonehenge. One of the fae, his name was Saffron Woodbloom, traveled to Earth through a portal in that area, and since he had the element of earth, he was able to literally grow those stones right where they stand, and they've been there ever since. He came back and bragged to everyone about what he'd done, laughing his head off as he told them how confused the humans were and worrying that it was giants. The story became well known, and it inspired other individuals to copy him."

I laugh loudly, not able to believe that I'm hearing the story of how something like *Stonehenge* actually came to be. And the truth of it is fucking *funny*. "So you think that's how we know about mermaids and elves and witches?"

"I think so. I have a theory that individuals went to your realm a long time ago, and showed themselves or their powers to the mortals. Either as some sort of prank, or it's also possible that they were lower powered and wanted to be admired or worshiped in some way. That's why a lot of the depictions and descriptions are similar, but not entirely accurate. It could also be that those individuals gave them false information on purpose so they wouldn't know how to kill them if they tried to."

I nod along as he talks. As interested as I am in what he's telling me, I'm exhausted. The combination of the soothing sound of his voice, the heat of his body, and the glide of the horse underneath me is making it seriously difficult to stay awake, and before I know it, I'm drifting off in his arms, feeling oddly safe.

I wake sometime later to the horse stopping. I look around blearily and see that we're coming up on a forest with a gentle river flowing through it.

"Why did we stop?"

"Horsey needs a break." I snort at him calling her that. "I also thought we could eat some lunch."

I nod as he gets off the horse first, and before I can help myself down, he reaches up and grabs my waist, lifting me like I weigh no more than a carton of milk. I slide down his body, feeling every single inch of him. I grip his arms and look up at him. From here I swear I can see a storm brewing in his gray eyes.

"Thanks," I breathe.

His muscles tense and he squeezes me harder for a moment before he breaks away, leaving me empty and disappointed. I huff in irritation. One of these days I'm either going to have to ask him what's going on, or put on my big-girl panties and make a move myself.

Now that I'm awake, I look around a little more and see the twin fangs in the distance. From far away the two mountains really do look like fangs, and I can't help but appreciate their beauty. Horsey is drinking from the river, and I walk over to her and stroke her back. She gives me an appreciative neigh in response and I smile.

"You're such a pretty, strong girl, aren't you?" I coo, making her snort happily.

She goes back to drinking her water, and I leave her in peace, turning to find Alexei staring at me, a smile pulling at his lips. "What?"

"Oh, nothing. I just think it's amusing how you talk to her."

"Well, she clearly likes it, in case you didn't notice. She's a good, strong horse. She deserves to be spoiled and pampered. Especially with this kind of a trip."

"Whatever you say." That stupid grin is firmly in place now, and it makes me want to punch him. Instead I head a little farther up the river to grab myself a drink.

"This water isn't going to make me laugh for half the day, is it? Or any other weird, crazy things I don't want?"

"No. You're fine drinking from the river."

That's good enough for me. I get on my knees and cup the water in my hands before taking a long drink. It's very cool and refreshing, and I immediately gorge myself on it, only now realizing how thirsty I am. When I've had my fill, I head back over to Alexei, who is getting some lunch stuff out. There's also a patch of earth that is slightly raised and circular, almost like a little cushion. It looks like that perfect spot to sit, and as I do I almost sink into it it's so comfortable. I don't know why or how this formed, but I'm grateful for it after sitting in the saddle all day. I look up to find Alexei smiling to himself.

"What are you smiling about?"

"Nothing."

I let it go in favor of eating because I am absolutely starving. Alexei passes me the food that he's taken out. We were able to bring some perishables along with us, and we will go through those before eating the food that will last a while. I have cheese, bread, meat that he cooked last night, and a peach. We eat in companionable silence, enjoying the scenery, the food, and the fresh breeze flowing through the trees. When we're all finished, I go to the stream and drink more water. We have canteens, but I figure this way we keep them full for when we need water on the road.

"Would you like to start training before we get back on the road?" he asks.

"Yes, please!" I exclaim, excited to learn to defend myself. "Which weapon are we going to start with?" I look at everything he brought and try to figure out what I'll be most comfortable with.

He laughs, shaking his head at me. "Nice try, little doe. You are not even getting close to those yet."

I frown in confusion. "But I thought you were going to train me?"

"I am. But there's a lot you need to learn before we start bringing weapons into the mix."

I nod along as if I understand, but I don't. At least not yet. I've never done anything like this before. "So where do we start then?"

"With balance. One of the most important skills to master is being able to stay on your feet during an altercation. If your balance is on point, then you will be knocked on your ass far less, thus ensuring better odds in a fight."

I think back to my yoga classes I used to take; I'd always been the worst with the balancing poses. Although, now that I'm thinking about it, the more often I went to class, the easier those poses became, so with some practice hopefully I will get better quickly.

"I want you to close your eyes." I do so, that simple act already kicking up my focus on balance. "Now, I want you to feel your feet connecting to the ground. Root all four corners of your feet to the spot you're standing in. Pretend that they've sunken into the dirt beneath you. Make sure to breathe deeply. Your breath is an important key to fighting as well. Your moves should flow from your inhales and exhales."

I do as he says, already comfortable with this. The techniques remind me a lot of yoga, and I try to drop into that headspace. I take some deep yogic breaths, and on my third exhale, my peacefulness is shattered when I'm pushed hard from the front. I grunt, my eyes shooting open as I stumble back, luckily catching myself before I end up on my ass.

"What the fuck?" I yell at him, pissed that he pushed me, especially when my eyes were closed.

"Next lesson: always be aware of your surroundings. An attack can come from anywhere at any time. Your attacker isn't going to wait for you to be prepared. They are going to come at you the second you are vulnerable and when you least expect it."

I scowl at him. What he's saying makes total sense, but this is not how I was anticipating this to go, and he totally ruined my peaceful mind frame I had going for me.

"But you didn't fall down. Good for you."

Despite myself, I inwardly smile at the praise.

"Now, close your eyes again. We're going to do the same thing, but this time try to anticipate my moves. Try to tell where I am with your other senses. But don't forget to breathe, and keep focusing on rooting your feet down."

This time I widen my stance a bit, bending my knees slightly to give myself a little more room to work with. Then, I focus on my feet, distributing my weight evenly throughout the four corners of each, and take a deep, cleansing breath to center myself. When I'm finally ready, I close my eyes.

Now that I know what to expect, I'm more aware of the things around me. I try to see with my other senses, since I can't with my eyes. The wind and sun are on my face, I smell the trees and catch a whiff of Alexei's scent (to my right?), I hear a bird chirping off in the distance, and a twig snap to my left. I tense in preparation of an attack from that side, but nothing comes. I widen my senses out farther, and I can feel Alexei's emotions. I can't tell which direction they're coming from, but I stay tuned in to them in hopes that I might be able to figure out when he is going to pounce. There's a slight trickle of amusement, determination, and what I think is pride?

I hear leaves rustle in front of me, smell a strong hint of him, and suddenly feel when he makes his decision to attack. I brace myself, almost certain he's coming at me head on. His hands slam into me, but instead of hitting me from the front like I think he's going to, he's slightly to my right. I stumble since I miscalculated, but I do much better than the first time around.

"Good. Now this time, I want you to tighten your core. Half the trick of maintaining your balance is to engage your core. If you have weak core muscles, then it will be much more difficult to keep yourself up, not to mention holding and handling weapons when we get to that stage."

I inwardly groan, but do as he says. I fucking *loathe* core work, but I know he's right. This time, it's a little easier to tune in. I don't know if it's because I've had my eyes closed for a while, or because I had success doing it the previous attempt, but when he attacks this time, I know he's coming from the back. After I take his push, and my body stays put, I swing my arm around, attempting to hit him. I don't know if I'm supposed to be doing this or not, but it seems natural to try to fight back.

My fist grazes him, barely missing. I sense his surprise that I almost got him, and definitely pride. I smile, feeling somewhat accomplished already. We continue practicing, and his shoves start getting a little more aggressive the longer we go, because I'm starting to get used to it. I stumble some more, only actually falling on my ass once when I completely misjudged where he was coming from, but during his final attack, I manage to get a solid hit in. He doesn't go anywhere, but I do a little happy dance.

"Very good, Ember. I think we will end it there for the day." He smiles genuinely at me and I beam back at him.

Things are just getting started, but accomplishment lightens my heart, and I can't wait to see where this training takes me. It will be a long time before I notice any big changes, but at least I'm already making a little bit of progress.

I need to take care of my bladder before we leave, especially since I drank so much water over lunch. While Alexei packs everything up, I try to find a good place to do my business.

"Don't go too far!" Alexei shouts at me, and I huff in frustration.

I don't want him to be able to hear anything, but it seems I don't have a choice. I find a nice tree that is tilted and on a hill. I pull my pants down, grab the tree, and lean, that way gravity takes control and I don't have to squat on already sore legs and potentially make an ass out of myself. Business done, I go back to my traveling companions. Horsey is already all packed up and ready to go, and we hop on and take off.

As soon as we start moving, I can feel how sore I'm going to be. My legs are already protesting the position, and my core muscles are like jelly, even though I've been leaning on Alexei for most of this ride. Combine that with today's training and my body is going to be pissed at me tomorrow.

"Want to practice your magic now?" he asks. I nod since we don't have anything else to do at the moment. "Okay, well first, let's have you identify my emotions and then we can see if you can manipulate them. So take a nice deep breath."

"Here we go again with the breathing," I huff under my breath, making him chuckle, but I do as he says.

When I'm centered, I expand my senses toward him. It's not hard to pick up on what emotions he's experiencing. At first it's subtle, but I can sense his intrigue and interest in what's going to happen.

"I can tell that you're curious about all this." His arms tighten around me. "Now I can detect your interest piquing, and your delight that I'm able to tune in to you."

I take another deep inhale, and my breasts subtly brush against his arms wrapped tight around me. I suppress the urge to moan and shift my hips to try to alleviate the heat building there. My backside brushes against something hard, and I suck in a sharp breath.

"Now you're lustful," I whisper, my voice rough.

He clears his throat, which sounds more like a growl. "Try to change it," he instructs, his voice gruff.

"What do you want me to make you feel instead?"

"Something appropriate," he murmurs against my ear.

His nose skims my neck, and I can hear him inhaling and know that he's smelling me. His bloodlust swirls through me and I can tell he wants to bite me. I try to focus on what I want to change his emotions to. The only thing I want from him is more lust, but he said something appropriate. My mind immediately goes back to when I drank from the river that made me giggle, and I figure that's pretty safe territory. I channel that memory, drawing it up and into me, seeing the pretty yellows and oranges of the sensation, intermingling with each until it's a swirl of happy color. I push it from me into him, and he starts chuckling. The deep rumble of his laughter flows through me, and it brings a smile to my face. His surprise and astonishment that I'm able to actually do it crash into me. I don't think he believed me until now.

"Wow. That's incredible," he murmurs. "How easy was that for you?"

"It wasn't hard. It did take me some time to imagine what the emotion looked like, and once I pictured it, a fair amount of concentration to move it to you, but I was able to accomplish it."

"Well, I had my mental barriers open to you. Now once you have that down, we can move on to you trying to get those emotions past my barriers." I nod because I didn't even think about it, but what he's saying makes a lot of sense. "So try again, and we'll keep going until you are comfortable with it."

I focus my energy again, deciding to go with excitement. I think of times when I've felt genuine excitement, and memories of Christmas Eve come to mind. I've always loved the holidays, but especially Christmas, and very especially when I was young. I picture it before pouring it out of me into a bubble. It becomes vibrant green with little streaks of gold running through it. With the bubble firmly in front of me, I reach out, curious if I can touch it or perhaps even turn my gift on myself. The moment my fingers come into contact with it, a shot of excitement runs through me, and I smile widely in response. I swirl my fingers through it, mixing the colors, and generally have fun playing with my new skill.

"What are you doing?" Alexei asks me, perplexed.

"I can see the emotions I want to portray. They come in the most amazing colors and patterns."

Without going into further detail, I push the brilliant cloud toward him. For a second, it looks like he has green and gold all over his tragically handsome face, and I giggle in response, but then he inhales, and it's like he breathed in the emotion. His features immediately light up, well, like a kid on Christmas morning.

We continue my training for the rest of the afternoon, and by the end of the day when we stop to set up camp, I think I've made some progress. I almost fall off the horse in exhaustion. I'm drained in basically every way I can think of. My body is killing me, not only from riding all day, but also from my first training session. My mind is fatigued from working with my abilities all afternoon. I wish I had a comfy bed to collapse into, but I guess the ground is what we're stuck with for tonight.

I help Alexei as much as I can, but I'm pretty sure that I'm being more of a hindrance. We get the little bit of bedding we brought down and pile it onto the ground. I was hoping that I would be able to sleep in my own spot, but between the fact that it's so much colder here and we will be needing all the extra body heat we can get, and that we are in the middle of the forest and should stick close to each other, I realize that won't be happening. *It will definitely do wondrous things for the sexual tension building between us*, I think to myself sarcastically.

Alexei starts a fire and takes out our food once again. I get our cheese, bread, and grapes ready, while he starts cooking up the meat that he had thawing all day, adding the spices he brought. I start eating the bread and cheese before the meat is ready, the smells making me too hungry to wait. He starts digging in too, clearly having the same problem. We finish off all of our appetizers as the meat is done cooking. I tear into it, still starving. I know it's all the training that I did today, not to mention the traveling. I'm not used to this kind of thing. The meat is delicious, and I'm done with it much too soon, wishing that I had another portion.

Alexei takes a blanket to lay over Horsey, before refining our bed. He leaves the fire going to keep us warm during the night, but then he does something truly spectacular. His fingers twirl around, but soon my eyes shoot to the ground in front of the fire. There's a slight rumble, and then earth springs right out of the dirt. His fingers keep twirling round and round, and soon there's a little shelter made out of dirt, leaves, and twigs. It curves up from the ground and is enclosed on all sides, except for the entrance. He then adds a large amount of leaves throughout the floor, making a nice bit of padding for us. When that's finished, he finally adds our bedding. Well, it might not be the supersoft mattress I was wishing for originally, but it's loads better than how I thought we would be sleeping tonight, which was out in the open on the hard ground with rocks digging into my back and a threadbare blanket. I use the restroom before going to bed, not wanting to get up in the middle of the night when it's cold and dark and I'm half-asleep wandering around the woods. That sounds like a disaster in the making.

Once I'm finished, I make my way into our little shelter. Alexei is already lying down, and the space seems so much smaller with him inside than it did while he was making it. I swallow audibly and head toward our bags instead, deciding to change into sleep clothes so I'm hopefully a little more comfortable. Then, I go back to the bed and stop in my tracks the second I spot Alexei.

He's lying on top of everything, leaving the blankets for me, but what stops me is the fact that he's passed out and his glorious torso is on display. I slowly walk toward him, like I'm afraid to spook him. I inch my way into the shelter, already warmer. The heat from the fire is creeping in and getting trapped with us.

I lie down next to him and pull the blankets up tight around me, trying to ignore the literally and figuratively hot man next to me, but before I can stop them, my traitorous eyes latch on to his chest. It's moving up and down steadily, his breathing deep in his sleep, and he's so toned it makes me want to cry. He has a six pack, and his pecs are so taut that you could bounce a quarter off of them, and my mouth waters with the idea of exploring the entirety of all that skin with my lips and tongue. He has a half-sleeve tattoo that goes over his shoulder and takes up his entire left pec. It looks almost Nordic, with intricately woven lines and swirls that make up a fierce-looking wolf. He has multiple scars as well, and before I think better of it, I'm dragging my fingers lightly over them. Besides the scars being raised, his skin is so smooth. Reluctantly, I remove my hand before he wakes up, and when I close my eyes my exhaustion takes over, and I pass out next to him.

Chapter 11

I wake the next morning, more comfortable and warm than I've been in a long time. I don't want to open my eyes yet, wanting to stay in the moment and enjoy this coziness for as long as I can. My cheek is resting on the comfiest pillow, and there's something supporting along my back that I equate to some sort of heating pad. I snuggle in a little bit more, but at that moment my bladder screams at me. I reluctantly open my eyes to find a man's nipple staring back at me. I'm so confused, until I realize that I must have snuggled up to Alexei in the night. I glance up at his face, moving as minimally as possible.

Luckily he's still sleeping, and I can hopefully finagle myself out of his arms before he realizes what happened. I start by lifting my head off his chest, and even that small movement has my core protesting from our activities yesterday. I realize the real problem is going to be escaping the arm he has wrapped around me. I slowly and carefully roll onto my back, pinning his arm underneath me. I sit up quickly before he notices the weight on it, and I give myself a mental high five that I accomplished it without him being any the wiser. When I glance down at him, I realize, much to my dismay, that I wasn't nearly as stealthy as I thought. His eyes are open and filled with amusement, and a knowing smirk gracing his perfect mouth tells me all I need to know.

Before he can say anything, I get up and walk out, my bladder still yelling at me. Once I've taken care of business, I come back to find him making another fire. Our shelter from the night before has disappeared, and our bedding is already neatly packed. Alexei is heating water in a pan, and he has two cups out. When the water is finished, he pours it into them, handing me one. I smell mint and I'm grateful that he made tea. He has another pan over the fire with what looks like oatmeal in it. I'm finished drinking my tea by the time it's done, and I eat quickly like I always do, almost burning my mouth in the process.

With Alexei still eating, I change back into my traveling clothes and splash some cool water on my face to wake myself up a bit more. I was going to pack some stuff up, but it seems that he's already done all of that, so I give some love to Horsey instead. I need to think of a name for her. I can't keep calling her Horsey, although I do like it when Alexei does. I stroke her snout as I think of good names for a gray horse. She needs something fierce. Storm immediately comes to mind, but I dismiss it. It's too cliché. Graphite is my next thought, but I would feel weird calling her that. It almost sounds too...formal? Not a name? I don't know what exactly, but it doesn't fit her. I think about my name for a moment, wondering if it would be too cheesy to have names that are related, and I try to think of names that could revolve around flames. Ash. Yes. That's it.

"How do you like 'Ash,' pretty girl?" She neighs in approval, snorting into my hand in her enthusiasm, and I chuckle in response. "Ash it is."

"Ash, huh?" Alexei says, sneaking up behind me and scaring the shit out of me.

"I think it's appropriate, don't you?"

"Ash," he says softly. She butts her head into his hand, asking for the attention that she's come to love. He chuckles before indulging her, petting her snout. Seeing him love her makes my heart squeeze. "Yes, it's the perfect name for her. Although, I still like 'Horsey.'"

I laugh loudly, and he gives me a fond smile.

"Are you ready to go?"

I nod, grasping the saddle and hoisting myself up. Alexei comes up right behind me.

"Let's roll, Ash."

I giggle at how he's adopting my phrases. I don't know if he's doing it purposefully or not, but I like it all the same.

We ride in silence for a while, and I take in our surroundings. We're traveling through the forest now, and it's getting more dense the farther in we go. The leaves overhead are so thick that it's getting much darker, the sun not able to penetrate nearly as well. We follow along the river that runs through, which is a relief, as we won't have to try to find water on our travels.

We continue on the same way for the next few days. Breakfast, stop for lunch, train, practice my magic in the afternoon, and then dinner and rest for the night. We end up tangled together every night, and every morning we both pretend that nothing happened.

Every training session I notice improvements with both my magic and my combat skills, and by the time the night comes around, I am so exhausted that I immediately collapse after dinner, sleeping through the night. After that first day, I start to notice that every time we are on the ground, whether we're sitting or lying down, the earth is extremely soft, almost padded. On the fourth day of our travels, I ask Alexei about it.

"I cushion us with my earth magic," he says simply.

I thought that was the case, but it still catches me off guard a little bit. "That seems like a lot of effort to put in every time we sit or lie down."

"It takes barely a thought from me. Honestly, building the shelter usually takes more effort."

"Well, I appreciate you doing those things for me. It may not seem like a lot to you, but it is to me," I tell him genuinely, smiling at him.

He returns the smile, looking almost surprised that I said thank you. "Well, you're welcome. Now, enough of that, and back to your training."

We're stopped for our lunch break and are working on combat skills. Alexei determines that I'm doing well enough with my balance that I'm able to move on to actually learning how to fight. I'm in my usual stance that he has slowly been correcting as I wait for his instructions.

"Today I'm going to teach you how to hit properly as well as to block."

Excitement builds inside me as I look forward to finally being able to inflict some damage.

Alexei starts out with blocking, showing me the best movements to counter certain attacks, like freeing my wrists if someone has grasped them, blocking his punches by swinging my arm out, and bringing my leg up and where to take the brunt of the kick if someone goes for the legs.

I copy him as best as I can, with him correcting me or demonstrating alternative movements. I'm grateful for all the work that we've put into my core and balance, because otherwise I think I would already be on my ass and feeling like a failure. We work together until I have the moves down pretty well and then we move on to delivering blows. We do this in basically the same way, me watching him first and then attempting the move and him making any changes or adjustments that I need.

These routines are more enjoyable for me, and he teaches me how to properly throw a punch (how to make a proper fist, and how to start at the feet to add power to my blow), and how to kick and where to aim to inflict the most damage. An hour and a half later, I'm confident I have all the offensive and defensive moves down, and we mount Ash and move on.

We start our usual routine of ability training while we ride. I've gotten down identifying his emotions immediately and being able to push different sensations on him with only a thought, but those have been with his shields down. Today he is going to start putting his mental barriers up and we'll see how well I do. I take a deep breath as my nerves start to kick in at this slight change.

"Okay, hit me with your best shot, little doe."

I close my eyes, as that usually makes it a little easier for me to concentrate. I open my senses to him, and don't pick up on anything. I try not to be too disappointed that it wasn't as easy as I was hoping. The problem is that I don't know how to get around the walls in his head. I take another deep breath and open my mind a little bit more. After a few minutes with no success, I switch up my tactic. Instead of opening my mind up, I push against his. His mind resists, and I struggle to maintain my concentration. I keep it up though, and push more. With a final grunt of determination, I break through his shields.

"I did it!" I cry, excited. His emotions finally spill into me, and I feel his pride and slight shock that I was able to do it.

"Well done. Now see if you can change them."

I immediately make him hyper as a result of my excitement. The bright neon orange color sinks into him, and he starts fidgeting slightly behind me, and I smile at my success. I do notice that he doesn't seem to be reacting as strongly as when his shields are down, and I'm guessing that it takes more effort to reach that same level with his shields up. Even though I already broke through them, I know he's trying to push me back out.

I concentrate harder, taking a firm grasp on his mind so I can mold it to the emotion I'm trying to force on him. This time it works better, the emotion actually taking root in him as opposed to being a fleeting thing that could fly away in the wind. He starts bouncing up and down behind me in an effort to expel some of his energy, and he kicks Ash into a faster pace. All of that combined activity has us rubbing up against each other, sending heat straight to my core. He wraps his arm firmly around my stomach and pulls me closer to him to make sure that I don't fall as we go faster and faster. I laugh loudly and enjoy the wind whipping my hair back, exhilaration at our speed making my heart pound. I let it continue for another few minutes, and when my ass starts to hurt from bouncing so much, I pull the hyperness from him. He immediately slows us and chuckles.

"Well, that was an interesting one. I needed to *move*."

"I could tell."

"You did well though. My shields weren't nearly as powerful or strong as I would normally have them, but I want to work up to that. It will continue to get harder and harder to get into my head, and eventually you may not be able to, but this way we can find out how powerful you really are, little doe."

I nod. I figured that he wasn't going full force right away after not shielding at all.

"Let's try again, and see if you can get through quicker this time."

His barriers slam up between our minds, and now that I know how to get through them, I have an easier time doing it. It doesn't take me nearly as long this round, and once I'm in, I immediately pour an emotion into him without thinking. I want to get it done quickly before he can force me back out.

I realize too late that I am pouring an inappropriate feeling into him. Lust. Bright magenta-colored lust. He grunts softly behind me, and he hardens against my backside. I suck in a sharp breath, heat building in me quickly. This is a mistake. I should pull back. After all the sexual tension that's been building between us, my body is reveling in the attention, but I don't want it this way. His hips flex against mine, and I fight back a whimper. His mouth finds its way to my neck, and I move my head to the side to give him access. His fangs drag down my throat, and even though I told myself I never wanted to be bit again, at the moment it doesn't sound like the worst idea in the world.

"Ember..." Alexei murmurs against my neck.

My name on his lips like a plea snaps me out of it enough to pull the lust back out of him. I want him so bad, but I don't want him under my influence when it finally happens between us. He immediately snaps his head back as if I burned him.

"I'm sorry," I tell him genuinely. Embarrassment and shame that I accidentally took advantage of him like that tinge my cheeks red. "I didn't mean to push that emotion on you. I was trying to act quickly before you could get your defenses back up, and I pushed the first thing that popped into my head. I'm so sorry."

"Ember, it's okay. It just took me off guard. I mean, I battle that emotion with you on my own on a daily basis," he says gruffly behind me, catching me by surprise.

"You do?" I ask quietly, almost afraid to startle him by speaking louder. Or maybe startling myself.

"Yes. Sleeping next to you is like my own twisted form of torture on myself. Having you so close but not being able to actually *have* you."

"Why can't you have me?" I ask, confusion knitting my brow.

He sighs heavily. "Ember, when I became a guardian, I took an oath. While I maintain this position, I'm not able to have intimate relationships with anyone. It detracts from my duty and distracts from my responsibility to this kingdom. Protecting the realm is the highest and most noble job someone can have. We guard Queridian so that it is safe from potential invasions from other realms. It is the most important job here, other than perhaps the king himself. So unfortunately, no matter how much I want to be with you, while I do this job, I can't. I'm sorry."

My heart sinks with his words. I knew he was attracted to me, but I figured that he wasn't ready to start anything yet. I should've realized that he had a good reason for it.

"I understand," I say softly.

And I do, but disappointment sits like a rock in my stomach, which is stupid because I hardly know him. Well, that's not exactly true. I've never had close relationships with people other than my mother before, so while we haven't actually known each other that long, I do feel closer to him than I have anyone else in a very long time.

"I wish things were different," he whispers, moving my hair over my shoulder to speak in my ear.

I can hear the longing and regret in his voice, and irrational tears build behind my eyes. He rests his head against the side of mine, and for one moment, I imagine what it would be like to be able to be with him. When more tears start to build, I push the fantasy away and force the tears back so they don't fall, and as much as it pains me, I pull away from Alexei. If this can't happen between us, then I need to stop the intimacy we've been starting to share with each other. He pulls back regretfully.

"Well, we can just be friends, then," I say when I've got a hold on my emotions.

"Of course. Now, let's focus back on your magic."

We redirect our efforts, and this time he's put up a stronger mental shield. It takes me a moment to concentrate enough to remember how to get through it, and it also takes more effort, but I eventually break through. He's disappointed, guilty, and sad, and I assume it's from our conversation. I push past it, already having an emotion ready so we don't have a repeat of last time. I don't want him to have any negative emotions since he's already experiencing so many, so I remove them and give him a sense of calmness that is the gentlest shade of lavender. As I focus on it, I can smell lavender too, and I inhale deeply, trying to imbue some of those feelings into myself as well. His body immediately relaxes against mine, and I push more and more into him until I'm sure that's the only thing he's experiencing. He takes a big, deep breath, and if it's possible, he slackens even more against me. I look back and see his eyes are closed, and it almost looks like he's sleeping.

I smile to myself until he starts tipping off the horse. I scream in fright, reaching around to clutch on to him, and my mind immediately retracts the emotion from his mind and inserts a sense of alertness. At once he shoots up as if nothing happened, looking as though he just had a shot of espresso.

"I guess that was too much?" I ask, laughing. I did not expect that to happen.

"A bit," he says, laughing too.

"But, my mind reacted instinctively, which is good, right? I was able to wake you immediately."

"You made me wake up like that? I thought that was from you screaming in my ear," he teases, but his question sounds genuine.

"Yes. My mind took away the calmness and gave you alertness so that you wouldn't fall off the horse. Of course, I started reacting physically at first and didn't even realize that my brain was doing that all on its own without any prompting."

He nods, looking impressed. "Yes, that is good news. You're developing more control over your gift. And you're fucking *strong*." I grin at his praise. "Tomorrow I will put up the strongest shield I can conjure, and I'll have you try to break through it. See if you can put the same amount of force behind it, *if* you can get through it," he says cockily. "If you can manage all of that, then we can start focusing on you building up *your* mental shields."

I'm excited for the prospect, and the challenge I'm going to have tomorrow. I think figuring out how to get past his barriers in the first place was the hard part, and now it seems to be getting easier every time.

Shortly after that, we stop for the night. Alexei sets up our camp like he does every night, but I notice it's a little bigger this time around, for which I'm grateful. I don't want to end up in his arms again tomorrow morning because of the conversation we had today. At least that's what I'm telling myself. The uncomfortable sensation in my chest at the thought is saying something different to me, but I disregard it.

We eat our dinner in tense silence. Things are a little awkward between us after this afternoon, and I keep my attention on our meager meal. We've gone through all the perishables, and are now onto the dried meat, fruits, and nuts. They're fine, but we've been eating them for a few days now, and I'm craving a hot cooked meal.

"We're almost through Elisora Forest. We should be coming up on the Moonlit Mountains pretty soon."

I nod. I had noticed the ground getting slightly steeper as we went, but I wasn't able to see the mountain range because of the denseness of the forest. We finish dinner, and I head over to Ash to give her some love before we bed down for the night. She nuzzles into me and I give her some well-deserved pets and an apple that we saved from an apple tree along the way. She eats it gratefully, blowing happily into my hand, and I drape her blanket over her as she drinks some water from the stream. When she's all taken care of, and I'm ready for bed and can literally do nothing else to stall, I head to the shelter.

Alexei is lying down already, the light from the fire making him look like some sort of god. His shirt is off like it always is when he goes to bed, but this time I wish he would sleep with one on. He's still awake and basically on the farthest side of the shelter. I take the other side and there's several feet between us, and I'm pretty positive that I won't end up like I have previous mornings. I'm so tense that I'm as stiff as a board and have no clue how I'm going to get to sleep anytime soon.

I know I'm making a way bigger deal out of this than I need to be. So what he can't be with me? So what a crazy sexual tension has built between us? That doesn't mean things need to be awkward and tense whenever we're around each other. We can push past it and find a new normal. We can do as I said earlier and be good friends. Because even though it sucks that we can't be together, he still means a lot to me, and I want him in my life, even if it's not what I was originally hoping for.

Without consciously doing so, my mind reaches for his. He has his shields in place, and with all the practice we've been doing, it's instinctive to burst through it, but I stop myself. It feels like a violation of his trust to do it when we aren't training. Besides, if our roles were reversed, I wouldn't want him snooping around in my head right now.

The heat from the fire finally relaxes me enough that I'm able to drift off, and right before I do, I hear Alexei whisper, "Good night, Ember," as his fingers softly caress my hand.

The next day, things return relatively back to normal between us, which I'm grateful for, especially after my revelation last night. We finally start to move out of the heaviness of the dense forest, and I'm able to see the start of the Moonlit Mountains. They're stunning, pale, and expansive. I have no clue how big they actually are, but they're definitely intimidating.

We stick to our routine, combat training at lunch, this time facing off against one another so that I can practice actually fighting someone. It's rough at first, but the longer we go at it, the more natural it is to me, the moves he taught me becoming more instinctual.

When it's time for my ability training, he does as he promised and puts up his strongest mental shields. Since I've been successful in the past, I think it's going to go smoothly, but I can't get past them. I push and push against his mind, usually cursing in my frustration, and hours later when it's almost time for us to stop for the night, my mind is exhausted and I'm more pissy than I've been on this entire trip.

"It's okay, Ember. You've done well up until now. Actually much better than I anticipated. If you would've gotten through my shields today, that would've been unthinkable. I'm sure you will at some point because I know you're that strong, but it's going to take practice."

"But I've *been* practicing. That's what we've been doing for *hours* every single day." I know how whiny I sound. And I hate it, but with my mood I can't help it.

"It's also going to take time. You aren't going to be proficient in everything with hardly any training. Be patient. It'll come. On a lighter note, there's something that is going to cheer you up." I perk up a bit at his words, waiting for him to continue. He doesn't, but as I'm about to ask him about it, we turn a corner, and an inn comes into view.

"We get to sleep there tonight?" I ask excitedly, and he nods and smiles in response.

I can't believe we actually get to sleep in a soft warm bed and I'll get to have a bath! I moan at the thought, and Alexei clears his throat uncomfortably, but at the moment I don't even care. He's right; my bad mood is completely gone, and I can't wait for a delicious hot meal.

A stable boy approaches, taking Ash from us, offering her lots of fresh hay and brushing after our long journey. Alexei hands him some coins and we make our way inside. An elderly gentleman behind the counter greets us as we come in, and Alexei tells him we want two rooms for the evening. I'm grateful that he's getting me my own room, but my heart sinks when he tells us that they have only one available. Alexei looks at me a little uncomfortably.

"It's okay. I can sleep on the floor," he tells me.

"Don't you dare. We've been sleeping on the ground for almost a week now. Besides, we've been sleeping next to each other this whole time and it's been totally fine. Really. All I care about is that I get to have a fresh meal, take a hot bath, and sleep in a warm bed."

He nods at my words, and the innkeeper takes us up to the room. There's already a roaring fire going, and while it's nothing special, it looks like utter bliss compared to how we've been spending our nights.

"I'll have some food sent up," the innkeeper tells us before shutting the door on his way out.

"Would you like to have a bath first?" Alexei asks me.

I notice then that the room is large enough to house a small bathing chamber around the corner. It isn't very private, as there is no door, but then I spot a little privacy screen that I can use to divide the rooms. I nod excitedly before I get the water going.

Alexei sits on the bed and takes his boots off. I set up the divider and start cautiously undressing. It's a little weird doing this with him on the other side of the partition, and I'm sure he can hear every move I make, but I push past it. There's a mirror in the corner, and I look at myself for the first time in a while.

I can already see subtle changes to my body from my diet and all the training we've been doing, and I smile proudly at the muscle definition that's started to peek through. When the tub is filled, I slowly sink down into the water. I don't think anything has ever felt this good. I dunk my head under, wanting to wash my hair right away and get as clean as I can after our week on the road. I look around for the shampoo, and I huff in frustration as I don't see anything to wash myself with. I guess this isn't like hotels back on Earth where they provide you with that kind of thing. I'm pretty sure we packed toiletries, but that would mean Alexei would have to bring them to me. I curse under my breath.

"What's wrong?" he asks from the other room, startling me. Damn vampire hearing.

"Umm...there's nothing to wash with in here."

"Do you need me to grab ours?"

"If you could. I would like to get clean."

He noisily rummages around in our luggage for a moment before his footsteps get closer and closer. When he's on the other side of the divider, he stops.

"How do you want to do this?" he asks hesitantly, as if he just realized that I'm naked and wet on the other side of the only thing separating us.

I sit up, hugging my knees to my chest and moving my hair to cover as much of my chest as I can. "I'm basically covered. I don't think you'll be able to see anything." The erratic pounding of my heart contradicts my blasé words.

He slowly inches his way around the partition. He meets my eyes and walks toward me. It seems like it's taking all his effort not to look down at my body. I hold out my hand for the soap and shampoo, and that finally draws his eyes down. He places them in my hand, and our fingers graze like there's an electrical current running between us. I keep my eyes on his face, and his gaze roams my body before he swallows hard.

"Thank you," I say in a rough voice. He nods and turns, walking away and leaving me to wash myself. Disappointment settles in me as he leaves.

I pour the shampoo in my hands and start lathering my hair as I try to ignore the heat that's built in my core from that little interaction. As soon as the smell of the shampoo hits me and my hair is full of bubbles, I moan again. It feels so good to be getting clean. I hear Alexei groan in the other room, and not in a good way. It almost sounds like he's in pain or something.

"Are you all right?" I ask.

He clears his throat. "Yes. I'm fine."

I don't believe him, but I leave it alone. I dunk my head under, rinsing out the shampoo. I make quick work of washing my body, anxious to get all the dirt off me. I hear a knock on the door, and Alexei answers. The innkeeper brought us food, and Alexei thanks him before bringing the tray into the room. The smell of something delicious and hot teases my nose, and I finish with my bath so I can attend to my growling stomach. I drain the tub and wrap a towel around myself.

I go into the bedroom, dripping wet since I have to grab my clothes and dress before I can wrap my hair in my towel. Alexei has the food on the bed since there's no table, and he's about to take a bite when he spots me coming into the room. The fork he's holding stops halfway to his lips, his mouth wide open. I smirk at him and dig through my clothes before selecting some clean items, not wanting to put my dirty ones back on after my bath. When I return to the bathing area, Alexei is still staring at me with his mouth open and the fork still in the same place. I chuckle knowingly, get dressed and wrap my hair in the towel. I consider braiding it, but I'm too hungry to take the time. This will do for now.

I come back in the room and sit next to Alexei. He has a plate already prepared for me, and the sight and smell is mouthwatering. He's already halfway through his dinner, but with me being me, I'll probably finish before him. I take a sip of the wine he's poured while I decide what food to start with first. It looks like mashed potatoes, greens with lemon, and some sort of roasted and seasoned meat. I've always been a sucker for mashed potatoes, so I start there, and an almost sexual sound comes out of my mouth before I can stop it. After days of eating cold, dried meat, along with some nuts and berries, this is heavenly. I quickly devour everything on my plate, taking short breaks only to drink the delicious wine, and sure enough, I finish right before he does. He smirks at me knowingly, and I blush, slightly embarrassed by how quickly I always seem to eat when delicious food is placed in front of me.

"How was your bath?" he asks.

It's an innocent enough question, but the heat behind his eyes tells me differently. This whole staying friends thing is going to be difficult for us both it seems. I know we should be backing off on flirting with each other, but I enjoy it too much to stop.

"Wonderful. It's so nice to be clean. And the hot water felt fantastic."

"Do you think there's enough hot water left for me?"

I nod. "It didn't seem to be cooling much by the time I turned it off."

He stands, taking his wine with him, and walks into the bathing chamber. I hear the water turn on, and then the distinct rustle of him removing his clothes. I take a big drink of wine as I try—unsuccessfully, I might add—not to picture him naked. There's the sound of him stepping into the water, and I make sure I didn't give him false information.

"How does it feel? Was there enough hot water left?"

"It's fabulous." It finally registers that he's completely naked, and heat shoots straight to my core. My brain conjures up so many filthy images that I can't stop them. Him stroking himself in the bath while I watch, us on the bed together with his wet body draped over mine, my hands tangled in his damp hair as he feasts on my cunt. *Stop it, Ember.*

Through pure force of will, I shove those images out of my head and try to concentrate on anything else. I unwrap my hair from the towel and start Dutch braiding it as I stare at the fire. It's so difficult to keep my mind off of him as I listen to him washing himself. The first image pops into my head again, slower this time, of him caressing his hard length as he gives me that sexy heated look he always seems to be wearing. I bite my lip and my hand starts drifting toward my pussy. The pressure equally awakens and alleviates my discomfort and a low moan slips out. Alexei stops moving, and things are utterly silent on his end. I jerk my hand away guiltily before I do something stupid.

"Ember? Are you all right?" Of course there was zero chance of him not hearing that with his stupid vampire ears.

"Yes. This bed is *so* comfortable," I say as an excuse. I mean, technically it's not a lie, it's just not the reason I was moaning.

He finishes up quickly and comes back in, a towel wrapped around his waist, as he clearly forgot to bring an extra set in with him like I did. I've seen him without a shirt plenty of times this week, but for some reason, it's different now. Probably because he's naked. And wet. I can't help but watch as a droplet from his hair travels down his chest and disappears underneath the towel. All I can think about is how it would be to trace that water with my tongue. Before I can watch another one, he takes a stack of clothes and vanishes behind the partition again. I take a deep breath and try to calm my racing heart before he comes back in. I move the tray off of the bed, putting it on the floor by the door so we can take care of it in the morning, and slide beneath the covers. The bed seems so small, but I know that it's similar to the amount of space we normally have between us when we sleep.

When my head hits the pillow, all thoughts of how small the bed might be fly from my head. I can already tell I'm going to get the best night's sleep of my life, and I'm almost asleep by the time Alexei climbs into bed. I can feel his body heat from here, and if possible, I become even more relaxed. Within two minutes, I'm asleep.

Chapter 12

The next morning, we have an equally delicious breakfast, and we each take another bath since we won't be able to for a while. As good as the baths feel, I miss showers. They're convenient, fast, and so enjoyable. But I'm not complaining. We come downstairs and the stable boy brings Ash out.

"Is she all taken care of?" Alexei asks.

"Yes, sir. I even gave her some fresh carrots this morning. She's a happy girl," the boy says affectionately. It looks like she caught someone else under her spell, and I smile as I move forward to pet her. She neighs happily at my attention.

"I think she missed me last night," I tell Alexei.

He chuckles as he and the stable boy load her up with all of our gear. When we're on the road I'm able to look around a bit more than I was last night. I can see everything more clearly since the sun is out and we are officially out of the forest. The mountains span from left to right endlessly, and I wonder exactly how far out they go. The mountains themselves hold a milky hue, and I have no clue what kind of stone they're made out of, or if it even exists on Earth. The effect is breathtaking, and I've never seen anything like it. I remember Alexei saying they were called the "Moonlit Mountains," and that name resonates with me now. There's a trail that we can follow up the length of the mountain, and I'm grateful that we don't have to do any hiking or climbing.

"When we work on your training today, I'm going to teach you how to use a bow and arrow."

"Really?!" I ask, completely surprised. I didn't think I had advanced far enough in my training yet for weapons, but I have to say that I am very excited at the prospect.

"Normally I wouldn't have you learning any weapons yet, but we're entering a dangerous area, and the more prepared you are, the better."

I swallow. I knew when we were going on this journey that there would be some danger, but up until now I haven't thought or worried about it at all. I remind myself that this is why Alexei is training me—so I can defend myself in dangerous situations.

"I'll protect you with everything I have, Ember. But I also want you to be able to protect yourself in case something happens to me or I'm not able to get to you."

I'm touched by his words. I know we're getting to know each other better, but the fact that he's willing to put his life on the line to protect me speaks volumes.

"Thank you, Alexei. I don't know if I've ever told you how much it means to me that you're training me and helping me with everything. And I appreciate that you're willing to protect me, but with all the training I'm getting, hopefully you won't have to. I want to fight by your side if something dangerous comes along, not hide behind you like some simpering damsel. I want to be a badass too. I want to be able to do some serious damage, and I can't wait for you to teach me everything you know."

"Everything I know, huh? That would take quite a while, little doe."

"Well, maybe you'll have to stick around long enough to do that."

It's something that I don't want to think about. I'm not sure what's going to happen when we get to the Immortal City. I know he's bringing me there to see what the king thinks about my arrival, but I don't know what that means for him. Will he return to his post when his duty is finished? Will he stay there with me? Or will the king immediately send me back to the Mortal Realm? So many paths, and I have no clue where we're going to end up.

"Maybe I will."

I try not to get my hopes up. After all, most of the outcomes are out of our hands.

We continue on in silence for a while before he asks me if I want to take control of Ash. I nervously take the reins from him, and there's not much to it. I pull on the right and she goes that direction, and same when I pull left. I pull on both and say "Whoa" like I've heard Alexei do, and she stops. Then I gently squeeze her with my legs when I want her to go again. There's so many new abilities that I'm learning with Alexei, and I'm delighting in it. I love being taught new things, and all of this is so different from what I've learned on Earth.

After we stop for our break halfway through the day and finish eating, Alexei takes out his bow. He brings it over to me and demonstrates how to hold it with his left hand before nocking an arrow with his right. He pulls the string and the arrow back to his mouth in one fluid motion. He takes a deep breath in and releases on his exhale, and the arrow flies through the air and embeds into a tree trunk twenty yards away. I marvel at how easy he makes it look and know that it won't be that easy for me, no matter how much I want it to be.

I take the bow from his grip and immediately grunt at the weight. How the fuck am I supposed to hold this up? I nock an arrow like he did and lift the bow into the air. I'm able to do it, but my shoulder and arm are screaming at me in protest. I ignore them and focus on the same tree that Alexei shot his arrow into. He comes up behind me and steadies my left arm before guiding my right to pull the string back. I pant at the effort, barely managing to pull it back to my mouth.

"Inhale," he commands and I do so. "Release on the exhale."

I let the string go and watch the arrow spring out before flopping to the ground ten yards in front of us. I sigh in disappointment, but before I can get discouraged, I remind myself that it was my first attempt and I have a great teacher behind me.

"What did I do wrong?"

"You're not putting enough tension on the string. You need to pull back farther so that when you release it you get a nice strong shot."

"I'm trying, but the bow is so heavy and the string is so hard to pull and cuts into my fingers."

"You need to build up calluses in your fingers. It will take time, but once they develop you won't even notice anymore. In the meantime, we can wrap them and it should help a little bit. I also have a smaller bow, which should be a little easier for you."

He walks toward Ash and rifles through our luggage before coming back with small strips of fabric and a smaller bow for me. This one looks quite a bit lighter, and I wonder why he didn't start me on this one to begin with.

He gently grasps my right hand in his, wrapping each individual finger. It's a little difficult to flex my fingers, but I do it a few times, loosening the wrapping, and it seems to be a little better. Then, I grab the new bow, already noticing a huge difference in the weight, nock an arrow, and pull it up. It's noticeably easier, and I'm relieved that I won't have to put quite as much work in to hold it. When I draw the string back I'm able to get it farther than the last, and the cloth is definitely helping with the bite of the string. I inhale and release on my exhale. This time, the arrow goes flying, but misses the tree entirely. I don't feel even a hint of disappointment though, because that was already loads better than the first time around.

"Why didn't you start me off on this bow? It's much easier."

"I wanted to see how you did with the heavier one first. Once you get used to shooting with this one, I may switch you back to the other.

Sometimes you don't have a choice in which weapon you get to wield and you need to pick up the first one you have access to. If you can learn to shoot with a heavier bow, then you can shoot with anything."

I nod. Even though it was kind of mean, his explanation makes sense. Damn him with his stupid logical ways.

"This time, when you pull the string back, touch the corner of your mouth. That is your anchor point. Then you need to close one of your eyes so that you can aim more accurately."

I do as he says, but I switch back and forth closing each eye to see which one is more natural to have open. I keep my left eye open and latch it on to where his arrow is still embedded in the tree. I inhale and release on my exhale. I yelp in pain and surprise when the string snaps against my left forearm. I put the bow down and see a huge red welt on it. When I look back up, I see that my arrow hit the tree! It's nowhere near Alexei's, but at least I hit the target. I do a little happy dance to celebrate, and Alexei gives me a strange look.

"What are you doing?" he asks.

"It's called a happy dance, Mr. Grumpikins. Not that you would know how to even do one," I tease, to which he rolls his eyes. I show him my forearm. "How do I stop this from happening?"

He gently takes my arm, and I hiss in pain as he runs his finger over it. He rushes to his bag and grabs a container. He brings it back and applies a small amount of ointment to my arm. It tingles a bit, but within a few moments the sting starts to fade.

"Your left arm is too straight. If you bend your elbow a bit, the string shouldn't snap you when you release it."

We spend the rest of the hour practicing. He critiques me when I'm doing something wrong, or when I forget to breathe properly. Occasionally, he will stand behind me and correct my posture, and his presence always fucks with my head a little bit. By the time we take off again, I'm more confident and can't wait to practice more. I'm already liking this better than the hand-to-hand training we've been doing. It's more natural to me, and I like having a deadly weapon that I can defend myself with.

"So, why are the areas that we're moving into dangerous?"

"This side of the Moonlit Mountains has pockets in them that house monsters. We have monsters all over Queridian, but these are particularly vicious and are native to this area."

"What are they?"

"They're called 'áspro vrykólakas.' They're huge white bats. They used to be vampires, but they went too long without feeding and they turned. Once that happens, we turn white as a sheet, our eyes grow red, we grow wings, and our bite becomes poisonous. Most people only have one day before they die from a bite." My eyes grow wide. They sound terrifying, and I hope we don't encounter any. Now I know why he's teaching me archery.

"How long does it take to become one of them if you don't feed?"

"It takes a while. When we start to get hungry, our body will start feeding off of our own blood. It can become very painful, and once there's no more blood left in our body to feed on, we turn. It's why they're white. But that usually doesn't happen for months. If there's a serious injury and we lose a lot of blood, it can speed up the process though."

"Is there any way to heal from their bite?"

"Nylaluna in the Healing Springs territory would do it. Luckily we aren't far from there, just in case."

"What's that?"

"It's a sacred pool in the elves' territory. Elves have the ability to heal, therefore they have water on their land that has the same power."

"So if one of us were to get hurt, we could go to this pool and it would heal us?"

"Well, technically, you aren't allowed in the Healing Springs. You would need a travel visa, or to have diplomatic immunity like me. I can travel to any territory because I am a royal guardian, but there are very few people who are able to travel to every territory legally. If something were to happen, I would need to sneak you in."

"Well, let's hope that nothing happens, then. Plus, I can shoot them now like a badass with my new bow and arrow." I wink at him over my shoulder with more confidence than I feel, but he chuckles all the same.

"Damn right you can. Now, enough questions. Try to get through my mental shields."

I resist the urge to complain and focus. I close my eyes, focusing only on his mind, pushing with everything I have against them, but they won't budge. I try every way I can think of, even mentally sneaking around the back side to try to get one past him, but his barriers stand firm. I snarl in frustration, not able to get so much as a brick to move. I open my eyes God knows how long later, and the sky is starting to darken. It frustrates me that I was making so much progress with my power, but now I'm stuck.

"Don't worry, little doe. You'll get it eventually."

I nod, a little dejected. We stop for the night and make our camp as usual, although I notice Alexei sleeping with his shirt on. I think he's trying to tone down the sexual tension between us, which isn't a bad idea.

The next day we continue on the same way, and when we stop for lunch to do more weapons training I realize how sore my shoulders, arms, and back are. I push through, determined to learn as much as I can in this short amount of time. By the end of practice, I'm able to mostly hit where I'm aiming, and I jump up and down excitedly. Finally, I'm making some progress with something and I can actually see a difference.

The magic training starts as it has for the last couple days. I push and push and push against his mental barriers until I'm exhausted and I feel like my brain has gone through a meat grinder. As I'm about to give up for the day, I think of a different tactic. Clearly pushing at it is not doing jack shit. What if I come at it in a gentler way? More subtle.

I take a deep breath to center myself before picturing his walls in my mind. Instead of trying to force my way in, I gently caress them, willing them to open for me. I promise that I'm trustworthy and that I mean no harm. I tell them that I'm a friend and that they don't have to be frightened of me. I coax and coax, and I finally see a little sliver that opens up. Instead of rushing for it like I want to, I take my time, petting the barriers as if they were a skittish animal. When I reach the crack, I slowly ease myself into it. When I'm through, all of his shields fall away, and I gasp at the sensation of his emotions flooding into me, stronger than I've ever felt. His contentment and a deep seated feeling of belonging seep into me. I also sense a strong bond of friendship and something that's a little deeper.

"I did it," I whisper, so as not to startle him. His surprise and pride that I was able to finally get through his walls hit me next.

"Push something onto me," he murmurs in my ear gruffly.

I usually try to push something positive onto him, but I should probably practice with some negative emotions too. I push frustration, and he instantly tenses behind me. He growls low in my ear as I watch his fists curl. Now that I know I'm able to do it, I switch to joy. I don't like making people have any negative emotions, especially him. He breathes a sigh of relief behind me.

"That's amazing that you're able to do that, Ember. It's such a strange sensation to have emotions thrust upon me like that. And the quickness with which you can change them is incredible."

His words light something up inside me, and I smile fully. I'm so relieved that I was able to accomplish the task, and his praise means a lot.

"Now we need to have you focus on building up your own mental shields. That way you'll be able to keep others out as well."

"What other races can affect the mind?"

"Well, humans, as you know, although you're the only one I've ever heard of who can actually change emotions. You can also be influenced by the mermaids. They hold the power of persuasion and allure, so most of them can convince you to do things they want you to. Some of them take on political roles so that they can easily sway others to their cause. Also, depending on how strong your shields are, you can protect yourself against mimics copying your form."

"They can do that?" I ask, shocked.

"Yes. If you come into contact with a mimic and you don't have your shields up when they touch you, they will be able to take on your form. They still might be able to copy some features if your shields aren't very strong, but won't be able to imitate your likeness completely. Mimics are feared among the other races because of that power. They're generally regarded as untrustworthy, so most of them end up staying in their own territory. I've only met a few myself, and they are strange. Probably because a lot of them are in their animal forms much of the time, so they aren't great at interacting with others."

"Are they able to shift into any animal?"

"No. They have only one animal that they can shift into. Usually that form carries through bloodlines, but not always. Sometimes someone will emerge as a random animal not previously held by their ancestors. They can switch between their one animal form and then their true humanlike form. Well, and others' forms like we just discussed. Their land is also imbued with that magic, so rarely does anyone go into their territory because it's so easy to get lost as the land shifts and changes. I do know there are landmarks that stay the same throughout, but the land itself shifts. So one day you might be looking up at a sprawling peak, and then next you'll be looking down into a valley."

"Wow," I breathe, unable to fully comprehend this new crazy realm I fell into.

We're about to stop for the night when we hear a pterodactyl-like shriek in the distance that makes my blood freeze. Alexei's whole body tenses behind mine.

"It's the áspro vrykólakas," he breathes.

Terror rips through my body and I force myself to breathe and focus.

He takes our bows out and hands me mine. "If they come into view, shoot them. Remember your training. I will protect you, Ember," he says seriously.

I nod, sitting up straighter. I conjure up confidence and bravery before pushing it into both of us. I grab my bow and nock an arrow so that I'm prepared. I keep breathing, trying to calm down as much as possible. I hear another screech, closer this time, and my heart pumps harder. Alexei nocks his own arrow as we continue on as quietly as we can.

We round the bend and they're flying in the air. There are four, and the image I had in my head is nothing like what I'm seeing now. I know he said they were huge bat-looking creatures, but I didn't realize how large they would actually be. They are the size of a full-grown man and as white as snow. Their wings span twice the length of their bodies on either side, and they are completely naked, making it possible to tell that three of them used to be men and one was a woman. They are extremely thin and emaciated, and the woman's breasts are so shriveled they're almost nonexistent. They haven't seen us yet, and we try to sneak around them, but I have my bow raised and pointed at them to be safe.

When I think we're going to be able to pass without them noticing, one whips its head around and its soulless red eyes meet mine as the loudest blood-curdling shriek I've ever heard pierces my ears. I let my arrow fly, and it sinks into one of its wings, making it go even more crazy. It crashes to the ground before running at us at full speed. I nock another arrow, but I don't think I'll be quick enough to shoot it.

Luckily, Alexei is ready and lets his arrow go. I watch in morbid fascination as it strikes right between the monster's eyes. It drops dead before us, but before I can feel relieved, the others start coming at us. I aim and fire, missing by a hair, and curse as I grab another arrow. Alexei shoots again from behind me and gets another right in the chest. It falls in front of us and Ash unexpectedly dashes to the right to miss the creature.

I lurch sideways and crash to the ground, but I still have my bow and one arrow with me. I get to my feet as quickly as I can, and the remaining two don't seem to notice that I'm not on the horse anymore. I turn to see one coming after Alexei, but he doesn't have his arrow ready yet, and the thing is getting closer and closer. I act quickly, shooting my arrow straight at it from behind. It takes a swipe with its clawed hands at Alexei right before my arrow sinks into its back and it falls dead before him.

I hear Alexei shout my name in terror, and I turn to find the last one coming right for me. I curse the fact that I have no arrows left and no other weapons. I try to fall back on my hand-to-hand combat training, but the creature is too fast, and its movements too unpredictable. I hear Alexei coming up behind me, but when I hear his arrow release, the creature grabs my arm and sinks its teeth into my wrist.

Pain shoots up my arm and immobilizes me right as I watch the arrow imbed itself in its skull. The monster falls away from me, its fangs ripping free of my flesh, and I look down at my arm in horror. I'm already dizzy and nauseous and the wound is ghastly. Alexei and Ash ride up next to me, and he jumps off the horse as I turn around to face him. His brows are furrowed in concern and his gaze latches on to my arm.

"*Fuck.*" I don't think I've ever heard him curse like that, and I know how serious this is. I look at him only to see that he has four bloody slashes on his shirt and through the cuts in the material I see how deep the wounds are. But he doesn't seem fazed by them at all, looking much more concerned about me. "We need to get you to Nylaluna immediately. We don't have time to rest tonight." He pulls me up on the horse with him, and we take off at once, much faster than we've ever gone before. The poison is already working through my body, and I struggle to keep my eyes open. "Hang in there, Ember. I'll get you there. I'm so sorry I was too late."

I force my eyes open and make myself stay awake, knowing it's important. "It wasn't your fault, Alexei. You still saved me." I grip his arm in gratitude. I grunt as the rough ride jostles my arm, and I bite my lip to keep from crying out in pain. "There was nothing you could have done. I was too far away." My head rolls back on his shoulder and my eyes close again.

"Stay awake, little doe. Keep talking to me." He shakes me slightly to keep me conscious. A burning sensation is traveling up my arm and panic starts to set in.

"Alexei, what if this kills me?" I slur, terrified. I still don't have answers. But as I think about it a little bit more, I realize that if I did die, I would get to be with my mother, and that wouldn't be so bad. I relax marginally and take a deep breath.

"It won't, Ember. I won't let it. I swear to you." The conviction in his voice makes me believe him, and I relax a little more.

The next thing I know, I'm passed out, but I'm still semiconscious; I can feel the horse moving underneath me and hear Alexei's panicked pleas for me to wake up, and for Ash to move faster.

We continue on for what feels like forever before we finally slow. I force myself to open my eyes and look around to see that we're bathed in shadow, and there's some sort of guard close by. I hear Alexei murmur words I don't understand, and all of a sudden it's like a cold black sheet has been dropped over me. I am still able to see, but it's a bit harder, and I don't understand what's going on.

"Ember, if you can hear me, whatever you do, do not move or speak." I do as he says, but I'm starting to be pulled under once more. The horse begins to move forward again.

"Halt." We do. "What is your business?" I hear a strange man ask.

"I'm here on secret business related to the crown," Alexei states importantly, leaving no room for question.

"Where are your papers?" the man asks.

Alexei moves around behind me, and I hold my breath, realizing that he's sneaking me in somehow, and it is vital that I remain undetected. "Well, everything seems to be in order. Move along."

He takes off slowly, I would guess so as to not raise suspicion, and before I know it, I'm fully unconscious, blackness pulling me under its grasp so far I can't even attempt to drag myself back out.

When I finally come to, I'm in warm bubbling water. I'm not awake enough yet to actually open my eyes, but I'm slowly becoming more aware of my surroundings. I smell something mineral, and a hint of some sort of herb, like eucalyptus or rosemary maybe? I breathe in deeply, letting the scents calm me. There's a dull pain in my arm, as well as a warm, firm body holding on to me. I'm so confused as to where I am or what's going on. I don't remember what happened or why I was unconscious and now struggle to wake up.

My hearing comes back, and a man is talking gently to me and stroking my hair. "It's time to come back around now, beautiful. Let me see those pretty eyes." Alexei.

That's the first time he's ever called me beautiful, and if I were fully awake I would be swooning. I take another deep breath and will my eyes to open. It takes a few minutes, but I'm finally able to manage it.

His face is close to mine, and relief fills his gray eyes. "Thank the Gods. Don't scare me like that again, little doe."

"What happened?" I ask, confused. My head is fuzzy.

"We were attacked by the áspro vrykólakas. We were able to kill them all, but the last one bit you. I had to sneak you into the Healing Springs, and I didn't think you were going to make it."

At his words, everything starts coming back to me. "You saved my life, Alexei. Again. I don't know how I can repay you."

"Well, you also saved mine. I would've died if you hadn't shot that one in the back when you did. So we're even."

I had forgotten that he almost died, and my eyes dart to his chest. The slash marks from the beast's claws are still there, but they're healed over, only scars now. It's then that I realize we're both naked and I'm in his arms.

I try to jump up out of his hold, but his hands tighten around me. "You need to stay still for a while. Let the water heal you, and relax."

As hard as it is, I stop struggling, knowing that I shouldn't be moving around a lot right now. "Why are we naked?"

"You cannot take anything into the springs that is not natural. It destroys the magic in the water. I had to remove our clothes in order for us to enter the pool."

"And why are you holding me?"

"You were unconscious. If I hadn't been holding you, you would've drowned."

"I'm not unconscious now."

He's silent for a moment, as if he's trying to make up a good excuse for him to keep me in his embrace while we're both naked. "Truthfully,

I was terrified that I was going to lose you, and I'm not ready to let go of you quite yet."

I'm taken aback by his honesty, and I squeeze his arm comfortingly. "I was worried I was going to lose you too." I run my fingers down his chest where the claw marks are.

"I'm a lot harder to kill than that, baby," he tells me cockily, to which I roll my eyes. He chuckles before he bends down and rests his forehead against mine. We close our eyes and breathe each other in. "How are you feeling?"

"Better. My arm is barely hurting now, and the brain fog is almost gone." I look down at my arm to find that the wound is almost closed. "How come yours closed faster than mine did?"

"Because yours had poison in it. The claws aren't poisonous, only their fangs. The water had to draw all the venom out of your body before it could start healing the wound."

"How long have we been here?"

"Probably about an hour and a half. We should stay another half hour to make sure you're fully healed before we leave."

I finally look around at the cave we're in. Ash is waiting patiently outside and is peeking her head in as if to check that I'm okay. I can see moonlight shining in, illuminating everything. There's steam rising from the springs and gorgeous stalactites and stalagmites everywhere. They also have some sort of natural light to them, like they glow from the inside. I also smell those herbs again, and that earthy mineral scent. I look around for where it's coming from, but don't see anything. It's hard to tell how deep the caves go, but the water and the glow from the rocks seems to follow them.

"What am I smelling?"

"The springs themselves have tons of minerals in them, which aid the healing process, and also produce eucalyptus and rosemary, which diffuse in the water."

I give myself a mental high five that I was right.

"Do these caves continue on? It looks like it, but I can't tell how far they go."

"It's rumored that these caves go all the way through the mountains, but it's easy for one to get lost. No one has traveled through them in a very long time, so no one wanders them anymore past these few rooms that house the healing waters."

The archaeologist in me is dying to explore, even though it's not a good idea.

We stay as we are for another twenty minutes or so, and when I'm finally completely back to normal, we get out and get dressed. I struggle to keep my eyes off his body, and I notice that he is having a similar problem. We get on Ash after she gives me a nuzzle to say she was worried about me, and as we're about to get going, a guard starts coming toward us.

"*Shit.* That's the guard who let us in. If he sees you we're in trouble."

I look around, finding no other way to go, and he's coming right for us.

"We need to take the cave route," I tell him. "It's our only choice, and if we go that way, no one will know that I was here."

He looks reluctant, but nods, and we head back into the caves.

Chapter 13

The water from the springs flows in a small stream, occasionally forming little pools, and the farther in we go, the less I can smell the herbs. Luckily the lights continue along the way, and I hope the water and the light stay with us for the journey, otherwise we'll be screwed, and it will completely be my fault. I marvel at the incredible sights surrounding us, and my eyes take their fill. We decide not to continue on too far since we already had quite the evening, but we want to make sure that we're far enough that no one will discover us.

We find a space to stop where we have a decent amount of room. Alexei grows a little patch of grass for Ash to eat, and softens the ground for us to lie on like always, and he's able to build us a small fire since he can conjure up some wood and brush with his magic, which I'm grateful for because now that we aren't in the warm water, the caves are fairly chilly. I cuddle up next to him, and he doesn't stop me, even going so far as to put an arm around me and pull me closer. Our brush with death tonight rattled us both. We're asleep within minutes, both of us completely exhausted.

When we wake, we have no concept of what time it is, since there is no sunlight, and it makes me a little unsettled. We follow the tunnels and I'm grateful there haven't been any forks yet, and I'm sincerely hoping we don't end up lost in these caves because of some rash decision that I made. We continue on with our normal routine, although with the limited space we aren't able to do any training with the bow and arrow. Instead we do more hand to hand, which I'm starting to improve in quite a bit. The moves and motions are becoming more natural, and I don't have to think as hard to produce countermoves to his attacks. I'm even able to land a strike against him, and I have to refrain from doing a happy dance.

He also introduces me to blade training, starting with daggers, first teaching me how to defend, and then how to attack. He shows me where they do the most damage depending on where the opponent is in relation to me. He also shows me the best places to strike when someone is wearing armor, obviously anywhere there would be gaps, like the armpit, the neck, and the low back. I like these, but not as much as the bow and arrow. But of course, different weapons are good for different things. At least that's what Alexei keeps telling me.

When we get back on Ash, he starts teaching me how to build up my mental defenses. Luckily, the caves are big enough that we can still ride on Ash.

"Start by picturing your mind. Now picture yourself building a fortress around it. Build it up around your mind brick by brick until everything is covered. When you have that, imagine adding a layer of concrete around the entire fortress."

I do as he instructs, taking my time to make sure that everything is covered. When I accomplish that, I tell him so.

"Good. Now, unfortunately, I don't have any type of powers that can penetrate the mind to test how it holds up, but for now, we can have you try to keep that barrier up as you try to get into mine and change my emotions."

I nod, although it sounds difficult. I reach toward him with my powers and find his strongest shields up, as I expected. Now that I know how to get into them, hopefully I'll have an easier time. Before I go further, I check mine to make sure they're still solid, and they are. I use the same technique I did previously, and I am able to get through his barriers more quickly this time. I don't know if it's because he's starting to trust me more, or because I'm getting the hang of it. Hopefully both.

Once I get past his, I check mine again. In all my focus on getting into his head, I lost my layer of concrete. I still have the bricks in place though, so it doesn't take me long to refortify them. That done, I identify his emotions. Excitement and adventure plow into me, and I smile to myself.

I realize suddenly that I already have experience in mental shielding. I learned long ago that if I didn't want to take on someone's emotions as if they're my own, that I needed to form a barrier between us, and this is very similar. Once I get this technique down, I will hopefully be able to sense others' emotions only when I want to, and the thought fills me with relief. I pump Alexei full of accomplishment and pride in himself. I want him to feel these because he *should* be. He's a fantastic teacher, and I'm incredibly lucky he's helping me.

We finally come to our first fork, and we stop here for the day. We can make up our minds about which direction to go after we've rested. He grows more grass for Ash, and she drinks from the stream that's still going through the caves. We eat our meager meal, and I'm asleep as soon as my head hits the pillow.

When we wake, we both have the urge to go right. Not only do we both have a pull to go in that direction, but that's also the way the stream runs. The farther in we get, the more claustrophobia closes in on me, hitching my breath, and I try not to think about the fact that there is literally an entire mountain on top of us right now. By the time we stop for the day, we finally come across something extremely interesting that calls to my archaeologist nature.

"Oh my God...there's fucking *parietal art*!" I say, completely stunned and amazed.

"What is that?"

"Cave art! It means that someone used to live in these caves." I go up to the cave wall reverently and closely examine them. "From what I can tell, they're at least a thousand years old."

I see what looks like all the different species together, and I can't tell if that means that they all lived in these caves with each other, or if the individuals who drew these were trying to tell the history of Queridian. There are some paintings that depict a huge structure, and I'm curious where this is located. It's not clear in the drawings, but it looks magnificent, and I hope I'm able to find out more.

The place we stop for the night has a fairly deep pool, and I'm grateful because it's been a minute since we came across one, and the mustiness of the cave is making me dirty. I grab the soap out of our bag and head over to the pool. I start stripping, and immediately hear Alexei drop something in surprise.

"What are you doing?"

"What does it look like? I'm getting clean. These caves make me feel disgusting."

"You should give me a warning next time," he grumbles, turning away from me.

"Well, you've already seen it all anyway."

He mutters something under his breath that I don't catch, and I chuckle as I make my way into the water. The stream isn't nearly as warm as the Healing Springs were, but it's not freezing either. I would equate it to being in a bath that has cooled quite a bit. Either way, it's amazing to get the dirt and grime off of myself from traveling, and I linger in the water even after I'm clean.

"Are you almost done?" Alexei asks in a frustrated tone.

"I'm already clean. I just enjoy being in the water."

"Well, can you get out then?" Pissy Alexei is back, and I have no idea what brought him on. He hasn't been in a mood like this since our first few days together, and now that I know him better, it's kind of cracking me up.

"No, I don't think I will yet," I goad him a bit and he snarls softly in response.

I run the water over my body, making sure he can hear me, and let that little visual sink in, moaning softly. I hear him make a pained sound and smile at the fact that I'm able to affect him so much. I might be a bitch for doing this, but for some reason, I have the urge to torture him. I think I'm a little frustrated with him that he refuses to do anything about the fact that we both want each other. I know he took an oath and *blah blah blah*, but I think there could really be something between the two of us. Surely it would be worth it to at least try? Or maybe I'm being unreasonable, but if he can't let anything happen between us, then he should stop giving me so many mixed signals.

When I'm done in the water, I get out, not bothering to cover my body. Like I told Alexei, he's already seen it all anyway. His eyes flick to me every few seconds, like he's trying to avoid looking at me but can't help himself, and I smirk. Once I have my clothes back on, I plop down and start braiding my hair. That seems to be my go-to hairstyle in Queridian, seeing as I don't have any hair products or tools to style it. Plus, being on the road so much, it's easier to have it out of my face. Despite not knowing what time it is, I'm exhausted. I ease onto my back and relish the soft earth underneath me. Apparently Alexei made our bed extra cozy tonight, and I can't say I'm complaining.

"What are you doing?" he asks.

"Whatever do you mean?" I reply innocently, batting my eyelashes at him.

He narrows his eyes at me as if he can see right through my virtuous act. "Never mind," he huffs as he lies down next to me and turns away.

I smile to myself, knowing that I'm getting under his skin. I don't know why I'm enjoying it so much; it's very unlike me. For a minute I think about how much I've changed since my mother died and realize that I am no longer the quiet, shy girl I used to be. I'm more fierce, and people's opinions matter to me much less than they used to, especially seeing as I never had any friends anyway. Maybe a part of me always knew that I didn't belong on Earth, and now that I'm in Queridian, I'm able to come into myself. Also, there's something about *him* that brings out this abrasive side of me.

His bad mood continues into the next day, and it makes me want to be even more obnoxious. I subtly shift my hips while we ride, and every time I hear him exhale heavily and he hardens behind me.

After the fifth time I do this, he finally asks, "What's wrong? Why are you shifting around so much today?"

"My body is tired from riding, that's all."

We do more training at lunch, and he's harder on me than he normally is, and while it's frustrating, I know it's making me better, so I take what he gives me. My magical training is also getting easier the more I do it. I'm getting used to keeping my own shields up while working to get into his. His frustration and lust all come together in a dangerous combo. They are both so strong that it isn't until we're about to stop for the day that I notice an undercurrent of something that I've been missing from him, and suddenly his bad mood makes so much more sense to me.

"You're thirsty," I state, not needing his confirmation, but wanting to ask why he hasn't mentioned it. I feel a pinch guilty that I've been goading him so much while he's clearly been suffering.

"A little bit." But I know he's lying because I can tell that it's getting worse.

"Is that why you've been in such a bad mood the last few days? You're hangry?"

His brows furrow in confusion. "What's hangry?"

I laugh loudly, still unused to him not knowing certain phrases.

"It's when you're so hungry that you're angry."

"I'm not hangry," he says like a typical man, and I guffaw. Why can men never admit or realize when they're hangry?

"Do you need to feed? I thought you wouldn't have to for at least another few days."

"Well, I was injured in the áspro vrykólakas attack and lost some blood. That sped the process up a bit."

"Why didn't you tell me you needed to feed?"

"Because I didn't want you to feel obligated to offer yourself up. I know you are uncomfortable with it after the vampire incident when you first got here. You did say you never wanted to be bitten by another vampire again after that."

It's sweet that he's sparing my feelings, but now that I have a bit more knowledge on the subject of vampires, l have a different opinion than I did before.

"Alexei, this is important. I know you won't turn for quite a while when you go hungry, but there's only us here. What if we're in these caves for longer than we hope to be? What would I do if something happened to you? What if you get injured again and the problem gets worse? Besides, you're in pain, and I don't like that. Will you let me help you?"

I hear him take a deep breath, and for a moment I think he might be smelling my neck, and I try not to shiver in response.

"Are you sure, little doe?" His voice is so rough it's like gravel.

I turn my head so I can meet his eyes, and they are so dilated they look almost black. His pet name for me feels all too real at the moment, like I'm his prey. Instead of responding verbally and possibly embarrassing myself, I simply nod and extend my neck for him. He skims his nose up my throat and now I definitely know he's sniffing me. He growls, and it reverberates through my back. His fangs extend and he drags them down my throat. Just as I think he's going to bite me, he pulls back.

"Not yet, Ember. We should stop first. The horse could jar my movements and I don't want to hurt you. Plus, if you get light-headed at all you can lie down."

I'm surprised that he's able to think so rationally while he was so close to doing it. We stop for the night, and when we're lying in "bed," my nerves start to get the better of me. I know he needs this and that he will make it as pleasant as possible, but I can't stop thinking about the only other time vampires bit me. My heart rate picks up, and I struggle to keep still. Alexei, of course, notices. Immediately.

"We don't have to do this, Ember."

"Yes, we do." I grab him and pull him close to me, moving my head to the side to give him room as I remind myself that this is my choice.

I want to help him, and even though I'm nervous, a small part of me is actually excited too. He keeps his weight off of me as he leans his head in. I take a deep breath, and when I exhale, his teeth pierce my skin. There's a sharp pinch, but then the pain is gone. It's nothing like my other experience, and I moan out loud as a heat builds in my body and between my legs. I wrap my fingers in his hair and pull him closer to me, and before I know it, his body is on top of mine. His mouth is hot against my neck, and I can feel the pull of my blood leaving my body. He groans low in his throat, and his hard length presses up against my hip. I wind my legs around him so he's right where I need him, and I start grinding myself against him before I realize what I'm doing.

With a grunt of effort, he pulls his fangs out of my neck. I stop moving, mortified by the fact that I was basically dry-humping him. Blood fills my face in a blush even though I was a human blood bag moments ago. We're both breathing heavily and we stay exactly where we are. In the next moment, his tongue glides up the bite to seal it, and it reignites a bit of the heat I felt. Nothing near as intense as the bite itself, but still noticeable. He pulls his head back and looks down at me. There's barely any space separating our faces, and his breath intermingles with mine. He's still hard between my thighs, and I struggle to focus on anything else besides how good he feels there.

"What *are* you?" His question takes me off guard, and a sliver of alarm sinks into my body.

"What do you mean?" I ask, breathless.

"You don't taste like a normal human. You taste like nothing I've ever had before. It's *addicting.*" He eyes my throat like he wants to bite me again, but then shakes his head as if to clear it. "What are you doing to me?" he asks, resting his forehead against mine.

I don't answer, simply breathing him in. I don't have an answer for him, because *he's* the one scrambling *my* brain. After a few minutes he moves off of me and lies down beside me.

"Are you feeling better?" I ask.

"Yes. Thank you so much, Ember. I know you felt like you had to do that, but you didn't. You helped me so that I wouldn't be in pain anymore, and I don't think you realize how much that means to me. I appreciate you more than you know." He looks over at me and runs his thumb down my cheek.

Tears burn behind my eyes, and I will them not to fall. I don't know why I have formed such a strong connection to this man in such a short amount of time, but he's become very important to me. Probably because he's saved my life twice. At least that is probably part of it, but there is a bond with him that I'm unable to explain. Luckily, it seems he senses it too. Unluckily, we can't do anything about it, and I curse his stupid oath for about the millionth time. We fall asleep like that, looking at each other with his hand on my cheek.

The next day is the same routine, but halfway through the day, we come to another fork. We take the one that feels natural to us, and soon after Alexei realizes something.

"We're in Mystic Mountain," he says suddenly.

"The fae territory?" He nods. "How do you know?"

"I just know," he states simply.

I doubt it's that straightforward, but at least we know we're heading in the right direction. And when we get out of this passage we won't have to hide, since Alexei is supposed to be taking me to the king.

By the time we start on my magic training, Alexei discovers something that will work to our advantage. Now that he's had my blood, he can attempt to get past my mental shields since he will have my abilities. He's already had some practice with it since he sometimes drinks blood with a similar ability.

I leave them down at first so he can get used to using them again, but he breaks it down pretty quickly and is able to identify my emotions within moments. I do as I've been practicing and build my barriers up before reinforcing them. I can sense him trying to get in, and he's not subtle about it. In fact it gives me a bit of a headache. It's like a battering ram, pounding on the walls surrounding my head, and I wonder if he had to endure days of this when I was trying to learn how to get past his own mental shields.

I sneak into his own mind and sense his frustration that he can't get in. I smile to myself before pushing amusement onto him.

He chuckles and shakes his head behind me. "You're getting really good at that, little doe. I don't even notice when you get past them anymore. The only way I know is that you push it onto me strongly, so I feel an immediate change in my emotions. You might want to start practicing going at it more subtly now. But remember to keep your own up since I'm still trying to get in."

After practicing for a while longer, he tries to switch up tactics, like I did. Finally, he caresses my shields like I do with his, even though I've never told him how I get through. I know what he's trying to do and I don't fall for it. I keep them firmly in place and reinforced. I like this method much better. The original felt like he was hammering against my brain, whereas this one is more like his mind is rubbing up against mine, almost like a cat rubbing against your leg.

With him still distracted, I slip past his barriers again and detect his determination. I try to think of how I can make a change happen more subtly. Since I was able to accomplish it with Shindar, I know it's possible, but it will be more difficult with Alexei since he has shields up and is aware of my ability. A simple switch that he probably wouldn't notice would be from determination to hope. I picture hope in my mind, and I watch as it becomes a mist in front of me of the palest blue. I slowly drift it toward Alexei and it starts seeping into him a little at a time. A small smile graces his lips before he looks down, meeting my eyes.

"I'm going to get through them eventually, little doe."

I smirk because I know it worked and he doesn't even realize it. I do it a few more times while still managing to keep him out, and he still doesn't notice. When we stop for the night, he mentions it to me.

"Well, I didn't manage to get into yours, but you weren't able to change mine either," he states, a bit smugly I might add.

"Is that so?" I raise my brows, and he narrows his eyes in response.

"I didn't notice you changing anything."

"Oh, Alexei, you're adorable." I pat his cheek in a patronizing way, making him snarl half-heartedly at me.

"Were you really changing them?"

"Yes, darling. I was being so subtle about it and changing them to something similar every time that you didn't notice I was even doing anything."

He stares at me for a moment before laughing loudly.

"Well, I must say, I'm impressed," he says, giving me a big smile. I give him one right back as I soak in the praise.

Just as we're about to bed down for the night, I notice that the caves up ahead seem quite a bit brighter, and when I strain my ears, I can hear something. I turn my ear toward it and lean in a little bit, and after listening for a few seconds, I realize it's the sound of water.

"Alexei, do you hear that?" He furrows his brow before nodding.

We leave Ash where she is and head around the corner where the next section of caves starts. As soon as we turn, I gasp. It's the structure from the parietal art! The cave opens up into a huge cavern, larger than any I've seen before.

The castle-like structure is back and underlit by the bright glowing natural lights that appear to be amplified from the other caves, giving the form a bluish hue. There's a small waterfall on one side of the formation that leads down to an enormous pool. When I go to the edge and look down, it's all lit up underneath and seems to go on and on. The thought of what might be lurking in the depths of the water sets my heart pounding.

"This is amazing. I wonder who used to live down here."

"Want to go explore inside?" Alexei asks, and I nod excitedly. This is an archaeologist's dream. I literally stumbled across a lost civilization.

"Did you know this was down here?"

"There are myths about a group living down here thousands of years ago, but since no one travels the caves, it was thought to be only a rumor."

We approach the front doors, and I'm bursting with excitement. Since the lost city has been down here a long time, it's not in the best condition, but much better than I would've thought. I wonder if some sort of magic was used to preserve it. Although, I'm unsure if that type of magic exists, since none of the species I've been told about has that ability.

"Do you think they used something to preserve this place? It does not look to be thousands of years old."

"I'm sure they used a preservation spell."

"Who can do spells?"

"Anyone can. It's called 'base magic.' Everyone living in Queridian has the ability to do it, the problem is, you have to know the spells, and unfortunately, most don't possess that knowledge."

"Why not?"

"There's a giant library in the Immortal City that contains all the spells you could think of. But only the royals have access to the Epitome Athenaeum, and they hoard the information. That's partly why they've ruled for so long. Some of the spells are fairly common knowledge, at least among the fae, but most of the other races don't know any of them. Well, I guess with the exception of the witches. Sometimes they're able to *see* how to do certain spells."

"Is that how you were able to sneak me into the Healing Springs? You put a spell on me?" I vaguely remember him speaking and then something falling over me, and clearly the guard hadn't been able to see me.

"Yes. I know only a few, and those were mainly taught to me in case of emergency situations like we encountered."

We enter the structure, and I'm too distracted by it to continue our conversation. This was legit a royal palace at some point, and I'm blown away by it. There are beautiful delicate details everywhere I look. A chandelier overhead that looks like it's been made from the stalactites and other gorgeous rock formations. Crown molding that's been carved all along the tops and ceiling. A huge winding staircase made of glass in the far corner.

We slowly walk around, taking everything in. There aren't many items in the structure itself. Most of the belongings were probably taken when whomever inhabited it left, but there are still random things that were left behind.

We come across an enormous room, and it contains the most massive chandelier out of any that we've seen so far. There's an extensive banquet table on one side, and an elevated stage off to the other, where six thrones sit. That seems excessive to me, but who am I to judge?

"I think this was the royal ballroom," Alexei says, and I nod in agreement.

"Can you imagine the balls that were held here?"

"I bet they were pretty spectacular. I can practically feel others dancing around us."

That brings a wonderful idea to my head. "Stay here," I tell him.

"Where are you going?"

"To go get something. Don't move. I'll be right back." I sprint off, not able to believe I haven't thought of this before. I head to where Ash is and see that she's passed out for the night. I rummage around in my purse as quietly as I can, so as not to disturb her. I grab what I need before turning and running back to the ballroom.

Alexei is right where I left him and I smile softly at him. I head over to the stage and turn everything on before setting my Bluetooth speaker down on the platform. Alexei's brows rise as Nat King Cole's "Unforgettable" starts playing. Since I have music downloaded on my phone, I don't need any kind of service for this. I slowly walk toward him, vulnerability coloring my cheeks. I want to dance with him, and it sounded like such a good idea in my head, but now I'm worried he'll think this is stupid. I woman up and ask him.

"Want to dance with me?" I look down shyly and resist the urge to open up my senses to him to spy on his feelings.

He meets me in the middle, and when I still don't look at him, he gently grasps my chin and tilts my head up so our eyes lock. His are warm and inviting, and filled with something that both terrifies and thrills me. "I would be honored to dance with you." He pulls me in close, and we hold on to each other as he whisks me around the room.

I'm shocked to learn that he can *dance*, like really dance. I smile brightly, and I realize I haven't been this happy since my mom passed.

He beams back at me, and when the song ends, Billie Holiday's "I'll Be Seeing You" comes on next. He swirls me around the dance floor, and I can see what he means. It's almost like there are ghosts joining us, but I don't take my eyes off his to look.

We continue on as my classic playlist plays one romantic love song after another. When it finally ends, he drops his forehead to mine, squeezing me tightly before releasing me. I gather my phone and speaker, turning them both off before we continue exploring. There's a permanent smile glued onto my face, and when I reach for Alexei's hand, he doesn't pull away, warming my heart even further.

When we're about to leave the ballroom, I have the urge to turn around, the sensation that I'm missing something important hitting me. It's then, when I'm at a distance from it, I see symbols all over the floor.

"Alexei, what are all of these markings?" I pull him back and point.

There are six symbols forming a circle in the middle of the dance floor. I recognize the one for vampires from when Alexei showed me the last time, the fangs with the drop of blood. There's also a large wave with a fin of some sort coming out of the water. The next are the four elements, fire, water, air, earth. Then, a circle with a small medic-looking cross in the middle. The fifth is a giant eye. And finally, the last is a great bird soaring through the sky. All of the symbols are incredibly detailed, and I know they all hold meaning. I have an inkling as to what they are, but I want Alexei to confirm it before I voice my theory.

"They're the symbols of all of the species. The only one that's missing is the humans."

"Which ones are which?"

"Well, you already know the fangs are vampires. The wave with the fin belongs to the mermaids. The elements, fae. The cross, elves. The eye, witches. And the bird, mimics."

"This means something, Alexei. I have a theory. This place was occupied thousands of years ago. Clearly the humans weren't here yet. I think that all of the races used to coexist here. Why else would they have all the symbols in this palace in the same spot? It represents them all." It's then that I remember the water outside of the structure. I drag him along with me until we're standing at the edge of the pool. "I bet this is where the mermaids lived." Now that I look more closely I can see things in the water that maybe they used to use, or areas they could have occupied. It looks like there are little separate pools within the water that could give each one their own sense of privacy. Shells line all along the walls and along the private areas. The rest of it continues down farther underground into the rest of the caves, and another theory comes to mind. "Alexei, what if this connects to their land? What if this was some sort of central place for everyone? They could travel here by land, clearly, or by sea."

I cup my hands and bring some water up to my lips. Sure enough, it's salt water, unlike the rest of the caves. I gesture for Alexei to try it, and he brings his lips to my hand. I try not to squirm as he locks eyes with me and licks my hand. I can see the surprise on his features at the taste of salt.

"You could be right, little doe."

"Don't sound so surprised."

"Apparently you're more than just a pretty face," he tells me with a teasing glint in his eyes.

I smack his arm, smiling despite myself. We head back in and do some more exploring. This time we go up the stairs, and excitement beats in my chest in anticipation of what else we might find. Whoever occupied this palace had to have put some sort of preservation spell on it, because not only does the structure look perfectly intact, but everything we find is as well. The only way I can tell everything has been preserved this long is because all of the items are covered in a fine layer of dust, and there's a musty smell to the air.

We stumble across some bedrooms, the beds still occupying the space, and with each room I hunt for anything that could tell us more about the occupants. There's not much, and it looks like they took most of their belongings with them, but I do find some old pieces of ancient-looking clothing. The ones left behind are of the extravagant variety, and I guess that they probably weren't able to take impractical objects with them. I have the urge to try them on, but the thought makes shame rise in my chest. These were people's personal belongings, and while I can admire them, trying them on would be crossing a boundary.

In the last room we enter, I find a journal in one of the nightstands. My breath catches in my throat, and I hold it reverently. I gently open it, worried about damaging its precious pages, but it's just as well preserved as everything else. The handwriting inside is elegant, but unsurprisingly, it's in a language I've never seen before.

"Alexei, what language is this?" I hold out the journal to show him.

He studies it for a few moments. "I'm not sure. A lot of the ancient languages died out right around when the humans showed up. Some of them still exist, but most have been forgotten."

Disappointment flickers through me. I was hoping that we would be able to read it and figure out exactly what this place was and who lived here. I almost put the journal back in the nightstand, but something stops me. I can't help but feel that there is something important in it. I open it again and study the writing as an idea strikes me. I wonder if I could decipher this. It would take me a hell of a long time, but I bet I could do it. Part of my schooling was in languages and how to discern patterns in them. I tuck the journal under my arm, my mind made up. At least it will kill some time on the road if nothing else.

We keep wandering and discover a kitchen. It's cozy and exactly what a kitchen ought to be. There's a great big fireplace with a decent size table next to it. It's nothing elaborate, but I know that's because it was used by servants. There would be no royalty in this part of the palace, but maybe that's what makes it so inviting. None of the pomp that seems to come with the rest of the structure is present. We check everything, and discover some dry foods that were left behind, rice, pasta noodles, things like that. I would be tempted to take them with us, but even with the preservation spell, I don't think it would be safe.

We see pictures in the hallways, including a giant map of what Queridian used to look like at the time when this structure was thriving. I don't see any area that could belong to the humans, to which I am not surprised since we already figured that this was before they arrived in this realm. I bring out my phone and take a quick picture of the map. My archaeology brain is itching for evidence I might need to reference later.

There's also a large room that has paintings of who I assume are the royalty who resided here. Strangely enough, each painting looks to have a different species as the ruler, and I can't tell if they all ruled together, or at different times. If they led together that would make a lot of sense, each ruler in charge of their own race. Especially since there were six thrones in the ballroom.

When we've made our way through most of the castle, Alexei takes my hand and pulls me toward the entrance.

"Let's go to bed." At his words my heart rate speeds up and a blush rises to my cheeks. He gives me a knowing look, and I'm sure he can hear my heart. "To sleep," he corrects me.

I nod and we head back to Ash. We talked about sleeping in the castle, but with all the dust and mustiness, I don't think it would be very healthy. I would rather sleep on the ground with Ash close by. Plus, I'm a little unnerved by this place, almost as if those who used to live here are still present in some way.

"Do you think we're almost out of the caves?" I ask. Of course he doesn't know, but I'm sick of being trapped underground, even though this whole thing was my fucking idea.

"I think so. Hopefully in the next day or two. And then I promise to find us a nice little inn where you can take a hot bath and have a fresh meal."

"Stop talking dirty to me." His face scrunches up in confusion, making me cackle.

He makes our bed for the night, and I drift off thinking about what it will be like to feel the sun on my face again.

Chapter 14

Alexei was right. It takes us another day to get out of the caves, and when we emerge into the fresh air and sunlight, I almost weep, although it does take me a few minutes to adjust to the brightness. Ash neighs excitedly too and starts galloping away.

"Someone's happy to be able to run around in the open space," Alexei remarks from behind me, a wide grin pulling at his lips.

I tilt my face up to the sky and delight at the heat of the sun caressing my skin. I don't know if I've ever felt anything this good before. Then I remember what it was like to have Alexei in between my legs and sucking the blood from my neck. The thought brings a rush of blood to my face and in between my thighs.

"I would give anything to know what you're thinking right now."

Ugh. Of course the vampire has to notice every single thing.

"I'm not thinking about anything," I insist, putting on my best poker face.

"Whatever you say, little doe." He smirks knowingly, and I have the urge to smack that smile off his face.

Not surprisingly, our internal circadian rhythm is disjointed because of the lack of sunlight from the caves. We keep pushing longer than we normally would to take full advantage of the sun. Since we now have ample space again, we can go back to training with the bow and arrow, and I have to say, I am really looking forward to it.

Also, since I'm getting more comfortable with my magical abilities, we're putting more emphasis on my combat training. In the remaining hours of the day, I spend a lot of time on the horse poring over the journal. I haven't been able to decipher anything yet, but I am starting to recognize words when they're repeated. I know I won't be able to actually start decoding it until I'm able to sit down and document my findings.

When I go to pick up the bow, it takes me a moment to get used to the weight and feel of it again. I would like to learn how to shoot while riding Ash so that I can also be accurate while we're moving, but since we are riding onward, it doesn't make sense. We can't waste the arrows, and we would have to retrieve them every time I made a shot. But it is on my list of things to practice when we're no longer traveling.

We divide our day into multiple training sessions, going between hand to hand, daggers, and bow and arrow. Needless to say, when we finally find an inn, I am so unbelievably grateful that we can sleep in a legitimate bed tonight. I am exhausted and starving. Big surprise.

Alexei tells the stable boy that Ash is to be given every luxury they have available, and I pet her neck lovingly before we head inside. We sleep in the same room again since that's what we've been doing for weeks now. This time I offer Alexei the bath first since I bathed in the caves a couple days ago. I do have an ulterior motive though, and that is that I am so hungry I do not want to be in the bath when the food arrives.

I'm pleased with my decision when Alexei gets into the bath right when there's a knock at the door. I quickly retrieve the food and thank the innkeeper. There's a bottle of red wine that I make short work of opening. I pour us each a glass and take a grateful sip. When I take the top off of the tray, steam wafts up to my face, bringing scents of butter and garlic to my nose, and I inhale greedily. Those are probably my favorite scents in the world. They have two big, juicy steaks on the tray, along with roasted potatoes, asparagus, and rolls with butter. I'm salivating and I dig in without any preamble.

"Save some for me, yeah?" Alexei asks from the bathing area, making me laugh.

"Only if you get out in time to claim it. Otherwise I'm finishing everything."

I would never do that, of course, but as I hear Alexei wash more quickly I laugh, realizing he thinks I'm being totally serious. The drain is pulled a minute later, and Alexei comes out in fresh clothing, having remembered to bring some with him this time. We're on our last set of clean clothes, and I'm pretty sure that means we're almost to our destination.

I finish up my food right as he sits down opposite me. I fill my glass again and take it with me to the bath. Luckily there's still plenty of hot water, and when I sink down into it, I promise myself that I will never take baths for granted again. It's absolutely heavenly. I enjoy lounging for a while, and I close my eyes and relax, letting the water soothe my sore muscles. I can hear Alexei in the other room, but I am so calm I barely notice him. Suddenly, I hear him talking to me, jolting me out of my serene state.

"Ember? You haven't drowned in there, have you? It's been almost an hour."

"Oh shit. Seriously?"

He chuckles. "Yes."

"Let me wash, and I'll be right out."

"You haven't washed yet?" Amusement trickles toward me from him.

"No I haven't, Mister I-Took-a-Bath-in-Five-Minutes. I was relaxing. Not that you would know how to do that."

"Well, I didn't have time to do that with you threatening to eat all my food."

"Sorry, I didn't hear that. I was underwater," I lie, and he huffs in frustration, making me laugh.

I quickly wash, basking in the smell of the shampoo that reminds me so much of Alexei. When I'm finished, I dress in my fresh set of clothes, rejoicing in being clean. I tip back the rest of my wine and come out to find Alexei lying on the bed. I join him as I start braiding my hair back in my usual style.

"I think we'll arrive in the Immortal City tomorrow," he tells me.

"We will?" I ask, stunned.

I figured we had at least a few more days of travel, but I suppose cutting through the mountains shortened the time that we had to travel through fae territory. Although I guess we technically *were* in fae territory during part of our cave trip, just not in an area where anyone else wandered.

"Yes. I'm estimating that we'll be there by dinner tomorrow."

Nerves and excitement fight for dominance within me. I'm definitely looking forward to not being on the road anymore and seeing a new major city of Queridian. I'm also excited about potentially learning more about myself and my ancestry, but I'm anxious about meeting the king. I have no idea how the interaction will go, or if he'll make me turn right back around and march my ass straight back to Earth. I hope not. I don't want to spend another few weeks on the road only to go back to where I came from.

Besides that, I'm starting to find a place for myself that I've never had before. Queridian feels more like home than Earth ever did. I'm also worried about how things will be with Alexei when it's not only the two of us anymore. I bet he could teletravel all the way back to his little home on the mountain and be done with me forever. I don't think that's what he wants, but I'm not going to count on him sticking around, especially since that decision will most likely be out of our hands.

"What are you going to do when we get there?" I ask quietly.

"Well, since I have a replacement guarding the portal, I would like to stay for a while if the king lets me. I have some things to catch up on with my father."

"Oh, right. I forgot your father was there." I'm stupid for thinking that he wanted to stick around for me.

"Plus, if he lets you stay, I would like to continue your training." My heart skips a beat, which I'm sure he hears, but he doesn't let on. I smile at him.

"I would like that."

We lie down, and he's asleep within minutes. It takes me longer, and I stare at him for an undetermined amount of time. My last thought before I drift off is how I hope this isn't the last night that I get to sleep next to him.

The next day seems to drag and go by at the blink of an eye at the same time. It's a strange sensation, and one that I don't enjoy. We stick to our normal routine, but we're both distracted, causing Alexei to cut our lessons short. We make our way up the mountain, and he informs me that the Immortal City is at the very top of the highest peak in Queridian. The fae have the high ground, and therefore the advantage for any battle that might come their way from other territories.

The mountain itself, Mystic Mountain, is lush, green, and altogether awe-inspiring. It is the most beautiful land I've ever laid eyes on, and I can understand why the fae have claimed it. Everywhere I look there's either trees, water, or incredible views down the mountain. I look up to where we're going, but the top of the peak is cloaked in the clouds.

By the time we're nearly at the summit, I'm practically bouncing in my seat from nerves and excitement. Alexei chuckles behind me, resting a hand on my stomach and pulling me close. The gesture settles me a bit, and I relax against him.

"Don't worry, little doe. The king isn't so scary. I actually think you'll like him."

I smile at his attempt to calm me. "Do you know him well?"

"I've known King Stavros my whole life. He's always been very kind to me. From what I've heard, he's much more amiable than those who ruled before him."

"Were the previous kings unfair rulers?"

He nods. "That's what I've been told. And they were always adamant about keeping the races segregated. King Stavros doesn't give an opinion one way or the other. I'm sure there's more he could be doing to try to bring the kingdom together, but he doesn't make laws to separate us like his predecessors did."

"What do you think he could be doing better?" I ask, genuinely curious.

He looks around nervously, like he's worried someone might be listening in on our conversation. "It doesn't matter what I think."

"It does to me."

"Well, for one, he could open up the territories so that everyone in the kingdom could go where they wanted and not be confined to one area. That would greatly improve communications between the territories and the races. He could also hear from the other species. He never gives others a forum to talk about how Queridian is being run, or about problems or ideas that they have for their own territories. He's fairly confined to this immediate area, and as a result, he doesn't realize how things are in the other parts of our world."

What he's saying makes a lot of sense, and it seems while King

Stavros is a kind ruler, he might be a little ignorant and all too happy to stick to his palace.

"Is he married?"

"He was. His wife died a few years ago."

"Kids?"

"No. They were never able to conceive."

"So, since he has no heirs, what will happen when he passes?"

"The crown would then pass to the next highest position of power, which would be my father."

I whip my head around so quickly to look at him that I think I give myself whiplash.

"So, you could potentially be king eventually?"

"I never thought about that, but now that you mention it, I guess so. But fae live for hundreds of years, so I wouldn't need to think about that for a very long time."

"Well, in theory, but you're not accounting for accidents or assassinations. Someone with that much power will always have enemies, and therefore will constantly have a target on their backs."

He nods, considering my words, but before he can reply, we pass through the clouds that conceal the palace, and my breath rushes out of me in a *whoosh*. Before us is a massive skinny bridge that is clearly used mainly for security purposes, and on the other end is the most grand structure I've ever laid eyes on. It's part stone, part metal, and part glass, all woven together to form something extraordinary. It's a strange juxtaposition between ancient and modern, as it has turrets and towers like a normal castle would, but the metal and glass work is what makes it look so modern. It forms domes in certain areas, and others it juts up, curving upward as if it can pierce the sky. There's a waterfall on the left side that pours into a river that runs in front of the castle and under the bridge we are currently making our way across.

"Welcome, my lady, to the Immortal City," he says dramatically, but I don't even have it in me to scoff at him, because this place is the definition of *dramatic*. "Make sure your mental shields are up and strong, Ember," he tells me seriously, and I'm grateful for the reminder.

When we finally reach the main gates, a few guards stop us.

"State your business," one says sternly, looking at me suspiciously before their eyes take in Alexei behind me. Recognition flares in both of their gazes, along with delight; they obviously know him and like him.

"Oh! Sorry, Alexei, we didn't see you there."

Alexei gets off the horse and walks up to them. They slap each other's backs, making me laugh at how the bro-hug transcends realms.

The other one gestures to me. "Who's the pretty lady, and what's she doing with you?" he teases, making me blush under their scrutiny as they all look at me.

"This is Ember," he tells them. "She accidentally traveled through the northwest portal."

The guards' eyebrows shoot up and they look at me in a whole new light, filled with curiosity, and their suspicion comes back.

"I need to take her to see King Stavros."

They nod in understanding, ushering us inside. Alexei moves to the front, taking Ash's reins and escorting me through the city. It reminds me a little bit of Twin Fangs, with stalls and vendors all over the street selling anything and everything you can imagine. In the center of the town square, there's a huge water fountain, and in the middle is a statue of what I can only assume is King Stavros. He looks handsome, and I'm guessing this was commissioned when he first became king because he looks fairly young. Although, now that I'm thinking about it, I remember that Alexei told me that fae don't age quickly at all, so he could potentially look my age but actually be a lot older.

He has a large crown on his head and is holding a sword, positioned in front of him and pointed toward the ground, almost like he's leaning on it. He has striking facial features that on most people would be too dominant, but he somehow pulls it off, with his sharp jawline, thick eyebrows, slightly elongated nose, and of course the heavily pointed ears.

As we make our way through the streets and toward the castle, my heart starts pounding harder and my palms begin to sweat. I have absolutely zero clue as to how this interaction is going to play out, and that always sets me on edge. People look at me curiously as we pass, clearly able to spot an outsider, and I try not to fidget.

I'm very aware of the fact that I have been on the road for weeks. I bathed last night, but my clothes are wrinkled and my hair is frizzy from the humidity and popping out of my braid. I try not to make eye contact, and instead focus on my surroundings. The castle, of course, sits at the highest part of the mountain, and we still have a bit of a trek to get up there. I can hear the waterfall to my left and the humidity leaves a heaviness in the air. As we get closer to the palace, there are fewer homes and shops, meaning that I'm no longer being stared at, which I'm grateful for.

"They don't get many visitors in the Immortal City," Alexei says from in front of me.

"I could tell. I'm a little self-conscious since I'm not looking my best from being on the road for so long."

He stops and looks back at me. "You look beautiful, Ember. That's why everyone is staring at you."

I blush furiously under his stare, but his words bring a smile to my lips.

We finally make it to the palace, and I dismount Ash, brushing my clothes to try to make myself more presentable, aware that it probably isn't helping. Alexei tells more guards that we need to see the king, and they usher us in. I would've preferred having some time to take another bath and change into some fresh clothes, but unfortunately that doesn't happen. I triple-check that my mental shields are firmly in place, and then we're taken into the throne room.

"The king will be with you momentarily," announces our escort.

I wander around the great room, not wanting to sit. Not that it would even be possible, considering the only seat in the whole room is the throne itself. The space is enormous, tall as well as wide, with huge columns that line either side. On the other side of the columns are little pools that seem to serve no purpose except for decoration. Generally, pools like that are used to cool the space, but since this isn't an arid climate, I doubt that's the case here.

There is a huge red carpet that spans the length of the room and leads up to a raised platform where the throne sits. The ceiling is intricate and astonishing, and I know that I could get lost in its detail for hours. The throne itself is gold with black upholstery that looks velvet from here, and the gold metalwork is exquisite and detailed. There are fresh plants throughout the room; some look completely unfamiliar, and I'm sure they're native to Queridian. The entire space is also incredibly bright, because there are windows lining the curved wall behind the throne, and a skylight up above it, which effectively gives the impression that the heavens themselves are shining on the ruler of this realm.

Surprisingly, we don't have to wait long, and I'm standing there gawking at everything when a small door on the right side of the platform opens and a man enters, escorted by multiple guards. I can immediately tell that this is King Stavros, even though he isn't wearing his crown. There's something about him that's so *regal*. He's wearing mostly red and gold, and I can tell the statue in the square was modeled after this man. The only differences are the goatee he is now sporting, and the fact that he looks a few years older, perhaps around thirty-five.

He takes his seat on the throne and looks down at us intimidatingly.

It's then that I remember that this man is fucking *royalty* and all I've managed to do is stand there and gape at him and his room. Alexei clears his throat behind me, and I take the cue and bow low to him. I don't know what the protocol is here, and in hindsight I wish I would've asked Alexei to school me on some of the proper court etiquette so I don't look like a complete ass.

"Your Majesty," Alexei says, and from the sound of his voice I know he's bowing too.

"Rise," the king says, and we do. "This is quite the surprise, Alexei. I'm sure there is an interesting story here." His eyes flick to me again, and he cocks his head, a peculiar look on his face. We are still a little distance away from him, considering how large the room is, so I can't quite decipher the look he's giving me. "Come closer," he commands. When we're right below the stairs to the platform, he sucks in a sharp breath, his eyes boring into mine. "Catalina?" he asks reverently, getting up from his seat and walking down the steps so he's right in front of me.

His hand reaches out as if he's going to cup my face, and I flinch back slightly. This man may be king, but I have never met him before and don't want him thinking he can touch me without my permission.

"My name is Ember," I tell him, confused. I don't know who Catalina is, but it sure as shit isn't me.

He looks at Alexei. "Who is she? Why did you bring her here?"

"She came through the northwest portal. She traveled here by accident, and I discovered she had a Queridian necklace, which is how she was able to enter it."

I pull my necklace out of my shirt and hold it out to show him. His gaze snaps to it, and tears fill his eyes.

"May I?" he asks, gesturing to look more closely at it. I'm surprised he even asked permission since he's the king, but I nod, taking it from around my neck and holding it out to him. "Where did you get this?"

he asks quietly.

"I found it in my adoptive mother's things after she died. She had a hidden box with items that belonged to my birth mother." His breath catches and more tears well in his eyes.

"This belonged to your birth mother?"

"Yes. As far as I know. I have some notes that she wrote my adoptive mother that were in the same box. This was in there too." I gesture to my hairpiece, and his eyes immediately latch on to it before widening.

"You're my daughter," he whispers, and my heart stops beating.

"What?"

"You're my daughter," he repeats tenderly.

My eyes nearly bug out of my head as he reaches forward cautiously to touch my cheek again. This time I let him, and the moment he does, it awakens something within me. I can't explain it, but a spark runs through me that reaches something I never even knew existed inside me. I've never known the love of a father before, and the fact that there's the chance for it now, with this man, brings tears to my eyes.

"How do you know?" I ask, to be sure. I can't get my hopes up if this ends up not being real.

"I gave your mother this necklace. It's been passed down in my family for generations, the kings always giving it to the woman who owns their heart. I gave it to her when she told me she was pregnant with you. She was also wearing that hairpiece the day I met her."

"What happened?"

"She died. I was told that neither of you survived the birth."

I let that sink in for a moment. I take some deep breaths, but it's not doing much to calm me. I break eye contact with him and step back. I can't handle this right now. I look for Alexei, only to see him standing far back, trying to give us the privacy he thinks we need. But I don't want that right now. I need his strength and support when I have no idea what the fuck this means for me. He must see the panic in my eyes, because he immediately comes to my rescue, walking up to me and putting a supportive hand on my back.

"Your Majesty, I think this is all a lot for Ember to process right now, and we've had an extremely long journey. Would it be possible for us to get some rest and maybe continue this conversation another time?"

The king looks like he's about to refuse, but then he looks into my eyes again, and must see that that wouldn't be a good decision, considering I'm about to freak the fuck out, and nods regretfully. "I'll have Humphrey escort you to your rooms."

"Thank you, Your Majesty," I tell him, not willing to call him anything else right now. "Would it be possible for our rooms to be next to each other?" I ask quietly.

His eyebrows rise and he looks between us, but it's not like I asked if we could share a room. He nods again before turning and heading back the way he came.

A moment later, a man who I can only assume is Humphrey walks into the room. "I can escort you both to your rooms, if you'll follow me."

Alexei still has his hand on my low back, and I'm so thankful because his touch is the only thing grounding me at this point. I walk on in a daze, not taking in any of my surroundings. I know we go up multiple sets of stairs, but I wouldn't be able to tell you how many. I should probably be concerned because when I leave my room I am going to be so lost, but I can't find it in me to care. Humphrey shows us our rooms, which as requested are right next to each other.

"Here you are. Let me know if you need anything at all, miss."

I nod in thanks, and I feel bad that I'm so unresponsive.

"Humphrey, could you please have meals brought up for us? We could use a hot dinner after the long trip," Alexei chimes in.

"Of course, sir." He bows and leaves us to it.

"Will you come in with me?" I ask, not wanting to be with myself quite yet. I was originally looking forward to having my own space when we arrived, but after that huge revelation, I need to talk shit through with someone, and like it or not, Alexei is the only person I can discuss this with.

"I don't know if that's such a good idea here, Ember. People might get the wrong idea."

"Just for a few minutes. Please. It's not like I'm asking you to sleep with me." I try teasing him a bit, but it falls flat. We both know I'm in no teasing mood.

He nods before following me into the room. I sit on the bed, not even looking at how opulent I know the room must be, considering I don't have the mental capacity for anything but this right now.

"Can this be true?" I ask him quietly, almost afraid to voice the question.

"He seemed pretty adamant. And even though we haven't heard the story yet, what he's told us makes sense. On the plus side, you'll be able to learn about where you come from, how your parents met, how they fell in love. That's what you were looking for, wasn't it?"

I nod as I digest all of that. "Yes, but I didn't think I would end up being the goddamn *princess* of a magical realm." My voice gets higher and louder as I talk, because up until I said that, it hadn't occurred to me.

My breath starts coming faster, and I'm glad I'm already sitting down because I almost pass out as a panic attack hits me full force. God, I wish they had Xanax here. When I start hyperventilating, Alexei kneels in front of me so we're eye to eye.

"Breathe, Ember. Slow, deep breaths. With me."

I watch him and match my inhales and exhales with his. It's difficult at first, but the longer we continue, the easier it gets. My lightheadedness passes, and my heart rate starts to slow. When I'm marginally calmer he goes back to the topic at hand.

"Everything will be okay. I know you're alarmed about what this could mean for you, but let's take this one step at a time. We have no idea what's going to happen, and I'm sure you will have a say in it too, so don't disregard that or think that any of this is out of your hands. And I know I already told you this, but I want to remind you again. If this is true and he is your father, you'll have a family again. *Blood* family. That's a big deal, Ember. You could find the love and support of one of your true relatives. Of course, it won't be like that right away, but maybe with time it will. I think you should hear him out, see how things go. What's the worst that could happen?"

I keep breathing as I think about what he's said. I've always wanted to know what it was like to have a father. And considering I'm his only child, and he thought I died in childbirth, I bet he's wanting the same thing.

"I'll talk to him tomorrow. Will you be there with me?" I hate that I sound so clingy, but my world has been rocked, and I need someone there who can ground me. And as frustrating as Alexei can be, he's sweet, supportive, and he's always looking out for me.

"Of course I will, little doe."

I smile at his pet name for me. I hated it at first, but it's definitely grown on me.

"Now, if you're done with your freak-out, I'm going to go get settled. If you need me, I'll be right next door."

As soon as he leaves, I sit and enjoy the silence and the privacy. Not long after, there's a knock on my door. A young woman comes in carrying a tray of food. She sets it down on a little table near the fireplace that I didn't notice earlier. The food smells delicious, but I don't have much of an appetite. I leave it where it is and head to the bathroom, which is larger than my bedroom back home. There's a huge tub in one corner, and for a moment I forget my problems and squeal in excitement when I spot a shower. I figured they didn't have showers in this realm because I haven't seen one yet, but maybe the wealthy have them? I'll have to ask Alexei next time I see him, but for now I take the longest shower I can manage. Luckily shower products have been provided, and I strip quickly after turning the water on.

I step in when the water heats and sigh in pleasure at the feel of the spray pounding on my back. Just as I promised myself, I take my time, and when I've thoroughly washed and groomed everything I can, I reluctantly turn off the water. I eye my dirty clothes with hesitation; I don't want to put them back on, but I don't know what else to do considering I don't have any clean clothes right now. For now, I wrap myself in a towel, and find a separate one for my hair.

When I get back into my room, I am finally able to look around and appreciate the beauty of where I am. There's a massive bed that has the comfiest plum-colored bedding known to mankind, and the frame is gilded and extravagant. There are magnificent pictures lining the walls, some of the Immortal City, and others that I imagine are other places in Queridian. I marvel at how immense my fireplace is. The ornate mantelpiece is entirely covered in intricate carvings and is topped with various little knickknacks. I find a closet, and I open it to find the only thing it contains is a big cozy robe. I smile as I drop my towel and wrap it around myself. I won't have to change back into gross clothes, for which I am extremely grateful.

Now that I've had a little time to relax and process things, my appetite is back, and I head over to the table so that I can eat the delivered food. I take the lid off to find something completely unexpected. Pasta. My literal favorite. There's also a salad, garlic bread, and berries covered in honey for dessert. I eat all of it in record time, which is saying something, and when I finish, I collapse into bed and pass out.

Chapter 15

The next day I'm more well rested than I've been in as long as I can remember. The bed is so comfortable that I did not wake once, which is unsurprising since I've been accustomed to sleeping on the ground. I stretch my arms over my head lazily before everything from yesterday crashes into my mind. I'm half dreading, half eagerly awaiting the necessary talk I will have with the king. I'm sure it'll be awkward, but Alexei is right; I'm excited to hear about how my parents met and to learn more about my birth mother.

I get up and take another shower because I can. I don't wash my hair since I did so last night, but I lather my body up in the jasmine-smelling soap and let the hot water work out any tension in my muscles. I wish I had my purse with me so that I could put on a little makeup, but I have no idea where our things are.

When I get out of the shower and put my robe back on, I see containers on the counter. Intrigued, I open them only to find exactly what I was looking for. It's not *my* makeup, but fuck it, it's better than nothing. I keep it minimal and natural, but it does wonders for making me feel more like myself.

Just as I start freaking out about the fact that I don't have anything appropriate for a visit with the king, there's a knock on my door, and Humphrey is on the other side holding a dress.

"Miss Ember," he says, bowing to me. "The king asked me to

bring this for you. He's under the impression that since you've been traveling, you do not have any clean clothes."

I take the dress from him, smiling.

"Thank you so much, Humphrey. He is right. I have no clean clothes. And the clothes I do have are for traveling. Nothing fit for a palace."

"I will make sure to bring you some more, Miss Ember. Also, the king has requested that you join him for breakfast when you are finished getting ready."

I take a deep breath as nerves flutter in my stomach.

"Yes, that will be fine. Can you notify him that I would like Alexei to be there too?" I don't know what protocol is for this, but I want to meet with him on my terms as much as possible. And I wasn't lying last night; I want Alexei there to support me in this.

"I will let him know. Would you like me to tell Mister Alexei as well?"

"If you wouldn't mind, that would be wonderful." I smile gratefully at him.

"I don't mind at all. I'll come to escort you after I've talked to both of them. Will that be sufficient time for you to finish getting ready?"

"Yes. Thank you so much, Humphrey." He bows again before heading toward Alexei's room.

I close the door and look at the dress he brought for me. It's simple, but elegant. It's floor-length and the entire garment is crafted from deep purple velvet, with a V-neck and loose sleeves that come down to my elbows. Overall, I love it. I also wonder if the plum color was intentional since I'm fucking *royal* apparently.

I put on the dress, and the material slides over my body like butter. This is already my favorite thing I have ever worn, and I have no idea how Humphrey knew. Or more likely, he didn't and I got lucky. Probably that one. I check over my appearance in the mirror, and am pleasantly surprised by the woman staring back at me. I look well rested, and my face is bright from the makeup I applied. My hair is smooth and shiny from the hair products, and since I didn't braid it the night before like I normally do, it has a soft, natural wave to it. The dress accentuates my body perfectly, and the color also matches the feather in my hair. Needless to say, I'm as ready as I'll ever be.

Ten minutes later, Humphrey arrives, and I suppress my nerves as I open the door. Alexei is standing behind him looking as well-groomed as me, and he must've been given some fresh clothes too. Although, since his father works in the palace, I bet he has a room here along with a full wardrobe. His eyes heat as he drinks in my appearance, and I blush slightly under his scrutiny.

"Ready, little doe?" The pet name helps to calm me, and I nod as Humphrey takes off down the hallway, us at his heels.

We arrive at a dining room a few minutes later to see the king already seated at the table. We bow to him as we come in, and he smiles lightly upon seeing me.

"Good morning. Please sit." He gestures to the seat next to him, and I rise before heading over to it.

There's every sort of food I can think of on the table before us, and I breathe in the heavenly scents. I take a seat to the king's right, and Alexei takes the seat across from me.

"Would you like something to drink?" Humphrey asks me.

"I would love some tea, if you have it. Thank you."

He nods and heads in the direction of what I assume is the kitchen. Within minutes, my tea is served, and I notice they have one for Alexei too. I gratefully breathe in the scent of spearmint and honey, as it helps to clear my head a bit. I take a sip to have something to do, since we're heading into an awkward silence that I don't quite know how to clear.

"You look just like your mother," the king says quietly. With those few words, tears already build behind my eyes.

"What was she like?" I ask, wanting to know everything about her so much that it almost hurts.

"She was wonderful," he says, a smile on his face. "She was so kind and caring, always thinking of others. And she was strong, her spirit the fiercest I've ever known. And she loved you."

I inhale sharply at the words. I know I had the love of Eve, my adoptive mother, but I always yearned to have the love of my birth mother too. For so long I never knew why I was given up, and I always felt unwanted, like a burden that was passed onto someone else. The fact that she loved me and wanted me fills a hole inside of me that has been empty for my whole life.

"How did you meet? And how did I come to exist? Aren't the fae not allowed to mix with other species?"

"Yes, well, I guess you could call ours a forbidden love. Years ago, right when I had become of age, my friends all talked me into going to the Mortal Sanctum for some fun. They all wanted to enjoy, well..." He clears his throat awkwardly, not meeting my eyes, and from what I know of how Alexei came into the picture, I think I know where this story is going.

"You went to the Abandoned Bliss?" I ask, trying to make it a little easier on him. I remember the name from when Alexei first mentioned it to me. I still don't know for sure what it is, and this is probably my opportunity to ask.

"Yes. Do you know about it?"

"I've heard it mentioned, and I have my theories as to what it is, but those theories haven't been confirmed."

Alexei cuts in, and I can tell that the king is grateful that he doesn't need to explain them to me. "There are two locations in the Mortal Sanctum. One is the Sacred Rite, and the other is the Abandoned Bliss. They are both brothels and run by the same female. The Sacred Rite is where the human conduits are located. Anytime someone would like to have the bloodlines mixed, that's where they go. Thorough records are kept to ensure that you are getting what you want. It's also expensive, and extremely strict, as you can imagine. You can't do whatever you want to the women, and the interactions are closely monitored to ensure that none of them are harmed.

"The Abandoned Bliss is your regular brothel. The girls who are employed there always have two human parents, and therefore cannot produce children with multiple powers. Things are much more relaxed there, and the whole point of it is to have fun. Occasionally, one of the girls there will end up conceiving, and the females always end up in the Sacred Rite when they become of age." I cringe. It's exactly what I thought it was.

"I'm assuming that the girls from the Abandoned Bliss have multiple clients a night?" I ask, a question forming in my mind.

"Usually."

"So, how do they know what type of conduit the child will become?"

Alexei looks slightly uncomfortable. "Well, vampires can identify the species types in the blood. They're bitten before they're recruited for the Sacred Rite."

"Lovely," I comment sarcastically.

"Right." The king steps in now that the awkward part has been explained. "So, my friends took me to the Abandoned Bliss as a sort of celebration when I turned twenty-eight, but I had no interest in being with any of the girls there. I went with them, and they all inevitably fell into bed with someone. Instead, I went to the kitchens, trying to stay out of the way so I wasn't propositioned anymore. All of the servants welcomed me into their space and brought food to the little table where I sat, and all of a sudden she walked into the room." He looks up as his eyes take on a dreamy quality, picturing that moment in his head. "She looked at me and then said, 'What does this asshole want?'"

I laugh out loud in surprise, not expecting her to be so vulgar.

"The entire staff looked ready to kick her out and all apologized profusely to me, claiming that she didn't know who I was, which I'm sure she didn't, but I didn't let them punish her. Instead, I had her sit down with me and we shared our first meal."

"Was she a prostitute then?" I ask. Not that it matters, and I would never judge her if she was, I simply want to know everything about her.

"No. She was actually a servant there. She wasn't of age yet, and after I met her the first time, I ensured that she would not be forced to take clients when she did turn twenty-eight."

"So then what happened?"

"My friends had planned for us to be there for the week, considering it took so long to travel there, and they wanted to make the most of the trip. During the day we would explore the territory, and at night, whenever they took up the company of women, I would go to the kitchens and spend time with your mother. Needless to say, we connected and fell in love quickly. When we left to head back home I promised to write to her regularly and come visit when I could. We kept in contact then, slowly getting to know each other more through our letters, and after about a year I was able to go back and visit her. That was when she became pregnant with you, and although it was highly unheard of, I planned to marry her. I knew my plans would not be well received, not only by the fae, but also by my parents and the council. I was willing to risk it for her. I sent her that necklace as soon as I found out about you, and I was going to propose the next time I went down to see her, but then my father and mother died unexpectedly, and things were very hectic here as I made the transition to becoming the king. By the time I was able to visit her, I received a letter saying that both of you had died during childbirth."

By this time, both of us are crying, and I reach over and clasp one of his hands. He squeezes back empathetically, giving me a teary smile. "After that, I had no choice. I had to take another bride, and the two of us were never able to conceive. She ended up passing a few years ago."

"I'm so sorry. How did she die?"

"She was eating dinner alone in her room and choked to death."

"Did you love her?" I ask, not sure why.

"I had a deep respect for Queen Amira, but I didn't love her, and we were decidedly not mates. My heart has always belonged to your mother, and I'm afraid she took it with her when she died."

"Mates?" I ask. I haven't heard that term here.

"Mates are very rare and a wonderful gift. The bond snaps into place the first time the two touch if both of their powers have been awakened. Since our gifts develop as we go through puberty, most of the time the connection happens as soon as they meet each other. A brand will magically be burned on each of them, the design always completing each other's. Your mate is the perfect match for you, and you will be drawn to them like a moth to a flame, never able to stay away from them."

"And it can be anyone?"

"It has only ever developed between two individuals of the same species. Although, in the case of some of the polyamorous races, they can have more than one mate, but that is extremely rare." While all this is extremely interesting, I realize I've gotten off topic, as I typically do when talking about Queridian.

"Do you know why you were told that I also died and then was taken to Earth?"

"Unfortunately, I do not. I have been trying to think of why since I met you yesterday, but haven't been able to come up with anything. I wish I knew."

After the heavy talk, we start in on our food. I try to be more mindful of the fact that I'm eating in front of the king, and eat more slowly and civilly than I normally do. Alexei notices immediately and smirks knowingly in my direction. I narrow my eyes at him, warning him not to say anything, and have the urge to give him a filthy gesture. When we're satisfied, and our bellies are full, we start conversation back up.

"So, tell me about yourself."

"Well, I'm an archaeologist."

"What's that?" he asks, looking confused. I chuckle, still not used to people being unfamiliar with what I'm talking about.

"It's my career path. What I do for a living. I study human history and perform analysis on past events and extinct cultures based on evidence that I find on human remains and areas that used to be inhabited, but no longer are." I inwardly chuckle to myself about how scripted my explanation sounds, but I've recited it so many times in my life that it's become natural to me.

"Oh! That's interesting. We don't have anything like that here."

"Really? 'Cause Alexei and I actually traveled through the caves from the Healing Springs and discovered an entire palace and society that used to occupy them."

His eyebrows rise in surprise and then furrow as he looks at Alexei. "You took her through the caves?" There's a dangerous tone to his voice.

"It was my idea," I cut in before Alexei can try to talk his way out of it. "We were attacked by the áspro vrykólakas and I was injured. He had to sneak me into the Healing Springs, and when we went to leave, we were almost caught. It was my idea," I reiterate. "And don't get upset with him about it. He saved my life. Twice actually."

There's an edge to my voice, and I don't care that I'm talking to the king. He's apparently also my father, and I won't let him punish Alexei for something that was my decision, especially since Alexei has had my back from the beginning.

I didn't think it was possible, but the king's eyes grow even wider as my words register. But then a huge smile graces his face. "Well, you certainly have your mother's personality too. She never took any of my shit either," he whispers to me, catching me off guard with his cursing.

"It sounds like she and I would've gotten along famously." The thought brings a smile to my face, and I wish I could've met her.

"I think you would've. She was extraordinary. She was so brave, always speaking her mind, even when it got her into trouble. She was incredibly kind as well, always helping anyone in need. She also had a wonderful sense of humor, she was constantly making me laugh."

I smile at the picture he's painting. I like to think that I share those qualities with her, at least to some extent. Tears start building again, and I change the subject to avoid them.

"So, what does this all mean for me now?" I ask. I've been dreading talking about this subject, but it's also been driving me out of my mind not knowing what's going to happen, or what will be expected of me.

"Well, as you're my daughter, I would very much like to announce it to the kingdom. It's also a possibility that you would be next in line for the throne, but at this point I think we need to get to know each other better before we make that decision. Now, I know that's a lot to take in, and it's got to be intimidating for you, but it is something to think about. Also keep in mind that because of the difference in our life spans, that might never even come to pass."

"I have a choice? It's not a requirement for me to take over since I'm your only heir?"

"Of course you have a choice. If I had known you'd existed from the start, things might be different. You would've grown up understanding that this was your future, and you wouldn't have known any differently, but since that's not the way things happened, I would never force you into this position. I would like you to think about it. I would also very much like to get to know you. Would you consider staying at the castle so I may have the opportunity to do so?"

My breath leaves my body in a *whoosh*. I didn't realize how much

I needed to hear all of that from him. So far he's killing it on the dad front. I smile softly at him.

"I would like that very much."

"So would I, Ember."

"Can I make a request?" He nods at me to continue. "Alexei has been training me in combat these past few weeks, and I've become quite good friends with him. Would he be able to stay awhile and keep training me instead of returning to his post in Twin Fangs?" I hold my breath. Of course I would be okay if Alexei had to leave, but I don't want that in the slightest. He's become my only person. I know that I'll meet new people and make new friends here, but the relationships won't be the same. He is the first person I've been close to other than my mother, and I'm not ready to give up whatever is going on between us.

"I don't see why we can't make that happen. I'm sure you have some business to catch up on here with your father too, don't you, Alexei?"

"Yes, Your Majesty."

"And you have a replacement at your station?"

"Yes. But since I'll be here for a while, we should send another replacement as backup, in case something happens with the current guard."

"Very well. I'll see that it's done."

"I've also been training Ember in her magical abilities, Your Majesty. Hers are very strong and unique." Alexei seems to be bragging about me, and it equally thrills and embarrasses me.

"What's unique about them? Not the standard human ability?"

Alexei looks to me, and instead of telling the king, I let him. I'm sure he'll be able to do so more eloquently than me anyway.

"Well, not only can she sense others' emotions, she can also change them."

The king's head whips to me, shock lining every feature of his face.

"I've also been working with her on mental shields, and she's now able to get through my strongest one, and keep a sturdy barrier up herself."

"Show me," the king demands of me.

I swallow nervously, not liking being put on the spot by him. I look at Alexei to find him smiling and nodding at me encouragingly. I close my eyes and push my senses out to my father. He, of course, has barriers up, and from what I can sense they are stronger than Alexei's, although not by much. I do as I've been practicing, and although it takes me slightly longer than normal, I'm able to get through them. I smirk to myself in triumph until his emotions hit me full force.

I gasp as I recognize so many feelings that it overwhelms me. He's intrigued, gloriously happy, sad, and shocked. I tell him everything I'm sensing, and come up with a strong emotion for him, settling on amusement. I want to hear him laugh, and let's be honest, it's one of my favorites to push onto others. I give him so much that it overwhelms him, my eyes popping open when I hear his deep throaty laugh. It almost sounds like he hasn't laughed in years, and the thought saddens me.

"Wow. That's incredible! I've never heard of someone being able to do this before."

"That's what I said," Alexei chimes in. "But then she demonstrated it like she did with you."

"Have you always been able to do this?"

I shake my head. "When I was back on Earth, I was able to sense others' emotions sometimes, but never affect them, or maybe I just never tried. But when I came here, my ability immediately sharpened. Well, and then, I got into a bad situation where I *needed* to change someone's feelings, and it worked. I was as shocked as you both were. Since then, Alexei and I have been practicing, and it's gotten as natural as breathing."

"Ember, this is unbelievable. You're so strong. I hope this isn't too early for me to say, but I'm so proud of you."

His words bring tears to my eyes, and although I barely know him, I get a rush of exhilaration that this extremely important man is proud to be my father. It's what I've always wanted. I've known the love of a mother, even if she wasn't my birth mother, but I have *never* known the adoration of a father.

"Thank you," I murmur as a tear slips free.

"Well, would you like a tour?" the king asks.

"I would love one," I reply, smiling at him.

"I'm going to leave you two to it, then. I need to meet with my father," Alexei says and heads in a different direction than us, bowing to the king as he goes.

"So, what would you like to see first?"

"How about you show me *your* favorite part of the castle?" He smiles at me and leads the way. I have no clue where we're going, but I'm excited to learn more about him.

We stop in front of a huge set of chestnut double doors, and he looks back at me, giving me a smile like a little boy. He pushes them wide and I gasp at what's revealed. It's a library! Like literally the library of my dreams. It reminds me of a darker *Beauty and the Beast* library. There are so many books here that I don't even know where to start, and I immediately wonder if this was the Epitome Athenaeum that Alexei was telling me about. When I ask Stavros, he tells me it's just the castle library, and the Epitome Athenaeum is much larger. My eyes almost fall from their sockets. I can't imagine one larger than this. He shows me around, and as we make our way up to the second level, it starts getting brighter.

"This is my favorite place in the whole palace. Right here." There are massive windows spread out along one wall, cozy chairs seated in front of them with an imposing fireplace to the left. "I will usually pick out a book and read it in this chair here, although sometimes I take it out on the patio so I can look down at the gardens."

I open the patio door and walk out into the sunshine, and am stunned silent by the gardens below. They sprawl out in front of me, and have every plant you could possibly imagine, including so many that I've never even seen before, so I assume they're native to Queridian. To the right of the gardens is the waterfall I saw upon entering the city, and it's glorious in its beauty. It flows down in a river in front of the gardens and continues off to the left and out of sight.

"Would you like to go down there?" he asks, gesturing to a spiral staircase with plants curling around the railing to immediately welcome you into the space.

I nod and we head down. Upon entering, I'm reminded of the secret garden, but with plants that are not on Earth. Everything is immaculately designed, and there's an enormous fountain in the center, a small pond off to the left side covered with lily pads, and a small bridge to cross over it. Sprawling trees, intoxicating lavender bushes, lilies, and roses as far as the eye can see. The scents overwhelm me, and I breathe them in deeply, only to sneeze.

The king chuckles. "Allergies?"

"Yes. I've always struggled with them."

"Your mother did too, even though she absolutely loved springtime. She adored seeing all the blooming flowers and budding trees." I smile at that because he could be describing me. "This garden used to be so bare. There was hardly anything in here, and no one ever visited them. After your mother died, I expanded it and planted all the things I knew she loved."

"What was her favorite flower?"

"She loved lajeldas. I was going to have a huge display of them when I proposed."

"What are those?"

He points in the direction of the pond, and I step up to get a closer look. They're large, wide, and open, all ranging in different colors, but the centers are all pink with a slight glow.

"She also loved translucent roses."

He gestures to the flowers next to them that I didn't even notice. Sure enough they're roses, but they're almost completely clear. The only visible colors are little spots of pink and green that are so light it's almost impossible to see.

"This is her section of the garden. I put all of her favorites in this immediate area." I also spot lotus flowers, peonies, irises, and more lavender.

When I start sneezing again, he laughs. "Want to go inside?"

I nod, and we go in a separate door, which leads to a large open hall. There are checkered tiled floors, and an immaculate hand-painted ceiling. It reminds me of the Sistine Chapel. We go through a door in the hall into what I'm fairly certain is the royal ballroom. I take it in with wide eyes. It is the most incredible room I have ever seen in my life. It's absolutely enormous, but that's no surprise since it's used to host a ton of people.

There are columns lining the perimeter of the room, connected with archways that soften the edges of the structure. The ceiling is delicately designed with intricate swirls and paintings. The floor is a sophisticated marble, and the fae crest is placed boldly in the middle. But the most amazing thing about this room is the diamonds that are embedded into the walls. The surfaces literally sparkle and shine, and when I go up to touch the wall, the roughness of the gems cut against my palm. I know that these are one hundred percent *real* diamonds. I mean, of course they would be in this palace, but the reality is shocking. Finally, I look to the platform at the far end of the room to see that there are two thrones, one covered in a black sheer fabric to symbolize the late queen and one for my father.

"We were able to explore the palace in the caves. It had a ballroom similar to this, although not nearly as extravagant, but there were six thrones and all of the species' crests, except for the humans. We think the palace was occupied before the humans arrived. There was also cave art that contained depictions of the races coexisting. Oh, and there were paintings of the various rulers, and they were all different species. I think they ruled together."

"I've heard about that," he says but doesn't seem happy with the direction of our conversation. "It wasn't what you're thinking, Ember. They weren't the rulers, even if that's how it appeared."

"Well, still, I know that things are segregated now, and I was thinking it doesn't have to be like that." I decide to air some of Alexei's ideas on how to improve the kingdom. "Maybe it might be a good idea to open the borders between territories?"

His gaze hardens, and he breaks eye contact before I can question him further. "I appreciate your input, but that would never work, Ember."

"What? Why do you say that? Clearly others tried to make it work in the past, even if they didn't rule the realm. Why not give it a shot?" I know that I don't know the history of this place. I also know that I'm probably pushing my luck with him, but I don't care. The parallels in this world to things that have happened on Earth in the past make me want to persuade him that things could be different. Better.

"Ember, there are a lot of things that you don't understand. You just arrived here, and you are so young. It wouldn't work."

The way he dismisses my opinion and tries to make me seem like a naive child pisses me off. I *know* that I just arrived here, but studying past civilizations and human interaction is my life's work. I mean, I guess that's technically more along the lines of anthropology, but the two really go hand-in-hand. I would say I'm rather worldly and have a good grasp on how societies and cultures successfully and unsuccessfully interact with each other. But apparently I'm only a young girl whose opinion doesn't fucking matter.

"My mistake. Your Majesty," I say disdainfully, bowing before I turn to leave.

He doesn't stop me, and I walk out. I take a few moments to calm down, heading back through the garden and the library before going in search of my room. I'm fairly certain I can find it on my own, and twenty minutes later, and multiple wrong directions, I finally do. At least I was able to do some exploring by myself. When I enter, I find a note on my bed.

Miss Ember,

I took the liberty of stocking your closet. There are now multiple sets of clothes for different occasions and needs, as well as more grooming products in your bathroom. If you require anything else, notify me and I will see that it is done.

Humphrey

I take a look in the closet, and am pleased to see the new clothes. There's not much here, but it's enough to get me by for at least a little while. He's also managed to find me different types of clothes in case I need to dress for something specific, which is nice to have that option. There are more casual training clothes, a thing or two for everyday wear, and finally a lavish gown I don't think I'll ever use.

I have no clue how he got this all together so fast. I bet they have a spare wardrobe for guests. Or maybe multiple wardrobes. Either way, I'm so grateful that I have a few more options to choose from for now. I'm tempted to try on the gorgeous over-the-top gown hanging up, but as I'm about to undress, I hear a knock at my door. Alexei is standing there, looking handsome as ever.

"I wasn't sure if you'd be back yet, but thought I would stop by and see if you wanted to stick to our training schedule today?"

The thought brings a smile to my face and I nod at him. I'm glad that I have a small piece of routine to return to when my life is a bit unfamiliar at the moment.

"Let me get changed."

I head back into the closet and find suitable training clothes. I pull on a pair of fighting leathers and a loose-fitting shirt that I tuck into my pants. I add my traveling boots since they're worn in now, and my look is complete. I head into the bathroom and find something to tie my hair back before going out to Alexei.

"Ready?"

I nod and he shows me to an outdoor area, which I can only assume is a training yard. Something like this would've never excited me in my old life, but since we started all this, I am surprisingly looking forward to utilizing this space. There are targets on one end for archery and dagger throwing, figures made out of some sort of durable material—rubber I think—for swords and hand-to-hand combat, and a whole range of weapons.

"What do you want to practice today?"

"Hmm. How about hand to hand and archery?"

We start with hand to hand, and we do in fact use the figures. Alexei starts and demonstrates some new moves, and I'm able to see precisely where he's striking. Then I give it a shot, and he, of course, critiques me, but soon I get the moves down, and we start incorporating them with the techniques I learned before. When I think we're getting close to switching to the bow and arrow, he leaves an opening. I don't know if it's intentional or not, but I take it all the same. I sweep my foot out, knocking him off his feet, and he falls with an *oomph*. Before he can get up, I pounce on him, straddling his hips and bringing my hand to his throat, squeezing lightly.

"I win," I say smugly, a smile on my face.

"Do you now?" he asks, and before I can reply, he wraps his legs around mine and flips us so suddenly that my breath catches. "Do you still think you won?"

I can feel his hardness in between my thighs; he's clearly as excited about our little sparring session as I am.

"Yes, I do," I say, grinding my hips against his.

I hear his sharp intake of breath, and his eyes latch on to my lips as I wet them. When I think he's going to lean down and kiss me, a throat clears behind us. We both break apart guiltily, and Alexei quickly gets to his feet, offering me a hand up. I take it and dust myself off once I'm standing. There's a tall man over by the entrance who has an air of importance about him. Whether he is actually important remains to be seen.

"Well, I see what everyone's been talking about," the man says, eyeing me up and down creepily. I try to hide my sneer of disgust, not knowing who he is. As he gets closer I can see a resemblance to the man next to me, and I realize this must be Alexei's father. They have the same dark blond hair, although his is cut much shorter and slicked back. They also have the same gray eyes and sharp nose.

"Father, this is Ember. Ember, this is my father, Mordecai."

"It's a pleasure to meet you, Ember," Mordecai says as he grabs my hand and brings it to his mouth. This guy makes my skin crawl, not to mention that he just caught me and his son rolling around on the floor.

"You too."

"Alexei, would you mind if I talk to you for a moment?"

"Sure. Ember, why don't you start practicing with your bow and arrow. I didn't bring the one you normally use because I want you to get used to using different ones."

He gestures to where the bows are and I pick a few up, testing their weight and seeing which one is comfortable to hold. I don't pick up the one that's similar to my normal bow because that would negate the purpose. I stand on the line marked on the floor and take aim at the target. I try not to eavesdrop on their conversation, but it's difficult.

"Alexei, what are you doing?"

"What do you mean?"

"She's the king's *daughter.* Not to mention that you took an oath. You looked pretty close to breaking it."

"I'm training her. We were sparring, that's all."

That definitely was not all, and I try not to be hurt that he denied it to his father, even though I understand why.

I release the arrow so I don't give away the fact that I'm listening in. Even though I'm distracted, I'm pleased to see that I hit the target, on the second innermost ring.

"I can see there's more to it than that, but I'll trust you not to take it any further, Alexei."

He nods and that's the end of the conversation. I release my next arrow, and it goes into the second ring again, but on the opposite side. I overcorrected.

"Nice to meet you, Ember. Keep up the good work," Mordecai says, gesturing to the target.

"Thanks. You too," I say simply, even though it was definitely not nice meeting him. He takes off, and luckily that's all I have to endure of his presence for now.

Alexei comes up to my right, although I notice that he keeps more distance between us than normal, making me bristle.

I line up my arrow again, attempting to ignore him and focus on the target. His eyes are boring into me, and it fucks with my concentration. Normally it doesn't bother me to have him watch, but after the conversation I overheard, I'm very aware of things between us. I release the arrow without putting too much thought into aiming or breathing, and I curse myself when it hits the outer ring of the target.

I huff out a frustrated breath.

"You weren't breathing. You also lined up your shot wrong, both of your eyes were open."

"I know. It was a little distracting having you watch me."

His brows furrow in confusion. "That's never bothered you before."

I latch another arrow so I don't have to meet his gaze. Instead of answering him, I line up my shot. This time, I take extra care aiming, and Alexei moves behind me so that I can't see him. Even though I know he's still watching, it helps for him not to be in sight. I close one eye, and when I'm ready, I take a deep inhale and release on the exhale. The arrow soars through the air before hitting the target directly in the center. I squeal in excitement. I've never hit the center before! I turn around to find Alexei looking at me with a big smile on his face and pride in his eyes.

"I did it!" I exclaim.

"I can see that. Well done, Ember."

I start jumping up and down before running to him and giving him a big hug. He catches me, although I can tell I've caught him off guard. He releases me more quickly than I would like and steps back.

"Why are you doing that?" I ask, even though I know the answer. I want him to know that I've noticed.

He looks at me uncomfortably before averting his gaze. "I think we need to put a little distance between us."

"Because your father lectured you about it?"

His surprise filters toward me. "You heard?"

"Every word. But apparently you don't need to distance yourself from me since you're just *training* me and nothing else."

"Ember, you know I can't, no matter how much I want to," he says quietly.

"Then why do you keep fucking with my head? One minute you're basically dry-humping me and about to kiss me, and the next you're staying away from me like I have the plague. Pick a goddamn lane, Alexei, 'cause I'm tired of being dragged around by you. If you can't ever be with me then cut this shit out now before you break my fucking heart."

Tears build behind my eyes, but I refuse to let him see them. I know he's a good guy, and that he's as torn up about this as me, but I'm suddenly so angry about it all, and it's not fair of him to keep stringing me along like this. "So, what's it going to be?" I ask.

He looks deeply into my eyes, and I can see my own hurt reflected in them. His hand moves a tiny bit closer to me like he wants to touch me or pull me into his arms, and for a moment my stupid heart flutters with hope, but then he clenches his fist at his side, and I know that it's never going to happen. The answer is on his face before the words leave his mouth.

"I'm sorry, Ember. I can't."

I nod, setting my bow down on the table before walking away from him. My heart breaks more with every step. I still don't cry, even as pressure builds up in my head with my need to release the tears, but I can't do that until I get to my room.

I finally make it to my quarters, and I immediately turn the shower on before stripping everything off and stepping inside. I collapse onto the shower floor and the water pounds over my body as I let the tears go at last. They're big and ugly, accompanied by body-racking sobs, and the water washes it all down the drain like it never happened. I don't know what happened today, if the men in my life are being completely unreasonable, or if I'm just confrontational right now, but the fight with my father and then with Alexei are too much for me to handle.

I don't know how long I sit there feeling sorry for myself, but when all my tears have dried up, I make myself get out. I wrap up in my plush comfy robe and throw my hair up in a towel before collapsing into bed. I know it's the middle of the day, but I'm exhausted and in desperate need of a siesta. I'm asleep within minutes.

Chapter 16

Sometime later, I wake to a knock at my door. Confused, I get up, making sure that my robe is securely fastened. The towel came loose while I slept, and I know my hair has got to be a mess, but I don't have time to do anything with it before answering.

I open the door to find a stunning woman on the other side, holding a tray of food. She is unlike anyone I have ever seen. Her waist-length hair is so white it has a purple sheen to it, her irises are a pale dusty rose, and her lips are full and a shade darker than her eyes. She has a flowy blue skirt on and an ivory lace top that shows off her perfect hourglass-shaped body, and of course she's as tall as a supermodel.

"Humphrey was about to bring this up to you, figuring that you might be hungry, but as soon as I heard what he was up to, I grabbed your tray and ran off with it before he knew I had it. I thought you could use some girl time?" Not only is she crazy good-looking, but she also has the most angelic voice I've ever heard. It's almost lyrical, even when she's talking it's like she's singing.

"I'm sorry, who are you?"

"Oh, silly me. Forgive me. My name is Pearl. I'm the king's ambassador. Well, technically he has several, but I'm the one from Mermacovia."

"You're a mermaid?" I gasp. I should've known because she has a very mermaid quality about her. It's also then that I look down at her clothing to see the mermaid crest on the breast of her shirt.

She giggles and the sound lightens my heart. As strange as it seems, she makes me want to do things for her. I realize then that this is her power, and I slam my mental shields up. The urge immediately leaves me, although I still find her just as beautiful. She smiles brightly at me.

"Do you mind if I come in?"

"Okay," I say, stepping aside to make room for her. "I'm sorry, I wasn't expecting company. I'm afraid I'm a bit of a mess at the moment." I self-consciously touch my hair. I'm sure it looks like a rat's nest, and of course I had to meet this dazzling woman when I'm looking my worst. My eyes are probably super red from crying in the shower earlier too.

"That's all right, darling. I know the look of a girl who had a breakdown," she says nonchalantly, and although I should be offended, I like her straightforward, no-bullshit attitude.

I laugh. "Yeah, having fights with the only two people in my life kind of hit me all at once as soon as I got in the shower." I don't know why I'm telling her this, but she makes me feel like I can share things with her. Also, it's been so long since I've interacted with another woman, I forgot how nice it is.

"The shower is also my favorite place to ugly cry," she says, nudging me. "Now, would you like to eat? Or I could also give you a makeover and we can girl talk about what's bothering you. Or we can do both, in whichever order you prefer."

I smile, but am a little suspicious. "Why are you being so nice to me?" I open up my senses to her to see if I can detect anything that might give me some insight. She has a barrier up, but it's weaker than Alexei's, and I get through it quickly. I don't sense any deceit or ulterior motive. Only curiosity and a bit of loneliness.

"Oh, believe me, it's for my own benefit. There are no women here my age, and as a result, I don't have any friends. I thought since you don't know anyone here either that we should get to know each other." The honesty in her words rings true with my gift, and I relax as much as I can with this stranger.

"I would like that," I tell her truthfully. While she's a bit intense, I like it, and I'm excited about making an actual female friend. God knows I've never had one before, with the exception of my mother. I sit down in front of the tray and start eating. Pearl sits next to me and starts stealing things off my plate.

"Good choice. I always start with food too." We quickly finish off the plate, and Pearl grabs us some wine. "Okay, are you ready for your makeover?"

"I don't know how you're ever going to get through this rat's nest in my hair, or how you're going to make my eyes less red and blotchy, but please feel free to try."

She squeals in excitement that I'm going to let her, and takes a seat behind me after rummaging through my bathroom for bottles, creams, a brush, and numerous other things.

She first applies an oil to my hair, and it smells so good I want to bathe in it. It reminds me of something you'd find in Morocco. I smell amber, cinnamon, vanilla, and orange. Then she sections out my hair and starts gently brushing through it. It's so relaxing I almost fall asleep. No one has brushed my hair for me since I was probably ten.

"So, do you want to talk about it?"

I think about that for a moment. I can't exactly tell her about my argument with the king. She works for him, and therefore would probably be obligated to tell him. Could I tell her about Alexei? I mean she lives in the palace, so she probably knows more than I do about this kind of stuff, but once again, I don't know what she's obligated to report, and I don't want to get Alexei into trouble.

"I promise, anything that you tell me will not leave this room," she says seriously, squeezing my shoulder, and once again her sincerity bleeds toward me.

I take a deep breath and nod. I do want to talk to a woman about this. At least the Alexei stuff.

"Do you know Alexei?"

"You mean the insanely hot guard who is the son of the advisor? Yes."

"He's the one who found me and brought me here. We were on the road together for weeks, and in that time we've gotten close. On the trip here, though, he mentioned that he took an oath not to get involved in any romantic relationships. And I understand, but maybe because I'm not originally from here I don't see why it's such a big deal. But either way, we've been flirting with each other, and getting close to one another, and now I think I'm almost past the point of no return with him. I got angry with him today because he keeps telling me we can't be together, but then he does something that shows how much he wants to be with me. I told him he needs to stop fucking with my heart or it's going to end up broken. He once again told me that he can't do it. Then I walked away and broke down once I got to my room."

All the time I'm rambling, Pearl calmly brushes my hair, listening intently, but not interrupting, which I'm extremely grateful for.

"I've tried doing the friend thing with him, but then he dances with me, or tells me how much he wants me, or holds me during the night, and I can't help but think that we're drawn to each other, and we can't do anything about it. I don't know what to do." Tears gather in my eyes again as I talk through everything. There's something that always triggers my emotions when someone touches me in an affectionate way.

She continues brushing my hair until it's all smooth, shiny, and gleaming. "I understand why you feel the way you do," Pearl says softly, her voice soothing my frayed nerves. "But you are right. It is different here. He would have to give up his position in order to be with you, and while I'm sure he's tempted, from what I've heard, the guard position is Alexei's whole life. It would be an enormous deal for him to do that, and he would need to do something else for a living, and honestly, I don't think he's ever thought about doing anything else in his whole life."

I give her a resigned sigh. "I get that. But then he needs to stop giving me so many mixed signals. If we can truly only be friends, then he needs to be my fucking friend, not break my heart."

"I completely agree. Want me to beat him up for you?" Pearl asks me conspiratorially.

I laugh despite the heavy conversation. Finished with my hair, she moves on to my face, first applying a moisturizer, then putting a special cream under my eyes, which apparently reduces puffiness and redness so no one will know I've been crying. My makeup is next, and I don't know what she's putting on my face, I simply close my eyes and enjoy my makeover. The last thing she does is give me a mani pedi. It's like I've spent a day at the spa, and I don't even care what I'll end up looking like, I'm so relaxed. It's been so long since I've been pampered, and I'm soaking it the fuck up.

"All done! Alexei is going to regret ever taking that oath," Pearl tells me, a gleam in her eyes. "Go look and tell me how amazing I am." She pushes me toward the full-length mirror in my room.

I gasp upon seeing my reflection. I don't know what kind of voodoo magic she's done, but I have never looked so good in my life. My hair is shiny, and she's brushed it so my waves are falling naturally around my face, almost looking like finger waves, which I have never been able to accomplish. She wasn't lying about the eye cream; I look well rested and not like I was crying in the least, and my eyelids are shimmering and bright in a seminatural way. My lips are painted a bold red that makes them look fuller than they've ever been. Overall my whole face is *glowy*. Lastly, my fingernails are neatly trimmed and filed to a slight oval shape, and painted with a polish that looks iridescent, changing between pearl white and pink in the light, and my toes match.

"Well? Am I amazing or what?"

"Pearl, *amazing* doesn't even cover it. How did you do this to me?"

"Darling, I'm a mermaid. We're very conscious of our beauty and we know how to make ourselves look as stunning as possible. I've learned a few tricks over the years, and even more since working in the palace."

"So, what exactly do you do here?" I ask. I mean, I know she's the mermaid ambassador, but I don't know what her duties entail.

"Basically, I help the king with any negotiations or deals."

"With your gift?"

"Yes. I use my beauty and allure to encourage arrangements he may need or garner support. Also, all of the ambassadors are on hand to consult about decisions that would be best for their territories. Basically like a council."

"Are you pretty powerful then?"

"Well, I don't know if I would say *powerful*."

"Bitch, please. You work for the man ruling the country. You wouldn't be in the position you're in if you weren't."

She blushes slightly under my praise, but it's not like any blush I've ever seen. There's a shininess to it, almost like her blood is glowing underneath her skin. It's mesmerizing.

"Fine. I'm decently powerful."

"Hey, speaking of that, I'm working on my mental shields." Her brows rise in surprise. "Would you mind helping me practice? I need someone who is strong who knows what they're doing to see how mine are holding up."

"Who taught you that? It's not a very well-known skill."

"Really? Alexei taught me, but I haven't had anyone to practice with who would actually be able to get past them. Also, why isn't it a very well-known skill?"

"It just isn't. Usually individuals in positions of power know how to do it, but if you're subtle enough with your gifts it's easier to get past someone's barriers without them even knowing."

"Well, you sound like the perfect person to practice with, then," I tell her with a smile.

"Okay," she agrees, "we have some time before dinner."

"Dinner?"

"Yes. The king has requested you join him. I'll be there too."

I nod, a little nervous after our interaction this morning, but with Pearl there hopefully it won't be as awkward. I focus on the task at hand and build up my shields carefully, making sure I'm extra thorough because of how powerful she is.

When they're solid, I tell her, "I'm ready. Hit me with your best shot."

She stares intently at me, and I keep my attention focused on maintaining my shields. I feel small nudges at my barriers, but they're subtle, and if I wasn't so focused, I'm sure I wouldn't even notice anything. But as it is, I do, and I'm able to keep everything firmly in place. She tries multiple times in various spots, but there's no altering to my mental state. After a few more minutes, her mind pulls back.

"Well, damn girl. You've got a strong mind. I wasn't able to get past them even a little bit."

I beam at the praise, glad that all of my training has paid off.

"But, you were prepared for me to do that. If you want to get better, you'll let me practice with you without warning, because that's how it's going to happen. You won't have time to prepare in real situations. So, if it's okay with you, I'm going to try to get to you at random times. Deal?"

I smile at her. I'm excited to learn more, and ecstatic that we're going to be spending more time together. "Deal."

We practice for a little longer, but like she said, I'm aware of what she's attempting, so she is not successful in any of her efforts. I'm sure she will catch me off guard at some point though.

"So, the final thing we need to do before dinner is dress you up so that Alexei eats his heart out instead of his food." She winks at me, and we head into my closet to pick out a drop-dead gorgeous outfit.

"Thank you so much for all of this, Pearl. I already feel close to you, and I'm so glad to have an actual friend that's a woman." I squeeze her hand to show my sincerity.

She returns my smile and squeeze. "I've been wanting a girlfriend for so long. We are going to be best friends, I can already tell."

"I've never had an actual girlfriend before. The only person I was ever close to was my mom, and she passed a couple months ago, and now Alexei. I think that's why it's so hard for me to be upset with him. He's the only person I have right now."

"Not anymore," Pearl tells me with a wink and a hip check, making a genuine smile cross my lips. "Now, let's pick out your outfit."

We head into the closet, and I peruse the options. Although Humphrey got me clothes for every occasion, there's not a lot of choices. There's a long black boring dress, and one that's entirely too fancy; I could totally see wearing it to a ball or something, but for a regular dinner it's too much. I think about putting on the dress that I wore earlier today, but then I remember my skirt that we bought before we went on our trip that I never got a chance to wear.

Humphrey, or someone else, brought up my things from the journey. All of my clothes have been cleaned, folded, and laid right inside my door. I'm guessing that whoever brought them either wasn't comfortable coming into this space while I was away, or they came when I was sleeping and left them inside so as not to disturb me. Either way, I'm glad to have my own things returned to me, and immediately grab the skirt from the pile. It's nothing fancy, but with the right shirt, I think it will be appropriate for dinner. When I head back into the closet, Pearl is looking at the clothes with a defeated expression.

"Well, there's not too much here to work with," she says dejectedly as she turns to me. She eyes the flowy plum skirt in my hands, her eyes lighting up. "We can work with this." She flips through the shirts hanging in the closet, finding a lace cream-colored top. It has long sleeves, and the collar comes up to my neck, but the back is practically nonexistent, dipping down into a low V at the base. "This will be perfect."

I quickly change into it, tucking the shirt so the high waist of the skirt is visible. Pearl claps excitedly when I'm dressed and leads me back into the bedroom, sitting me on the bed before running into the bathroom to grab what I'm assuming is more grooming products.

She throws some stuff on the bed, but before I can look at what it is, she turns my head and starts braiding my hair, although not like any braid I've ever given myself. She goes round and round my head until she's back at the front where she started. I reach up to touch it, but quick as lightning, she swats my hand away. After lots of pulling and pinning, she deems me ready, and I look in the full-length mirror. She's given me a braid crown, loosening it until it's the largest braid I've ever had, making my hair look incredibly voluptuous. It goes well with the high collar of my shirt, and I think that a pair of dangly earrings would complete my look.

"You need jewelry," Pearl says, reading my thoughts. "Let's go to my room and you can borrow some and I can change for dinner too."

I'm pleasantly surprised to find out that Pearl's room is right down the hall. The setup is similar, but she has way more personal things, which is understandable considering this is legitimately *her* room, and she's been here a hell of a lot longer than I have.

Everywhere I look there is something water related, whether it's shells, paintings of the ocean, or random things that have a mermaid vibe to them. I'm also surprised to see that she's kind of a slob. There are clothes strewn everywhere, like she just tosses them off as soon as she enters the room with no care as to where they fall. She doesn't seem to mind that I'm witnessing her messiness though, and while I find it endearing, it also makes me cringe to think of living in this chaos.

She drags me into her closet and guides me to her jewelry collection while she heads over to the clothes. She strips quickly even though she still has yet to find something to wear, and my eyes widen as I admire her body. It is the perfect hourglass shape. Like I'm fairly certain that her body was used as a guideline for the ultimate fantasy for every man alive. I hate that I like her so much, because I am supremely jealous of her at that moment.

I turn my attention back to the task at hand so that I don't drive myself insane. She has so many accessories that I don't know where to begin, but figure I should start with dangly earrings, and soon I've found multiple sets that I can't decide between. The first set has delicate chains on the fronts and backs. The fronts have a small black teardrop at the bottom, and the backs have a white one. The second set has a crescent moon for one, and a star for the other. And finally, the third set are long arrows pointing down.

I grab each of them, intending to ask for a woman's opinion, grateful that I'm able to, and when I turn around Pearl is getting dressed. She's wearing a white one-piece; the under part is all solid material, almost like a tank top, but the top portion is see-through and has little pearls all over it. Next, she adds a navy pencil skirt. She looks the epitome of professional and sexy. I'm unsure how she's able to combine them both so seamlessly, but that is exactly what she manages. Her hair and makeup is already done, so she doesn't need to bother with either.

When she's finished getting dressed, I hold the earrings out to her.

"Which ones?" I ask.

She plucks the chain teardrops from my palms and extends them out to me. While I'm putting those in my ears, she skirts around me to her collection and grabs something else, and fastens it around my neck. I reach up to touch it, and frown at the simplicity. It's just a small chain, but before I can comment, something settles in the middle of my back, and I realize it's basically a backward necklace.

"What am I wearing?" She grabs the pendant and holds it over my shoulder to show me. It's the symbol for woman on Earth, and I wonder if it means the same here. "Does that mean female here too?" She smiles and nods, and I'm surprised.

"Okay. You're all set. Gods, you look like a queen with that braided crown." She winks at me, and my stomach bottoms out at her words.

I'm unsure if she knows exactly who I am or not. That comment could be totally innocent, or it could mean that she knows I'm related to the king. Either way, her saying I look like a queen makes me uncomfortable. What if the king takes it that way too and thinks that I've made up my mind about everything? I still haven't had time to process it all, or to decide what I'm actually going to end up doing. I'm still pissed at him for this morning, and am unsure how to act at this dinner. And I'm sure Alexei will be there as well. Before I know it, I'm starting to hyperventilate.

"Hey, what's wrong?" Pearl asks me, and I want to brush it off and pretend I'm fine, but the words get stuck in my throat as my panic sets in. It's then that a dazzling aura surrounds her, and even in my anxious state, I can't help but notice how beautiful she is. I have the urge again to want to do things for her. "Will you take a deep breath for me?" she asks me, her voice taking on even more of that melodic quality. I nod, doing as she says. "Good," she praises, and I soak it up. "Take some more and keep looking at me, okay?" I nod again, breathing in and out deeply. My heart rate starts to slow. "Calm down for me," she keeps instructing. Finally, I'm almost back to normal, and I realize she was able to get past my mental shields. I slam them up, and she gives me a small smile.

"Thank you," I tell her sincerely, grateful she was able to pull me out of my panic, even if I'm disappointed she was able to get past my barriers.

"You're welcome. Feeling better?" I nod. "Well, at least now we know what you need to work on with your shields. I was able to get through them with your panic. My theory is that when you are experiencing strong emotions, you don't think about it, and therefore don't notice when someone is attempting to get past them."

"I'm sure you're right. Come on. We should go or we're going to be late."

I don't actually know if it's true or not, but I don't want her asking why I was panicking, and it's the perfect opportunity to steer the conversation away from me, even if the thing we're about to go do is why I'm so anxious. She nods all the same, taking my hand and leading me out the door. We loop our arms together like school kids, and I'm almost tempted to skip down the long hallways. I smile to myself at the image, and can already tell that Pearl and I will end up becoming close.

"So, who's all going to be at this dinner? Do you know?"

"Well, I wasn't originally supposed to be here, but I begged the king to let me come, and I know you don't know me well yet, but it's *really* difficult to say no to me." She smiles innocently, and I bust out laughing, knowing she's probably the least innocent person around. "And then the king, obviously, and then I think Alexei and the advisor Mordecai."

Thank God Pearl is going to be there, otherwise it would probably be the worst dinner in the world.

We approach the doors for the dining room that we were in this morning, and I take a deep breath before we enter. I have to remember that I'm angry with them. I have to hold on to it. I do *not* want to be the one who caves with either of them, because I know that if I do it will set the precedent for how future interactions go between us. So I grip on to that emotion with all that I have, pushing away any awkwardness, hold my head high like the queen Pearl says I look like, and strut through the door.

The king has yet to arrive, but Alexei and his father are here. My eyes meet Alexei's across the room, and pain and conflict swirl in them before they ignite with so much lust as he takes in my appearance that I fear I'm going to burn up from it. I break eye contact, not wanting the guilt to bubble up over standing my ground or to see the want in his eyes, and harden my heart. I'm starting to understand, especially after talking to Pearl, but I still can't keep getting jerked around like this.

My eyes slide to his father, and I fight a cringe. Something about this man gives me the creeps. I can't put my finger on it. It's not his looks, because he is one handsome man. He's basically a carbon copy of Alexei, but more put together. No beard, short slicked-back hair, no scar, pristine clothing. No, it's not his looks. He locks eyes with me, giving me a smile like a spider, and I'm caught in his web. I fight down a shiver.

"Ember, how lovely to see you again, dear." He walks up to me, grabbing my hand and kissing the back of it. I smile back politely, but inside I'm cringing and trying not to wipe the back of my hand on my skirt. "I trust you enjoyed your afternoon?"

"I did, thank you. I actually made good friends with Pearl here." I gesture to her, hoping that it will get his attention off of me.

I open up my senses to see if I can discover anything about him. I find strong mental shields in place, and I huff in frustration. I attempt to get past them, but they are surprisingly resilient. No matter how I try, I can't sneak in. He must keep them up all the time in order for them to be this impenetrable, and I wonder what he's hiding.

"Oh, how wonderful." He turns his leering gaze to her, and even though I'm grateful to not be the center of his attention anymore, I'm sorry that Pearl is now getting the brunt of it.

She, however, takes it all in stride, not looking fazed in the least, and I remember that she probably has dealt with him more often than not because of their positions.

"Advisor," she says, addressing him. She's definitely not rude, but the bubbly personality that I've come to know today is nowhere to be found. It's obvious that she does not care for him.

The door at the other end of the room opens, and the king strolls in. We all bow, but he doesn't pay attention to anyone else besides me.

"Rise," he says quickly. "Ember, you will sit next to me tonight."

I grind my teeth at having to follow his orders and not getting a choice in where I sit. He doesn't direct where anyone else needs to be, and I'm thankful that Pearl takes the seat next to me. I'm also lucky that Alexei takes the seat across from me, and even though I'm upset with him and intend to ignore him for the duration of the evening, I'm glad I don't have to be across from his father.

"How was your afternoon, Ember?" King Stavros addresses me again.

"Fine, thank you" is all I say.

His brows furrow. "What did you do?"

"I trained for a little while, and then went back to my room and took a nap before I had the pleasure of meeting Pearl." I smile at her genuinely. I'm so happy that she's here with me.

"How did training go? Did you help her out, Alexei?"

I scowl at both of them. It's like he's cutting me out of the conversation and talking about me as if I'm not here. Plus, he's insinuating that I need *help.* Or maybe I'm just pissy and reading too much into things. Probably that.

"It went well. She's getting more adept in all of the combat skills I'm teaching her."

"So, she's improving?"

"Excuse me," I butt in. "*She* has a name, and is sitting right here, thank you very much." I can hear Pearl's sharp intake of breath next to me, but I don't give a shit.

The king's eyes widen in surprise, and I doubt that anyone has talked to him like this since my mother. The thought makes me sad. I wish I could've known her, and from the sounds of it, we're quite a bit alike. He takes it all in stride, a smile barely peeking through at me.

"My apologies, Ember. How do *you* feel your training is going?"

I take a deep breath to rein in my temper. "It's going well, in my opinion. I was able to hit the center of the target today for the first time, and I also took Alexei to the ground," I say smugly. I sneak a glance at him, and his eyes heat at the memory and a slight smile graces his perfect lips.

The king speaks up before I can get lost in his gaze. "Well, that doesn't happen very often." He nudges Alexei, who smirks at him.

"No, it certainly doesn't. If I didn't know any better I would say he lost on purpose. It would certainly be a good excuse to get underneath her," Mordecai teases, winking at his son. The statement makes me see red. I'm about to say something when both the king and Alexei cut in at the same time.

"I never hold back with Ember. She accomplished that all on her own," Alexei defends me.

"That's enough out of you, Mordecai," my father spits; the "getting underneath her" comment was apparently not appreciated.

"My apologies. I meant no offense, Your Majesty," Mordecai says, bowing his head, but I can see right through him. I barely know him and I can tell he's a fucking *snake*.

"So, where's your wife, Mordecai?" I ask, even though I know he never married.

"I never found someone I wanted to spend my life with."

"Oh, is that it? I figured it would've been along the lines of not finding someone who would put up with your misogynistic bullshit," I say with a sweet ass smile on my face. I bat my eyelashes innocently for good measure.

I watch the rage take over his face, but before he can respond, the king laughs boisterously.

"Someone to finally give you a run for your money, old friend," the king says, amusement dripping from his words. "Mordecai is usually the one to tease everyone else, but he rarely gets a taste of his own medicine."

Mordecai quickly throws up a mask of amused indifference. Pearl catches my eye next to me and gives me a look that's part delight, part shock, and part worry. I smile back, giving her a wink. After that, things are fairly tame. Everyone eats their meal, the men talking about stupid political stuff that is of no interest to me. They're discussing other important people who need to be schmoozed or met with.

I rein in the urge I've had since I got here not to scarf everything down, and considering we're dining in the royal palace, the food here is fucking delicious. So is the wine, and I quickly make my way through multiple glasses. I should probably be careful so that I don't end up making an ass of myself, but then I remember that I don't care what anyone here thinks because I'm still pissed, and have another glass.

By the time dessert is served, I'm fairly buzzed, and I start forgetting about why I'm so upset with everyone. I lock eyes with Alexei across from me, and before I can help myself, I'm eye-fucking him. A blush rises to my cheeks, and I bite my lip. His gaze immediately locks on my mouth and his eyes heat.

"So, Ember, when are you going to be heading back home?" Mordecai asks, clearly ready to be rid of my company.

"Well, I don't have any plans of returning to Earth anytime soon. As long as the king is okay with me staying?" I ask, looking at my father.

His eyes light up and he gives me a genuine smile. "I would like for you to stay for as long as you wish."

I return his grin, letting go of some of my anger. I have to remember that things here are different than on Earth, and there's a lot about this realm that I don't understand, or that may not make sense to me. I also don't know him that well yet, and there are probably a good many things that he can't share with me, or doesn't trust me enough with yet. I mean, I barely know the man. Hopefully we will get to the point where we can actually discuss things, and where we're comfortable sharing more and more with each other.

"How wonderful," Mordecai says with the fakest smile I've ever seen on anyone's face. "Well, as stimulating as this dinner has been, I think I'm going to retire for the evening." He stands, bows to the king, and takes his leave.

That prompts the rest of us to turn in for the night as well, but before I can leave, Stavros grabs my arm, gently stopping me.

"Will you join me for breakfast tomorrow? Just the two of us?" I notice that he's asking me this time instead of ordering me.

I nod. "I'll be here."

"Until tomorrow, then." I bow and head back to my room, not hating the idea of spending more time with him.

Chapter 17

I'm standing in my closet, wishing I had more outfit choices. I need to talk to Humphrey about expanding my wardrobe. I mean, I've never been a woman who had a *huge* closet, but I do like clothes, and I like to have options, and ever since I arrived in this realm, there hasn't been much for me to choose from. That was fine on the road when I didn't care what I looked like most of the time, but now, in a *castle*, around a *king*, I'm starting to care.

I settle on a plain pair of black pants and a flowy olive green blouse that's a bit on the longer side. I add a brown belt around my waist, giving me more of an hourglass figure. I do simple hair and makeup, and when I'm ready, I head down to the dining room to meet with Stavros. I know he's my father, but considering we only met recently, I'm not too comfortable thinking of him like that yet. So for now, it's either the king or Stavros in my head.

Like the day before, the king is already here when I walk in. I bow before taking a seat next to him.

"Good morning, Ember. Did you sleep well?"

"Morning. I did, thanks. My bed is the most comfortable one I've ever slept in."

"I'm glad to hear it."

Things stall out there, and we're plunged into a bit of an awkward silence after that. While I'm not as upset as I was yesterday, I'm still not as friendly as I normally would be, and have no desire to fill the quiet.

"Have you thought any more about what you want to do?"

"What do you mean?"

"Would you be willing to let everyone know that you're my daughter? I would like to have a gala soon to announce it to the kingdom and celebrate, if you are."

"What would that mean for me? If we were to tell the kingdom I'm your daughter, would I then be pressured to take up the throne? Because I definitely don't have an answer to *that* question yet, and I know I won't for a while."

He nods understandingly. "That all makes sense, and I would never pressure you into a decision this life-altering. If we were to tell the kingdom you are my daughter, I would also notify them that as of right now no changes are being made. There will be no pressure for you to take up the throne if you decide against it. Besides, we still need to get to know each other better."

"And that will be acceptable? I figured that because I'm your sole heir that I would be forced to take it if we acknowledge the fact to the rest of the kingdom."

"Normally, that would be the case, but as these are special circumstances, I will make sure to notify everyone that just because you are my daughter, that does not automatically mean you have to take over."

"Well, in that case, I would be honored for you to make the announcement," I tell him, a genuine smile gracing my face, and he beams in response.

"Excellent. I will get preparations underway for the ball, then, and we can make it official."

I nod and start eating.

"Now, I would also like to talk to you about yesterday."

"Yesterday?" The memory stirred a lingering pang of unease. All at once, an odd sensation washes over me, as if I'm a young child being scolded by their parent. I was familiar with that kind of reprimand from my mother, but this new experience of an absent father's lecture is distinctly different.

"Yes. We started discussing things that I wasn't quite ready to share with you yet. And I wanted to apologize," he says quietly, but sincerely.

The words hit me with such impact that I'm left speechless. All I can do is blink at him, wondering if my face is mirroring the shock I'm experiencing.

"I didn't mean to make it seem like I don't value your opinion, or to say that you're too young to understand. My words came out wrong, and I know that I made you feel inferior and naive, and I'm sorry. That was never my intention. But there *are* things that I'm not able to discuss with you that affect a lot of the situations in the realm. All I can tell you is that current circumstances, while they aren't exactly *pleasant*, are in fact for the betterment and protection of the kingdom. If we ever get to the point where you *do* take over ruling, I'll be more than happy to share those details with you, and discuss other options."

I considered that, and it was fairly close to the conclusion I had come to last night. "You're forgiven. I understand that it's different here and that there are things that you aren't able to share with me yet, or ever. Next time please explain it to me the way you did now. I'm a big girl. I can be logical."

He chuckles. "I suppose you are. I know this is no excuse, but I'm not used to people questioning me, or having to explain myself to anyone. It's going to take some practice for me. Be patient, please."

I nod. "I can do that. I want to let you know that I'm well educated back on Earth. I happen to have a firm grasp on history and how certain civilizations died out, and *why* they died out. You might want to take advantage of that knowledge. I'm aware that I don't know the history *here*, and that circumstances in Queridian are obviously very different from Earth, but that doesn't mean that the same mistakes can't be made. Something to think about. And I'm available whenever you're able to talk about what's affecting the realm if you want another opinion. Or if you want to ask about certain world events that I think would be important to understand so you don't make those same mistakes here."

"I appreciate that, Ember." He leaves it at that, and I notice he doesn't offer me any more information, or ask any questions, but that's fine. We've cleared the air, and now we both have a better understanding of each other. "So, on to more pleasant topics, how are you enjoying your time here?"

"It's been amazing. Pearl and I have already become close friends, which is a new experience for someone like me who's never quite fit into the Mortal Realm. I've never understood my misfit status, not until I arrived here."

He nods in understanding.

"And I love the palace. It's wonderful here. It's been rewarding getting to know you better." I hesitate, treading into uncharted territory. "I haven't had any sort of father figure in my life before. This is going to be a bit of a learning experience for both of us."

He chuckles again, and I'm glad that I can make him laugh. "You've got that right. I already screwed up during one of our first interactions," he teases.

"Well, I'm sure we will both have plenty more of those."

He nods in agreement.

"I'm looking forward to exploring the palace a bit more. Also, Humphrey has been exceptional. You should give him a pay raise." I think the way everyone is talking is starting to wear off on me. Since when do I use the word *exceptional*? "Which reminds me, I do have a favor to ask. I was hoping to expand my wardrobe a bit more now that I'm going to be here awhile. Humphrey brought me a selection of clothes, but it won't last me very long. Should I go shopping outside the castle? Or is there a better way to go about things?"

It's then that I remember I don't have any fucking money. I don't want to ask him for any. It's awkward, even if he is my father, and can clearly afford it.

"It's up to you. There are a few options. If you would like to go down and shop you certainly can. I'm sure you will need funds since you only have Earthly money, which I can supply you. I can also send the palace seamstress up to you and she can make you an entirely new wardrobe, although that will take a while. Perhaps you should consider purchasing some essentials in town while she's making your new items."

Wow. Have someone make an entire wardrobe for me? Custom? Never thought that would be something that would happen to me. I can't say I hate the idea, even if it makes me a bit uncomfortable.

"I would appreciate that. And I also am grateful for you offering me money, but I'm not the type of person who likes to take things without earning them. Is there anything I can do to earn the money? Some way to help out around the castle?"

He looks taken aback by my request, and I guess it's strange to him that a princess would want to work for her funds. "I'll consider the request and try to devise something suitable for you to undertake if you'd prefer, but please know that it is unnecessary."

"I would like to do something, if that's okay. Taking the money makes me uncomfortable. Plus, I like being busy. I get bored if I have nothing to do."

"Okay, well, I will let you know when I have tasks for you. In the meantime, tell any of the merchants that they can charge the palace for whatever you want to buy. I'm sure Pearl would love to go down into the city with you to shop, and she will be good to consult on different clothing options since you aren't sure of the fashions here."

"Are you saying I have bad fashion sense because I'm from Earth?" I ask, totally kidding, but the way his brows rise and his eyes widen in panic probably means that he hasn't figured out my sense of humor yet.

"No! Of course not! I only want to make sure you have everything you need."

I smile at him before I start chuckling over his reaction. "I know. I'm teasing you, Stavros."

He smiles back, his face red in embarrassment. "Yes, well, I don't get too much of that here. On a separate note, I know you're doing your combat training with Alexei, but I thought you might want to start training with me for your mental shields? Alexei's are sufficient, but you'd be hard-pressed to find someone in the kingdom who can rival mine."

"Oh. All right, then. I would appreciate it. Although, I was able to breach your defenses at breakfast yesterday when you asked for a demonstration."

"Oh, that? I wanted to see what you could do, so I weakened them significantly so that you would be able to get past them."

I don't respond for a moment. That shouldn't take me off guard, but for some reason it does.

"You can try again now if you don't believe me?" he asks, a small smirk gracing his lips.

I sense the challenge in his voice, yet I willingly take the bait. I extend out my powers to find a shield more powerful than any I've encountered before, even greater than Mordecai's formidable defenses. I employ every trick in my arsenal, and after a few relentless minutes, I exhale a breath of defeat.

"All right, fine. I guess they're pretty good." He laughs at my less-than-enthusiastic response.

"So, what do you think? Would you be willing to train with me?"

"Yes, I would. That would be greatly appreciated. I'm trying to learn everything I can."

"Ah, you get that from me, I'm afraid. It's a nice trait to have until you're overwhelmed by the amount on your plate."

I laugh because that's exactly what I'm experiencing right now, but I can't say I mind. I like being busy. It keeps my mind occupied.

"I won't be able to start training you quite yet. My next few days are fully scheduled, but maybe at the start of next week we can begin?"

"That would be wonderful," I tell him honestly.

It's a little strange, but exciting at the same time, getting to know him. For so long, a masculine influence was absent from my life, which I now realize was a void I'd always known was there, but tried not to acknowledge. It's unfamiliar terrain, but it's a path I want to take. We continue to dine in silence, an unspoken understanding shared between us. We're both in uncharted territory, but we're eager and willing to nurture this new bond. The initial awkwardness is inevitable, but the outcome will be worth it.

"So, I know you told me that you were going to marry my mother, but I have to wonder if you really would've been able to realistically with how the kingdom is, and how I'm assuming your parents were."

"Ah, yes. Well, in my young, naive brain, I was determined to. She's the love of my life to this day. And I know she would have made an exceptional queen. She was strong, determined, kind, and didn't take shit from anyone. A trait I've come to discover you share with her." He smirks at me knowingly, and I smile in return. "Truthfully, I'm unsure whether the kingdom would've accepted her or not. My parents were thoroughly against it, declaring that I shouldn't be marrying anyone who wasn't fae, especially not a human. I guess we will never know if it would've worked out or not."

"Well, what will happen if I were to become queen? Would they approve of me since I'm basically only a human?"

"I think so. You are half fae after all, and my daughter. I think they would be more welcoming because you are my potential heir."

I absorb his words, knowing my own acceptance within the kingdom isn't certain. I sense his optimism that everyone will embrace the change willingly, yet I can't help but suspect that if we choose this path, we will have our work cut out for us.

We finish our meal and reluctantly part ways. Both of us have things to do, and will only be able to see each other for breakfast and dinner. I decide to go down to the town and shop, and Pearl will be the perfect companion to accompany me. I knock on her door, and she answers.

"Hey. Want to go shopping?" I cut right to the chase.

"Yes! Give me two minutes." She slams the door in my face before I can say anything else.

I don't know what else she needs to do with herself. She already looks perfect. While I'm waiting, Alexei comes out of his room.

"Oh, hey."

"Hey," I reply.

"I was coming to see if you wanted to train today?"

"I'm about to go shopping with Pearl."

"Oh." He nods dejectedly. "Okay."

"Maybe before dinner?" I ask, not able to help myself. I can't stand that look on his face.

He immediately brightens. "I'll see you in the training ring. What are you going shopping for?"

"More clothes. Humphrey brought me some, but I figure since I'll be here for a while that I should probably have a respectable wardrobe, since I am the king's daughter and all." Pearl opens her door as I say that.

"You're the king's daughter?!" she all but yells. I wince, realizing that I probably shouldn't have announced it like that, but it's too late now. Besides, we're going to be having a ball soon to broadcast the news to the kingdom anyway, so she might as well hear it from me, here and now.

"Erm, yeah. We found that little tidbit out when I showed up and met with him for the first time." I find I'm a little nervous to see how she reacts. Will she be upset I didn't tell her? Pissed that the king has a human daughter?

"That's wonderful!" she exclaims, immediately calming my nerves. "Now the king has an heir! Oh my Gods, Ember, you're going to be queen!" With that one sentence she's brought them back full swing.

"Settle down, Pearl. One step at a time. We haven't decided anything like that yet."

"But you're the heir," she says with a confused look on her face. "Don't you want to be queen?"

"I don't know yet, Pearl. It's all a lot to take in. A month ago I didn't even know Queridian existed, let alone that I had a father here who was king of the damn realm. Right now I want to get to know him, and spend some time here. And he wants to get to know me as well. He's not going to simply give Queridian over to a woman he knows nothing about. Even if I am his daughter."

"I guess I can understand that."

"But, he wants to throw a gala and announce to the kingdom that I'm his daughter."

"Oh! That's fantastic! It's been too long since there was a ball here. Right, Alexei?" she asks him excitedly.

"There was one three months ago," he replies, clearly not sharing in Pearl's enthusiasm. Just as well. Most men seem to have that in common, no matter what realm they're from apparently.

She ignores him. "Well, we need to start planning! I bet I can convince the king to let the two of us handle it."

"You know, I did ask him if there was something I can do around here to earn the money he's giving me. This would be the perfect opportunity."

Pearl looks at me strangely. "Why do you want to be put to work? You're a princess. You don't need to earn your living here, it's part of your inheritance and your birthright."

I huff in frustration. Clearly no one here understands why this is important to me. Either way, planning the ball needs to be done, and it will definitely keep me busy. And on the plus side, I'll get to spend some quality time with Pearl and get to know her better.

"Well, either way, I need more clothes. King Stavros said I could go to town and buy some, and he's also sending the seamstress up soon so she can make me new clothing as well."

"Oh, perfect. She's exceptional at her craft and will make you the most stunning dress for the ball."

Nerves and excitement battle for dominance in my stomach. I've never been to a gala before, and certainly don't know how to act, let alone dance. I inhale sharply as that thought hits me, causing panic to spread.

"What's wrong?" both Pearl and Alexei ask at the same time.

"Am I going to be expected to dance at this thing?"

"Probably," Pearl says nonchalantly. I want to scream at her.

"I don't know how to properly dance!" I exclaim. Sure, Alexei and I shared a dance before, but it was nothing compared to the grandeur that awaits at the gathering. Not to mention the entire fucking kingdom will be watching me.

"You don't know how to dance?" Pearl asks, confused.

"Not properly. We dance on Earth, but nothing formal really."

"You did fairly well when we were in the caves," Alexei chimes in.

Pearl immediately gives him a knowing look, half smirking, half glaring at him, and I love her for it. His cheeks pink, but that's the only sign he's uncomfortable.

"Fairly well is not going to be good enough for the ball, Alexei."

Pearl nods in agreement.

"Well, I can teach you. I'm an excellent dancer."

His words cause relief to trickle in, as well as lust, and something I don't want to put a name to. I try to squash the inappropriate rush of sensations, but the thought of him holding me close, his hands on my body, even in an innocent way, makes heat flare between my legs, and I mentally slap myself to get my shit together.

"You wouldn't mind? You're already training me in practically everything," I laugh. "Although, Stavros told me he would take over my training on my mental shields, so we won't need to worry about that anymore. And Pearl has been helping me with that as well."

"I don't mind at all. Honestly, being here, there's not too much for me to do. They're already fully staffed on the guards, so I haven't had to take any of those shifts, and I don't tend to do too much business with my father, so it'll keep me occupied. Do you still have that music device? We can practice with that."

I almost laugh at him calling my speaker a music device, but nod all the same. Unfortunately, that will kill my batteries pretty quickly, but the end result will be worth it.

"When?"

"Whenever you'd like. We're combat training before dinner, but maybe after dinner?"

"Okay. I'll make sure to bring my *music device* with me to supper so we can go straight from there."

He narrows his eyes at my mocking tone, but before he can respond, I grab Pearl's hand and start walking away.

"See you soon!"

He shakes his head at me, but there's a smile on his lips.

When we're a good distance away, Pearl asks me, "What was that?"

"What?" I ask innocently.

"You two were totally flirting with each other, and now on top of already giving you combat training he's going to be teaching you to dance? That's a lot of time to be spending with him, especially when you're trying to distance yourself. *And* you'll be in close contact with each other during both activities."

"I know. It'll be fine. I'll be careful."

She gives me a look that says I'm full of shit.

"Look, I know that it's not ideal that it's Alexei, but I need to learn both of these things. I don't want to make an ass out of myself at the ball, and I need to learn how to fight. I'm not going to be defenseless ever again."

Her eyes soften at that last declaration. "Okay. Be careful. I don't want you to get your heart broken."

"I won't," I promised. "But thank you for being concerned for me. It's nice having someone to watch my back."

"As long as you watch mine." She winks at me, bumping my hip with hers.

By this time, we're leaving the palace, and the guards nod to us as we do. I observe the city with new eyes this time. When Alexei and I first came in, I was worried about meeting the king, and was overwhelmed by the enormity of the city that I didn't take everything in. This time, I'm able to notice more details, like the openness of the square, children playing in the streets and by the fountain of my father, the wonderful-smelling food (that's somehow different to the food in Twin Fangs), the crisp mountain air, and the general peace of the city. The kingdom itself may not be very united, but the cities and its residents seem content.

"So what are you looking to buy?" Pearl asks.

"I'm not sure. Primarily everyday necessities. I expect the seamstress will create my outfit for the ball, and any higher-end attire I might need, but my daily wardrobe is lacking."

She nods, leading me to a shop showcasing practical, everyday attire along with a few upscale options. There's nothing excessively extravagant. It's exactly the store I need at the moment.

As we step inside, we're greeted by a busy crowd, leaving us to our own devices as there is no one available to help us. I prefer it that way, especially with Pearl appearing to know her way around the store. We start with dresses, which is fitting considering I currently live in a castle.

We find some typical princess-like dresses. The first one is a floor-length wine-colored dress with long sleeves, a V-neck with gold detailed trim, slightly poofy shoulders, and a metal gold belt.

The second, a deep cerulean, floor-length gown, with alternating red and brown trim that circles the collar and cuts down the middle between my breasts almost down to my belly button. The blue portion of the sleeves is short, but there's a white fabric that starts where it ends, which comes down to my elbows before splitting wide and hanging on the back sides of my arms down to the wrists.

The third is by far the most bizarre. The top portion above my breasts is a forest green, the two sides overlap in the middle and come up to my throat, and it is also long sleeved. Then from the breasts down is almost a separate dress, in a dark sage. It has a sweetheart neckline that sits on top of the forest green portion, and is tightly fitted all the way to the waist, where it then flows out, the outsides stopping at the knee, but the center ends about middle of the shins. There are brown straps across the waist, under the bust, and one going from the top of my left shoulder and crossing over to my right breast where it connects to a bronze metal cup that covers only the right side of my chest. There's also a matching shoulder cap on the same side.

The fourth is fairly plain, and I probably won't start wearing it quite yet. It's more of a wintery dress, tight-fitted, gray, and thick. Of course, it's floor-length with long sleeves, since it's designed for the cold. We also managed to find a matching gray cloak with a large fur collar held together by a circle and a chain, and a thick dark brown belt to go with it.

With the dress selection out of the way, we dive into a range of more practical attire. Skirts in shades of gray, brown, and black. Simple shirts in white, brown, and black to match. The local fashion appears to lean toward layering, so we include a collection of over-tops, corsets to complement the shirts, and an array of scarves to accessorize my hips and neck. And, of course, an additional assortment of belts.

Overall, it's a successful outing, and I find my new wardrobe more to my liking. We instruct the cashier to charge everything to the palace—a deduction they had already made given Pearl's presence. They assure me the clothes will be delivered later that day, and we thank them before stepping back into the courtyard's sunlight.

"You hungry?" Pearl asks.

"Yes. I'm starving. Shopping always makes me hungry."

"Gods, me too. Let's get something to eat." She leads me over to a stall, and the man running it greets her by name and asks if she wants her usual. She replies that she wants two. I have no idea what she ordered for me, but I guess I'm about to find out.

"I take it you come down here often?" I tease. Everyone seems to know her.

"Yeah. I get cooped up in the palace and like to explore the city. Plus I love shopping and eating, so it's the perfect combination. Or maybe a dangerous combination is a better description," she chuckles.

A few minutes later, our meals are handed to us. The mouthwatering aroma is incredible. The dish resembles naan, topped with meat, peppers, onions, an unknown sauce, and sprinkles of feta cheese. We're also given a cup of warm milk complete with cinnamon on top.

After devouring my first bite, I recognize the dill sauce—a favorite of mine—and I understand Pearl's preference for the dish. Upon finishing my wrap, I take a drink of the milk, only to discover that there's also rice and sugar in it. I drink the rest and then Pearl gives me a spoon so that I can finish off the rice at the bottom.

"Holy shit. This realm is going to kill me with food. At least I'll die a happy death," I joke.

"Is the food better here than where you're from?" Pearl asks.

"Yes. So. Much. Better."

"Why do you think that is?"

"Well, I think one of the biggest reasons is that where I'm from, they add a bunch of chemicals to the food so that it doesn't go bad as quickly. It cuts down on food waste, but it's terrible for you, and as a result the food doesn't taste nearly as good."

Pearl wrinkles her nose in disgust.

"I also have a theory that because there is so much magic in this realm, it also applies to the land and the crops, making them taste more magical, if you will. Alexei also mentioned that my senses are stronger here, so I'm sure that makes a difference too."

"I would like to see Earth someday, I think," Pearl says, surprising me.

"You would? Why?"

"Because, although we have magic here, Earth has its own magic. I've heard about technology, for instance. We don't have anything like that here. It's almost like since the humans there didn't have access to magic, they used their minds to create some of their own."

"Well, maybe someday I can take you. I can show you all the fun things to do on Earth. Maybe I'll take you to a club," I muse.

"What's a club?" she asks, confused, making me giggle.

"It's kind of like a tavern, where they play loud, shitty music and everyone dances in clothes that are basically nonexistent."

"I thought you said you didn't know how to dance?"

The question makes me think of people at the ball dancing like you would in a club, and I bust out laughing.

"I wouldn't call what we do at home 'dancing.' At least not like you're used to. It's basically people swaying their hips and grinding up against each other."

"Maybe we should start incorporating that, 'cause that seems like it would be fun," she says suggestively, winking at me.

"Yes, it can be very fun. Especially when you've got a few drinks in you."

"I bet I could have a good time with a good-looking male or female like that."

My brows shoot up in surprise, although I don't know why. "Are you bisexual?" I ask, even though it's probably rude of me to do so.

"Yes. And polyamorous. Most mermaids are. We're so into beauty that we like to be with multiple partners, and don't discriminate between sexes."

"Are you in a relationship then?"

"No. I was back in Mermacovia, but then I got the job here, and we decided to end the relationship rather than continue long-distance. We ended things on good terms."

"And you haven't found anyone here who catches your eye?"

"Not yet. But it's hard in the castle. Most of the individuals who work there are older, and I'm a young soul. I need someone, or someones, who can keep up with me."

"Well, maybe you'll meet someone at the ball. Or someones as you like to put it."

Her eyes glint in excitement at the possibility. "Yes. Maybe I will."

"Do you have a dress in mind?" I ask her.

"Hell no. I'm going to have Imelda make me something new after we have a theme and color scheme sorted."

I laugh. Of course Pearl is going to have her design something only for the gala. I wonder if she'll ever wear it again after.

Our shopping excursion continues, taking us to a jewelry store next.

I'm captivated by a few pieces. A bold bronze necklace with a dark stone nestled in its center. A pair of intricate dangly earrings, a perfect complement to the necklace. And a chunky silver bracelet, still delicate because of the artful swirls etched into it.

I also spot a few pieces that remind me of Pearl's collection that I'm drawn to—arrow-shaped earrings, and a unique necklace designed to drape down the back, showcasing a crescent moon and a star at its base.

As we're preparing to leave, one more item catches my eye and I'm instantly obsessed—a circular brooch with a wicked-looking dagger descending from the center. It's an addition I can't resist.

The last of our shopping done, we head back to the castle. Pearl and I part ways, promising to meet up tomorrow to start planning the ball. Although, now that I think about it, I still haven't run this by the king. Oh well. I'll bring it up to him at dinner.

I change into some practical clothes and head down to the training ring. Alexei isn't here yet, but that's fine with me. I want to practice a bit on my own before he arrives, so I'll be warmed up, and hopefully show improvement. I start with some deep breathing and warmup exercises.

When my heart is pumping, I move into the various hand-to-hand combat techniques he's shown me, flowing from one to the other. Once I feel more confident in my movements, I step up to the fighting mannequins and replicate the moves. The satisfaction of striking a tangible object offers me a sense of how a genuine fight would feel.

After about thirty to forty-five minutes, I'm thoroughly winded, but I'm noticing a definite improvement of my skills and techniques. It's been different here in the castle because Alexei and I haven't been able to train as much as we did on the road, but I'm still noticing a difference. I take a break, get a drink of water, and then pick up my bow and arrow. I use the one that's the most comfortable for me, but once I'm in the groove, I decide to switch it up to get more practice with different weapons, like Alexei suggested a while back. I take aim, breathe, and release. It hits the third ring, and I curse under my breath. I pick up another arrow and go again. After ten minutes or so, I finally hit the bull's-eye and whoop with excitement. Since no one's around, I do a little happy dance.

I exchange my bow with a heavier, bulkier version. I'm already grunting at the weight, and know this won't be enjoyable, but who said training would be fun? Oh, that's right—every bullshit movie or book scene that made this seem easy. The reality is far from it, but at least there is noticeable progress. My newly developed strength allows me to hold the bow steady without feeling like I'm going to drop it.

I nock an arrow and take my stance. My deltoid is straining at the weight, but holds firm without a hint of the quiver that used to seize it when I was a newbie. I draw the string back, immediately noticing that it carries more tension than my previous bow. Hopefully I have enough strength to take a more powerful shot. This time when I release, the arrow hits one of the outer rings, but the *thwack* it makes upon impact is louder than any of my previous attempts, confirming the increased power. I reload, release, repeat. After who knows how long, I'm finally back where I started with the first bow, hovering on the line between the second and third rings. Not bad.

"You're using a larger bow," Alexei says as he comes up behind me. "And handling it well, from what I can see."

I beam at the praise. "I thought I would come down a little early and see what I could do with this bad motherfucker," I reply, gesturing to the monstrous weapon still in my grip.

"It's good that you're practicing with different bows. And you'll be surprised how much easier it will be when you go back to your old, lighter bow."

"I want to practice shooting while I'm riding Ash soon. Do you think

I'm ready?"

"Not quite, but you're getting close. Once you can hit the bull's-eye regularly with that 'bad motherfucker,' as you call it, we'll talk."

I nod.

"So, daggers?" he asks.

I put the bow down before grabbing an astonishing set of daggers. They have dark, nearly black blades with a decorative design on them, a dainty curved dark brown cross guard, and ivory grips. I'm slightly tempted to take these for myself. Alexei sees me admiring them.

"Gorgeous, aren't they?"

I nod in agreement. "I want them."

"Take them. You should have weapons of your own anyway, and it's not like the palace is short on blades. Plus, you basically own them since you're the princess." He winks at me.

I try not to react. I truly do, but that sexy look in his eyes coupled with the wink sends heat straight to my core. I turn around before he can notice my reaction.

"So, what are we working on today?" I ask, wanting to distract myself.

"Well, actually, before we start with them, I want to demonstrate something essential when using daggers." He goes back over to the weapons table and finds two holsters. He hands me one and takes the other. "Put that one on your left leg."

Before I start to follow his instructions, he kneels in front of me, causing my breath to catch, and starts putting the other one on my right leg. I shake off my shock quickly, not wanting him to see how much that simple sight and touch is affecting me, and attach the other one. The only outward sign of my affectedness is that my hands are shaking. As we stand upright, both sheaths secured, he hands me my daggers, gesturing for me to tuck them in their respective holsters on the outsides of my thighs. With the blades firmly in place, a feeling of fulfillment washes over me as if these weapons were destined to be part of me my entire life. Almost like I haven't been fully complete without them, and I wonder if every species in this realm is the same way in that regard, or if it's a sign that I'm meant to be a warrior. Although, every woman is a warrior in her own right.

"So, today I want to demonstrate the easiest and most effective way to attack your opponent with daggers." He positions me, one foot slightly in front of the other, knees bent, right hand in front of my face and forward slightly. He then takes a step back from me. "What I want you to do is try to slap me across the face."

My eyes widen in surprise. I did not expect that.

He continues talking before I can attempt it. "But I want you to really focus on the area of your body you move first. So this time I positioned us far enough away that you'll need to step in order to get to me. Be very conscious to move only your feet first."

I nod. I wait, trying to throw him off a bit. Before I can overthink it, I step forward and reach out my hand, but Alexei leans back in plenty of time to avoid my strike. He smiles knowingly, and the urge to slap him gets stronger. Good thing this exercise allows me to.

He moves a little bit closer to me. "Now, this time, concentrate on moving your torso first. You don't need to step forward since we're close enough."

I wait again, and after a long ass time, I lean forward, only to miss him by an inch or so.

"Good." He moves even closer so he's standing right in front of me. "Now, move your hand first."

Instead of waiting this time like he expects me to, I whip my hand out, hard and fast, and even though he attempts to dodge the blow, it strikes true. The stinging slap fills the space between us, and a bright red handprint blooms on his cheek. But even though I slapped the shit out of him, he has a huge smile on his face, causing one to rise on mine as well.

"Nicely done. The whole point of this was to demonstrate that you will always be quicker with your hands than your feet or body, especially if you're in close contact like this. So, when you're working with daggers, you should always be striking with your hands first, feet and torso following, otherwise your opponent will almost always be able to dodge your blows."

Next, we practice with the blades, both the offensive and defensive moves that he's already taught me, with the occasional new one thrown in.

By the end of the lesson, I'm sweating and all my muscles are aching.

"Pick up the bow again. The heavy one," he tells me, and I groan.

I thought we were done. But then again, I did this to myself by coming here early. It's good though. I'm building my stamina. I do as he says, and my shoulder screams in protest, but I push past it. I slot an arrow and line it up, remembering to breathe. My arm is shaking, but I focus my aim, not letting my fatigue get the better of me. I pull the arrow back as far as I can, and release on my exhale. It hits the second ring, and it's the closest I've gotten with this bow. I smile at my success but refuse to celebrate until I hit the center. I keep shooting, waiting for Alexei to either stop me or to hit the bull's-eye. I'm not disappointed. After twenty minutes, I finally achieve it. I drop my bow on the weapons table and jump up and down after yelling "Yes!" and pumping my fist in the air. "Take that, you bad motherfucker!"

Alexei chuckles behind me. "You sure showed him, didn't you?"

"Damn straight!" I make sure to maintain my distance with him so we don't have a repeat of the last time. "Well, on that note, I think I'm going to head to my room."

"Oh no you don't. Hand to hand. Now."

I shouldn't like his bossy tone, but I find myself picturing him telling me what to do in the bedroom, and I can't help but flush in response.

But then reality pulls me back. He's insisting on continued training despite my absolute exhaustion. His gaze on me is challenging, as though he's expecting me to object. I know he would relent if I felt like I couldn't continue, but I want to defy his expectations. I want to prove to myself that I can keep going even when I'm dead on my feet.

"All right, let's do this."

Surprise and pride flare in his eyes before he comes at me. I block and duck, swinging my leg out to try to knock him off his feet. He's prepared for it and easily sidesteps me before attacking again. He comes at me again and again, and while my defense is holding up, I'm getting more and more frustrated that I can't land a hit.

"You're better than this, Ember. Hit me."

I growl at his words. Legit growl. I'm tired and fed up and frustrated.

"Or are you too tired, little doe? Do you need to stop?" He asks me like I'm a child, only angering me further.

"Fuck you."

"You'd like to," he taunts, smirking at me, making me snarl and bare my teeth.

I've gone full animal, and I don't give two shits as I feel the surge of adrenaline pumping through my body to give me renewed strength.

Instead of continuously countering his blows, I go on the offensive, shoving him farther and farther back as I advance. He blocks every single thing I throw at him. It dawns on me that he knows all of my moves because he taught them to me. He can tell how I'm going to counter, how I'm going to attack. I come up with a quick plan. Since we've been practicing together for a while now, I also know some of his moves. I know that when I swing my right leg out to knock him off his feet, he dodges back and then presses forward on the same side while I'm standing back up.

I wait for the opportune moment, the one where I typically *would* execute that move he's anticipating. Finally the opportunity arises, and I position myself, pretending to launch the anticipated action. But as he retreats, I shoot forward, snapping my fist straight into his face. I hear a crack, and his nose starts spilling blood. I gasp in horror.

"Oh my God, Alexei, are you okay? I'm so sorry."

"Ember, I'm fine. You did great! I was trying to get you to finally land a hit. You needed to be worked up properly."

I take in his words, and I smile despite how angry I was moments ago. That smile fades when I look at him to see more blood leaking out of his nose.

"Alexei, I think I broke your nose."

"You sure did, little doe. I'm so proud of you."

"Enough about me! We need to get you to a doctor."

"What's a doctor?" he asks, making me laugh.

"Someone to take care of you when you have something medically wrong with you."

"Oh. We have healers here. They will have this fixed in five minutes flat. Nothing to worry about."

"Okay, well, let's go, then."

"You don't need to come with me. Why don't you get some rest before dinner? All teasing aside, I know you trained hard today, and you must be exhausted."

"We didn't do that much more than we normally do."

"True. But I saw you when you came here, and know that you trained quite a bit before I showed up."

"You were watching me?" I ask, horrified and embarrassed. I was acting as if no one was around. I did a happy dance! Although, this isn't the first time he's seen it, so it's not that big of a deal.

"Yes. I've been waiting for you to start training on your own. It's how I knew you were ready to take things to the next level today. I had to make sure you were properly motivated." He makes it sound as if I wasn't motivated before this.

"We're getting off track. I injured you, and I don't care how tired I am, I am going to come with you to get it fixed. End of story, Alexei."

He looks a little surprised by my vehemence. "Very well, then." He leads the way back into the castle, heading to an area that I've never been in before. "This is the healer's wing," he explains.

It's nothing like I anticipated. I was expecting something like a hospital, but instead, the hallways are wide and full of windows, which allows sunlight to stream into the space. There's no chemical smell at all, only a hint of herbs, like when we were in the caves.

We step into a room with walls practically built entirely of windows, several of them ajar, allowing the sound of the nearby falls' cascade to fill the air. A woman strides in, her appearance severe and imposing. Her brown hair is pulled into an impressively tight bun, accentuating her heavily pointed ears. She appears middle-aged, but from how slowly everyone seems to age here, I know she must be ancient. She doesn't acknowledge us as we arrive, engrossed in her own activities, although I'm certain she's well aware of our presence.

"Good afternoon, Agatha," Alexei says when he's tired of waiting on her.

"Alexei. I see you somehow managed to damage that charming face of yours again," she says sarcastically, disdain dripping from her voice.

Wow. I wonder if all elves have this attitude, or only her. Or maybe she doesn't like Alexei?

"Only so we can have these moments together." I know he's goading her, but I cut in before she can reply.

"I'm afraid that's my fault. We were sparring and I managed to get him on the nose," I say apologetically.

She turns to face me, scrutinizing me closely and apparently finding me lacking. "Ah yes, the *human girl*," she sneers. "Well, thank you for burdening me with more work."

At that moment, it becomes clear that her distaste isn't exclusive to

Alexei. She appears to harbor disdain for everyone.

"You're just as pleasant as always, aren't you, Agatha?" Alexei comments, and I have to hold back a laugh at the look she gives him.

"Sit down." She gestures to a comfortable-looking bed. "And don't bleed on anything," she says sternly before walking away.

"She's great with people," I remark.

"Pretty much all elves are like that." Well that answers that question.

"That's very strange. I would assume they're all caring and compassionate since they, you know, *care* for people."

He guffaws. "You'd think so, but it is definitely the opposite. Maybe because they're always taking care of everyone else, they've lost that piece of themselves that feels any sympathy."

We stop talking when we hear Agatha coming back in. She sets some things down on the bed next to him before standing before him and tilting his head up so she can assess the damage. I try not to blink so I don't miss the magic. She brings her thumb up and grazes it down his nose. He hisses through his teeth, and then his nose is straight, but pouring more blood.

"Why is it bleeding more? I thought you healed it," I ask, instantly filled with regret when she looks at me as if I'm stupid.

"The nose always bleeds after being reset." That's the only explanation she gives me as she shoves a cloth at Alexei's face.

He holds it up to his nose, stopping the blood before it drips onto the bed and earns him a reprimand from Agatha. She puts some salve on his nose and cheeks, presumably to help with swelling and bruising, before sending us on our way.

"See, little doe? No big deal. All fixed up, and my pretty face will be back to normal by dinner. So why don't you go get showered and try to get some rest before then?" I huff, but nod as we make our way toward our rooms.

"So, we're still on for tonight after dinner?" I double-check.

"For what?" he asks me, although he has a bit of a glint in his eye.

"Alexei Dreymonde, why are you teasing me so much today?"

"I don't know what you mean." He's full of shit because that glint is in full force in both eyes now, and there's a smirk pulling at his lips.

"Fine. I'll see you for dinner." I turn and walk into my room, but before I can slam the door I hear him call out to me.

"Don't forget to bring your music device."

I roll my eyes and shut my door before heading for the shower.

Chapter 18

I take a nap after my shower. Alexei is right, today's rigorous training session coupled with my shopping trip has sapped my energy. I collapse on the bed and am asleep within minutes. No dreams visit me, but I swear I can hear the ethereal voices of my mothers whispering to me again.

Beware of the snake.

Hours later, I wake to someone knocking on my door.

"Ember! It's time for dinner. Hurry up!" Pearl's yelling on the other side. I open it, and she looks at me in horror. "Girl, what are you doing? You aren't ready at all and we're supposed to be downstairs for dinner any minute now."

"Shit. I fell asleep after training with Alexei this afternoon, and I guess I overslept."

I'm thankful my new clothes were delivered before I returned from training. I quickly rummage through them, choosing the blue dress I found earlier today. I slip it on and swiftly style my hair in a diagonal braid that drapes over one shoulder. It's quick, simple, and elegant.

As I attend to my hair, Pearl does my makeup quickly but efficiently, and within five minutes I'm ready to go, appearing as polished as if I spent a half an hour getting ready. I grab my phone and speaker before leaving, and we hurry out of the room.

We waltz into the dining room precisely on time, earning a sly smile from Pearl. I return her grin, feeling like we pulled one over on everyone. Unfortunately, Mordecai is present again, or, as I've started to call him in my mind, "Moldy Mordy." Despite the lust evident in his gaze—which thoroughly creeps me out—there's also unmistakable disdain etched in every line of his face. I know without a shadow of a doubt that his animosity matches my own for him.

Unable to resist, I flash him a taunting smile and a little wave. I'm aware I'm poking the beast, but I can't help it. I want him to know his facade doesn't fool me. The look on his face swiftly morphs into one of polite indifference, all prior emotion cleverly concealed.

"You're looking well rested, Miss Ember."

I know he's trying to insult me, but I paste on a sweet as pie smile.

"Thank you. I had to take a nap after your son wore me out this afternoon. He thought I couldn't keep up, but I proved him wrong. Didn't I, Alexei?"

Alexei chokes on his wine and his face turns red, but he takes it all in stride.

"You did. She broke my nose in training this afternoon," he comments, completely skipping over my sexual innuendo.

The king arrives in that moment, and he laughs loudly, pride glowing in his eyes. "Is that right?"

"Sure is. And she hit the bull's-eye with the biggest bow we had in the training yard."

If possible, the king's eyes grow even wider. "Well, if I didn't know you were my daughter before, that would do it."

That gets my attention. "Are you skilled at combat?"

"Of course. But shooting was always my specialty."

I smile at the connection we've found between us. The moment is interrupted as a bevy of servants flood the room, bringing a spread of food with them. As soon as they set it down, I pile my plate high. The intense training earlier today has left me famished, and although I am always careful not to overeat in the king's presence, I do allow myself to eat more quickly than I normally would. Alexei sees everything and gives me a knowing smile.

I've noticed the cuisine in the Immortal City more closely resembles the food in Greece, whereas in Twin Fangs, the food was more similar to medieval fare. I'm suddenly curious about what the food is like in other territories. I believe it's natural that each territory would have its own unique cuisine, influenced by the local geography, culture, and even history. The archaeologist in me hums at the thought.

When my plate is empty, I turn to my father. "So, I thought of something I could do to earn my keep like we talked about earlier. Pearl and I would like to plan the upcoming gala."

"Oh, wonderful! I'm sure you'll add some interesting details since you're from Earth and will think of things that we won't. Pearl, we will need to invite everyone important from all the territories."

"I know, Sire. I have the list already." She smiles kindly at him.

"Of course you do. And I'm sure you already have everything planned in your head as well," he says fondly, and I have an irrational moment of jealousy. "Oh, also, just to notify you all, the mimic ambassador told me yesterday that he will be retiring. I have already selected a new one, and he will be traveling here from the Everchanging Glades next week. He should arrive in time for the ball."

"Is he going to be another old man who I have nothing in common with?" Pearl complains next to me.

"Actually, no. He's thirty and his name is Xanto."

Pearl's eyes gleam in excitement. Before the conversation can continue, Humphrey comes in quickly, leaning down to whisper in the king's ear.

"Your Majesty, there's an urgent matter that requires your attention."

"What is it, Humphrey?"

"There have been more disappearances. From all the territories."

The king's expression shutters as he suddenly stands. "Forgive me, but I have things to attend to."

Mordecai follows him, and suddenly it's only the three of us at the table.

"Do either of you know about these disappearances?" I ask.

Pearl shakes her head. Instead of answering, Alexei doesn't meet my eyes. I zero in on him.

"Have there been more?" I ask him, not bothering to pretend I don't know that he knows.

"Ember, I'm not supposed to talk about it."

"It's just the three of us here. What harm could it do? Besides, we all heard Humphrey."

From the look on his face he knows I'm not going to let this go. "Fine. Yes, there have been others."

"From all over?"

"Yes."

I sigh in frustration. I wish he would tell me what he knows instead of giving me the bare minimum.

"The same from each territory? Or some territories more than others? Are there patterns? Older, younger, women, men?"

"They're not discriminating on who they're taking. And there's about the same number going missing from each territory."

"How long has this been happening?" Pearl asks.

"A while. It started out so small that they didn't even notice a pattern at first. But it's been steadily increasing over the years."

"Is it possible that these individuals are traveling to Earth? Maybe trying to escape or something?" I ask.

"No. First of all, many of them had lives and families. They didn't take anything with them, or tell anyone anything. Second of all, all entrances to the portals are heavily guarded, as you well know, and they would have to provide a permit before being allowed to enter the portal."

"Do they go missing at separate times?"

"No. There's always a group taken from each territory within a day of each other."

"So that means there's multiple people involved in this. Unless it's a vampire and they're teletraveling to all the territories. Although that couldn't be the case either because you can't take anyone with you when you do that."

"They wouldn't be able to anyway even if we were. At least they wouldn't be able to get to Mystic Mountain. There are wards around it that prevent teletraveling, unless you're very special and have permission to do that. But I think the only one who can is the vampire ambassador."

"You don't have permission?"

"No. Otherwise I would have teletraveled here to the king directly when you came through the portal instead of having us travel all the way across the country. Plus, there are few vampires who are strong enough to teletravel that far."

"Well, we definitely know it's a group then as opposed to one person."

"It would have to be," Alexei agrees.

"Wait, you said there are wards around Mystic Mountain?" He nods. "How did they do that?"

"Do you remember our earlier conversation about base magic?"

I nod in affirmation.

"As it turns out, the fae have access to all our records of it, housed in the Epitome Athenaeum. However, only the royals and those who have been granted special permission can access that information. At some point one of the royals discovered a spell to create wards around the city, and they've been in place ever since."

I digest all of that. It seems incredibly selfish of the fae and the royals to hoard crucial information. It should be a right, not a privilege, for everyone to have access to base magic if they possess the ability. Besides, the withholding of this information deprives the rest of the population of valuable knowledge. And all for what? Power? Ridiculous.

"But enough heavy talk. Are you ready for your dance lessons?"

I nod, standing up.

"Can I come watch?" Pearl asks, and I cringe.

"Sure," Alexei says before I can tell her hell no. "I could use the extra help so I can demonstrate."

The three of us head to the ballroom, and it's as opulent as I remember. This room isn't in use regularly, so there will be no staff around to see me make an ass out of myself. I turn my speaker and phone on and look through my music, trying to figure out what we're most likely to hear at the ball. I enjoy classical music so I select that playlist and scroll until I find the soundtrack to *Pride & Prejudice*, since there's quite a bit of dancing in that movie.

"Watch first. I'll teach you the steps, and then you and I can try." Alexei pulls Pearl into his arms, and I tamp down another flare of jealousy.

They look so good together it's unreal. Before I can think too much about it, they're gracefully swirling around the dance floor. I try to watch their feet, but it's difficult to keep up with their pace. The song ends, and they break apart before Alexei motions me over to him.

I stand next to him as he demonstrates the steps. I follow slowly, occasionally missing steps, but eventually I'm able to grasp the basic steps reasonably well. This time Alexei pulls *me* into his arms, and I can't help but think of us dancing in the abandoned palace. We lock eyes, and I can tell he's thinking the same thing. His gaze dips to my mouth, and I lick my lips in anticipation, although I know by now that he's never going to do anything about this attraction between us.

"I can help guide you from behind!" Pearl exclaims, breaking the tension between us. I know she did it on purpose, for which I'm equally grateful and resentful. She puts her hand on my upper back and her other hand on the hip that Alexei isn't holding.

"This is just like *Dirty Dancing*," I laugh, the scene popping into my head.

"What?" Pearl asks.

"This isn't *dirty*," Alexei says at the same time.

"Ughh. You guys don't get *any* of my references. It's so frustrating."

They give each other a perplexed look, but then the next song starts and we move. It's a little sloppy at first, and there are definitely a few times where I fumble and step on Alexei's feet, but they're both patient with me.

After an hour or so, I have reasonably mastered the steps, and we stop. "So, that's the easiest of our dances. It's called the Whisper. I'll teach you as much as I can before the ball."

Of course there are more and not simply this one. And of course this is the easiest of all of them. Jesus.

"Will you show us how you dance on Earth? Like at one of those clubs you were telling me about?" I laugh loudly, but agree. This will be too good to pass up.

Before I change the music though, I decide if we're going to do this, then we need to have the whole vibe. I have Alexei grab us a bottle of liquor while Pearl and I blow out half the candles so it's nice and dark like a club would be.

"Is this all really necessary?" Pearl asks me.

"Well, you can't dance like this with a ton of lighting and no liquid courage. Trust me."

Alexei finally returns with some whiskey, and all of us take shots right out of the bottle. When we start getting a buzz, I head back to my phone and find another playlist called "Dance." I turn the volume waaaaay up, and both Alexei and Pearl flinch as the music starts. The first song to come on is "Cheap Thrills" by Sia.

I stand in between them and start moving my hips and swaying to the music. They both look at me strangely and don't move. I fight the urge to stop, and instead wrap my arms around Alexei's neck. I start grinding myself against him, and he reluctantly starts moving with me. I beam at him before untangling one of my hands and grabbing Pearl and pulling her close behind me. I rub my ass against her pelvis until she starts moving with me too. Soon, the three of us are dancing together, and wouldn't you know it, it actually starts feeling like a club.

The next song to come on is "She Wolf" by Shakira, and I laugh, thinking of Shakira as a mimic. By this time, the two of them are more comfortable and moving on their own without my guidance. I snag the whiskey bottle from Alexei and drink another couple shots. I pass them the bottle, and the booze seems to help them loosen up a bit more.

A classic comes on next. "Beat It" by good ole MJ. It's strange to me that they know none of this music. Music that my entire world knows is not something that they've ever heard before. Until now, that is.

Throughout the evening we drink more whiskey, dance more, listen to more classics until they're both moving freely, enjoying the natural rhythm of our bodies. The three of us sway in sync, grinding and rubbing until we're panting, sweaty, drunk, and honestly excited too. Every rub of my nipples against Alexei's chest shoots heat straight to my core, and every grasp of his hands on my hips makes me wish we didn't have clothes on, especially when the evidence of how much he likes this too is pressed firmly against me.

Then there's Pearl. I don't know if it's the alcohol or the camaraderie between us, but having her behind me is almost equally as thrilling. I've never been with a woman, but I can see the appeal in her gentle caresses of my shoulders and back. I turn to look at her, wrapping my arm up and around behind her head, and find her glowing softly, making my breath leave me in the wake of her incredible gift. She smiles seductively, as if she knows what the sight of her lit up like a star does to me. The three of us are about to cross some arbitrary line, and I'm not sure if it's a good idea or not. The liquor, music, and general fun we're having is clouding my senses, but I don't have it in me to care right now. My eyes lock on to Pearl's lips, and as she starts leaning in and Alexei's hands tighten on my body, pulling me closer, the door bangs open.

"What's going on here?" the king booms.

We all jump apart guiltily, and I quickly head over to my phone, shutting off the music.

"What's the meaning of this?"

"I was teaching Ember how to dance for the ball," Alexei says quietly, and I almost laugh because we clearly weren't doing that anymore.

"Oh, and is that how you're planning on dancing at the ball?"

"They requested that I teach them how we dance on Earth. That's all we were doing," I jump in. It's my fault things got to this point anyway. I'm the one who pulled them both close and demanded we drink. Speaking of which, hiccups have now started, making the king narrow his eyes at me.

"And the whiskey?"

"I thought it would be beneficial for them to get the full experience, which usually includes copious amounts of liquor," I snip. He's pulling the dad card, but we are definitely not there yet.

"Yes, because drinking and dancing like you were always leads to good decisions," he quips.

I turn to Alexei and Pearl. "Why don't you guys head to your rooms? This is clearly an issue that involves me, not you, and this was my idea anyway."

They look back and forth between us, seeming unsure. The king is furious that I dismissed them, and I doubt that anyone has dared do anything like this with him before. But I do not want them being punished for this, and the conversation we're about to have needs to be private. The king nods to them, effectively releasing them. When they are out of the room, I turn back to him.

"What exactly are you upset about?"

"You were acting extremely inappropriate."

"First of all, all we were doing was dancing—"

"That didn't look like dancing to me," he interjects.

"Like I told you before, that is how we dance on Earth. There is nothing inappropriate about it. It's just good fun."

"Yes, the way you appeared ready to rip their clothes off looked extremely appropriate," he cuts in sarcastically.

I roll my eyes like I'm sure every daughter has in response to her father at some point, but keep going. "Second of all, there was no one here to witness our behavior."

"Well, the entire castle can hear that ridiculous *music* you were playing."

"Third of all," I say, not even addressing *that* comment. As if he's any judge. Besides, no one listens to club music because it's *good.* That's not the point. "I am a grown ass woman, and am perfectly capable of making my own decisions. If I do want to drink and dance and act inappropriately, I will, because that is *my decision.* I have not had a father my whole life, and I don't need the dad lecture now that I'm all grown up. Okay?"

His face pinches in pain, and guilt knots my stomach for a moment, but I push past it. He doesn't get to act like I'm being a disobedient teenager right now when I'm almost thirty years old. It isn't my fault he missed out on that part of my life.

"Maybe I overreacted a little bit, and I'm not trying to lecture you, but the fact of the matter is, you are a princess now, Ember. You have to be extremely careful what behavior you show to those outside of your inner circle. And while you claim that the interaction I witnessed was perfectly normal and platonic, you are not on Earth anymore, and if anyone else were to have witnessed that, it could've been a scandal. Keep that in mind. You are in the public eye now, and your behavior will be scrutinized."

"I didn't think of that. I'll be more careful in the future."

"Is that seriously how humans dance on Earth?" he asks, and his scandalized facial expression has me laughing.

"Yes. That's usually what it's like at a club, or even a school dance like prom or homecoming."

"They dance like that in school?!"

"It's older kids, like fifteen and up. The schools hold special dances, and usually that's what it ends up like."

"Well, Earth is an interesting place, it sounds like."

"Have you ever been?"

"Me? Definitely not."

"Why not? Haven't you ever wanted to go?"

"Maybe someday. It's never been a priority though."

We stand there awkwardly for a moment.

"Well, you should probably get to bed. I imagine you're tired after the day you've had."

I almost argue, because he's basically ordering me around again, but then I think of how he ended that statement and realize that he's attempting to care for me. I smile at him.

"Yes, it has been quite a day. Breakfast tomorrow?" I've actually started enjoying our private meals together in the morning. It gives us an opportunity to get to know each other without having anyone else witness the awkwardness.

"Of course. That's the best part of my day," he tells me sincerely, and I soften even more toward him. I know it hasn't been long, but

I'm glad that we're starting to develop a relationship.

"Until tomorrow, then."

Pearl and Alexei are waiting outside my room when I finally get there.

"How did it go?" Pearl asks.

"Fine. He was mad at first, and so was I, but we made up in the end. He's fine. We're fine." Jesus, I'm saying that word a lot, but because of the drinks I've had, I can't think of a more dignified way of describing the interaction.

"Sorry I got you in trouble," Pearl says.

"Oh, please. That was not your fault in the least."

"I'm the one who asked you to show us."

"Yes, but if you remember correctly, I was the one who pulled both of you closer." Now that we're out of the moment, I'm a little embarrassed about that, and I'm sure I'll be more so tomorrow when I'm sober, but fuck it. Nothing I can do about it now. "I was also the one who got us all liquored up."

Alexei chuckles. "That's true, but we weren't exactly objecting."

"It's fine. Like I told the king, we did nothing wrong. Besides, we had fun, didn't we?"

Pearl nods enthusiastically while Alexei answers verbally. "We sure did. I can see why you do it that way on Earth. It's much more relaxed."

"Well, maybe I'll have to take you two there sometime and we can go clubbing for real."

"Do you think you're going to stay here? Or do you think you'll eventually go back home?" Pearl asks, and I look at Alexei to find him watching me intently, waiting not so patiently for my answer.

"Well, there isn't much left for me back on Earth, is there? I have no family, no friends. Jesus, I don't even have a job."

"Who's Jesus?" Alexei asks, and I let out a surprised laugh.

"Never mind. My point is, I probably will stay here. I have you guys and my father now. I would like to get to know all of you better. There are some things that I left at home that would be nice to have though. Maybe one day I'll go back there and bring you guys with me to see it. If you want, that is."

"What else would we do while we're there?" Pearl asks excitedly.

I think about that, but I have no idea where to start. I guess they don't have any technology, so maybe they'd enjoy going to the movies?

"I would probably take you to see a movie."

"What's that?" Alexei asks.

"It's a story that's acted out and recorded. You can watch them anytime at home if you have a TV, but the new ones are played in the theater. They have huge screens, and very loud surround sound so it makes it seem like you're *in* the movie. They also sell food and beverages that are way too expensive, but are part of the whole experience. As for what else, I'll have to think about it, but I would make sure you would love it."

"Well, count me in," Pearl says enthusiastically, although I already knew she would want to.

"That would be fun," Alexei agrees. "When we went to Earth for my training, they didn't show us anything enjoyable. We basically observed people so we could know what they were talking about."

"That sounds miserable. I bet you watched us entranced in our phones and maybe driving a bit?"

He laughs. "Basically. It was a very boring week. But what you've mentioned sounds enjoyable."

"It's a deal, then. When I go back to get my things, I'll bring you both with me and we can make a trip out of it." On that note, we all break up for bed, and I'm asleep before my head hits the pillow.

During breakfast, the king and I are slowly but surely becoming a bit more comfortable with each other. The conversation flows more naturally, we find out new things about each other. He asks about Eve, my adoptive mother, and how my childhood was. At my description, he says he believes that he remembers her from his short time spent at the Abandoned Bliss, and I make a mental note to show him some pictures when I have my phone on me next.

I, in turn, ask about his parents and what it was like growing up in a castle. He tells me all about the shenanigans he used to get into with an entire palace as his playground. I smile at the picture in my head, and can only imagine the destruction left in his wake.

"So, I thought tomorrow after breakfast we could begin your training with shields?"

I nod my enthusiasm. I'm looking forward to learning everything he knows about them, and getting better at strengthening mine and breaking through others' more easily.

"I was also going to ask you if there's anything you're wanting or needing for the ball? I was going to meet with Pearl this morning to start planning."

"I don't get asked that very often. Most of the time I tell the party planners to throw a ball and they plan it on their own without my input. Which is convenient, not having to worry about all the little details, but sometimes I think it would be nice to have a little bit of a say in it."

"So do you have any requests? Now is the perfect time to tell me about them," I say to him, smiling. It will be fun to have some of his flair at this party too.

"Well, fall is around the corner. Maybe something with an autumn theme? Nothing over-the-top, but perhaps some fall and winter color palettes?" He looks so out of place trying to come up with something for the party. It's adorable.

"Absolutely! Fall is my favorite season and has the best colors. We can definitely work with that." He smiles, looking relieved.

"So, I understand if you aren't able to tell me, but I was curious what business you had to attend to last night? I heard Humphrey say there were disappearances?"

His face falls at the change of subject, and for a moment I regret bringing it up. "Yes, well, it's not common knowledge. Actually we're keeping it on a strict need-to-know basis, but seeing as you're my daughter, I don't see the harm in telling you. Keep it to yourself, though."

I nod in agreement. I know I heard about this from Alexei yesterday, but I'm curious if the king would be willing to share any new information with me. I'm pleased that he's starting to trust me more. He tells me the same thing that Alexei did, and I soak it all in, trying to think of any new questions to ask.

"So, how many disappearances were there last night?"

"So far we've discovered fifty, but usually it takes longer before we find out that there's more. My guess would be around seventy total." My eyes almost bug out of my head. Seventy? I was thinking like ten.

"They were from every territory?"

"Yes. They always take the same number of people from each territory."

"How long has this been going on?"

"We discovered it happening about fifty years ago, but at that point, the disappearances were so minimal that it took us a long time to notice. It probably started before that, and it's been steadily increasing as the years pass."

"So, the group taking them is either getting bolder, or more desperate, depending on why they're taking them in the first place."

We talk more about it, but it's clear that despite how long this has been occurring, they don't know much.

Half an hour later I meet with Pearl. It's awkward seeing her after our drunk interaction the night before, and I figure we should probably clear the air a bit.

"Before we start party planning, I want to talk with you about last night."

"Oh, sure," she says, looking completely normal and unfazed.

"So, I know things got a little"—I search for the right word—"heated between us last night while drinking and dancing. I know that you like women, and I can't say I wasn't tempted to see what might happen, but I value your friendship too much. I don't want to cross that line with you because I worry what it could do to our relationship."

She smiles kindly at me, not looking in the least bit put out. "Ember, I value your friendship too. And I agree with you. It's probably mostly my fault anyway. We mermaids are like water, fluid. Unfortunately that usually translates to us being sexually fluid as well, and sometimes, especially when I have drinks, I let my powers out to play a bit, and it can draw people to me unintentionally. Besides, the kind of dancing you like to do on Earth is pretty damn intimate."

I laugh. "So, we're good?"

"Yeah, we're all good, babe. Now, about this gala. I have a lot of ideas."

"Before you get too crazy with them, the king has requested we do a bit of an autumn theme. Nothing too intense, but maybe the color scheme?"

She whips out a notebook and opens a page with so much already written on it. Not just notes, but *thorough* notes. I have no idea how she did this. We just talked about this *yesterday*.

"Yes, that should work. I was thinking something along those lines anyway. So, for the color scheme, what if we use mainly gold, with some darker accent colors, such as plum, maroon, and maybe black?"

"That will be especially luxurious. We could blend darker flower arrangements, and then place gold chargers and silverware with black plates and wineglasses and plum napkins?" I can envision everything coming together in my head and am already so excited for this event. "Ooh and what if we have candles in little glass bulbs that we can hang. Maybe we can bring some trees in the ballroom and hang the bulbs from them."

"I'll have to see about the trees. I can execute the other ideas though. Here's the guest list." She hands me a list that's pages long. "I have it organized by species type, and obviously we will have to have separate tables for each."

"Wait, why do we have to do that?"

She looks at me like she doesn't understand the question. "The races are always separated and seated at different tables."

"What if we have open seating? So they could sit anywhere they wanted to? They shouldn't be forced to segregate. Obviously if they want to sit with their own kind that's fine, but they shouldn't *have* to."

She considers my words, but her facial expression is unreadable.

"Let me think about it. That *would* be less work for us. Then we wouldn't need to come up with a seating plan. But moving on, for invitations I was thinking either black lace envelopes with gold calligraphy, or rolled-up parchment with gold lettering and plum ribbons."

"I think the black and gold would be a little more classy."

We continue on for hours, going through every detail we can think of, and I'm pleasantly surprised to find that we already have a decent amount accomplished. I wonder what the seamstress is going to create for me at the ball, and excitement bubbles in my stomach. I love a good dress.

Lunch is waiting for me in my room when I return, as well as the seamstress.

"Hello, my dear. I'm Imelda. I was hoping to get your measurements and speak with you about what kind of clothing you would prefer."

"Oh, wonderful! Yes, now is the perfect time."

She smiles kindly at me, grabbing her measuring tape and getting straight to work. She takes notes while she works, and she's finished within fifteen minutes. "We're all done, dear. You should eat your lunch while we talk so it doesn't get cold."

I do as she says, grateful for her suggestion because I'm hungry.

"So, what are you envisioning for your wardrobe?"

"Well, I did go to town and make essential purchases yesterday. I was able to find dresses as well as some training clothes." I gesture to where they are still on my floor by the door. I know I should've hung them up as soon as they were delivered, but what can I say? I've always been bad about putting away my clean laundry.

"May I?" she asks, going over to them.

I nod, and she picks up each piece, examining it before hanging it in the closet. I flush with embarrassment that she's cleaning up after me, but I can also tell she's cataloging the clothes in her mind so she can determine what I've already chosen and note my preferences.

"So, it looks like you still need quite a bit of daily wear, as well as multiple gowns suitable for balls and other formal occasions. What kind of style would you prefer? Are there cuts, colors, or fashions you gravitate toward?"

I think back on my wardrobe at home, and almost tell her that I want something tame and conservative, because that's always been what I've worn, but now that I'm here, I realize that my personality is changing, and with it, I would like a new look.

"Bold. Daring. Fierce."

Her eyes light up with the challenge, and I already know she's going to enjoy this. "Any colors you avoid or dislike?"

"Yellow." I make a face. It does not look good on me.

"All right. I can definitely work within those parameters. I'll send things up to you as I finish them." She leaves, and I'm excited to see how my wardrobe turns out. I always love women who dress boldly, and I am ready to join them. I think.

Chapter 19

"You're not concentrating, Ember," Stavros chastises me during my training session. I bite back the snippiness that wants to work its way free. I don't want to sound like a child.

"I *am* concentrating. It's just not working." I'm sure he can tell by the sound of my voice how exasperated I am. I thought I had this skill mastered, but every time I come across someone with a stronger shield, I realize I have a long way to go.

"You need to understand that all minds are different, as are the relationships that you have with those people. You will need to slip past their barriers in alternate ways. Sometimes subtlety is the better option, but occasionally it requires brute force. At that point you have to know that your mind is more powerful than theirs."

"But what if it isn't?"

"Well, it won't be if you don't tell yourself that it is. You have to believe with your entire being that your mind is more capable than anyone else's on the planet. It's the same with maintaining your own mental barriers."

"But I don't know that. My mind clearly isn't as strong as yours, for example."

"Ember, the more you tell yourself that, and continue to doubt yourself, the weaker your mental shields will be. I'm going to be honest with you. The only trick to this is what I'm currently telling you. The only reason you can't get past my barriers is because you're telling yourself that you won't be able to. You need to believe in yourself. Believe in your wonderful mind. *Know* that you can do it. That is the key. Confidence and belief. Nothing else."

My eyes tear up at his words, because while I've never been an insecure person, I do have my doubts about myself. And I have never possessed the conviction that he seems to.

We continue the training for another hour, and by the end I feel like a complete failure and am on the verge of tears. His pep talk seems to backfire, amplifying my insecurities rather than mitigating them. Maybe it's from a whole life of never having friends? I've never felt popular, or strong, or even *liked*. Hell, maybe I *am* insecure.

"It was a valiant attempt, Ember. You're doing well. Don't let today discourage you. We will keep practicing, and you *will* achieve your goals. I'll make sure of it."

I give him a small smile and a nod before departing to my room.

Pearl arrives shortly after, and we attempt to make plans for the ball, but my heart's not in it, so we decide to end things early. As I lie in bed listening to "Everything I Wanted" by Billie Eilish, a deep longing for my mother takes hold. I miss her so much. She would have known the right words to soothe me, and then we would have shared a drink and laughed until my worries seemed insignificant. I give myself ten minutes to cry and miss my mother, before forcing myself to seek a distraction—anything to do other than wallow in self-pity.

I pick up the journal I found in the abandoned palace, and now that I have access to a pen and paper, I'm able to write out patterns. I start by jotting down all the repeated words I find, as well as letters that I think may be vowels. I don't know how much time has passed when I hear a knock at my door. Alexei is standing on the other side.

"Hey, what's up?" I ask him.

"You didn't show up to the training yard. I wanted to check and make sure you're okay."

My eyebrows rise in surprise. "I'm sorry. I'm fine. I got caught up trying to translate that journal we found and must've lost track of time."

"Have you made any progress with it?"

"A little bit. I have a few letters that I think may be vowels, and found some repeated words. Hopefully I'll be able to figure it out eventually."

"Well, let me know if you make any discoveries."

"I will. Is there enough time left to train at all today?"

"Not really. Dinner is in thirty minutes."

I nod, and he heads to his room. I can't believe I was wrapped up in the journal for that long. I should probably change and freshen up.

I take a quick shower and put on one of my new outfits, this time donning a skirt, shirt, and corset combo before weaving a few mini braids throughout my hair. I look in the mirror to see a Viking warrior bitch staring back at me. With a smile, I playfully stick out my tongue at her before making my way to the dining room.

Dinner unfolds similarly to our previous meals, yet it grows more comfortable each day as I become more familiar with everyone.

"So, Ember discovered a journal when we found the palace in the caves. It's in a language I don't recognize, but she's been attempting to decipher it," Alexei tells my father.

"She did? I would like to see it. Maybe the language will be familiar to me."

I almost hit my head with my palm. Why didn't I think to ask him?

"But if I don't, I can always take you to the Epitome Athenaeum. We might be able to find something there to help us."

I also didn't think to do that either. Jesus, what's wrong with me lately? That should've been the first place I went.

"Yes, I would absolutely love that. I'm very excited to see the library anyway, even if you recognize the text." The prospect of visiting an extensive library scarcely anyone has access to? Getting to read through the history of this realm? Discovering base magic spells that I can perform? Who wouldn't want to go? I'm practically bouncing in my seat with excitement.

The king smiles as if he knows what I'm thinking. "All right. I won't be able to take you until next week though."

I try not to let my disappointment show on my face, but it's difficult, and I force myself to nod.

"How are the gala plans coming along?" he asks me and Pearl.

"They're coming along wonderfully!" Pearl chimes in. "And we put in some autumn colors for you, Your Majesty. Gold, plum, maroon, and black."

His eyes light up. "I'm sure with you two in charge, it will be the most magnificent ball we've ever had."

After dinner I'm about to head back to my room when Alexei stops me. "Dancing?"

"Oh, right. I'm sorry. I am all over the place today. I'll grab the speaker."

"No repeats of last night," the king reminds us, a teasing glint in his eyes.

"Of course not, Sire. We will be on our best behavior," Alexei cuts in before I can come back with some smart-ass comment.

"Want help again, Alexei?" Pearl asks, and he nods.

I run to my room and grab my speaker before meeting them both in the ballroom. I turn the speaker on and play some classical music. Alexei informs me that this one is faster and more complex, and is called the Alton. Pearl and Alexei start moving, and sure enough, this one is definitely more difficult. I can already tell I'm going to fuck this up real quick. The song ends, and we do the same thing as last time: Alexei shows me the steps and then we attempt to dance together with Pearl guiding me from behind. It's as hard as I thought it would be, but I don't make as big of an ass out of myself as I had expected.

By the end of practice, I'm able to roughly do it, stumbling only a few times, but I count that as a win. We cut out the club dancing; you're welcome, Stavros.

The next week passes by quickly. I train daily with both Alexei and Stavros. I'm getting exponentially better with my combat training, and I'm more confident every day in my skills. Although, my training with Stavros has been very slow going. I still haven't been able to breach his mental shields, and it doesn't feel as though I'm getting any closer.

I've also been practicing on random people throughout the castle and have noticed a slight improvement. I'm still unable to get past Mordecai's defenses, which infuriates me every time I try. I know he's hiding something, and I want to know what it is, but until I can get into his mind, I won't have an idea. Or maybe I simply don't like the guy, and am being completely paranoid, but my intuition says otherwise. Pearl has also been subtly trying to sneak past my shields as well, but has been unsuccessful except for when I had my panic attack in front of her.

The plans for the ball are also coming along marvelously, and my excitement grows with each passing day. It's going to be beautiful and inspiring, and I can't wait to see all of our careful plans come together. Pearl is almost ready to send out the invitations. We're apparently inviting the most important people in all the territories, but obviously I don't know any of them. This should be interesting.

The day finally arrives for Stavros and me to go to the Epitome Athenaeum, and I'm thrilled to be able to explore it with him. I think I love books more than Stavros does, which I've found is rare. Because I never had any close friends, I always felt a connection to the characters in the novels I read. They were always there for me and understood me unlike anyone else. And I could pick them up to comfort me anytime I was in need.

I dress in one of my new favorite things to wear—a skirt, shirt, and corset combo, before adding a sweater since it's starting to get even chillier here. Seated in the carriage next to me, Stavros is dressed more comfortably and appears to be more relaxed than I've ever seen him before. I wonder if he's more at home in the library than in the palace.

Luckily, it's not far, and we're riding for only ten minutes before we stop. I look out the window, and am thoroughly confused. I don't see any buildings here, nothing that would indicate we had arrived at the library.

"Are we in the right place?" I ask Stavros.

He smiles secretly at me before nodding and stepping out of the carriage. I follow him until he stops before a waterfall that's flowing down the side of the mountain. He looks back at me, beckoning me forward over his shoulder as he walks straight into the pouring water, taking me aback. I reluctantly follow, but am pleasantly surprised when no water hits me. I stop directly underneath the spray, but still don't feel any moisture. I look up to see that the liquid is stopping about an inch from my skin, and even when I move, the water follows, and is repelled.

"Come on, Ember." My head snaps toward Stavros at his words, and an amused smile is gracing his lips.

When I'm through the illusive doorway, my eyes widen in wonder. I'm already in love with this place. It's beyond magical. There are cave walls on either side of me, but water on the floor. Fake stone books that look incredibly realistic sit on top of the water, making a pathway. I giggle as I make my way across them, and we arrive at another entrance. There's a dark brown door that makes me think a hobbit might actually live here, except books line the curved archway. Stavros turns the knob, opens the door, and gives me my first glimpse of the Epitome Athenaeum.

I am literally speechless. Stavros gestures for me to enter, and I barely pay him any mind as I step through the doorway. The first thing I notice is the immense tree in the center of the room, rising higher than conceivably possible since we're in a mountain. As I look up, I don't see a ceiling—only a gorgeous sky, complete with sunshine, birds, and clouds that also make their way down to the books and surround the room. Books are everywhere. As far as I can see. There are multiple spiral staircases throughout the room that lead up to higher levels.

The smell hits me next. One of the best smells in the world. Books. Old parchment. Leather. When I finally blink, a tear glides down my cheek. This is unlike anything I have ever seen before, and it has literally brought me to tears.

"Pretty incredible, isn't it?" Stavros asks from next to me. I don't have the words, so I nod at him. "All of this section is for fiction. There are other rooms here that are organized by theme so you can find exactly what books you need."

I reluctantly let him lead me to other areas. I do want to see everything here, but fiction is my favorite. I'm sure the fiction section is divided by genre as well, but it's not as obvious as the themed rooms.

The rooms are all incredible. One room houses books on the universe and astronomy, which is clear as soon as you open the door and find the books floating around you, with the night sky and galaxy on the ceiling above. Another room showcases the botany of the planet. There is another tree here, with ivy and greenery that winds up through the bookcases. And yet another that depicts all of the monsters and creatures living in this realm, including an enormous stone dragon in the center of the room. When I ask Stavros about it, he tells me that dragons have been extinct for thousands of years.

We enter another room where the subject isn't immediately clear to me. There's a statue of a woman, elevated in the middle of the room. She has a crown on her head, and looks regal in her own right. There's a book floating above her hands and more that spiral down around her.

"What's this room?"

"This is our royal room. It has all the records we have on the lineage of the royal line."

We finally find the language room, and the walls themselves as well as the spines of the books are covered in every language I know, along with other languages I don't recognize, although none of them appear to be the language from the journal. We start sifting through all of the books we can. I've shown Stavros the journal, and he couldn't identify the language, but he looked at it long enough to be able to recognize it while we search. After hours of exploring, we still haven't found anything, and the suspicion I had when we first entered is essentially confirmed. There is no record of it here. I sigh in disappointment.

We leave the language room and head to one containing spells and potions. There are old glass bottles everywhere, but they hold no ingredients. This room is dark and dingy, as I would expect a potions room to be. Fog travels through the room at our feet, and I have to keep myself from shivering. I'm unsure whether the room's creepy aura is intentional, but it clearly has an ominous feel to it. It calls to my allure for the macabre, along with my adoration for Halloween, my favorite holiday. Needless to say, I love it.

"Do you think there will be something here that will help?"

"There might be. Honestly, I don't even know half of these spells, so there very well could be something in here that will."

"Thank you for helping me. I really appreciate it. And this place is fantastic. I've never seen anything like this. It's incredibly special. Thank you for sharing it with me."

"I'm glad I finally have someone to bring here with me. I've always come here by myself, with the exception of my parents when I was young."

I look down at the fog at my feet, and the shock of the place finally wears off for something to occur to me. "Doesn't the moisture in the clouds and fog damage the books?"

"There's a spell on the entire library. The books are perfectly preserved and unable to be damaged."

We continue to scour the room similarly as we did in the language chamber, but this one is far more fascinating. I've been sidetracked nearly a dozen times already, but I can't help it. I'm tempted to experiment with what I find, but that's not why we're here. I came prepared with a pen and paper, and am able to jot down some of the intriguing spells I'm itching to try out later.

I write down spells for glamouring (altering the appearance of people and objects), finding lost belongings, eliciting truthful confessions, invisibility, and finally, one for pausing time itself. While I immerse myself in the array of spells, Stavros directs his attention to the potions. After a period that feels like minutes, but is probably hours, his voice calls out to me.

"I think I found something we might be able to use."

Excitement pounds through me as I make my way over to him and look over his shoulder.

Deciphering Potion

This potion is used to translate any type of writing or code. Simply mix the ingredients together, and once it's completed, pour it over whatever you would like to interpret.

"This is perfect!" There are quite a few ingredients required, but the act of making it seems pretty straightforward.

"Oh no. We won't be able to use this, Ember," he says regretfully.

"What do you mean? Why not?"

"About half of these items are on the black market. We won't be able to get them."

"You have a black market here?"

"Yes. And it is *not* a place you want to go. I'm sorry, Ember. This isn't an option. We can keep looking though. Maybe we'll find something similar."

He puts the book away and moves on to another one. I sit back in my spot and try to come up with a plan. We found exactly what we need. I know he's trying to protect me, and obviously is worried about being seen at the black market since he's the king, but no one knows me here yet. I could go myself. I just need to find someone who can tell me where it is. Something my father doesn't know about me yet, is that I have a fairly photographic memory, especially when it's this fresh in my mind. I quickly scribble down the instructions, checking them over. I should probably find a way to look at the actual book to make absolutely sure that I got everything right.

An hour later, we still haven't found an alternative, and we reluctantly head back to the palace. As we walk out of the room, I stop.

"Oh, I forgot my pen. I'll be right back." I quickly hurry back inside, find the book the potion was in, and flip to the page. I compare it with what I wrote down, and as expected, they match. I mentally high-five myself before shutting it and running back to Stavros.

When we leave, the carriage hasn't moved, and I wonder if they've been here the whole time, or if they left and came back. My guess would be the former, since it is the king with me.

"I'm sorry we didn't find anything, Ember."

"That's all right. It was a long shot anyway."

As soon as we get back, Stavros takes off to attend to some official business, and I head to my room to eat my lunch that always seems to be waiting there for me. When I'm finished, I meet Alexei in the training yard. Once I've confirmed that there's no one around, and we're in close contact with hand-to-hand combat, I ask him.

"I have a favor to ask you."

"What is it?"

"Firstly, I need you to keep this conversation private. Do *not* tell anyone. Especially the king."

His eyes narrow in suspicion, but he nods for me to continue.

"I need to go to the black market," I whisper.

His head pulls back in surprise. "Why?"

"I found a potion that will translate that journal for me."

"Ember, I think you're putting too much into this. It probably belonged to a young teenage girl who was whining about her crush and the drama between her and her friends."

"That's definitely possible, but what if there's something important in there, Alexei? What if there's information that we can use? Or better yet, bring the kingdom together?"

"How would anything in that journal manage to bring the kingdom together?"

"You were in that palace, Alexei. You *know* that the species were intermingling, and even living together. What if there's something in the journal that can convince the king to change the way things are done here? It's worth a shot, isn't it?" I give him my best puppy dog eyes, and he cracks within ten seconds.

"*Fine,*" he grumbles.

"Thank you!" I yell, hugging him excitedly. "So, when can we go?"

"We'll go tomorrow night. We'll have to sneak you out. I'll be able to go on my own, but you leaving at night would be suspicious as hell."

"Can you do the same spell from when you snuck me into the Healing Springs?"

"No. That only worked because we were on the horse and Ash was carrying both of us. I was able to blend you in as my cloak. It wouldn't work with us walking."

It's then that I remember what I found at the library. "Oh! I found a spell for invisibility earlier. I have it in my room. I can try to master it before we go."

"Perfect. If you manage it, meet me at the front door at midnight tomorrow."

I nod, and we finish up our training, but I'm distracted. I'm thinking about trying out the spell tonight after dinner, and about what the black market is going to be like. Alexei takes me to the ground numerous times.

"You're not focusing, little doe."

"I know. I can't stop thinking about what we might find and all we have to do."

"When you're distracted, that is the time you're going to be most vulnerable. Remember that." We continue training, and after his reminder, I'm able to concentrate a little bit more, and improve slightly.

That night, I head up to my room and look over the sheet I brought back with me from the library. They are all fairly simple, and evidently all I need to do is speak the incantation. I look at the one for invisibility, stand in front of the mirror, and utter the words.

"*Ginomai Caecus.*" I look in the mirror and still see my reflection. I almost admit defeat, when I see that I've also written that I need to gesture with my hand to what exactly I would like to be invisible. I try it again, but this time, I sweep my hand over myself. I'm amazed when a moment later, I disappear entirely. The sheet of paper I'm holding seems to float in midair. I look back down at it to see how to make myself visible again.

"*Ginomai Conspectus.*" I sweep my hand over my body, and I'm once again staring back at my reflection. My eyes are exhilarated, my cheeks are flushed, and there's a beaming smile on my face. This is unbelievably cool, and I can't wait to try out the other spells I found. For now, I put it in the drawer of my nightstand and head to bed. I want to get some rest for the black market tomorrow, and ensure that

I'll be able to properly cast the spell so our plan will work.

Chapter 20

Throughout the day, nerves and excitement pound through my body, intensifying as midnight draws near. Stavros mentions that I seem distant during breakfast and our training session. Pearl asks what's wrong with me during our party-planning meeting. I take pains to ensure their curiosity doesn't bloom into suspicion—especially with Stavros. While I have no doubt Pearl would want to come with us, if Stavros discovered our plan, his reaction would be unpredictable. I'll find out soon enough what it would be once I prepare the potion and am able to translate the journal. By then it will be much too late for him to intervene.

To divert their inquiries, I simply tell them that I think my cycle is starting soon. Stavros, of course, acts like a typical man and starts spluttering some nonsense before hastily changing the subject. Pearl, however, true to form, commiserates with me about the shared plight of womanhood. Alexei, understanding the true reason behind my behavior, fortunately adjusts our training intensity.

The only thing he asks is if I figured out how to turn invisible. I reassure him that I have, and I'll meet him tonight. After dinner and dancing, I head back to my room and change for tonight. I want to look inconspicuous, so I don dark clothing: tight black pants, a loose black shirt with a tight black vest, and top it off with a dark purple cloak with gold embroidery around the hood. I also opt for darker, heavier makeup than I usually prefer, adding an extra layer of disguise. While I doubt anyone at the market would recognize me, it's better to err on the side of caution. I also secure my lovely new daggers to my thighs, flushing slightly when I remember Alexei attaching one of them to my body.

With two hours to spare, and nothing to do, I pace, growing more and more nervous as the time passes. I can't stop looking at the clock and it's driving me insane. I swear it's been like four hours, but of course only one has passed. I sit on my bed as I try to calm down.

I pick up a book that I got from the palace library the other day, but it's not catching my attention. I've been researching Queridian and it's been enlightening to say the least. Even though Stavros does things differently than I would, I will say that he's made enormous strides in how the realm is run. Things used to be much worse. The species weren't allowed to fraternize at all, and the only time they were was for very specific reasons, and you needed to get it approved beforehand. Of course, it probably happened much more than was "allowed."

The previous rulers were also incredibly strict, and as a result, the realm and its residents suffered. When Stavros was crowned, the kingdom rejoiced. He had always been beloved by his subjects, even when he was only a prince. After I've come to learn more, I realize how harsh I was with him when I first showed up. I still don't agree with how certain things are done, but I can appreciate that not everything can happen all at once. And should I ever rule, he has effectively laid the groundwork for further change and transformation.

It's finally quarter to midnight, and I leap up and head to the mirror, reciting the spell and making sure that I am fully invisible. I quietly head to the front door, but Alexei isn't here yet. I planned it so he wouldn't be waiting around for an invisible Ember. This way, as soon as he arrives I can whisper to him that it's me, and then we can leave. He shows up exactly at midnight, and I come up behind him, getting close to his ear.

"Psst."

He whirls around, but his eyes move right past me. I've startled him, and I almost start laughing, because I don't think I've ever witnessed that emotion from him before. "Ember?"

"Right in front of you, big man."

"You scared the shit out of me. Ready?"

I nod, but then remember he can't see me. "Yes," I whisper.

He starts walking, way too slowly, and I realize that he can't tell where I am and is worried about leaving me behind. It's not like I can exactly shout at him. I reach out and clasp his arm. No one will be able to see, but he can feel that I'm right there with him. I hear his sharp intake of breath at the surprise contact, but he picks up his pace. He nods at his fellow guards as we take off, and soon we're in front of the stables.

"Would you mind bringing Ash out for me?" he asks the stable boy, who scurries in and returns minutes later with my favorite horsey.

She comes directly up to me and sticks her snout in my face, sniffing me. I reach up and pet her quietly, and she snorts happily.

"Thank you," he tells him.

I climb up as quietly and carefully as I can, trying not to move too much and draw any attention. Luckily, no one is around, except the young stable boy, who isn't even looking in my direction, but is staring at Alexei like he's his hero. A moment later, Alexei reaches up, feeling that I'm in position, before making his way up after me. It's been a while since we've been on a horse together, and there's something comforting about it to me. We spent weeks like this, and getting back to it is like coming home. When we're far enough away from the palace, Alexei whispers in my ear.

"I've missed this," he tells me, echoing my thoughts.

"Me too," I whisper back. We're still in town, so I decide to wait until we're far enough away to remove the spell.

"I'm so sorry for everything, Ember. It's been so hard being close to you all the time and not touching you like I want, or telling you what I want. It's like you're right in front of me, but still so far away." With me invisible, and no one around, it seems like he thinks this conversation almost isn't happening. Like he's talking to himself.

"What do you want to tell me?"

"How much I want you. How much I wish I could worship you. And I *would* worship you if I could, Ember. You have never experienced pleasure like the kind I could and yearn to give you. How much I adore you, and find comfort in your presence. How much I wish things were different. How we should go back to Earth and forget about all of our responsibilities here so that we can be together." His lips brush my ear and trail down my neck.

A tear slips free of my eye as I bite back a whimper. Fuck. We always fall back into this, and I'm so tired of stopping it.

"Would you ever do that with me?"

"I've definitely thought about it."

"Is it too selfish of me to ask you to give up your guard position? Then we could be together, right?"

"I've thought about that too, Ember, and I don't think I could with the way things are right now. My father would...well, I don't exactly know what he would do, but it would *not* be pretty. And your father... fuck. I...I'm nobody. I'm not deserving of being with royalty. I'm a half breed for gods' sake."

"Well, he hasn't been in my life until this point. I know he's my biological father, but he needs to earn the right to be my dad, which he hasn't yet. And even if he didn't approve, I don't give a shit. I am a grown ass woman, and I can make my own goddamn decisions. So don't make that out to be an issue, because it's not."

At this point, we're far enough away from anyone that I'm able to remove the invisibility, and Alexei almost falls off of Ash in his surprise.

"Can you warn me next time you're going to do that?"

"Absolutely not. This way is more fun."

I can almost hear him rolling his eyes from behind me.

By this time, the world around us is cloaked in darkness, with the exception of the full moon above, and we're in the middle of nowhere. Ahead lies a sparse black forest, its shadows deepening under the night sky. I shiver instinctively, and Alexei pulls me closer to comfort me. Above us, the moon hangs large and heavy, impregnated in the sky, its size and radiance unlike anything I've ever seen before. It adds a surreal, ominous vibe to our venture. Red clouds hug the moon, swirling and winding around it tightly, and the scene from *Practical Magic* when Gillian Owens panics about there being blood on the moon flashes in my mind. I'm not a superstitious person, but I hope this isn't an ill omen for the rest of our night.

Roughly ten minutes later, we stop in the middle of the woods. I scan our surroundings, and drawing on my knowledge from the library, I suspect that this must be the black market's covert entrance. In front of us looms a massive sinister tree. Stripped of leaves, it seems utterly lifeless. Its trunk is so wide it could encompass my living room. As it stretches upward, the branches twist and intertwine into a snarled, knotted mess.

Alexei gets off the horse before helping me down, leading Ash over to a different tree, and tying her up. He speaks a few low words that I can't hear and moves his hand gently over her.

"What did you do?"

"Placed a protection spell over her. This isn't the safest place to be, and while I think she'll be fine, I would rather be on the safe side."

He grasps my hand and leads me over to the creepy ass tree, and as we stand before it, I wait for something to happen, but nothing does. I'm about to ask when Alexei pulls his dagger free and drags it across his palm. I cry out in alarm.

"What on Earth are you doing?!" I exclaim.

"The black market requires blood to enter," he replies nonchalantly, as if he didn't cut his fucking hand open out of the blue.

He closes his hand into a fist and holds it over the ground right in front of the trunk. At first nothing happens, but then the blood starts pouring out from the bottom of his fist, and when it falls on the ground, it hisses and the ground smokes, leaving an acrid scent behind. When I think we're in the wrong spot because nothing else is happening, the tree opens up, and there's a dark stairwell that spirals down underground. I swallow, but refuse to let my nerves get the best of me. I plow forward before Alexei, and down, down, down we go. There are little stones embedded in the walls that are lit, similar to the caves that Alexei and I traveled through, and they leave *just* enough light that I can barely see, but not nearly enough to be comfortable, and I'm sure that's intentional.

We finally reach the bottom, and the stairwell opens up into a huge courtyard. It reminds me a bit of the marketplace in the Immortal City, but it's much darker, more ominous, and the wares they're selling range in all manner of wickedness. I already know that I can't show any weakness here or I'll be eaten alive, so under my cloak where no one can see, I rest my hands on my daggers, pull my shoulders back, and hold my head high as I walk forward, looking as confident and comfortable here as I would back on Earth.

Alexei steps up next to me and leads the way as we wind through the crowd. And it *is* crowded, which surprises me. There are all sorts of things that I would like to scrub from my eyes. I'm horrified when I see the áspro vrykólakas in cages, their shrieks making my blood freeze. The bite I obtained from one pulses and burns slightly, as if in recognition. There are other monsters too, and I cannot fathom *why* someone would want to buy any of these poor creatures, and I can't help but pity them. Even though they're monsters, they don't deserve to be locked up in cages waiting to be sold off to God knows who for some sinister purpose. As we walk by them, Alexei whispers things about them in my ear.

There's your classic hybrid monster, which Alexei tells me is called a fright morph. They come from the Everchanging Glades (mimic territory), and that's why they have so many different forms attached to them. Apparently, no two are the same as they can take on characteristics of up to three animals, but once they take on the shape, they're stuck with it, unlike the mimics, who can switch back and forth at will. We see a few, one that is mostly a bear body, with gigantic antlers and huge wings. Another that is smaller, about the size of a deer, but has the head of a lion, and instead of paws, it has extremely large talons. The last one we see is in a tank full of water, and has the body of an eel with a fin on top that looks sharp enough to cut, the head is almost sharklike, but fits the size of the body, and it has a stinger on the end of its tail.

The next monster we see is called a vexmouth (pronounced like *vermouth*), and is from Wickshire (witch territory). It's basically a freaky-looking blob with lots of tentacle-like arms that surround its body, and in the middle of the blob is one giant eye. Apparently, this one is mostly psychologically dangerous. It can still do damage with its arms if you get close enough, but the real danger is the eye. If it snares you in its gaze, it can torment you in all sorts of ways, showing you your worst fears as if they're reality, making you believe that you're being tortured, all manner of things. I don't even glance at it as we walk past.

The last monster we come across is from the Healing Springs. This one is the most terrifying, in my opinion. It's a dark emerald green, and on all fours it's as tall as Alexei, but it can also stand on its hind legs. It has large spines and spikes that protrude from its back, and its soulless black eyes seem to see straight into my mind. When it opens its mouth, there are multiple sets of sharp-ass-looking teeth that remind me of a great white shark, and I can see venom dripping from them that hisses and burns as it hits the ground. Then there are the claws. They are long and massive, and I would bet that they also have poison in them. Alexei tells me they are called abyss hounds. The claws and teeth are lethal. One swipe or bite from either will not heal, and the poison will quickly spread through your body. The only cure is amputating whatever was damaged before the poison travels to the rest of your body, or if a team of elves heals you immediately.

I'm glad once we make it past the monsters, and am excited to see all sorts of dark magic books until we get closer, and I can *feel* their absolute evilness. I don't want to get near them with a ten-foot pole. I swear there's one that has a human's face on the cover, skin and all. There's some bound in chains, and I can only imagine the wickedness that's inside if they need something to restrain it. There's multiple with runes covering the entirety of the covers, and I wonder if that's another form of binding them.

We finally arrive where we need to be: the forbidden objects of the realm. Most of them look like they've been taken directly from different species. I would hope that all of the contributors were dead, but actually witnessing this place, I wouldn't count on it. The items on our list are all here—mermaid scales, witch eyes, and, finally, vampire teeth. Alexei visibly cringes when we are handed the teeth, and I hate that I had to bring him with me for this.

We're able to pay mostly in money, but then we both have to contribute a memory of our choosing. I make sure to pick something that I won't miss. I think of a time when I was young. I was being chased around the playground by some mean boys, and I thought they liked me, but the one I had a crush on pushed me down and spit on me. That was one of the times that I truly realized I was different. When I told my mother about it when I got home, she was sympathetic, but I remember her telling me that those boys weren't worth my time, and that I had so much more in me than they would ever comprehend. I always thought she was simply being a good mom, but now that I'm here, I understand that in her own way she was telling me that I had something in me that they would never have. Something special. Magic. That thought brings a smile to my face as the vendor holds a jar up to my mouth. I originally chose this memory because I always hated being bullied, but now that I realize what my mother was actually telling me, I wish I chose something different, but there's no time to change it.

"Open wide," he tells me, unnervingly, I might add. I do as he says, and am amazed when I can see the memory fall out of my mouth and into the jar, as if it's a movie reel playing at superspeed. Alexei tells me there's magic in the jar that pulls out the memory you're thinking about. I'm interested to see if the same thing happens when Alexei goes next. Instead of seeing it like a movie, all I see is a black smoke-like substance getting sucked into the jar. Our jars are next to each other, and now that the process is over, I can't see mine anymore. It looks the same as his does, and even though I try to think hard about what it was, it's gone. It's like smoke slipping through my hands, and even though I know I picked something unpleasant, I don't like that something was taken from me. Something that was *mine* alone, even if it wasn't something I liked.

Ten minutes later, we're making our way back up the tree staircase. I can't wait to get the *fuck* out of this place. I completely understand why Stavros refused to bring me here and said it was not an option. I hope he's not too upset when he finds out we came here anyway.

"I didn't know you could pay in nonmaterial ways like that here."

"It's not something you want to do often. Regularly giving up memories, even negative ones, isn't recommended. While it served our purpose for now, there are those who resort to it routinely because they can't afford to pay monetarily. After a while, they begin to change the essence of who they are, as they're surrendering the experiences that have shaped them. There are other ways of paying as well. Years taken off your life, giving up a personality trait, blood. Never give blood as a payment unless you *absolutely* have to. Blood can serve as a potent tool, and in the hands of the wrong person it can be very dangerous."

All of that sounds terrible, and not something I would ever do unless I was desperate and had no other options. We climb out of the top, and the entrance is still miraculously open, but I would guess that's because the magic recognizes that we already gave blood to enter. Ash is thankfully right where we left her, although she seems more antsy than normal and is equally as relieved to leave as we are. We quickly mount and take off, getting out of this creepy place as quickly as possible.

As we approach the castle, I cast the invisibility spell on myself, and Alexei moves closer so it doesn't look like he's awkwardly hanging off the back of his horse. I can't say I hate it, since every part of his front is pressed firmly against every part of my back. It's like we're glued together, and we fit so nicely like this.

We dismount, Ash is taken to the stables, and Alexei and I walk side by side. I grab his hand instead of arm this time, even though it doesn't matter if we walk together, but we still do all the way back to our rooms. When I get to mine, Alexei gives my hand a gentle squeeze before letting go, and it feels like he's squeezing my heart instead.

Once inside, I carefully put our bag of goodies in my nightstand. It's too late and I'm too exhausted to start the potion now, and after what we went through to get these ingredients, I do *not* want to mess this up. Alexei said he would stop by in the morning before breakfast to help me put it together. According to the recipe, it needs a week to brew, and then we should be able to use it. Excitement boils in my stomach at the thought of finding out what's in the journal, bringing some energy back to me.

My inner archaeologist is screaming to finally decipher the writing. It will also serve as an exciting opportunity to compare the notes that I took earlier to validate my findings and document a new language. Once everything is translated, I can compare it to the original text. Hopefully, if we encounter anything else in this language in the future, we won't require a potion, and we can directly translate the text from our documented notes.

I wake to an insistent knock the next morning. I groggily get out of bed and open the door to find Alexei on the other side. He looks thoroughly confused and pokes his head in the room, almost head-butting me.

"What the hell are you doing?" I ask, making him jump a foot in the air like a cat.

"Ember? Where are you?" He reaches out his hands, like he's a child playing Marco Polo. I look down, only to see nothing. I laugh loudly as his hands connect with my tits. I do the visibility spell, obviously having forgotten to reverse it last night in my exhaustion. As soon as he can see me, he realizes where his hands are, and he jumps back, blood filling his cheeks in his embarrassment. "Sorry, I couldn't see you," he says, stating the obvious.

"I figured. I forgot to take the invisibility spell off when I went to bed and didn't realize it when I opened the door."

Alexei comes fully into the room carrying the other ingredients that he was able to sneak from around the castle and a small cauldron as promised. We add everything as instructed, gently putting the potion over the fire halfway through, before taking it back out, adding the rest, and sticking it back on the fire for another half an hour. The potion produces a pungent odor, and I open my windows, hoping it doesn't stick around in my room. After we take it off the heat, we're done. There's nothing else that it needs, except to sit for a week. I put the cauldron in the back of my closet and cover it with a small blanket so that the smell hopefully doesn't seep out and taint my clothing, although it does seem to be less potent since we removed it from the fire.

We head to breakfast, and the moment we sit down, the king asks what the strange smell is. We deflect, saying we noticed it too, but can't figure out where it's coming from. Then, Pearl asks where I was first thing this morning. My eyebrows knit in confusion.

"I gently knocked and opened your door to show you the table settings for the ball, and you weren't in your room." I realize she opened the door while I was sleeping and was invisible, and I simply didn't hear her. I can't tell her that though, especially not in front of the king, so I lie.

"Oh, I stopped by Alexei's room this morning to ask him if we were still on for training this afternoon."

Her eyes widen, and I can tell she doesn't believe me. It's then that I realize my stupid mistake. She no doubt thinks that I slept with him last night and I made it worse by saying I was in his room. I can't back down now though. I look at Alexei imploringly. He looks ready to laugh, but jumps to my rescue.

"That's right. I told her originally that I wasn't sure if I would be able to do training this afternoon or not, so I asked her to come by in the morning in case we needed to train before breakfast. But it turns out I can do it later." He sounds much more convincing than me, and I give him a grateful smile.

Stavros nods in understanding, changing the subject, but as I look at Pearl, I know she does not buy one second of it. I give her a pleading look to let it go for now. She seems to understand that I can't talk about it here and gives a small nod, but the narrowing of her eyes tells me that I'm going to have to give her the real details later.

When we meet up for party planning, she immediately sits down and starts grilling me.

"Spill."

I tell her everything. About the journal, the library visit, the spells I found, the black market, and finally the potion that is currently brewing in my closet. When I'm done, she doesn't even say anything, just stares at me for what seems like minutes, even though I know it's not.

"Well. Firstly, you're damn lucky you both got out of there without something awful happening to you. I went to the black market in Mermacovia and was almost kidnapped. Secondly, are we sure that this journal is important enough to warrant all this? And lastly, why the hell didn't you let me know so I could come with you?"

I almost laugh out loud at the absurdity. "But you were almost kidnapped at the one in Mermacovia?"

"That doesn't mean I don't want to see all the black markets."

"How many are there?"

"There's one in every territory."

"And you've only been to the one?"

"Yes, but I've heard the one in Wickshire is particularly depraved. That's the one I've always wanted to go to."

"Why are you so interested in them?" I ask.

"I like taboo things, for one. I also enjoy dark items, even though they aren't legal. I never actually buy anything, but I like looking at them."

"Well, next time I go to a black market, I'll be sure to invite you along," I say sarcastically.

After that, we continue with preparations for the ball. Everything is almost all figured out, but we still need to smooth out the details. Needless to say, I think it's going to be elegant and entertaining, and I'm getting more and more excited for it by the day.

When it's time for training, I get changed and head down to the yard to meet up with Alexei, but as I'm walking through the halls, I hear him talking with someone. I don't consider myself a snoop, but at the moment, I can't help it. They're whispering, and I draw closer as quietly as I can.

"I don't know about that," I hear Alexei say, more clearly now that I'm closer.

"Son, you know that we don't have another choice. I told you what will happen if we don't."

Well, that answers that question. He must be talking to Mordecai. Probably about palace business.

"I know, but are you sure that it's accurate?"

"How often are the witches incorrect in their prophecies? And I know this one to be a very insightful female. When she makes a prediction, it comes true. End of story, Alexei. There are no other options."

"Well, let me at least think about it."

"You need to make a decision before the ball. That is your deadline."

I start walking quickly because it sounds like their conversation is coming to an end, and I don't want to get caught lurking. I hurry down to the training yard, and as I go, I can't help but think about what I overheard. There's not much to go on, but I get a sense that it's important. Mordecai's up to something, I know it, and it worries me. I wonder if he's planning some sort of action for the ball. Maybe stirring something up with one or multiple of the other territories? Something strikes me then. I wonder if he's somehow involved in the disappearances happening throughout the realm. If he wanted to stir up drama, or plan something at the ball, something that Alexei does not seem on board with, it would make sense that he could be. I mean that would be the perfect opportunity since all of the races will be there.

I realize that I'm probably being dramatic. I barely heard anything, and there's no way that Alexei would be involved in something nefarious. I can't help but be suspicious of Mordecai, but it's probably because he unnerves me. But he wouldn't be the first creep I've come across. That doesn't mean that he's actually evil. I'm tempted to ask Alexei, but then change my mind when I realize he would know that I had clearly been spying on him, and dismiss that idea.

When he shows up to meet me, he seems off and won't quite look at me. I'm sure I'm reading too much into it. It didn't seem like he agreed with whatever his father was trying to persuade him to do, and he's not sure what to do. I realized a long time ago that he's very torn about Mordecai. He wants his approval, but he also harbors some resentment toward him for not being there when he was growing up. I think he also feels like his dad never wanted him because of the situation between Mordecai and Alexei's mother. Needless to say, Alexei seems conflicted, and the relationship he has with his father is complicated, so it makes sense that he's not himself. I try to not think about it, it's not my business anyway. With that in mind, the two of us begin training.

Chapter 21

Alexei remains in a weird mood all week, but we maintain our normal schedule. The days seem to drag by, and I'm so excited when the potion is ready. I let Alexei and Pearl know, and they follow me to my room after dinner so we can find out what the journal says together.

I've been trying to push the potion to the back of my mind all week, but it's been difficult since I see it in my closet every time I change. I bring the cauldron into the other room and set it down on my table before I take out the journal, and when I'm ready, I finally take the blanket off to reveal the contents within. I haven't uncovered it all week, so I have no clue what it looks like.

We all let out a collective gasp at what's revealed. It is the most astonishing liquid I have ever seen. It's a deep navy blue that shimmers, glitters, and seems to change color slightly when you move it. It's like I'm staring into the galaxy, and despite the reek it was producing when we first started making it, it has a pleasant aroma now, almost like cinnamon. It has a slightly thicker consistency to it, but not so much where I can't move it or pour it. I lay the journal out flat on the table and open it to the first page. There's not a lot written, and I'm guessing it's basic information about whose journal this is. I'm not sure how much I need to use, so to not waste any, I pour one drop on the center of the page, and that seems to do the trick. The liquid seeps into the paper, shimmers for a moment, then the words transform, and we're suddenly able to read it. It's the strangest thing, like I can still see the original writing almost shadowed underneath, with the translated writing over the top. How it knows what all of us can decipher is beyond me, but I suppose that's part of the magic.

Zenobia Faellia
Year 15 birthday present
1850

"What do you think 1850 refers to?"

"Maybe the year?"

"How long ago was that?"

"Two thousand years ago."

"That would fit from what we saw in the caves, especially since we know there was a preservation spell on the palace."

They both nod and we turn the page, not gathering anything else. I repeat the same process. There is much more writing on this page, but it still needs only one drop.

I was gifted this journal for my birthday. I became fifteen today, a great milestone, Mother tells me. I'm still getting used to having visions since my powers awakened only a few moons ago. Not that we can see the moon in the caves. We venture outside on occasion, but it's been a long time since I gazed upon it.

We've resided in the caves for two years now. We came here for the promise of a better life. Things outside the caves are not good. The species are all segregated, not even able to interact with each other at all. Then Mother heard about this secret society living here. It took a significant amount of time for us to be able to learn everything we needed to, and for us to leave our old lives behind.

Things in the caves are significantly better. The races here all coexist. We each have a leader to represent us, and they all rule us together. I enjoy mixing with the others, and am grateful that I have the opportunity to get to know them. It was strange when I first arrived, but then I met Rose. She's my closest friend, and we met shortly after I arrived here. I wasn't sure about her at first, because as I've learned, elves are not very kind, but she's better than most, and I've come to get used to their attitudes.

I've also come across a few males I'm interested in, but there's one in particular. He's a mimic, and is named Darren. His shifted form is a stag, and it's fascinating to watch the change. I had never seen it before coming here. He asked me to accompany him to the ball that's being thrown for Shanubi, and I've accepted. Now I need to decide what to dress up as. Maybe something to match Darren's stag form?

"What's Shanubi?" I ask.

"It's a holiday we have here where you dress up like someone or something else. The mimics usually go as a different animal to what their shifted form is. It's one of our darker holidays. You know, kind of scary and spooky. There's always a lot of creepy decor and most people take it as an opportunity to scare each other."

"Oh, like Halloween?"

"I've never heard of that before. That's a weird word for that holiday." Pearl wrinkles her nose in disgust, and I try not to take offense.

"Excuse me? And Shanubi isn't?" She rolls her eyes at me. "Well, we were at least able to learn one thing from that teenage flashback: the species used to coexist in the caves. *And there were leaders for every race.* Our theory was right, Alexei!"

"That's all well and good, but we basically already knew that. And I don't know what other information we're going to be able to gather from this journal. It seems like it's going to be a lot of teenage drama, and I don't think she will go into more important details," Alexei says like a total crab.

"Well, we will have to read and find out. And you never know, she could tell us something significant. Just because she's a teenage girl doesn't mean that she didn't witness something important. She's part of a secret society that most of the kingdom didn't even know about."

Alexei does not seem happy about having to read this entire thing, and I can't say I blame him. There's going to be lots of teenage girl drama in here, and I don't see a grown man having any interest in it. Pearl and I however. . .

We read for hours, each new page getting a fresh drop of potion, and I am starting to get discouraged. We have not gained anything so far, other than having our theory confirmed earlier. Pearl, on the other hand, seems to be loving it. She is so interested in the drama between Zenobia and Rose, and is always excited when there is a new crush that develops and inevitably always goes to shit, usually causing the drama between the two girls.

The further in we go, however, the entries start becoming less frequent, and she starts talking about more significant things. Years pass. Not only is her writing more mature, but everybody knows that as you get older, you don't typically write in your diary as often. After two hours we have finally come across something pertaining to the palace and the politics, giving us a better idea of what was happening at the time.

Things in the caves are starting to get strange. There have been many more to join us here, clearly wanting the same unity that we do, but we've noticed that the larger our group, the more things here are changing. It's not something I can describe. More like a feeling that our lives are being threatened by some unseen force. It's nefarious, and it builds with each passing day.

My partner has a theory that civilization outside is aware of us since our group is getting larger. He thinks that maybe they are planning an attack, which would be devastating. We are a peaceful culture. It is why we moved into the caves to begin with. Let's just hope he's not right.

The entry is fairly short, but we're able to determine that something isn't right, and I wonder if we'll ever learn why they felt threatened. There are only a few more entries; the next couple don't provide anything of value, but it's the last entry that gives me goosebumps. I'm guessing she felt the need to write it down because she couldn't believe it was happening, and the act of putting pen to paper helped her come to terms with it.

It's official. We're leaving. The entirety of the caves. The leaders have decided that it's not safe for us here anymore. With the way the world is outside, we know we're going to have to go to our separate territories, even though we don't agree with it. The dark ones are coming. Ma has seen it. If we stay here, they will come for those in the caves first. We will be out by tomorrow or they will find us. Our little oasis we have formed and loved living in is over. Gone.

That's it. There's nothing else that might tell us what or who "the dark ones" are, but I am dying to know. All this journal has done is give me more questions. It's so frustrating. I was hoping we would be able to get some answers, which I guess we did. We now know that they for sure all used to live and coexist, and the reason they left the caves, but we don't know who the dark ones are, or what kind of threat they posed, or if they still do.

I also can't tell which emotions are mine and which are seeping from Pearl and Alexei. I think we're all very raw after forming this connection with Zenobia after reading her innermost thoughts. The thoughts that she most likely didn't share with anyone else. There's a vulnerability in that. Not only for her, even though she's dead, but also for us. It's a very personal thing, reading someone's journal, and now it's over with no closure. Sadness forms tears behind my eyes. Not just for her, but also for this wonderful community that all lived and breathed this equality. They had it perfect for a while, and in a few years, it was shattered.

My eyes trace back over her words, my fingers following, before stopping on "the dark ones." The writing here is more harsh, and a stab of fear strikes me as I linger there. Who were they? Were Zenobia, her family, and the rest in the caves able to escape them? When Alexei and I were there, I don't remember seeing any signs of struggle or attack, but that doesn't mean that nothing happened. I wish I could know what else became of them. A drop of wetness falls from my face onto the page before I feel the tears on my cheeks. I stand up, walk away from the journal, and head over to the window, opening it to get some fresh air and some space from all the emotions smothering the room.

"What do you think happened to them?" Pearl asks softly from where she's standing next to the fire.

"I don't remember seeing anything in the caves to suggest they didn't make it out. Do you, Ember?" Alexei asks, clearly thinking the same thing I am.

"I don't think so. I think they made it out. Not to mention that Zenobia's mother was a seer. I mean, she basically alludes to them having to leave when they do because she can *see* them getting attacked at a later point there. If they left before then, I think they were fine. And at this point, we aren't going to figure it out, so I think we need to believe that they were okay in the end." I have to believe this. Even though I didn't know her, there's a connection between me and Zenobia, and since I won't be getting any more details, I need to tell myself they survived and continued living somewhat happy lives.

"Are you going to show this to the king?" Alexei asks me.

I stare at the journal from across the room, debating. On one hand, he will probably go apeshit that I didn't listen to him and went to the black market. On the other hand, maybe he can shed some light on "the dark ones" and I can also show him that the races used to all live together in harmony and sing "Kumbaya."

"Yes, I think I'm going to. He might be able to give us some more information. In the meantime, I would like to save this potion in case we need to translate anything else. There's quite a bit of this left, is there something we can save it in?"

Pearl takes it from the table. "Yes. I can find something. I'll bring it back to you tomorrow after I get it taken care of."

"Actually, can you keep it in your room? I'm a little worried that when I tell Stavros, he's going to want to take it. If you take it, I can tell him that I don't have any. It won't technically be a lie, but he will think that we used all of it on the journal."

She nods in understanding, sending me a wink as she walks out with the cauldron.

When it's only me and Alexei, awkwardness descends on us, and I have no idea why. We were on the road together alone for weeks. We also slept in the same bed, out in the open, and in those couple lodges we stayed in. So, to have things be so weird between us is taking me off guard. Maybe it's from the back and forth that always seems to be between us.

"So, when are you going to tell him?" he asks me.

"Probably tomorrow at breakfast. That's the only time that we're alone and can talk. We don't really have the opportunity when we train."

"Okay. Well, let me know how it goes."

"I will," I agree. We stand there, not knowing what else to say.

"I guess I'm going to head to bed. It's been a long day."

"Okay, good night."

He walks out as I try to figure out what the fuck is going on. It takes me forever to get to sleep, what with our interaction, and how we spent the last couple hours, but I finally get there.

I, of course, dream of Zenobia and her family. I can see how things were when everyone lived in the caves. I can't tell if it's actually how it used to be, but it's incredibly realistic. I can also see the progression of how everything plays out, the almost utopia-like living beforehand, and then fear and quick retreat of the massive group of people that lived there. Zenobia is the last one out, but before she leaves, she looks back at the caves with regret. Her eyes latch on to mine, and her brows shoot up in surprise.

"Can you see me?" I ask. She nods. My belly tosses as my nerves spike. What is this? "Zenobia?"

She nods again. I can't help but notice a familiarity about her. I don't know what it is, if it's her looks, or the fact that I read her journal, but there's a kinship with her.

"Who are you? And how do you know my name?"

"I think we're both having a vision or something. I'm from the future. Two thousand years from now. I read your journal."

Her cheeks redden a bit in embarrassment, but she doesn't break our stare. "How is it in your time?" she asks hopefully.

"Segregated," I tell her, and her face falls. "I'm trying to find a way to bring everyone together. That's why your journal is so important."

"Zenobia!" one of her parents calls, sounding a bit panicked. She turns to go to them.

"Wait! Who are the dark ones?" I ask.

"They are coming" is all she says before she leaves.

When everyone is gone, I expect to follow the group, but instead I remain in the caves. I don't understand why, until I sense a dark presence here with me. I turn, but can't see anything other than darkness. It's almost like a large shadow that invades the space, and even though I know this isn't real, and it happened in the past, at the moment I swear this is real and that whatever this is can see through me. I take a step back, but it doesn't make any bit of difference. If anything, it seems to draw its attention to me more. The darkness envelops the space, and I can't breathe or see. I scream, and it shoots down my throat, choking me.

Just when I think I'm going to die from not being able to breathe, I'm shaken awake.

"Ember!" When I open my eyes, Alexei is above me, hands on my shoulders. "Are you okay? I could hear you screaming from my room."

"I had the most realistic nightmare. I dreamed of the caves, and saw Zenobia and her family, and it felt so vivid that I swear that what I was seeing actually happened. And then when everyone left, I think the dark ones came. Zenobia told me they would. Darkness invaded the entirety of the caves, I was stuck there with it, and it started shooting down my throat and choking me." My voice breaks at the end, and tears gather in my eyes.

"It was only a dream," he comforts me, running his fingers through my hair.

"Will you stay with me? I don't want to be alone right now," I whisper, vulnerable and terrified that he will reject me again and I'll be alone with the memory of that dream.

He looks like he's about to say no, and I prepare myself for it, but then he reluctantly nods, and I scoot over so he can join me. I don't move far because I need to have him pressed up against me. He seems to know what I need and wraps his arm around me, pulling me close. I breathe a sigh of relief as his warmth seeps into me, and I relax as much as I can. We lie there, and I let the sound of his heart pounding steadily underneath my ear calm me further. He rubs a hand up and down my back, and takes a deep breath as if he's about to tell me a secret.

"You know, I've been alone most of my life. My father was never around much, and the memories I do have of him are of the lessons he taught me, always strict, always wanting me to be better, be the *best*. But there is one memory I have of him where we had the perfect day together. There was no training, no politics, no expectations. It was one of those random days where you don't plan anything, or think that it's going to be anything special, but this was the best day. The two of us were in Twin Fangs. He was showing me where I was going to be sent one day. I was probably about eight or so. I had done a lot of my schooling here, but he also wanted me to go learn from the vampires, so I was going to be studying there for a while.

"We had already looked at the school and housing unit I would be in, and my father hadn't planned it right, thinking we'd need more time when we didn't. We had a whole day before we were supposed to leave, and we had already seen everything we needed to. So instead, we explored the city together. He took me to the market, and he bought me a few little trinkets and toys, and we sat at the fountain and ate our sweet ice. There were performers there that day, and we watched a show and laughed together. That was the first time I drank from the river. The same one you did that made you giggle so much. It was the best time I had ever had with him. The one time I didn't feel pressure from him about anything at all."

I don't know why he's telling me this, maybe to paint a nice picture in my head to distract me from my nightmare. It's working because between the deep, lulling timbre of his voice, and the beautiful, fun scene I can see playing out in my head, I am almost asleep.

"The next day, things went back to normal, and I've never had a day like that since with him, but it will always hold a special place in my heart."

By the time he's done talking, I'm fully out, knowing I'm safe and protected with a smile on my face.

The feel of a warm body fully plastered to mine wakes me. I'm momentarily confused, but then I remember the night before. I reluctantly open my eyes, not wanting the moment to end. I expect to find Alexei asleep, but he's peering down at me like I am the most wondrous thing he's ever seen. Our faces are only inches apart, and my eyes dip to his mouth as I lick my lips. The urge to kiss him has never been so strong. I know I shouldn't, but I lean in closer. I flick my eyes up to his, and that same want is mirrored in his own gaze. He doesn't stop me as I press myself against him and gently brush my lips across his. It's not exactly a kiss, but he groans all the same, and it causes the dam to burst.

He pushes me onto my back and follows so he's on top of me, his mouth never leaving mine. His tongue traces the seam of my lips in question, and I open willingly for him. It's a collision of lips, tongue, and teeth, the culmination of all of our sexual tension finally breaking, making our kiss sloppy, messy, and intense. It's everything I wanted it to be and more. I have goose bumps peppering my skin, and my nipples pebble where they're pressed against his chest. I wind my arms around his neck, trying to pull him closer to me, even though I know it's impossible. My legs wrap around his waist, and his hardness presses against the most intimate part of me. I shamelessly grind myself against him, and my insides clench at the sound of his growl, which vibrates against my chest, and I bite his lip in my excitement. He breaks away and looks down at me.

"Savage girl," he says, his voice husky.

Before I can respond, he dives back in. We're just as feral, and I drag my hands all over his chest. He wasn't wearing a shirt when he came in to wake me in the night, and I have never been more grateful that he sleeps without one. His hands make their way to my own shirt, and he pushes them underneath, his warm hands on my bare flesh igniting the most intense fire inside me. I moan in encouragement, but as he reaches below my breasts, he stops. He breaks our kiss and rests his forehead against mine. I know what's coming before the words leave his mouth.

"I can't, Ember," he whispers.

I close my eyes as hot tears build behind them, but I push them back. "I know. I'm sorry I started it."

"I'm not. I wouldn't trade that moment for anything."

I smile at him. I'm not mad. I understand. I bring my hand up to cup his cheek. "It's okay, Alexei."

He nods and gives me one more sweet, soft kiss before getting off of me. He moves to the door, but looks back reluctantly at me like he doesn't want to leave. Neither of us say anything. There's nothing *to* say. We stare at each other, full of want and regret that nothing can happen, until he finally turns and walks out.

I force the tears back. I know he keeps telling me that we can never happen, but I'm starting to believe that we're inevitable, and it's only a matter of time until we end up together. I need to be patient. And that kiss. There are no words. I have *never* had a kiss like that in my entire life. There's slickness in between my thighs from it, and I can only imagine what it would be like to have his mouth in other places. I flush thinking about it, and am tempted to curb my sexual frustration with myself in the shower. I do exactly that, because if I don't take care of this now, then I will not be able to concentrate all day.

Half an hour later, I'm showered, dressed, and have makeup on my face. I throw my hair in its usual braid before grabbing the journal and heading to breakfast. I've already gone back through and dog-eared the important pages so it's all ready to show Stavros. I'm more nervous the closer I get to the dining room. My palms grow slick, and my heart starts to beat faster. I know that he is going to be upset with me for directly disobeying him. Plus, I have to try to deflect, but not lie about the fact that it was Alexei who took me. I don't want him getting into any trouble when all of this was my plan.

I walk in to find the king already seated. His face lights up upon seeing me, and while I think it's incredibly sweet that he enjoys my presence so much, at the moment it's kind of like pouring lemon juice into a fresh paper cut. Things have been going so well between us lately, and I'm nervous this is going to escalate into a big fight. I smile back, although it probably looks more like a grimace, and take a drink of my tea to distract myself. Instead, I end up burning my tongue. Well done, Ember. We're getting off to a great start.

"Did you sleep well last night?" he asks.

"Not really," I respond. The opportunity is presenting itself, and I need to take it, but fuck if I'm nervous.

"Why not?"

"I had a nightmare." I take a deep breath. "I read the journal last night, and it gave me some interesting insights. My mind was so overwhelmed with everything that it carried over into my dreams."

"You read the journal? How?"

Another deep breath. "I was able to make the potion we found."

I watch his face for the change in his emotions, since I can't fucking read them like I would like to. He's pretty good at keeping his mask in place, but I can see him clench his jaw and his eyes harden slightly.

"And how did you do that?" he asks evenly.

I look down, not wanting to meet his gaze. "I wrote down the recipe while you weren't looking."

"And how were you able to make it?" His voice is getting deeper, and he's barely hanging on to his anger.

"I went to the black market and got the ingredients."

I hear him take multiple deep breaths, and when I finally work up the courage to look at him, he has his eyes closed, jaw clenched tight, and is breathing heavily through his nose. I wait for the explosion, but it never comes. He finally opens his eyes and looks at me.

"Ember, I am reminding myself that you are new to this realm. I'm not going to lie, I am furious with you right now, but I also know that you probably did not understand how dangerous that was. Not only do they sell horrible and illegal things, but if they knew who you were, you could've been killed, or kidnapped. Not to mention the way to pay for things there can be incredibly foolish and unpleasant, which I'm sure you witnessed. I wish you would've listened to me when I told you that it was not an option."

"I know, and I'm sorry that I went against what you said, but I felt like this was something that I had to do."

"Well, was it at least worth it?" he asks, gesturing to the journal in my hands.

"We found some stuff out, but it created even more questions."

I show him the important stuff: those in the realm wanted to live among each other so they formed a secret society no one knew about, that the species used to coexist, and finally how they all had to leave because of the dark ones. He lets me explain it all without a word, listening intently, which at least isn't telling me to shut up. When I'm finished, I look at him to see his mask back in place. It's impossible to tell what he's thinking right now, and I wish I could read his damn emotions for probably about the tenth time since entering this conversation.

"Well? What do you think?" I finally ask when I can't stand his silence anymore.

"It's all very interesting."

"*Interesting?!* That's all you have to say? You find out that the races used to live together peacefully, and that's *interesting*? You find out that they went against the rule of the king and queen to unite, and it's *interesting*? And what about the threat of the dark ones? That sounds *interesting* to you too?" My voice is getting higher in pitch and volume as I lose my shit.

"What do you want me to say, Ember? I've told you the species need to stay segregated. It's the only way. I know you don't understand that, and I'm sorry. I wish I could explain it to you, and someday I will, but today is not that day. As for the dark ones, this was written thousands of years ago. I highly doubt they are a threat to us now."

I know there's something he's not telling me, but I have no clue what it is, and I also know that pushing will get me nowhere.

"I don't know about that. When I had my dream last night, I was able to see all of this play out, and at the end, after everyone was out of the caves, the darkness came for me. It felt like a very real threat."

"Ember, it was a dream," he says gently, putting his hand over mine.

I let him for a moment. He thinks it's just a dream, but I'm positive it wasn't. It felt very real, and the memory of that foul presence choking me reignites my fear. My breath starts coming faster, but before I can start panicking, Stavros squeezes my hand.

"Ember, look at me." I do. "I will always protect you. Do you hear me?"

I can see the sincerity in his eyes, and it calms me. Before coming to Queridian, I had never had someone protect me like he and Alexei are willing to. I mean, I, of course, had my mother, but it wasn't the same. There's something about the protection of a man who cares about you. It's what they were born and bred to do, and it makes me feel incredibly cherished and safe.

I nod. "Thank you."

We leave our discussion at that. We clearly aren't going to agree, and I don't think either of us are up for a fight, especially when we are building this tenuous relationship. The smallest thing could damage it, and I don't want to weaken our bond.

"How's your training going with Alexei?" he asks me, steering the conversation toward more neutral ground.

"It's been going well. I'm a lot more confident, and it's starting to become natural."

"That's wonderful. You should start noticing more and more progression." He stops, looking like he wants to say more, but looks hesitant. "You know, I'm pretty good in combat too. I know Alexei is very adept, but if you're ever wanting a different opinion or to learn a new technique, I would be willing to spar with you once in a while."

"That would be fantastic. Would you maybe have time today after our mental shield training?"

He immediately brightens. "I would indeed."

"Okay," I reply with a smile.

I don't know why I didn't think of this. He's right, I will benefit from training with multiple teachers. Everyone has a different style, and I could learn something new from him. After that, we eat our breakfast. My stomach finally settles enough from my nerves that I'm able to consume something. We then proceed with our normal training, but I'm slightly distracted thinking about what he's going to teach me in combat training. Of course, I know that's ridiculous, because the whole point of any training is to stay present so you can actually learn what is being taught, which is easier said than done.

"Ready to head to the training yard?"

I nod. When we get there, I look around, grateful no one is here to witness this. I'm nervous again about showing my skills to someone other than Alexei. "What would you like to train with today?"

"Well, we've been training with daggers, bow and arrow, and, of course, hand to hand."

"Would you like to do one of those, or do you want to start something new?"

My ears perk up at the mention of something new. "What did you have in mind?"

"How about swords?"

My eyes widen, but I can't deny that the prospect excites me. I will be such a badass if I can start wielding one of those fucking things. I pick one up, selecting a smaller size so that I can manage it and get used to its weight. Even though I picked a smaller one, I'm surprised by how heavy it is, although by this time I shouldn't be. I know by now how heavy most weapons are. Stavros first shows me how to hold it. I'm, of course, tempted to swing it around like I've seen people do in movies, testing its weight and swiftness, but I know that I'll end up chopping my leg off or something if I were to attempt that right now.

Once I've established a good grip, he shows me some basic moves. His teaching technique is similar to Alexei's, which I'm grateful for when learning unfamiliar concepts. I tend to do well with this kind of training. The key difference lies in their communication. Stavros is more descriptive, articulating precisely how each movement should feel. Alexei relies on demonstrations, making corrections if necessary. Stavros starts me off with arm motions first, insisting that we will learn footwork separately, combining them only when I've grasped them individually.

Having repeated the strikes to his satisfaction, Stavros decides I'm ready to experience the clash of steel against steel. The initial contact is jarring, and I'm not quite prepared. The impact reverberates through my arm and into my shoulder, but with each strike, my body starts to adapt to the sensation. Stavros moves slowly, allowing my instincts to anticipate his next strike.

We pick up speed as we go, but still keep it fairly slow. When my arm feels like it's ready to fall off, he shows me the footwork. This is more difficult, although I will say that it reminds me a bit of my dancing training, and I'm grateful that we've been practicing so much because it makes me a bit more graceful than I would be without it.

"So, is it time to combine them?" I ask.

"Not even close. We have a while still before you're ready for that."

I nod, a little dejected, although I don't know why.

"Hey, you did well, Ember."

"Thanks, Stavros. I appreciate all your help and training."

When I get back to my room, my new dress for the ball is on the bed and I have a total girly moment, squealing in excitement before I go across the hall to get Pearl. She comes running over and I quickly shower so I don't get it all dirty and sweaty from training.

"Hurry up!" Pearl yells at me, clearly as excited as I am to see it on.

I come back out in a towel and run over to the bed. She's already holding it up, ready for me to put on. It takes us a few minutes to don the dress, but then I look in the mirror and am stunned. I've never seen a dress like this before in all my life. I take it all in from head to toe.

"Ember, you look like a queen," Pearl says quietly behind me, and I have to agree.

Regal is the only word I would use to describe this dress. It's floor-length with a train in a soft black fabric, but there is silver and white fur around the sleeves and around the hem, coming up in little sections. It's long-sleeved, but where it's tight up to the elbows, it then flares out and the bottom portion comes down to my knees. The neckline is curved and runs from shoulder to shoulder, but the breasts are what make it so spectacular. They are covered in rose gold. Literal rose gold, swirling and crisscrossing over my chest. As the rose gold gets farther up and separates from the fabric, it starts looking like fire crawling up my chest and connects to a rose gold choker. She's also made wrist and hand pieces that match the neckline. There are no words. All I can think about is how Imelda absolutely nailed it, and I can't wait to see Alexei's face when he sees me at the ball.

Chapter 22

The long-anticipated day of the ball has finally arrived, leaving me a mess of excited, nervous energy. I have little time to dwell on it thanks to the whirlwind of preparations that Pearl and I are overseeing together. We spend the day primarily delegating tasks, but it doesn't spare us from our fair share of lifting, shifting, and arranging.

When the party is only two hours away, Pearl and I head back to my room to get ready. Given that Pearl is going to do both our hair and makeup, we're going to need every minute. I hop in the shower and scrub myself down, ensuring I've removed every bit of excess body hair. When I'm cleaner than I've ever been in my life, I emerge to find that Pearl is already completely ready to go, with the exception of her outfit. I can't help but admire how utterly captivating she is. I know that she's letting her powers free to play tonight, and it's magnified her beauty tenfold. She is luminescent and shimmery, her smile radiating like the full moon. Before I put on my robe, she whips off my towel, making me cry out in outrage and shock.

"Pearl? What the fuck are you doing?"

"We need to apply this on you so it has time to sit and do its magic. It needs to go on every inch of your skin. You apply the front and I'll apply the back."

She sets to work before I can protest and then hands me the bottle. It's a glittery lotion, and when I put it on, my skin looks like Pearl's.

Within moments we have it applied everywhere, and she finally allows me to put my robe on.

She then applies my makeup in a very bold fashion to match my dress: dark smoky eyes, and bold red lips. She fashions my hair into an extravagant Dutch fishtail braid, elegantly pulled back to connect with an intricate bun. She then intersperses delicate gold leaves throughout the arrangement.

I make a quick decision to strap my daggers to my thighs prior to dressing. Since taking them from the training yard, I've become somewhat accustomed to their presence. Perhaps it's the recent surge of unsettling dreams, but I've been feeling a bit anxious. The comforting weight of the daggers against my skin provides me with a sense of security.

Pearl raises her eyebrows at me, but makes no comment. Next we tackle the challenge of dressing me in my gown, which proves to be a bit complicated. When I look in the mirror, I don't recognize the woman staring back at me. She is stunning, regal, confident, *royal*. Pearl gets dressed in her own gown, which is just as lovely. It's, of course, in a mermaid style, and ivory. The top is fitted like a corset and has a deep V neckline, and over the top is a shiny see-through fabric with lines of pearls cascading down. I've never seen anything like it.

"Did Imelda make yours too?" I ask.

"Of course. I don't let anyone else dress me for occasions like this. She is a genius, and I would be a fool not to take advantage of her skills."

After we're ready, we head back down early to make sure everything is set up properly. I stop short upon entering the ballroom. It is *immaculate*. There is no other word for it. It always has been, but with all the decor and the candles, it's like being in a fairy tale.

"Oh my God, Pearl. Look at what we did."

"It is pretty incredible, isn't it?" she muses, her tone not reflecting the same level of astonishment.

Then I remember she's likely attended countless balls in this castle, and probably contributed to planning a few as well. What's leaving me awed is the fact that this event is a product of our planning and vision. *We* planned this! It is even more spectacular than I could've dreamed. I imagine this is how many women feel on their wedding day after months of meticulous planning. The only difference here is that no one is getting married, and we had an unlimited budget. We could spend as much money as we wanted to, and boy did we. It did help that much of our desired decor, such as the solid gold chargers, were already available from previous events.

The band is already set up in the corner, warming up for their performance, and I delight in it. The music is different from Earth, but has a very Victorian vibe to it. I think everything looks perfect, but of course Pearl finds multiple things that are not up to her standards and rushes off to fix them before the guests arrive.

"Wow. You both did a phenomenal job," the king says from behind me as he enters, taking it all in. Then his eyes finally land on me. "Ember. You are so beautiful. You look like your mother." Tears fill his eyes, making my own start to water, but I push them back, not wanting to screw up my makeup.

"Thank you." I haven't called him "Dad" yet, but the temptation has been there, especially now.

I walk over to him, though, and give him a hug. He stiffens slightly at first, before relaxing and wrapping me tightly in his arms. I have to fight the urge to cry even more now. I can't explain it, but there is something unbelievably special about this moment between us. When we pull away, I can see a few tears that have fallen free from his eyes, and I know it's the same for him.

"I was thinking we could start the ball with our big announcement. What do you think?"

Nerves flutter in my belly. "Yes, that sounds good."

"Perfect. So, once everyone is present, I will call you up on stage. And remember, no pressure, okay?"

I nod.

Twenty minutes later, everything is perfect, and the guests start arriving. At this point, no one knows who I am yet, so I take the opportunity to sit down wherever I damn well please, considering we ended up not going with a seating plan. Pearl sits next to me, and we watch as the people who enter look around, taking in the splendor of the room before looking confused and nervous about where to sit. They were notified upon entering that they could choose whichever seat they wanted, and I am so curious to see how it plays out. I'm sure most of them will end up sitting with their own anyway, but there's a chance that a few might deviate.

As Alexei makes his entrance, I can't breathe for how magnificent he is. He's wearing all black, his shirt is embroidered around the edges with delicate silver detailing. He has a black and silver belt over the top at his waist, black pants, shiny black boots, and a black cape with silver silk lining. His hair is braided back out of his face, and his beard has been neatly trimmed. The moment he steps into the room, his gaze instinctively finds mine, as though guided by an unseen force. It's as if we're two magnets, perpetually aware of each other's presence and drawn together whenever we share the same space.

His eyes heat as they take me in, and they drag across every inch of my body as if they were his hands. A blush rises to my cheeks, and he takes a deep breath in through his nose, and I wonder if he can smell my blood, arousal, or both. He walks over to me and Pearl, but his eyes never once leave mine. When he's close enough to touch, he stops. Pearl clears her throat at the silence that ensues, but to the two of us, it's not awkward.

"You look absolutely devastating, Ember."

I furrow my brows because that doesn't sound like a compliment.

"I think you used the wrong word there, Alexei," Pearl cuts in.

"Not at all. She is so stunning that her beauty could level cities. That's why every man in this room can't take their eyes off of her. They would all destroy each other just to get a hint of her attention." Alexei is clearly talking to Pearl, but his gaze is fixed on mine, and I know the words are for *me*.

"Thank you. You're looking pretty devastating yourself. In fact, I might have to fuck some bitches up with all those fighting techniques you taught me."

His eyes heat in pleasure, especially when I give his body the same perusal he gave mine.

The music starts up as the guests trickle in, and I'm both nervous and excited at the prospect of putting my new dancing skills to use. Everyone comes in quickly, and we make sure to grab a glass of champagne from the champagne tower that we built. That was my idea, and I have to say it looks pretty spectacular. The king left the room to make his grand entrance once everyone arrived, which should be any minute now.

We take our seats, and moments later, Humphrey comes on stage to announce him, and he comes in through a doorway located on the platform. Everyone claps and bows as he waltzes in, and his smile is genuine for his subjects. It's obvious how much he adores them, and loves this realm. It's then that I realize he would do anything for them, which means that he has a damn good reason for keeping them segregated like he is. I hope he tells me. Maybe then I would understand, or be able to help come up with a solution.

"Thank you. You may rise and take your seats. And how lovely to see you all on this fine evening. Now, believe it or not, I actually *did* have a reason to host a ball besides wanting the company." The room chuckles. "First off, I would like to thank the lovely Ember and Pearl for putting together this wonderful event. Ladies, I believe this may be our most magnificent event to date."

The room claps for us.

"I do have an announcement to make. A very special one, in fact. But in order to do that, I will need to have Ember come on up here with me."

The room gasps, and I assume that no one is allowed on stage with him except the queen when she was alive. With all the grace I can muster, I stand and make my way to him as quickly as possible without making an ass of myself in front of the entire kingdom. I'm successful, thank the Gods, and when I'm standing next to him, he looks at me fondly, a question in his eyes, giving me the opportunity to back out if I want to. I nod at him to continue.

"Before I met Queen Amira, there was a lovely woman I met in the Mortal Sanctum named Catalina. It was not well known, but before I became king, I fell in love with Catalina."

I hear a collective gasp from everyone in the crowd.

"I planned to make her my queen, but she then died in childbirth. I was told my child perished with her. But about a month ago, I learned that our wonderful guard of the northwest portal, Alexei, had quite the surprise for me. Apparently, this young woman next to me is from Earth, and one day she fell through the portal into our world. Alexei brought her to me, and I could immediately tell that she was my daughter."

There is zero noise from the crowd this time. They look at us, stunned into silence.

"When she was born, she was taken to Earth by her adoptive mother, and was never told about our world. She has been learning quite a bit since she arrived, and has been living here in the palace with me. As you all know, I was never able to conceive with the late queen, and I was so pleased to discover that I have a child!"

He finally stops speaking, and the silence is deafening and endless, before the entire crowd erupts into applause and celebration. Stavros squeezes my hand, and I smile at him.

"I have a surprise for you," he whispers to me, and I look at him questioningly.

Humphrey appears next to him holding a velvet box. The king opens it, and inside is the most exquisite tiara I've ever seen, and so me, it's not even funny. It's rose gold, and there are pear-shaped black diamonds through the middle portion, more metalwork, and then it's topped off with little black diamonds coming up in points above the pear-shaped ones. He takes it out of the box, and in front of the entire kingdom, he places it on top of my head. I inhale sharply as the weight of it settles and reach up to feel it sitting there like it was always meant to.

"I originally had this made for your mother when I thought I was going to marry her," he says quietly just for me.

Tears gather in my eyes at the idea that I'm wearing something that was meant for her, and that it fits my style so perfectly. I guess I'm more like her than I realized. Stavros grabs us two glasses of champagne from Humphrey, Gods know where he got them, and hands me one before lifting his own in the air. Since when do I say "Gods?" I guess Queridian is wearing off on me.

"To the new princess of Queridian, Ember Solis!"

"To the new princess of Queridian!" the crowd echoes, holding up their own glasses and toasting each other.

The king clinks his glass with mine and we drink as the party really gets started. I head back to my seat as the staff starts bringing out the food. Pearl planned all of this since she has more experience with the menus at Queridian galas. We start with a bowl of soup. It's orange and reminds me of butternut squash, but it's not quite as sweet. Then they bring out a spinach and cheese bread that is to die for. By the time the main course is served, a delicious chipotle and cream pasta, I'm already full, but I devour it anyway. Finally, it's time for dessert, a blood orange and fig molten lava cake with vanilla ice cream. This idea was *mine*, and I'm pleased to say that I think this is the best dessert choice ever.

"Girl, this is the most delicious thing I've ever tasted," Pearl comments and I wink at her.

When everyone is finished eating, and gone through quite a bit of champagne I might add, the dancing starts. The first dance is only me and Stavros, and I am so nervous that I'm going to trip and fall on my face in front of everyone, but it seems all my lessons have paid off.

"You're doing wonderfully, Ember. The kingdom loves you already," he says as he sweeps me around the room.

"Do you think everyone is going to accept me though? Surely not everyone can be happy about this. I am *human* after all."

"I'm sure there will be some who aren't pleased about it, but there's always people in the kingdom who aren't happy about something."

I think he's overestimating people, but I hope he's right.

"Your dancing is coming along very nicely. I have to say, I'm impressed with how motivated you've been with all of your training. I hope this doesn't sound cliché, but I'm proud of you. I'm so proud to be your father, Ember."

Tears well in my eyes. I have wanted to hear that from a father for my entire life. This time I can't help it, and a few tears leak free. He smiles fondly at me, gently wiping the water from my cheeks.

The song ends, and I'm both relieved and disappointed. That was such a special moment we shared and I'm sad it's over, but I'm also glad the entire kingdom didn't witness more. I want my personal matters to stay personal, and if the conversation had continued, I can almost guarantee that there would have been more crying, and hugging, and Gods know what else. I want to have that moment with Stavros, and we will soon, but privately.

He squeezes my hand as we break apart, and Alexei taps him on the back to take his place. Alexei sweeps me away as the music starts, the rest of the dance floor filling up, but I don't see anybody but him. Our eyes lock, and there's so much that passes between us. I can see regret in his eyes, and I know that he's upset about how things are, like I am.

Song after song plays, and we keep on moving, never speaking or breaking eye contact. I don't know how much time has passed, or how many songs, but eventually Alexei gets tapped on the shoulder. We stop abruptly as if coming out of a trance.

"Mind if I cut in?" a man whom I've never seen before asks. He's equally as tall as Alexei, and is devastatingly handsome. His hair is as black as a raven and short, and his eyes are amber, smoldering as if they have an inner fire. He's well built, filling out his emerald green tunic.

"Sure." Alexei steps back but his gaze meets mine again and it's as if he's trying to tell me something. I remember then that I don't know this man and make sure to check that my mental shields are reinforced.

"It's so nice to meet you, Your Highness," the man says, bowing.

I don't think I'll ever get used to that. It's also the first time I've been addressed like that.

"My name is Xanto. I am the new mimic ambassador."

I notice then the mimic symbol on his lapel. With that, he grabs my hand and starts expertly whisking me around the dance floor. I'm so grateful that I reinforced my shields because he's now touched me, and I don't want him to be able to copy my form.

"Yes, I heard that you were going to be here this evening. How are you enjoying the ball?"

"It is lovely. I heard you had a hand in planning it?" His accent is strange, as is the way he talks. Almost a little choppy? I can't quite put my finger on it.

"Yes. I planned it with my friend Pearl. She's the mermaid ambassador." I gesture with my head to where Pearl is drinking and charming a whole group of people. They're all eating out of the palm of her hand, and I almost laugh at how clueless they all seem to be.

"Ah yes. The one who is more striking than this ball itself. Although, it would be difficult, if not impossible to manage creating something more exquisite than she is."

I whip my head to his, and see his gaze glued to her. I smile coyly. Pearl wanted to have some fun with people our age. I wonder how old he is.

"If you don't mind me asking, how old are you?" I feel like Stavros mentioned it, but I don't remember the answer.

"I'm young. Only thirty," he answers, still entranced by her. I might have to play matchmaker.

"If you're so smitten with her, why did you ask me to dance instead?"

"Well, I know that you are also new here, so I thought I might try to make friends since I don't know anyone, and you probably don't know many either."

"Ahh yes. The king's daughter is always a nice friend to have," I reply.

He has the decency to look a little sheepish. "While that is true, I am not lying. You seem nice, and also have a very stunning friend."

"Oh, so your real intention is to have me put in a good word for you with Pearl?"

He starts blushing, but doesn't deny it. I laugh good-naturedly, and he smiles at me.

"I can introduce you after this if you'd like?"

He brightens, nodding enthusiastically. He reminds me a bit of an excited puppy dog. I wonder how accurate I am, thinking he might be something along those lines in his shifted form.

"Are you excited to be here at the palace?"

"I am, but honestly, I'm a bit nervous."

"I understand. But everyone here has been wonderful and nice. I'm sure you'll fit right in."

"We mimics don't fit in well. And most people don't trust us."

I nod in understanding. "Well, being from Earth, I know exactly what it's like not to fit in. I think we're going to get along just fine. I am definitely willing to give the friend thing a try," I tell him genuinely.

And maybe that is the real reason he came over to me. I mean, sure, it's an added benefit that I'm the princess, and that I'm friends with the woman he has his eye on, but I bet he saw a kindred spirit when he looked at me. Someone else who has *never* fit in, and is now in a huge palace with lots of intimidating people. The song ends, and I take him over to Pearl.

"Ember! About time, girl. I thought you and Alexei were going to be on the dance floor all night."

"Pearl, I've met the mimic ambassador. I thought I'd bring him over to meet you since the two of you will be in close contact with each other soon. Xanto, this is Pearl." I gesture between them. I watch as Pearl's eyes light with interest.

"Well, hello. It's so nice to meet you, Xanto." Pearl has adopted her mermaid charm voice, and I can tell that he is even more taken with her than he was from across the room.

I leave them to it, deciding to grab another glass of champagne and sit down for a moment. My feet are already killing me from all the dancing, and I resist the urge to take my shoes off. Princesses aren't supposed to do that, I don't think. It seems as soon as I'm seated, everyone and their mother takes that as an invitation to come and meet me. I shake so many hands and learn so many names that I've forgotten them almost as soon as they walk away. It's extremely overwhelming and exhausting, and I'm already over this. There's finally a lull in people coming up to me, and I thank whatever god is listening.

"Want to go get some fresh air?" Alexei whispers in my ear.

"Yes, please. I need a break from all of this."

He offers me his arm and escorts me out. We go to the gardens that Stavros showed me when I first arrived, and I admire their beauty at night. I breathe in the fresh cool air, grateful that I have a warm dress on. The weather is definitely starting to get chillier, especially at night.

"You are too dazzling to look at sometimes."

"Is that possible?"

"Yes. It almost blinds me from how brilliantly you shine."

I blush at the compliment, unsure of how to respond. I reach out my gifts to see what he's feeling. I don't do this often because I don't want to invade his privacy, but I'm being drawn to at the moment. My mind connects with his, and I'm overwhelmed by everything I'm sensing. There's lust, guilt, indecision, and all-consuming *want.* I draw closer to him without realizing, and then he grabs me and pins me against the nearest column. I cry out as his lips meet mine. It's as intense as our last kiss, and I fall into it whole-heartedly. The contact between us is as essential as the air I'm breathing, and I can't get enough of it. We moan and groan and rub against each other, seeking as much contact as possible, but the amount of clothes in the way makes it difficult. All I want right now is to go back to my room and worship him. Or maybe, considering I'm wearing the crown, I'd make him worship me. He makes me feel like a goddess, and I want to prove to him that I am.

When we finally come up for air, my heart is playing its own symphony in my chest, and it's like I've run a mile. I meet his gaze, trying to convey all I feel for him in one look, but all I see in his is sorrow. I'm about to ask him about it, when all of a sudden he holds something up, covering my nose and mouth.

"I'm so sorry, Ember," I hear him whisper as I lose consciousness and my heart shatters.

Chapter 23

I wake slowly, my mind sluggish with a haze of confusion. The heavy pit in my stomach tells me that something is wrong and sets my heart beating harder. There's a fog covering my head, preventing me from thinking clearly. I can't open my eyes yet, but figure I shouldn't even if I could. I'm in something moving, like a car. I'm lying on my side, my arms have fallen asleep, and my head pounds uncomfortably. It's then that I remember that I'm no longer on Earth, so it's impossible for me to be in a car, but maybe I'm in a carriage or something?

"Why did we have to bind her?" I hear a familiar voice ask, and I realize that my hands are tied together in the front of my body, making my panic build as the haze starts to clear the slightest amount.

"I told you, son. When she wakes she is going to try to get away, and we can't let that happen." That voice makes my skin crawl. I know I don't like this man, but for the life of me, I can't remember who he is.

"I don't like it. I think it might scare her when she wakes, and I don't want it to do that. I don't want to cause her any unnecessary grief."

"When she finds out that you betrayed her, she is going to be feeling plenty of grief," the creep says mockingly. "Stop here."

"Why?"

"Just do it!" Whatever we're in stops moving. "Stay here."

I'm then lifted into a pair of strong arms, one resting under my knees, and the other supporting under my upper back. My head lolls back in an uncomfortable position, but since I still don't have control of my body, there's nothing I can do about it.

"What are you doing?"

"She should be waking any moment now, and I want to talk to her to tell her what's happening. I think it'll be best if I do it since she knows she can't trust you now."

The other doesn't reply, but I can sense that he's hurt and upset. I once again try to force my eyes open, and I barely accomplish it; they're slit just enough to allow me to see that I'm being carried into a forest. My breathing comes faster as my panic increases.

We walk for a while, long enough that I know we're not near the carriage anymore. I'm placed up against a tree, the rough bark cutting into the exposed skin of my shoulders, and suddenly, there's something pulling my arms up over my head. My mind starts to rebel when I realize that I'm being restrained. It takes too long for my body to react, and it's only when my panic mounts that I'm finally able to fully open my eyes through sheer force of will.

The face staring back at me makes me recoil, Mordecai's twisted features unleashing the trapped memories of what came before. My eyes search for Alexei, even as my heart shatters, the pieces lacerating me from the inside as I remember that he was responsible for this. Whatever he gave me knocked me unconscious. Betrayal is a cold realization within me. How could he? I don't know what's going on, but I know that it's not good. What is Mordecai planning?

"Ah, you're awake."

"What are you going to do to me?" I ask, terrified as nausea turns my stomach and my chest tightens. I wonder if anyone will realize I'm gone and come looking for me.

"All in good time, my dear." He's moving, drawing my eyes down to see him crafting earth magic to bind me to the tree.

I take stock of myself, endless scenarios of women being drugged only to wake and find their clothes torn or missing running through my head. Luckily, all of mine seem to be in place, giving me some measure of comfort that he hasn't done anything sexual. Hopefully that's not about to change. He reaches up and takes the tiara off of my head, throwing it on the ground beside him.

"Did you really think that you were going to be a princess? That I would *let* you take advantage of the kingdom like that?" he asks, his voice tight with anger as he takes a knife out. My blood freezes. He notices my fear, and his eyes light with malicious glee.

The sound of footsteps coming toward us draws my attention. My heart beats faster in hope that someone is going to rescue me. Then fear strikes again as I realize that it's probably someone coming to help *him* and not me.

Mordecai curses softly, his face scrunching up in frustration as Alexei walks into the wooded area. His eyes meet mine, and there is so much guilt and regret there. I harden my gaze and my heart against him. He made his choice. His eyes then sweep the rest of my body, taking in my bonds, and his brows furrow in confusion. He looks to Mordecai and sees the knife; realization and horror dawn on his face as he steps forward to do something—what, I'm not sure, but it's clear this wasn't the plan.

Mordecai is quicker though, moving like lightning to stir up his earth magic and bind Alexei where he stands. Vines snake up to hold his hands and legs, even as he fights with all his might against it. He grunts and cries out with the effort, fighting for all he's worth, but the vines holding him are too strong, and with his hands completely encased, he can't access his magic or do anything against his father. He's slammed up against the tree next to mine, and bound even tighter than I am. He continues to struggle in vain, his face turning red and veins bulging with the effort. I can see the magic cinching so tight around him that it cuts into his skin. My composure starts to slip in the wake of the effort he's putting in to protect me, and I fight to maintain my detachment.

"You motherfucker. You said we weren't going to hurt her! That's the only reason I agreed to this!" he yells, his face contorting in rage, but Mordecai looks completely unfazed, as though he was expecting Alexei's reaction.

I harden my resolve again at the mention of his involvement and turn my attention to Mordecai instead.

"I know. I lied. This bitch clearly doesn't trust me. I needed you to lure her out of the castle for me, and you did such a wonderful job. Did you actually think I was going to have you take her back to Earth? Foolish boy," he chuckles darkly, his eyes shining. "She knows too much, and would more than likely try to sneak back here at the first opportunity, and tell Daddy dearest what we've done. We can't risk that. This way, the issue is taken care of, and the king will think that she's one of the disappearances happening around the realm."

I figured that he didn't want me to leave this situation alive, but the confirmation of it sends my heart racing, and sweat builds on my brow. "Why do you need to get rid of me at all? I'm not a threat, and I don't even know anything!" I finally speak up, now that I know at least some of what's going on.

"Darling girl," Mordecai coos as he gently runs the blade over my cheek. I inhale sharply in terror, but am very careful not to move. It's enough pressure to be threatening without actually breaking the skin.

"Don't touch her!" Alexei yells from beside me, which Mordecai ignores. I can see how angry he is. He's practically spitting venom, and he's bleeding from how hard he's struggling against his bonds.

"You've been a threat to this kingdom since before you were born. That's why that whore of a mother of yours sent you to Earth and everyone was told you died in childbirth along with her. She heard the same prophecy I did and thought she could protect you. She didn't count on you finding your own way back here," he sneers, a look of pure disdain on his face.

"What prophecy?"

"She was told a prophecy by one of the most intuitive witches alive before you were born. It told of how she would die giving birth to you, but the most important piece was that *you* will be the end of the fae reign. I can't let that happen. I have worked too hard for too long, and now that I am this close, I am not going to let a filthy little human *bitch* get in the way." As his latent rage grows, the words become harsher, spittle flying from his mouth and hitting my face as he leans in closer.

"No! Father, don't! We can still take her back to Earth. I'll never let her come back through the portal. You don't have to do this!" Alexei fights with all his might to break free and protect me, his muscles bulging and straining against his restraints as sweat breaks out on his forehead. He's fighting equally as hard with his words, hoping to break through to his father.

But the darkness, determination, and dementedness is evident in Mordecai's eyes, and I know he's not going to let us go. His bloodlust will only be sated with my death—his twisted desires filled by some prophecy I'm unaware of. No matter what we say or do, it seems he's beyond reason, consumed by his dark intent. Terror surges through my system, and I struggle against my own bonds, the vines cutting into my skin, painting it with bruises.

Mordecai moves as quickly as lightning, and I see the glint of the blade a second before it pierces my chest. My eyes widen in surprise, and when I try to take a breath, or scream, or *anything*, I can't. Mordecai's eyes light with sadistic glee as he watches me struggle. He twists the blade and I'm being shredded alive, and I know I would be screaming if I could. All I can feel is the sharpness of it, the ache spreading through my body and then the blood that inevitably *pours* out of my wound as he rips the knife out, the heat of which is scorching me as it slides down my chest. My lungs are burning with the need for oxygen, tears stream down my face, and as I realize I'm dying I can hear Alexei screaming and crying my name like a prayer. I don't have it in me to answer...

There's nothing but an infinite expanse of blackness around me. I find myself wondering if this is what death is—a void filled with nothing, stretching into eternity. The thought is terrifying, as is the emptiness that seems to have seeped into my bones, rendering me numb and listless. I drift aimlessly, the passage of time losing all meaning in this place of nothing.

Two figures appear in the distance. They're blurred and indistinguishable at first, but as I drift closer, they gradually come into focus, almost like tuning into a fuzzy radio station, the sounds slowly becoming clear.

I inhale sharply when I realize who they are. The numbness that has enveloped me since I arrived here suddenly shatters, and I'm overwhelmed with a flood of emotions. Joy, grief, shock, relief—they all crash into me at once, leaving me breathless.

One of the figures is so familiar, and a face I never thought I would see again. Evelyn, my adoptive mother. She's smiling at me with tears in her eyes, sparkling like twin sapphires. Her hair, a glossy sheen that's almost too radiant to behold, frames her face. She exudes a healthy glow that I'd never seen during her lifetime. It's a vision that fills me with a surge of emotions so profound that they're impossible to unravel. My breath, if it can be called that in this place, quickens, catching in my throat as I take in the sight of her.

Next to her, it's almost like looking into a mirror, and I know immediately who she is. My birth mother. She has the same shade of hair color, although without the white streak, and the same face. Our body types are similar, but she has a much more graceful way about her. The only other differences between us are the color of our eyes—hers are dark brown—she doesn't have a beauty mark, and she has rounded ears instead of pointed like mine.

"Hello, my darling child. I've waited so long to meet you," Catalina says softly with a smile, looking at me like I've always imagined. Tears well in my eyes. How long have I wanted to know who she was? I run up to them and they both wrap me in the warmest hugs. Their touch breaks me apart and remakes me all in the same moment.

I look at Eve and see the same adoring face I've always loved. "Mom"—my voice cracks—"I've missed you so much."

"I've missed you too, honey. I'm so sorry."

"Why did you never tell me?" The anger I've felt since I found out about my birth mother surfaces, albeit not as strong with her in front of me.

"You have been in danger since you were born. I was keeping you safe."

"But you could have told me. I would've understood that I needed to stay on Earth." My voice rises as my temper does, and I have the urge to pull back from her a bit.

"You would've?" she asks with a knowing motherly look. Damn it. Sometimes she knows me better than I know myself. She looks at Catalina as if to say she knows how similar and stubborn we both are. "If I would've told you, you would've insisted we come here."

"But I ended up here anyway! And now look at where I am. I'm fucking dead." Pain pinches her face, but before she can respond, my birth mother chimes in.

"You're not dead, my child."

"I'm not? Then how is this possible?" I run my hands over my body and look around to see if I can glean any answers, even though the only ones who can give them to me are standing right in front of me.

"Well, technically you are dead."

My heart sinks at her words, and I struggle to keep my breathing even.

"But you're not going to stay that way. And don't blame your mother for not telling you. I made her take a vow of silence with me about it when I entrusted her with you. I couldn't bear the thought of anything happening to you. I've always loved you so much, and I know how cruel this realm can be."

It's then I recognize the haunted look in her eyes, and know that she must've had such a hard life before my father showed up. I wish I could tear down the world for her and shred anyone who caused her harm.

My hands clench with the need to do just that, but her words break that train of thought. "Ember, you have more to do. There are so many counting on you. You have so much power in you. You have to be strong. You have to go back. You're about to awaken, and with that, you will be able to bring about much needed change." I swallow nervously, not knowing exactly what to expect when I wake. "For though her blood will be the call." Her voice takes on an ethereal quality, as if she's quoting something important. The prophecy maybe?

"But I just met you. I want to get to know you," More tears fall at the thought of leaving this incredible woman I finally met. Both of these women. I hold on to them tighter, as if I can keep me here with them, or bring them with me. My heart breaks at the thought that this will be my last interaction with them until my actual death.

"It's okay, honey. We will always be here. We've been watching you grow. You've gotten so strong. We're so proud of you." Eve curls an errant strand of hair behind my ear.

I lean in to the touch, missing it so much. I wrap my arms around them once more, holding them tight to me, but I can feel them slipping away. I grasp at them with all my might, wanting one more moment, but they go faster and faster until I can't see them at all...

The sudden burst of sensations brings a fresh wave of energy through me, as if I am now aware of every inch of my body, and of an immense power stirring within. I get a quick flash of all of the species' symbols behind my eyelids, and before the confusion can set in, something starts to awaken inside of me. It feels like a great slumbering beast rousing from a deep sleep, opening its eyes for the first time. The awareness surges through me, removing the remnants of the drug that knocked me unconscious, leaving my mind clear. It's like a wave of sunlight banishing every shadow inside of me, cleansing and purifying.

I can feel the wound in my chest beginning to heal, the skin and flesh slowly knitting itself back together. My heart, which was once still, begins to palpitate again—slowly at first, as if it's just learning how to beat once more. I am in awe of this impossible ability that is pulsing through me. Is it possible that I have elf blood in my veins, enabling me to heal my own injuries?

The beats of my heart grow stronger and faster, the rhythm in sync with the resurgence of my awareness. The first sense to return is my hearing. I can hear Alexei, his raw screams echoing in my ears. The vines that had bound me to the tree no longer hold me upright; I am lying on the ground, my wrists still tied.

I have no idea how long I've been unconscious, but probably minutes by this point. I'm guessing that Mordecai is about to bury me, or maybe burn me, and my heart beats faster at the thought, my hands twitching slightly as I try to pull myself and all of my willpower together. I am not done yet.

"No! Ember! Stay with me! Don't leave me," Alexei is still screaming, and even though I'm assuming that I'm not actually dead or in danger of it, I hang on to it with all my might, letting it bolster my strength. "This wasn't supposed to happen. We were supposed to go to Earth together. We were supposed to build a life there away from all of this." His voice cracks, and it splits me apart even more.

"Oh, shut up, boy. I told you not to fucking get attached. But you can never do what you're told, can you?" Mordecai's disdain is evident, making my hate for him burn even brighter.

"You murderous traitor filth!" Alexei spits at him, and I can literally hear him spit. "I can't wait to bring you to the king and have him rip you to shreds."

"What a shame. I was hoping that we would be able to move on, but it looks as though I'm going to have to kill you too if you're going to betray me like this. Can't have that now, can we?" He doesn't sound like he's regretful in the slightest, and I wonder if his plan was to kill Alexei all along.

It's then, when I'm fearing for Alexei's life, that the thing I've felt stirring inside me since I awoke bursts free, like a phoenix out of a flame, and I fully come back to consciousness, my eyes popping open.

I stand as a tornado whips through the space, knocking the knife free from Mordecai's hand. A spark ignites in my fingers, and I watch in fascination as a small flame burns through the rope connecting my wrists. Luckily, my hands weren't bound like Alexei's, only my wrists, because otherwise I wouldn't be able to conjure my air and fire magic. I'm equally stunned and unsurprised that I have elemental magic.

Alexei's eyes meet mine through the windstorm I've created, and his gaze is so full of relief. He's smiling widely, tears spilling down his cheeks. I take stock of the rest of him, seeing that besides the bruises and lacerations from him struggling against the vines, he's unharmed. I harden my entire being against him, because even though I don't want to see him killed, and I understand that he was lied to and manipulated, I'm still in this mess because of him. Because he chose his father over me. He didn't even *talk* to me about it. The broken pieces of my heart shred painfully in my chest.

I break his stare and look at Mordecai, who has fallen to his knees in front of me and looks stunned silent. His eyes are wide and fearful, and I revel in it. I reach for his mental shields, and finally understand what my father has been telling me. I *know* that I am better than this piece of shit in front of me. I know I'm stronger, braver, more capable. With a confidence I've never felt before, I rip through his barriers like they're made of paper and cringe at the foulness that reaches me. I can almost smell it and wrinkle my nose in disgust. I can sense his surprise and fear of me, but I can also sense his wickedness, his need for power, and his determination to do anything to get it. I wipe it all away, except for his fear.

My skin starts to glow and shimmer, like Pearl's does when she's charming someone, and his face widens and softens as he's taken in by my allure. I get a brief but vivid flash of an image, and I'm sure what I'm seeing is the future. I smile savagely, ready to make it come to pass. I'm beginning to realize what my mothers were talking about as my mermaid and witch abilities present themselves, and a small part of me is scared by what this is all going to mean for me after this is over.

I use the wind I'm harnessing to lift my crown from the ground, floating it to my head and settling it there as I embrace the goddess I am. Mordecai and Alexei dip their heads in reverence, bowing, and the power in me purrs at the recognition.

My voice takes on an ethereal quality, and their eyes glass over like they're hypnotized. "Mordecai, tell me what you want and all you've done to accomplish it." If possible, my voice sounds even more angelic than Pearl's.

He meets my eyes, hesitation making him pause. I increase my allure and push feelings of trust and honesty onto him. His mind immediately caves to my demands, and he starts talking, telling me all the vile things he's done in his quest for power.

"I want to be king. I've taken out all those in my way to make that happen. The last one was supposed to be Stavros until you came along. I had the help of another ensuring that the king and his wife were never able to conceive. I didn't know about him having a relationship with Catalina until it was too late. I had plans to take care of you long before now, but then we were all told you'd died, and I didn't think to investigate further." He's struggling to speak, as if he doesn't want to tell me any of this, but can't help himself.

"Who helped you?" He flinches, and I push him with my powers.

He cringes more, as if he's in physical pain. "I can't tell you! We bound each other to silence!" he screams. I push as hard as I can, my body trembling with the effort, and he yells in pain. When it becomes clear I won't be getting that answer from him, I pull back. We both take a deep breath.

"You said you've taken out those in your way. Who?"

"Stavros's parents, and his wife, Amira." I blanch in horror. My poor father. I hate the thought of telling him, but maybe it will give him some closure.

"How?"

"Queen Amira I poisoned easily enough. Everyone thought she choked. I staged a carriage accident for the king and queen. They were supposed to be dead when I arrived, but they were only injured. I ensured they didn't survive and made it look like the injuries I gave them were from the accident."

This *horrid* man. His eyes take on a dreamy quality, and I know he's reveling in his past actions. I knew he was a snake. It's then that I remember the words my mothers spoke to me in my sleep.

Beware of the snake.

The fire inside me rises, and it comes to the surface, barely a flicker, but I fan it with my air and it spreads around us. I guide it to where Mordecai is kneeling on the ground and it catches his clothing. He shrieks as it burns his skin and he attempts to wrap me in his earth magic again. I burn the vines away as quickly as they manifest and let my allure drop so he can experience all the disdain toward me he can. I want him to know that I beat him. This *human* girl defeated him.

Vengeance is pounding through my veins, and I bask in it. Maybe if I were myself right now I would be unnerved about that fact, but as it stands, I let it fuel me even more. Rage ignites his eyes, but before he can get up and attempt to attack me, I teletravel behind him, grabbing the blade from my thigh as I go, which is easy since the bottom half of my dress has been burned off. I thread my fingers in his hair, ripping his head back as I drag the dagger across his throat. His screams turn into garbles as he chokes on his blood, which sprays the front of me as he turns and falls to the ground.

I spit on him and smile ferociously as I watch the life leave his eyes and the fire consume him. This is the vision I saw at the beginning when my powers awakened, and I now know for sure that I also have witch blood in me. When he's nothing more than ash at my feet, I cut off the air to the fire and turn to Alexei, still strapped to the tree. The reality of what I did soaks in, and I struggle not to collapse in a mixture of terror, relief, and sheer exhaustion.

He looks at me with awe written on his face, not looking scared in the least, even though I'm covered in his father's blood, and my own for that matter. He bows his head again reverently, and I know that I must look like a dark queen seeking vengeance. I burn his bonds off, freeing him. He falls to my feet and brings his lips to my hands, kissing each of them before looking up at me with tears in his eyes. Something burns my inner left wrist, and I gasp at the same time he does. I pull my hand back and look down to see a star tattooed on my skin. The same one I had a vision of on Earth when I was about to get my tattoo on my birthday. I look to see a crescent moon tattooed on Alexei's. I'm so confused as to what's going on, but his eyes light up with joy, silver lining them.

"Ember, you're my mate," he whispers, a smile in his voice. I flinch back away from him.

"Bull*shit*. I am not your *anything*, Alexei Dreymonde. I fucking *died* because of you!" I scream at him, tears streaming down my face in rivers, streaking through the blood. My careful composure shatters in the wake of his revelation.

"I know, little doe. I'm so sorry." He reaches for me again, panic bleeding toward me from him. I block him out, refusing to feel anything. I rip away the arm that he managed to grab.

"Don't call me that! Never again!" I shriek, hysteria bubbling inside of me and spilling over now that everything is done.

"Ember, I'm so sorry. I never thought that he would do this. I was going to take you back to Earth. I was going to come *with* you so that we could be together," he begs me. Even though I'm not connected to his emotions anymore, the panic and desperation are written plainly on his face.

"And you didn't think to ask me about any of this? Or let me say goodbye to the only father I've ever known? Or the only friend I've ever had? If you had asked me, I would've gone with you willingly, but you did the same thing as my mother and treated me like a child, never giving me any say, and it ultimately led to my fucking *death*. How can I ever forgive you for that, Alexei?" My voice rises as my anger mounts.

"I'll spend the rest of my life making it up to you. Don't you understand? We're *mates*. That's what these marks mean. We're meant for each other." His words ring true, but I refuse to accept them. "The mate bond must've snapped into place when your powers awakened."

"I'm not going to be mates with someone who doesn't trust me enough to tell me what's going on and then kidnaps me because he's made his own decision. I'm fucking done, Alexei. Leave me alone. I won't tell the king what you did because I don't want you to end up killed, but don't come near me again."

"Ember, please." Alexei tries to grab me and pull me to him, but something stirs in me again. In my desperation to get away, something ripples across my skin, ice sliding through my veins. With a cry, my whole body shifts, and suddenly I'm looking down at myself and am amazed to find that I'm in a bird's body. A purple bird no less, and I remember the feather in my hairpiece from my mother, realizing that I have the last species of mimic in my blood as well. I have them *all*.

My clothing and tiara are nowhere to be found, and I'm assuming they are still with my human body and will reappear when I do. I look up to find Alexei staring at me in shock.

I spread my wings and Alexei shouts at me, "Ember, no!"

I take off into the night. My flying is clumsy and clunky at first, but the more I beat my wings, the easier it gets, and the more natural it becomes. Alexei is running behind me, still shouting at me to stop, but I pay him no mind. From the air I can see the castle and I fly straight to it. I'm grateful that birds can't shed tears, but I let out a cry that sounds just as tortured as it would in a human's body as I continue into the night.

Author Note

Thank you for reading *An Ember in the Dark*! Ember's next book, *A Blaze in the Shadows*, will be released soon, and she can't wait for you to read her story.

If you enjoyed this book, please leave me a review. I can't stress enough how difficult it is being an indie author. Any type of support we get from our readers helps tremendously. Please help me make it possible to keep bringing you amazing stories.

If you would like updates on my upcoming books, please sign up for my newsletter!

http://eepurl.com/hRZzz5

I love hearing from my readers! Find me on...
Instagram: @L.J.Burkhart.author
FaceBook: @L.J. Burkhart
Pinterest: @LJBurkhartbooks
Email: LJBurkhartbooks@gmail.com

Acknowledgments

Wow! This book went by *so* quickly, and there have been a lot of people who have made this book possible.

Firstly, to my husband. You have always believed in me and my dream. Thank you for always being in my corner and rooting for me. I love you more than words can express.

To my sister and mother, this book would not be what it is today without all of your help and input. Thank you for believing in this story when others didn't. Thank you for brainstorming endlessly with me, and always having my back no matter what. You ladies are the most wonderful I have ever known, and I'm so lucky to have you both in my life.

To my dad, thank you for your support and your talent you passed down to me for story-telling. I still remember sitting on your lap, and having you tell me magical tales.

To my brother, thanks for always being in my corner. I'm grateful to have you in my life.

To Iris, once again, you always are so excited to read what I write. Thank you for always texting me back immediately, helping me address all of my book concerns, and booktalking with me every single day. You have been such an immense help in this story and I'm so grateful to have you in my life.

To my llama bitches, Tracey, Cheyenne, and Mandy. Thank you for all the writing sessions, helping me come up with words and phrases I can never think of, motivating me with our weekly check-ins, and reading through this while also giving me much-needed feedback. I'm so lucky to have found you all.

To Beth, my editor, once again, thank you for all the hard work you always put into my novels. They are much cleaner and make much more sense thanks to you. I appreciate you.

To my graphic designer, Les, thank you for the gorgeous artwork you contribute. You're always able to turn my vision into reality.

To Sheba, my sweet little yorkie girl, thank you for lighting up my life and always keeping my life interesting. I'll always love you and have a special place in my heart for you.

Finally, to you, dear reader, thank you for coming on this journey with me. Thank you for giving me and Ember a chance, and hopefully a place in your hearts. I appreciate every single one of you.

About the Author

L.J. Burkhart is the author of the new novel *An Ember in the Dark*. She writes contemporary romance and fantasy romance. She has also published a contemporary romance trilogy called the Fire series, which includes *Fire & Ink*, *Light Me Up*, and *The Fire Inside Me*. L.J. has been a lifelong writer, starting with songs and poetry in the third grade, before eventually moving on to novels in her early twenties. When she isn't coming up with dramatic plot twists and steamy sex scenes, you can find her doing yoga, hanging out with her best bitches, baking, or reading, curled up on the couch with her husband and dog with a big glass of red wine.

You can connect with me on:

🌐 https://www.ljburkhart.com

📘 https://www.facebook.com/l.j.burkhart

🔗 https://www.instagram.com/l.j.burkhart.author

Subscribe to my newsletter:

✉ http://eepurl.com/hRZzz5